Four lessons on love from four extraordinary authors!

From Sabrina Jeffries . . .

Look before you leap.

When Eliza flees her evil guardian, she unwittingly steals (oops!) a horse from Colin Hunt, a newly minted earl who wants nothing more than to send her home . . . or to keep her forever.

From Liz Carlyle . . .

At least *pretend* to be innocent.

After a passionate encounter between Martinique—the daughter of a French courtesan—and the notorious rake Lord St. Vrain, there is talk of a proper courtship . . . though there's nothing proper about either of them!

From Julia London . . .

Don't be naïve.

Sent to London to attract a match among the *ton*, Grace finds herself drawn to rugged Barrett Adlaine—an entirely inappropriate mate who will never meet with her father's approval.

From Renee Bernard . . .

Break free of the gods of mischief.

With her constant mishaps and chaotic ways, Alyssa is no match for Mr. Leland Yates, who is ruled by logic and reason—or is she?

The SCHOOL *for* HEIRESSES

SABRINA JEFFRIES
LIZ CARLYLE
JULIA LONDON
RENEE BERNARD

POCKET **STAR** BOOKS
New York   London   Toronto   Sydney

An *Original* Publication of POCKET BOOKS

 A Pocket Star Book published by
POCKET BOOKS, a division of Simon & Schuster, Inc.
1230 Avenue of the Americas, New York, NY 10020

This book is a work of fiction. Names, characters, places and incidents are products of the author's imagination or are used fictitiously. Any resemblance to actual events or locales or persons, living or dead, is entirely coincidental.

ISBN-13: 978-1-4165-1611-8
ISBN-10:   1-4165-1611-5

This Pocket Star Books paperback edition January 2007

10   9   8   7   6   5   4   3   2   1

POCKET STAR BOOKS and colophon are registered trademarks of Simon & Schuster, Inc.

Illustration by Craig White

Manufactured in the United States of America

For information regarding special discounts for bulk purchases, please contact Simon & Schuster Special Sales at 1-800-456-6798 or business@simonandschuster.com.

Contents

TEN REASONS TO STAY

Sabrina Jeffries

To Rexanne, who always saves me from myself.
And who really, REALLY deserves a season on Survivor.

One

The new Earl of Monteith, Colin Hunt, had been in possession of Chaunceston Hall less than a day and already trouble was afoot.

Surrounded by unpacked boxes, Colin watched through his study window as a cloaked form darted across the lawn to slip into the stable. It was after midnight; none of the servants he'd hired in London should be about. And since the stable was filled with prime horseflesh he'd purchased at Tattersall's earlier this week . . .

Confound these English thieves to hell! Unearthing his pistol from a box, he loaded it and shoved it into the waistband of his trousers before hurrying into the hall.

Why wasn't some groom outside guarding the stable? Because this wasn't India, of course. In Colin's home country of twenty-eight years, the weather was so balmy that a *syce* could sleep across the stable doorway very comfortably. But here in England, no sane man slept outdoors in such weather.

Grumbling to himself about the brutal English winter, he donned his heaviest wool surtout, lit a lantern, and headed out. The gust of icy wind that greeted him made him swear vilely.

He missed the hot Poona days, the sultry Calcutta nights, where a man could lie naked in his bed and still be comfortable. A wave of homesickness swept him. He missed spicy pickles and cinnamon-scented tobacco and jackal hunts with the local *jemadar* and other fellows from the native infantry. . . .

Who would just as soon slip a knife in his back as breathe.

Colin sighed. He didn't miss *that*, the suspicions and spying, the petty grievances that erupted into violence, the ever-present threat of marauding bandits, of mutinies and rebellions. Of women cowering beneath the sword—

He shuddered. No, there was nothing left for him in India, no reason to stay where the persistent memories of his wife's slaughter at Poona could torment him. He wanted peace, and he'd hoped to find it in the sleepy English countryside.

This wasn't a promising start. It was only his first night at the Devon estate he'd inherited from his late, unlamented grandfather, and already the local rogues were robbing him. But they were in for a surprise. Half-Indian or no, he had every right to live here, and they would soon learn that he meant to hold on to what was his.

With that resolve beating in his breast, he slid open the stable door. At first he could see nothing, just his new Cleveland Bays sleeping in their stalls. But the faint acrid scent of a recently snuffed candle hung in the air, proving that the cloaked figure probably still lurked here.

He swept his lantern in a wide arc, then came back to where his pride of purchase, a chestnut Arabian, stood wide-awake. She was saddled and ready, with a cloth sack slung over the pommel.

His temper flared.

"Come out now, whoever you are!" Colin demanded, setting the lantern on a hook. "If you force me to go stall by stall to find you—"

"No need for that, sir," said a decidedly young voice as a short figure emerged from the stall. Colin glimpsed riding boots and breeches before the fellow shrank into his voluminous cloak like a turtle into its shell. "Beg pardon, but I didn't mean to wake you. I was just seeing to the horse."

"Seeing to stealing it, you mean."

"No!" The lad's head jerked up, though the hood of his cloak still shielded his face. "I-I merely wish to borrow it. I know the owner personally, and I assure you he'd happily loan it to me if he were here."

Colin didn't know whether to laugh at the bold devil or shoot him. "That, too, is a lie."

"Honestly, sir, the owner's wife is a good friend of mine."

"That's impossible." Furious that this thief persisted in his pretense, Colin slid his hand inside his surtout to grasp his pistol. "The owner's wife is dead."

"Dead!" The lad sounded genuinely upset. "How did it happen? Did the duchess die in childbirth? I can't believe—"

"Hold up there, lad. What duchess?"

"The duchess of Foxmoor. You said that the owner's wife—"

"The owner of this horse, of this entire estate, is the Earl of Monteith."

"Who's lying now?" the fellow retorted. "The earl has been dead for six years or more."

If the boy knew that, then he wasn't some wandering horse thief. Which also explained why he thought that the duke owned the estate; Foxmoor had managed it for the heir. "The *new* Earl of Monteith is alive and well, I assure you."

"The new—" The lad broke off with a groan. "Ohh, I forgot. The duke's cousin inherited the Monteith title. But he's over in—" He stared at Colin. "Blast."

"Exactly." Was it usual for a country boy to know so much about a duke and his family? "*I* am the owner. And *you* are trespassing."

"I-I suppose that means you won't lend me a horse."

"That's exactly what it means."

"I understand. Don't blame you a bit." The fellow turned his head toward the open door beyond Colin. "I won't keep you any longer. I'll just go—"

"The hell you will," Colin bit out and took a step forward.

A hand suddenly appeared from beneath the fellow's cloak, bearing a rather substantial flintlock pistol. "S-stand aside," he said as he pointed the gun at Colin.

Colin's fingers tensed on his own weapon . . . until he noticed that the thief's pistol wasn't cocked, and the barrel was an ancient rusted relic. He'd lay odds that the thing hadn't been loaded in twenty years, much less fired. "An unloaded weapon won't do you much good, lad," he said dryly.

The fellow's hand shook. "How did you know it isn't loaded?"

"I didn't." Colin taunted him with a smile. "But I do now."

The lad groaned. Without warning he hurled the pistol at Colin. As the heavy weapon glanced off Colin's brow and the boy dashed past him, Colin let out a roar and lunged after him.

Catching the fellow's hood, Colin yanked him back, then slammed him against the stable wall and pinned his arms at his sides. "Now see here, you little devil—" he began as the lad's bared head shot up and their gazes met.

The words died in Colin's throat. Because the nearby lamp flooding the thief's face revealed porcelain features and a tumbled-down length of thick, golden brown hair that were decidedly not male.

"I'll be damned," Colin murmured. "You're a woman."

And quite a woman, too, judging from the full mouth, rosy cheeks, and long silky lashes. Not to mention the ample breasts crushed against his chest. No wonder she'd worn a cloak. No one would ever mistake her for a boy without it, breeches or no.

A series of sweet-scented breaths stuttered from between her pretty lips and her lightly freckled cheeks flushed. For the first time in a long while, his blood stirred.

"Get off of me, blast you!" she cried. "You've no right—"

"I wouldn't be talking about rights just now, if I were you," he warned, trying not to be affected by the soft, feminine body plastered to him from thigh to chest. "Last I heard, they hang horse thieves in England."

Her chin trembled. "You know perfectly well I'm no horse thief."

He did know. Despite her oaths, her speech was that of a well-bred miss. And if her tale about borrowing a horse from the duke was true, she had the connections of one, too.

But why was she out at midnight dressed as a boy? "Tell me who and what you are."

"I'd rather not."

"And I'd rather not release you, so it appears we'll be here all night," he said, deliberately pressing his body into her.

"It appears so," she said, but with less bravado.

As he gave her his fiercest glare, she began chewing on her lower lip, and the girlish gesture made him feel like a scoundrel for bullying her. With a curse, he released her arms and shoved away from the wall.

"Thank you." She pulled her hood back up to cover her hair. Warily she edged out from between him and the wall, then slid toward the door. "I'll be sure to tell Louisa of your kindness."

If the foolish wench thought he would free her simply because she'd tossed out the name of his cousin's wife, she was mistaken. "Oh, no, you don't." He whipped out his weapon. "*My* pistol is loaded. And *you* aren't going anywhere until you tell me why you were 'borrowing' my horse."

Her eyes fixed on the gun, and even in the lantern light, he could see her flinch. "You . . . you wouldn't shoot a woman."

She was right, but he didn't put the pistol away. "You never know what a foreigner might do when faced with a lying thief."

"I'm not lying! I really was borrowing it!"

"Why?"

A frustrated breath escaped her lips. "If you must know, I need to ride it to Honiton. But once I get there, I plan to pay a post boy to return it."

He snorted. "Right. You can't afford a mount of your own and don't have the wherewithal to rent one, yet you can afford a post boy."

"Oh, but I can! I can even rent the horse from you if you'll let me."

She reached into her cloak, but he waved his gun at her. "Keep your hands where I can see them. I don't need another conk on the head."

Which was beginning to throb. He gestured to the

door. "Let's go. We'll continue this discussion inside."

"But I don't have time for that!" she cried. "I must reach Honiton by two!"

"I'm not lending or renting or otherwise giving you a horse, so get that idea right out of your head." He snuffed the lamp, then strode up to grab her by the arm. "Nor am I going to freeze to death while you try convincing me to do so."

Hustling her out of the stables, he led her across the well-clipped lawn dotted with topiaries. "I suppose you know your way, since you're such a grand friend of Louisa's."

"Well . . . um . . . I've never actually been to Chaunceston Hall." She gazed ahead to the battlemented turrets and parapets of the manor house that dated back to the Middle Ages. "It looks positively gothic, doesn't it?"

"If that's the word for a moldering old pile with drafty halls and monstrous pieces of ancient furniture, then yes." He shot her a quizzical glance. "And if you weren't familiar with the place, why did you come here?"

"I overheard the servant talking about preparations for a hunting party's arrival next week, so I knew—"

"There'd be horses," he clipped out. "That were easy to steal."

"Obviously not *that* easy," she grumbled.

He choked back a laugh. She certainly behaved like Louisa's friends, those young ladies who'd flitted in and out of his cousin's town house in London during the month Colin had lived there after arriving in England. And his little captive had servants: more evidence she wasn't the sort of female to steal a horse. Unless—

"Why are you running away from home?"

Her head swung around, her eyes full of panic. "How did you know I was run—" She broke off with a groan. "That trick of yours grows more tiresome every time you use it."

"So you might as well tell me everything. I'll get it out of you eventually."

"It has nothing to do with you!"

"It does if you're trying to entangle *me* in your scheme."

"You're the one insisting on an entanglement. Just let me leave, and I'll *walk* to Honiton."

"The hell you will. I'm not letting some fool of a young woman out on the road alone to be raped or killed."

The harsh words made her tense. "Fine. Then be a gentleman and drive me there in that cabriolet I saw beside the stable."

"Not a chance." He hurried her up the front steps. "Not until I know what you're up to." He led her into the house, releasing a grateful breath to be out of the infernal cold. "Hand me your cloak and gloves," he ordered as he shut the door.

She blinked at him. "Why?"

"You'd be an idiot to run off without them in this weather, and I'm not taking the chance that you'll knock me over the head while my back is turned."

With a roll of her eyes, she peeled off her gloves, then untied her cloak. When she drew it off, the sight of what lay beneath struck the breath from him.

He'd guessed her to be a girl of about sixteen. He'd guessed wrong. God help him, that was a woman's body half-bursting out of the ridiculously tight male apparel she'd apparently "borrowed" from a man much thinner than she.

It was impossible not to stare at the fetching picture

she made in a waistcoat half-unbuttoned to make room for her plump breasts and a pair of breeches too snug for her hips. Her unfortunate choice of a tailcoat made matters worse, too, since the nipped-in waist only accentuated her curves.

So did the shimmering cascade of thick hair that fell to her waist unfettered, although a few lingering hairpins twinkled in the candlelight.

This time it wasn't just his blood that stirred.

Confound her. Why had she come along *now*? In the first years after his wife's death, he'd felt nothing but grief and anger. But in recent months, especially since he'd arrived in England where his memories didn't plague him so, his desire for feminine company—in and out of his bed—had begun to return.

So the last thing he needed was a reckless runaway firing his blood. She was too much like Rashmi, his late wife. When he married again, it would be to a steady, quiet female who wanted peace as much as he. Maybe even some settled widow who wouldn't be bothered by his mixed blood. Certainly not an impudent wench with more curves than sense.

"What's wrong?" she asked, coloring beneath his intense scrutiny.

"You thought you could pass for a man in that costume?"

"Well . . . no. I'm too plump in . . . er . . . certain places for that."

Plump? Luscious, more like.

"But that's what the cloak's for. And even without it, from a distance—"

"—you'd look like a cherry ripe for the picking," he snapped. "Just how old are you, anyway?"

"Nineteen." She cast him a mutinous glance. "Old enough to go where I want and do as I please."

She had a point. In India, she would already be married. And her lucky husband would already be happily initiating his blushing bride into the pleasures of the bed, unveiling those creamy breasts and that dimpled belly, winding himself in the luscious silk of her dark honey hair as he buried his flesh inside—

He swore under his breath. What was he thinking? She was trouble. The chit was probably running off to elope with some equally clod-pated idiot. Although if that were so, why hadn't the idiot come to fetch her?

Whatever her reasons, no young female with her attractions and rash tendency to land in trouble should be roaming the English countryside at midnight.

The last time a woman had convinced him to let her travel without his protection, she'd ended up dead. He wasn't about to let that happen twice.

"Old enough or not, you shouldn't be on the road alone." He held up his free hand. "So give me the cloak and the gloves."

Rebellion flared in her face. Taking him by surprise, she tossed the gloves at him. As he lunged to catch them, she deftly swung the cloak to cover his head and pistol, then took off.

He swore, momentarily blinded, but managed to fight free of her cloak just as she sped past him toward the door. "Oh no, you don't," he growled as he reached out and snagged her about the waist, then jerked her up against him.

When her furious gaze swung to him, he added, "Nice try, my dear. But it would take a better 'man' than you to best me."

"Very . . . funny," she gasped as she struggled against him. "Let me . . . go!"

"You're plucky—I'll give you that."

Also incredibly foolish. And it was time he made

her aware just *how* foolish. "But my patience is at an end." He stuffed his pistol inside his waistband, then caught her by the throat. "You have one minute to tell me your name, where you live, and why you're running away."

Although she stopped struggling, her hazel eyes narrowed to slits. "Or what? You'll throttle me?"

"Tempting as that sounds, no." He slid his thumb down to brush her top shirt button. "I'll simply remove the rest of your clothes piece by piece until you do."

Two

*W*ith alarm beating wildly in her chest, Eliza Crenshawe stared up into Lord Monteith's glittering gaze. For a moment, she'd actually forgotten that the new earl was half-Indian and a foreigner, but this close it was hard to ignore the man's swarthy features and the inky slashes of eyebrows drawn in a frown.

Or the large hand encircling her throat with potent menace. She swallowed, which only made her more aware of his grip. Surely he was bluffing. He was the duke's cousin—he'd never assault her virtue. Would he?

Blast it—she didn't have time for this! By morning, her uncle, Silas Whitcomb, would surely have discovered her gone, no matter how drunk he was. They were supposed to head to Cornwall in a hired coach at dawn, so once he came to fetch her from her bedchamber—

"If I tell you my name, will that satisfy you?" she offered.

She'd throw the dogged earl a bone to get him to release her. Giving him her name was probably safe, since both of them were new to the area. He wouldn't know that her uncle had a niece . . . if he even knew her uncle at all.

"I want more than your name." The earl's arm still anchored her against his side and his hand still clutched her throat. "I want to know where you live—"

"My lord, is that you?" came a voice from below, followed by footsteps coming up the servant's stairs.

They both froze. They'd awakened someone. And if they were caught together in the middle of the night, she'd be ruined for certain. Which would only give her uncle more of an excuse for going through with his heartless plans.

"Please . . ." she whispered, but Lord Monteith was already releasing her.

"Yes, it's me!" he called down as he scooped up her cloak and gloves, then tossed them into the nearby closet, which he locked with a little key. "I couldn't sleep, so I went for a walk. No need for you to come up."

They heard the servant hesitate on the stairs. "Very good, sir. If you need anything—"

"I'll ring for you. Go back to bed."

They both held their breaths until they heard the door close below. Then Lord Monteith pocketed the closet key. "We'd best continue this discussion somewhere more private." He gestured toward a long hall. "I believe the parlor is that way."

"You believe?"

He scowled at her. "I just arrived this afternoon. Too bad your spies didn't pass on that bit of information."

"Too bad indeed," she shot back, "for I'd have tried harder to avoid you."

Turning on her heel, she headed off down the hall he'd indicated, but with every step she felt the time racing by. Much longer, and she wouldn't make it to Honiton on foot. She could try to run from him . . . no, he could outrun her easily. Besides, he still carried that nasty pistol. She didn't think he'd use it, but—

How the devil had everything gone so wrong? Her plan had been simple: borrow one of the duke's horses, ride to Honiton, catch the mail coach back to school in Richmond, and appeal to Mrs. Harris for help with her mad uncle. Running afoul of the new owner of Chaunceston Hall hadn't been part of the plan.

And what was she to make of him? She could feel his eyes on her as he followed at a more leisurely pace.

You'd look like a cherry ripe for the picking.

Judging from the audacious way he'd raked her body with those black-as-hell eyes, he wouldn't mind doing the picking, either.

An errant thrill coursed down her spine before she squelched it ruthlessly. This was *not* one of her favorite gothic melodramas. This was real. Real trouble.

Besides, men didn't think of her like that—she'd always been too full-figured and freckled to be fashionable. It was just this ridiculously gothic house and gothic situation making her imagine such things.

But it didn't help that Lord Monteith made the perfect gothic hero, with his brooding stare and his piratical features, and those threats he kept making that she was sure he wouldn't follow through with.

Almost sure, anyway.

"In here," he bit out as he thrust her through the door of a well-appointed parlor.

He closed the door behind them, then strode across the room to build a fire in the enormous hearth while keeping a suspicious eye on her like the gothic hero he was.

Or gothic villain? She wished she could be sure. So far he hadn't hurt her, though he'd nearly given her heart failure half a dozen times. Like when he'd first caught her in the stables, with his ebony eyes gleaming and the shadowy light darkening his olive features.

And when he'd drawn his sleek, well-oiled pistol—

A shudder racked her. Perhaps she should have better heeded the lesson Mrs. Harris had set for her to learn over the holidays: *You have a tendency not to look before you leap, Eliza. It's time you stopped letting it land you in the briar bushes.*

Lord Monteith made quite a fearsome briar bush. As he crouched to feed the fire, the flames lit his fierce warrior's face, and his broad shoulders and muscular thighs impressively strained the confines of his wool clothing. She had no doubt of their strength after being pinned against the stable wall. This wasn't a man to be toyed with, Louisa's relation or no.

He rose and strode to where a carafe of brandy sat on a console table. She instantly stiffened. "I'd prefer that you not drink." She'd already had to deal with one intoxicated male this evening; she had no wish to wrangle with another.

"I'd prefer that England not be so damned cold, but since it is, I'm hoping the brandy will compensate." Arching one silky black brow, he held up the carafe. "I'm happy to share."

"A lady never partakes of strong drink," she recited, one of the few lessons that had actually stuck with her. She cast the carafe a pointed glance. "And English gentlemen don't imbibe strong drink in front of ladies, either."

To her annoyance, he still poured himself a glass, then turned to eye her speculatively as he sipped from it. "What makes you think I'm a gentleman?"

Certainly not his looks. With his thumb thrust inside his waistband and his hand brushing the pistol tucked there, she could easily mistake him for one of the ruthless sultans so popular as villains on the stage.

Except that his surtout and perfectly tailored wool

suit, not to mention his confident bearing, were pure English aristocracy. Even his speech was precise and cultured as any lord's, with only a hint of a foreign accent. And if he *wasn't* a gentleman, why was he trying so hard to keep her from traveling alone?

Perhaps if she appealed to the gentleman in him, she could convince him to let her go. There was still time.

She met his gaze squarely. "Louisa told me all about you."

"Ah, yes, my cousin's wife, your 'good friend.' What exactly did she say?"

"That her husband regarded you highly when you served as his aide-de-camp. That's why he worked so hard to have your rightful inheritance and title given to you after all this time. She said you were educated in one of the best schools in Calcutta and raised a gentleman, that you fought valiantly for England during the Battle of Kirkee despite—"

"My Indian blood," he broke in coldly.

"I was going to say, 'the hard loss of your wife before the battle,' but clearly you know my mind better than I."

His gaze softened a fraction. "Touché."

"And as I understand it, your blood is only half-Indian."

"That certainly hasn't prevented my countrymen—or you, for that matter—from regarding my dusky features with suspicion," he said with a hint of bitterness.

"It's not your dusky features I regard with suspicion," she said dryly. "It's that loaded pistol shoved in your trousers."

He blinked, then laughed. "Clever girl." He lifted his glass in a toast, but didn't take the hint and remove the pistol as she'd hoped. Instead, he took another sip of brandy before pacing closer. "How odd that I never met you in London. God knows I met any number of Louisa's other 'good friends.' "

"I've been in mourning for my father the past few months," Eliza explained. "He died when his landau lost a wheel and he was thrown into a—" She blinked hard, forcing back tears before going on. "Into a stone wall. It broke his neck."

"I'm sorry for your loss," he murmured.

"Thank you." She swallowed her sobs. She couldn't dwell on Papa right now. "Anyway, that's why you didn't see me at Louisa's. I've been rather reclusive."

"Until tonight." He swirled the brandy in his glass. "Does your father's death have something to do with why you're running away?"

He was fishing for information again. "You could say that."

"Come now, Miss— Damn it, I still don't even know your name."

"Eliza," she offered. "Just . . . Eliza."

"And where do you live, Just Eliza?"

A small smile touched her lips. "In Hampstead Heath."

"Very amusing. Even *I* know that Hampstead is near London."

"And that's where my home is. Or used to be, anyway."

"Where's your home now?" The clipped military command reminded her that not only had he once been a soldier, he was also the son of a soldier.

She weighed her choices. She could continue to tell him nothing, hoping he really had been bluffing about the strip-her-clothes-off thing.

But refusing to answer wasn't getting her anywhere. So perhaps if she told him everything, he might recognize her desperate situation and be willing to lend her a horse or drive her to Honiton. It was rapidly getting to the point where she'd never make it in time, otherwise.

Then again, he might just decide to return her to Uncle Silas. And then she'd never get another chance to escape.

Very well, she'd tell him only enough to convince him to help her. She'd leave out the part that might ruin her plan for escape. "My home is yet to be determined, actually. This is *my* first day in this area, as well. My . . . er . . . guardian and I only arrived here this evening."

"And what is *his* name?"

"I can't tell you." When frustration scored his features, she added, "But only because I can't go back to him, and if I tell you who he is, you'll try to make me."

He muttered an oath under his breath. "Eliza, it's late, it's cold, and I'm in no mood for playing games."

"Nor am I. But my guardian is determined to marry me off to a stranger. He means to force me into it, whether I want it or not."

Casting her a skeptical glance, he sipped more brandy. "I thought this was enlightened England, where no one is forced to marry against their will."

"I thought so, too," she retorted. "But that was before my new guardian left me at my school after the funeral, while he apparently went off to arrange some marriage without my knowledge or permission."

Her uncle's betrayal still made her reel. The Uncle Silas she remembered from childhood visits had been amiable and affectionate, a country squire held in high regard by the townspeople of nearby Brookmoor. Not the drunken bully he'd become.

"The day before yesterday, he came to fetch me for

the holidays," she went on. "But when we arrived in Brookmoor, he informed me that I couldn't have my Season in London next spring after all. Instead I was to marry some friend of his."

Worse yet, the marriage was to occur as soon as they arrived in Cornwall. Uncle Silas had said he intended to marry her to his friend no matter what, and would use any means—even force—to make sure she complied. He knew she had no recourse, with all her friends being in London.

"So you ran away," the earl said.

She thrust out her chin. "Yes. I didn't see any way around it."

He swore under his breath. "No, you thought it better to steal a horse and hie off to London alone in that outrageous costume. How about simply informing your guardian that you won't marry his choice?"

"I tried that. He slapped me."

"Slapped you!" Anger flared in his dark eyes, and his hand paused in midair as he was lifting his glass to his lips.

"Yes. He was drinking. Heavily." She touched a hand to her cheek, still mortified to remember it. No one had ever struck her, not her father nor any teacher or tutor. That a beloved uncle could do it— "And I fear what else he might be capable of if I persist in refusing to marry his friend."

A muscle ticked in the earl's jaw as he glanced from her to the brandy, then set his glass down. "What was your father thinking to give such a man charge of your life?"

She sighed. "I gather that my guardian's drinking has only become a problem in recent years. I'm sure Papa would never have appointed him if he'd realized that the man had become a sot."

But Papa's will had been drawn up before Aunt Nancy had followed Mama, her older sister, to the grave two years ago. Since then, Uncle Silas had refused to visit, saying that he still grieved too much.

Now she wondered if he'd had other reasons for refusing. When they'd arrived at Uncle's manor this evening, her aunt's once elegant parlor had been littered with bottles, and a horrible stench had pervaded every hall.

"So you see, I can't go back there."

"Then we'll take you to the local magistrate. He'll make sure that your guardian does his duty."

An alarm seized her that she struggled to hide. "You can't do that."

He eyed her closely. "Why not?"

Because my guardian is the local magistrate. "You just can't." When the earl raised an eyebrow, she added hastily, "The magistrate is sure to be on my guardian's side, so if you take me to him I'll be worse off." She met his gaze squarely, praying her answer would be enough to convince him to help her.

Apparently it wasn't, for he now regarded her with clear suspicion. "I see that my house isn't the only gothic thing around here."

She caught her breath. Good Lord, had he somehow guessed her fanciful speculations about him as a gothic hero? "I-I can't imagine what you mean," she said, unable to suppress a blush.

That only seemed to rouse his suspicions further, for his expression grew positively menacing. "I may be foreign, Eliza, but I do read books and attend the theater. I know all about the present passion for gothic literature that you young ladies pursue. So I recognize a trumped-up tale when I hear one. The drunken guardian. The late, lamented father. The forced marriage."

Her blood stilled in her veins. She hadn't realized until he said it that she'd begun *living* in a gothic play. Oh, how the other girls would laugh! They'd always teased her about her enjoyment of the absurd plots and excessive characters.

And they were right—it *was* absurd, all of it. Absurd that Papa had died in such an awful manner. Absurd that Uncle Silas had become a sot and was up to some wild scheme to marry her off to his friend.

Absurd that Lord Monteith, whom she'd begun to think might actually be reasonable, had returned to playing the arrogant and slightly scary gothic hero. Minus the wicked mustache and cape.

Well, she'd had enough of the play for tonight. She wasn't going to sit here quarreling while the minutes ticked by, bringing her ever closer to a marriage she didn't want. "So you don't believe me," she said. "Fine. Think whatever you want. Because it's not going to change anything. I, sir, am leaving."

Three

$\mathcal{M}$uttering a curse, Colin moved to block Eliza's march to the door. "I can't let you do that."

He was already furious with himself for listening to the spoiled chit's nonsense about a drunken guardian. How many of his wife's exaggerated complaints had he acted upon before he realized she'd say anything to get her way?

"You said you wouldn't let me leave until I told you everything," she protested, looking every bit the outraged gothic heroine. "So I did. It's not my fault you refuse to believe it."

"Nor mine that your tale left out so much," he countered. "The name of your guardian and where he lives. Even details about your dastardly suitor, like who he is and why you object to the match."

"I object to the match because he's a stranger to me! And that's why I can't tell you who he is. Why would I lie about it, anyway?"

"Because you think exaggerating your situation will enable you to talk me into helping you run away."

She looked genuinely appalled. "I would never—"

"If your guardian is shirking his duties, you should be happy to speak to the magistrate. Yet you refuse. So I know you're hiding something."

A guilty flush touched her cheeks. "Don't be ridiculous."

"There's another fellow involved, isn't there? Your guardian whisked you away from the city to keep you from marrying a penniless nitwit who's claims he loves you for yourself—"

"Absolutely not," she said with a sniff. "Mrs. Harris would skin me alive if I married a penniless nitwit after all her lessons."

Mrs. Harris. Where had he heard that name? Ah, yes. "So you're one of her little heiresses. From her School for Ladies."

"Yes." She eyed him warily. "What of it?"

"That makes your tale even more unbelievable. Why the blazes would your guardian marry you to a stranger when you could have your pick of suitors?"

"I said the same thing to *him*! But he claims I don't even have enough money for a Season, much less my dowry—which is ridiculous, because I know Papa left me adequately provided for."

"So that's what this is all about. You're angry that he isn't giving you a Season."

"No! That merely showed me that something is dreadfully wrong." She cast him a pleading glance. "And there was another odd thing—my guardian told me that after seeing me in the park, his friend was smitten."

"And that insulted you?" he said, all at sea.

"Blast it, no!" She looked exasperated. "Don't you understand? My guardian never introduced me to this man. So if the suitor had been in town, why didn't my guardian bring him to meet me?" Her eyes flashed. "I'll tell you why. Because he's some . . . horrible, decrepit fellow who has made a dastardly arrangement that my guardian refuses to reveal."

"And *this* is the tale you plan to tell your friends in

London to gain their help. Well, perhaps your friends would indulge your whim, but I'm not fool enough to do so."

This was the sort of impetuous act his wife had regularly indulged in, which was how she'd ended up dead. He wouldn't be a party to it. "I've heard enough. Give me your guardian's name; I'm bringing you home. If you wish, I'll speak to him on your behalf, but that's your only choice."

"Oh, for pity's sake, I don't have to put up with this! You have no right to keep me here, no right to stop me—"

"You were stealing my horse, remember? That means I have every right to haul you off to the local magistrate. He'll know what to do with you."

Though her face went ash-white, she planted her hands on her hips. "I should like to see you explain to him how I ended up in your company in the middle of the night. Since you insist on believing me a liar anyway, I might as well take my 'gothic tale' to its extreme. When I finish wailing about how you accosted me in the woods near my home and dragged me back to your lair to have your wicked way with—"

"What!" he roared. "You would dare to lie about a man's good name?"

"If I have to."

"You stubborn little troublemaking . . ." He forced himself to remain calm. "They'd never take your word over mine."

She arched one eyebrow. "Are you sure? My guardian would rather believe I was assaulted against my will than that I was shameful enough to run away."

Damn the chit, she was probably right. "Seeing you dressed as a boy will confirm my claims," he said, grasping at straws.

"Not if I tell them you forced me to wear a servant's clothes after you ripped my own off." She drew herself up, a determined glint in her eye. "I participated in amateur theatricals at my school, and gothic heroines were my specialty. I can even cry at will. Shall I show you?"

She screwed up her face as if to cry, and he rolled his eyes. "Spare me, please."

What a mess! Taking her to the magistrate became less feasible by the moment. He didn't actually know the magistrate . . . or anyone else in town. His new servants didn't know anyone, either. He'd come to the estate in advance of his cousin and the hunting party so he could grow acclimated. Simon was to introduce him about Brookmoor next week.

So if he took her into town and she did make spurious claims about his character, they might be believed. Her guardian might even be a prominent local figure. Despite Colin's title and connections, the townspeople would still regard him as a stranger and a foreigner.

Confound her to hell. How could he have a peaceful life in the country if she put him under a cloud of suspicion from the start?

"So you see," she went on, "*you're* the one with no choice, unless you want to be carted off to prison for assaulting a poor innocent."

God, he hadn't even considered that possibility. "They wouldn't take an English peer to trial on the basis of your fabricated tale," he said uneasily.

"Perhaps not, but they could make you marry me." Her eyes narrowed. "That would certainly solve my dilemma, so if you're eager to take a wife—"

"You? Never."

A flush touched her freckled cheeks. "You don't have to be insulting."

"Forgive me, but I don't want a wife whose favorite pastime is dressing in men's clothing and stealing horses. What I want is peace and quiet. And I daresay any husband of yours would have to give that up."

She tipped up her chin. "If it's peace you want, you should let me go." Shoving her hand into her coat pocket, she pulled out a wad of pound notes. "Since you won't drive me to Honiton, at least rent a horse to me."

His temper flared. The idiot meant to traverse England alone with a fortune in her pockets and a disguise only a blind man would believe. And she was mad enough to try blackmailing him into letting her do it.

What if she tried such foolishness with an unscrupulous innkeeper or coachman? In the two days it took the mail coach to reach London, she could be robbed and assaulted half a dozen times, for God's sake!

Fine. She wouldn't tell him who her guardian was, so he'd have to scare her into it. It was time he showed the woman exactly what she risked.

"You've just threatened to ruin my character—do you think I'll let you go *now*? You've given me no choice but to keep you locked up as long as it takes to silence your lying tongue."

That certainly got her attention. She blinked at him like a cat caught in candlelight. "Wh-what do you mean?"

He stalked toward her. "I can't have you voicing false accusations or forcing me into marriage. So what's it to be? A few nights in my attic while I starve you into compliance? A week in the dungeon? I'm told there is one, although a cellar would suffice."

At least she had the good sense to back away. "If you're attempting to play the villain, it won't work," she said with a nervous laugh. Yet she darted around the heavy baroque sofa to put it between her and him. "You would never lock anyone in an attic. And you aren't the sort to bully a woman."

"How would you know?" he asked as he prowled along the sofa.

"I heard all about your brave exploits in India from Louisa." She quickly moved to evade him. "Your reputation for heroism and fine deeds has preceded you, and I can't believe you'd tarnish it by hurting—"

"You forget that no one knows you're here. Not your guardian, nor my servants. I could haul you into the woods, shoot you, and bury you so that no one would ever find you." If *that* didn't frighten the little fool, nothing would.

"You could." Her gaze flitted about the room as if in search of a weapon. "But you wouldn't."

"Why not?"

"Because you'd have to catch me first." Grabbing one of the cushions, she threw it at him and darted for the door behind her.

Confound the woman! He leaped the sofa to capture her, and tossed her to the floor. With the wind knocked out of her, she couldn't stop him when he threw himself on top of her, pinning her beneath him.

For the first time since he'd found her in the stable, sheer panic showed in her face. "Get off me!" she cried, shoving against his chest.

"Do you see how easy it is? How quickly a man can subdue you?"

"Only if I let him," she spat, lifting her hands to scratch his face.

But he caught them and pinned them to the carpet, too. "Now what?" He glowered down at her. "You're well and truly trapped, admit it."

She struggled against him, but it took ridiculously little effort to keep her restrained by her wrists and to clamp her thighs between his so she couldn't move.

When she stopped her futile struggling, he continued his warning. "*Now* do you understand what I could do to you if I had a mind to it? I could rip your clothes off, and you couldn't do a damned thing to stop me. I could ravish you . . ."

"Oh, for pity's sake, you're worse than any gothic play." Her expression had turned mutinous. "If you'd meant to ravish me, you would have done it in the stables the second you discovered I was a woman."

He couldn't believe his ears. She was pinned to the floor completely helpless, and instead of acknowledging the danger, she was even more stubborn.

She actually had the audacity to taunt him! "It would have been far wiser, you know. Less messy— you wouldn't have spilled any blood on the furniture."

"Spilled any—" He let out a vile oath. "I swear, you're the most maddening female I've ever met! Don't you realize what trouble you're in?"

"Yes, I do. That's why I won't let you take me back to my guardian." Her eyes glittered up at him. "You won't murder me. If you won't risk having me falsely accuse you, you certainly won't risk a murder investigation."

Christ, how far must he go to intimidate the stubborn woman into revealing the truth and giving up her mad scheme? Clearly, farther than he had. "Perhaps not, but that won't stop me from making good on my earlier promise."

"What promise?"

"To strip your clothes off piece by piece until you tell me what I need to know."

At last he got the reaction he wanted. Uncertainty

flickered in her face, and she bit down on her lower lip. Her pretty coral lip, plump enough to devour—

He swore under his breath. Having her beneath him, with her lush hair spilling about her face and his groin flush against her soft flesh, was beginning to affect him. He'd better finish this while he could still control himself.

Clasping both her wrists in one hand, he dropped the other to her borrowed waistcoat. With a dire glance, he flicked a button loose. "We'll start with this."

"Stop that," she whispered as he opened another.

"Tell me your guardian's name," he said, pausing.

She thrust out her impudent little chin. "It's Peter," she said sweetly.

He jumped on that eagerly. "And his last name?"

"Pumpkin-Eater. He lives down the road in a pumpkin shell with his wife—"

"Damn it, this is not a joke! Tell me his name!"

"I don't remember."

With a foul glance, he worked loose another button, then another.

She glared at him. "Let me see—it was Jack something. Jack Sprat? Little Jack Horner? Look in the corner and see—"

"I swear, it won't be the corner you'll be sitting in if you don't tell me your guardian's name and where he lives," he warned.

"I'm not going to tell you."

Eyes gleaming with threat, he released the last few buttons, then reached for the ones at the collar of her shirt. "You think not, do you, Eliza?"

Though her breath came more quickly and her delicious lower lip trembled, her pretty eyes still shone resolutely. "As long as you're calling me Eliza, I shall call you Colin. It *is* Colin, isn't it? Colin Hunt?"

"Colin, yes." He caught himself. "It doesn't matter what you call me, confound it!"

"It certainly does. If you're about to see me entirely naked, then I should at least call you by your Christian name."

He froze. Damn her for putting that image in his head! "Have you no sense of danger, you little fool?" he exploded as he bent close. "No idea of how you tempt fate every time you open that reckless mouth of yours?"

"Not where you're concerned," she shot back. "Perhaps you alarm others with that black scowl, but I can tell a gentleman when I see one, and you—"

He cut off her words with a hard kiss.

He'd meant it to shut her up, to shock her. Unfortunately, it did far more than that. It made him conscious of her as a woman. A desirable woman. Whom he'd secretly lusted after from the minute he'd felt her curves beneath her cloak.

She wasn't helping, either, for she didn't struggle, didn't even turn her head away. She lay there frozen, letting him kiss her, taste her.

Desperately reaching for sanity, he lifted his head to stare at her, hoping to see fear or alarm or anything on her face that might bring him to his senses.

Instead, she was watching him with wide, astonished eyes. With a sinking heart, he saw in them the same awareness of him as a man that he'd felt for her as a woman.

And in that moment, he knew he was done for.

*C*olin's second, rougher kiss stunned Eliza. Especially when he slid his tongue between her lips and inside her mouth.

Lord save her. The girls at school had whispered of such outrageous kisses, but she hadn't known . . . she hadn't expected . . . He seemed to be trying to violate her mouth the same way he'd threatened to violate her body, but it didn't feel like a violation. It felt . . . amazing. Blatantly erotic, blatantly enthralling.

Oh, what was wrong with her? She mustn't let him do this, even if he *was* just trying to frighten her into letting him cart her back to her uncle's.

Frighten her, yes—the way the pistol digging into her thigh was meant to frighten her. This was not a *real* kiss. She must pay it no mind, even though her heart hammered in her chest, and the thrusts of his tongue did funny things to her insides, making her want to open her mouth further, tangle her tongue with his—

He jerked back with an oath. "For God's sake, what are you doing?"

"I-I don't know," she answered honestly. "Whatever it is, I don't *mean* to do it. It's just that no man has ever kissed me like that before, and you . . . that is . . ."

She was babbling, blast it. She couldn't help it—the

way he looked at her unsettled her. Excited her. Good Lord.

It only got worse when she chewed nervously on her lower lip. His eyes darkened to a smoky black, and he uttered a heartfelt groan.

Then he kissed her. Again. And she let him. Again. By tomorrow, she might very well be hurtling toward Cornwall, so she had to know what might lay ahead. That was her foggy reasoning, anyway.

This time he still took possession of her mouth like a hungry, marauding army, but gone was the roughness, the insolence. He kissed her like a man who meant it, his tongue delving inside with slow, sleek strokes.

So this was what it felt like to be thoroughly kissed: hot and heady and too tempting for words. Even his whisker stubble scraping her soft cheek and the threat of his pistol merely reminded her he was a man, and not some local lad trying to steal a kiss at a picnic. Every inch of the body plastered to hers was firm, muscular, demanding . . . the way a man's body should be.

Oh, Lord, she could never do this with just anyone, certainly not with some suspiciously secret friend of her uncle's. Never! No matter what it took, she would make sure that the only man she kissed this intimately was a man she desired.

A man like Colin.

She groaned against his lips. Had she lost her mind? Colin meant to cart her back to her uncle! And he'd made it clear he had no interest in marrying her.

Not that she would marry the stubborn ass. He refused to believe her, and he ordered her about, and . . . and . . . oh, blast, he kissed like something out of a gothic play. A very *good* gothic play. His mouth enticed her, and the press of his very masculine body against hers roused forbidden urges in her breasts and belly.

When he suddenly released her wrists, her arms slid automatically about his neck as if drawn there by a puppeteer. With a sigh of pure pleasure, she buried her fingers in his thick, silken hair.

He slipped his hand inside her open waistcoat to cup her breast through the thin linen of her shirt.

Good Lord, what was he doing? This went too far. And yet . . .

It felt so good. Shocking and appalling and absolutely marvelous.

"We must end this," he choked out even as he trailed kisses along her neck, and his thumb swept her nipple with a delicacy that made her breath catch.

"Yes," she breathed, though his hand now kneaded her breast, sending delightful chills along her spine.

"Tell me who your guardian is, sweeting," he murmured, a hint of desperation in his voice. "Tell me where he lives."

The question cut through her sensual haze like a knife of ice.

Blast, another few minutes of this, and she'd tell him everything he wanted to know! And then she'd be doing this with her uncle's horrible friend, whether she wanted to or not.

No, never. She jerked his hand from her breast. "Stop that," she whispered.

He pushed himself up, looking as dazed as she felt. At least she hadn't been the only one caught up in their touching. Though that proved hollow comfort when his scowl turned black as the devil's. "What game are you playing, Eliza?"

"Me! You're the one who's playing a game, touching my body and trying to distract—" She broke off. She didn't want him to know how close he'd come to succeeding, or he'd use that to his advantage. Forcing nonchalance into her voice, she said, "If you're trying to teach me the dangers of ravishment, it's not working."

"Damn it, I'm not playing!" He thrust his lower body against her, pressing something thick and rigid into the flesh between her legs. And it wasn't his pistol, either. "*This* is what happens when a man is aroused. Shall I show you what happens when he satisfies that arousal?"

He was bluffing again, wasn't he? She was almost sure he was. Still, it took all her will to cast him a sweet smile and call his bluff. "Go ahead."

He tensed, the bulge below his waist swelling against her, a bold, heavy threat that she couldn't quite discount.

Then he swore and rolled off of her, his breath coming in urgent gasps and his chest heaving to contain them.

Dropping her head back, she strove for calm. She'd won *this* round. But how many more could she manage?

It took her a moment to regain her equilibrium. Then she sat up on the carpet and cast him a furtive glance. "Thank you." *For being the gentleman I knew you were.*

Muttering a coarse oath, he rose, glared at her, then perversely held out his hand to help her up. She released it as soon as she was on her feet. The feel of his arousal against her soft flesh hadn't left her, and she very much feared she'd have let him do as he pleased with her, if he'd forced the matter.

She winced. Curse him for that. The few men she'd met at school functions had seemed appalled by her bold manner, abundance of freckles, and inappropriate cursing. Yet Colin seemed to like all of it, despite his railing against her.

As she buttoned her waistcoat, he watched her with

a fearsome scowl. "You do realize that if I'd been any other man—"

"I know," she said to forestall another lecture.

"So what am I to do with you?" He prowled the room like a panther, his agitation evident in every terse step. "You won't go to the magistrate with your tale, and I can't let you ride off to Honiton alone."

Her "tale?" Blast him, he *still* refused to believe her. "You could take me to Honiton in your cabriolet. You could ensure that I get onto the mail coach safely."

"And after that? Anything could happen on your trip to London. *Anything.* One look at that body of yours and that hair—"

"I'll keep my hood on."

He snorted. "To and from coaching inns or in a carriage, with people jostling you? You'd never manage it." With a glint of purpose in his coffee-hued eyes, he stalked toward her, his surtout flapping open to expose his pistol. "If you won't let me return you to your guardian tonight, I'll have to lock you up here until morning, when I can go into Brookmoor and ask around to find out who he is."

Panic pressed upon her chest. "And once you know?"

"I'll have a word with the gentleman, see if what you say is true."

"He'll just lie to you," she said glumly. "The way he lied to Mrs. Harris about my coming back in a few weeks for my Season."

"Credit me with some sense," he said. "I can tell when a man is lying."

"Really?" she snapped. "You think *I'm* lying, and I'm not."

"Exaggerating," he said, his gaze growing shuttered. "Not lying."

"So once you talk to him, then what?"

"It depends on what he says."

Her temper flared. "Right. And he's a man, so you'll take his word over mine, of course."

"I didn't say that."

"But you thought it." She glared at him. "I'd rather take my chances on the road than with you."

"And I won't let you. So let's find you a place to sleep."

She searched for another argument to convince him, but what was the point? Nothing swayed him. He was even more stubborn when sober than her uncle was when drunk. He left her no choice but to let him lead her from the room.

Now what? Colin would never lower his guard long enough for her to escape. And once he learned that she was the magistrate's niece, he would wash his hands of her. Because what foreigner new to town would champion her when it meant tangling with the authorities?

Unless . . .

He *did* seem to find her attractive, despite his insulting comments about the sort of wife she'd make. Why not use that? If she could get him even a little enamored of her, then perhaps he wouldn't be so eager to throw her back to her uncle in the morning. She might even convince him to take her to Honiton.

Could she do it? She'd watched other girls at the school flirt and tease fellows into doing things for them. She'd never been good at it herself—not enough opportunities for practice—but it couldn't hurt to try.

She slanted a glance at him as he led her to the stairs with an iron grip on her elbow, his dark eyes resolute and his jaw set. Colin wasn't some fawning suitor or a friend's shy younger brother whom a woman could tease endlessly with impunity. He was a virile, volatile man. If he lost control of himself with her—

She ignored the sudden and very wicked current that pulsed through her. She didn't want that; she *didn't*. All she wanted was to escape her uncle. And she could do it, if she were careful. After all, if Colin hadn't lost control when he'd had her subdued beneath him, he wasn't likely to do it in response to some teasing.

And if he did?

It was a chance she'd have to take.

Colin lay staring up at the canopy of his bed, wishing desperately for sleep to rescue him from his misery. But until Eliza stopped moving about in the adjoining room, sleep was impossible.

The last place he'd wanted to stow her was in his dressing room, especially since it was half-filled with boxes and had only a chaise longue for a bed. But it was the only room in the whole damned place that he could easily monitor. It had just one door and a transom window, both of which led into his bedchamber.

He couldn't risk her attempting an escape from this floor. And she was liable to do it, climb out some window and fall and break her pretty little neck. Then he'd have that on his conscience, too.

She hummed as she moved about, and he groaned. Confound the stubborn chit. Was she *trying* to drive him insane? Given that he'd nearly seduced her in the parlor, she ought to keep quiet, if only to soothe his temper. But no, after arousing him with her sweetly innocent response to his unwise kisses and then still refusing to tell him what he'd needed to know, she'd waltzed up the stairs ahead of him like a queen. While he'd followed behind, trying futilely to tear his gaze from those seductively swinging hips.

Then when he'd tried to stash her in the dressing room, she'd kept him there with questions about India, her soft, knowing smiles perfectly blending the innocent with the naughty. Clearly he didn't intimidate her one bit.

And why did she seem so damned convinced of his gentlemanly character? Other Englishwomen acted slightly afraid of him. Eliza melted in his arms.

The little fool was fearless. And sweet, a temptress in the making. He wanted her. *Very* badly. Which was why when he couldn't silence her magpie tongue, in desperation he'd shut her into her cage, before he gave in to the urge to stop her mouth with his own, again.

God, he could still taste her, still feel her breast ripening beneath his palm, and her thighs parting to allow him to cradle his aching loins between the delicate softness of her—

Don't think about it, he told himself as his cock hardened.

As if that were possible. He must be cursed. It was as if Shiva himself had sent down a delicious morsel of a female to destroy his resolve to settle in England. No matter what decision he made concerning her, it was bound to come back to trample him.

But oh, what luscious lips she had. And that bosom . . . a man could die happy caressing those breasts, as tempting and womanly as any *devadasi*'s. He could well imagine her as one of those Indian dancing girls, draped in a filmy gauze veil, with kohl lining her eyelids and henna staining her pouting, seductive mouth—

Damn it, he'd never get to sleep if he didn't find relief from his obsessive thoughts and this cursed arousal. Casting a furtive glance at the closed transom, he turned onto his side and took hold of his cock.

With her pretty humming still sounding in his ears, he began to work his flesh. He imagined her naked, beckoning him to suck her nipples and lick her belly and drive his eager cock inside her harder . . . faster . . . deeper . . .

As he reached his release, he muffled his cries with the pillow. After that he was finally able to fall asleep.

But he dreamed of her, of those delicate hands caressing him, and that hair of rumpled velvet entwining his limbs as she brought him to ecstasy with her hot, silky mouth. So it was no wonder that when next he awoke, he was half-hard again, aching for the dream that evaporated as soon as his eyes shot open. As soon as he realized that something in particular had awakened him.

For a moment, he lay there alert, waiting, listening, as early dawn brushed the room with the faintest wash of light. Then a loud thump sounded from the dressing room, and he jerked upright. What the blazes was she up to now? She should be sleeping—he'd given her a mountain of blankets. He'd also left her with candles and a flint box, so there was no need for her to be stumbling into things.

He slipped from the bed and shivered as the chill hit his bare flesh. He would have to resign himself to wearing nightclothes. Though he'd slept naked in India, it was too cold for that in England, even with the fire blazing high.

After donning his drawers, he threw on his banyan and knotted the tie, hoping that would be enough not to offend Eliza's maidenly sensibilities. Then he lit a candle and knocked on the dressing room door. "Eliza? Are you all right?"

"I'm perfectly fine!"

Her cheery response gave him pause, especially

when it was followed by another loud thump. "Are you dressed?"

"Yes, why?"

Swiftly, he unlocked the door, then swung it open to find her busily unpacking a pile of pasteboard boxes. A lit candle atop one box cast a lurid glow over the scene.

He'd expected to find her sulking, the way his wife would have over being thwarted, not happily exploring his belongings.

And doing it in style, too. She had shed her male attire to drape herself in a length of gold-shot silk that he'd brought from India to use as a gift for female relations. His mouth went dry.

Not only did it enhance the warm color of her skin and make her honey-brown hair fairly sparkle, but she'd wrapped it only just high enough to cover her nipples. Then she'd thrown the extra bit over one shoulder, leaving the other creamy shoulder exposed, along with a healthy portion of her breasts.

It was even more alluring than her too-tight male clothes. What he wouldn't give to run his tongue down into the shadowy crevice between her plump—

"Did you want something?" she asked.

You. In my bed. Now.

He swore under his breath. "What the devil are you doing in here?"

She shrugged her half-bare shoulders, apparently not the least perturbed by his burst of temper or her outrageous costume. "I decided to amuse myself by seeing what you brought with you from India."

He surveyed the boxes with their contents in various stages of disarray. "You had no right to unpack my belongings," he bit out.

"I didn't think you'd mind." When he glowered at

her, she added mischievously, "It's not as if I had anything else to do."

"How about sleeping?" he snapped. "That's what most people do in the wee hours of the morning."

"Most people don't have my worries." She tossed him a challenging glance. "I had to keep my mind off of my dire future somehow, didn't I?"

Confound it, she was like water on stone with her persistent tale. And damned if he wasn't beginning to believe her. She certainly seemed desperate to escape, so desperate that she'd refused to reveal her identity even after he'd manhandled her.

He shook off that thought. Women like her had a talent for making men believe their fabrications. This was a game for her, and he wouldn't let her win it.

"So what did you find to 'amuse' you?" he asked, determined not to give her the satisfaction of drawing him into another discussion of her claims.

She hesitated, then deliberately turned to rummage through something. "Oh, I found quite a number of interesting items. A lovely ivory comb . . . some leather slippers . . . and several fascinating pictures."

She faced him again, her expression resolute. "Tell me, sir, what exactly is the 'congress of crow'?"

What? Had she found—

"Because that's the title on this particular picture." She held up a print, and he saw several others scattered atop the box behind her.

Confound the woman to hell, she'd found his erotic Indian prints.

Five

Colin's expression was so comical, Eliza had to smother her relieved smile. *Finally*, she had the reaction she needed. She'd begun to think he would *never* respond to her feminine wiles, given how he'd ignored her for the past few hours.

She arched an eyebrow at him. "Well? Will you tell me what it is?" She held up the print. "The title didn't explain, although I must say the picture itself is very naughty—"

"Give me that!" Colin set his candle down on a box near the door and strode into the room. "That is not for a lady to see."

"I don't know why not," she shot back, though when she'd first found the prints, she hadn't been able to stop blushing. But shock had given way to fascination, and then to a plan. A very risky plan. "You found them perfectly acceptable to carry around with you."

Snatching the print from her, he pushed past her to gather up the others and stuff them back into the box. "They were a farewell gift from an artist friend. He thought it a grand joke."

"And of course, you kept them anyway. Out of loyalty to your friend. Certainly not because you like naughty pictures."

He glowered at her. "I must have twenty books in

these boxes, and *this* is what you chose to look at?"

She shrugged. "I looked at the books, but they were horribly dry. Frankly, Colin, I don't understand men's fascination with recitations of who won what battle and how. Now, if you'd had any books or prints concerning fashion—"

"Why?" His dark-eyed gaze trailed insolently down her body. "So you could invent an even more scandalous costume for yourself?"

"Is this scandalous?" She batted her eyelashes at him in perfect innocence. "I didn't think it any worse than an evening gown. And you were so outraged by my male attire that I figured I should put on *something* feminine. Under the circumstances, this was the best I could do. If you have a better gown, then by all means give it to me. Because this does have a deplorable tendency to slip down."

She tucked her thumbs beneath the top and pretended to tug it up, instead dislodging the silk another fraction. When his gaze swung inexorably to her bosom, she had to stifle a laugh.

"Please tell me you're wearing something underneath that," he said hoarsely.

"Of course." She waited until he released a sigh of relief, then added, "I found a pretty jeweled chain to go about my waist. It's the most darling thing, although I don't think it's really supposed to be worn against a woman's naked skin."

"God help me," he muttered under his breath.

"Is something wrong?" she asked, sidling nearer.

"I have to be in Brookmoor in a few hours," he said curtly, whirling toward the door. "And before then, I would like to get at least a *few* hours of sleep—"

"I've been thinking," she said, to keep him from leaving. The man wasn't cooperating, blast it. He was forcing her to be more shameless. "We could work out a trade. If you'll agree to take me to Honiton, then I'll do something for you."

"Like what?" he growled as he marched for the door. "Manhandle the rest of my belongings? Steal my hunting dogs? Tell the magistrate—"

"Pleasure you," she blurted out. "I . . . I could pleasure you."

He froze just short of the doorway.

Gathering her courage, she came up behind him. "Your prints reminded me of the harem tales we girls secretly read at school. According to the tales, it's possible for a woman to pleasure a man by—"

Abruptly he swung around, then backed her against the wall of the dressing room, his eyes glittering dangerously. "Are you *trying* to end up in my bed, Eliza? Because that's precisely where you're headed."

He'd turned into the gothic villain again, and that wasn't what she'd wanted. "I didn't mean—"

"Not that I'd complain, believe me," he said in a rough rasp. Laying his hand on her hip, he swept it up to caress her waist, her ribs . . . the sides of her breast. "But if you're hoping that seducing me will trap me into marriage, think again. I may ruin you, but I'll be damned if I'll marry you."

She fought not to show how sorely his cruel words wounded her. "Thank you for your candor, my lord," she managed to choke out. "But it's quite unnecessary. I'm not interested in seducing you." She tipped up her chin. "Nor have I any wish to marry a man who considers me utterly unsuitable to play the role of his wife—except in his bed, of course."

"I didn't say you were . . . I only meant that . . ." He muttered a curse. "Never mind. And if you don't want to share my bed, then what do you intend?"

With her blood in a dizzying stampede, she forced herself to soldier on with her plan. "From what I read, it's possible for a woman to give a man pleasure without . . . losing her virtue. That's what I'm offering."

He leaned so close to her that she could feel his arousal through the flimsy silk. The reality of it momentarily shook her, but it also reassured her that her plan could work. At least he found her attractive.

Emboldened by his reaction, she slid her hand between them. "I could use my mouth or my fingers . . ."

He caught her hand. "You could. That's true." His eyes bored into her. "But then what? Once you're done pleasuring me, I mean."

"You take me into Honiton in your cabriolet."

"Ah, yes." He released a shuddering breath, then turned his gaze to the door. "Tempting as your offer is, I cannot in good conscience accept it."

"Why not?" she cried. "I know I'm not the most attractive woman, but I thought . . . that is . . . you do seem to desire me."

"Yes." A faintly regretful laugh escaped his lips. "But not enough to ruin my future and yours."

"It wouldn't—"

"The cabriolet is a gift from my cousin, sweeting," he said softly, his gaze swinging back to hers. "He had the Monteith crest emblazoned prominently on the panels. By the time we reached Honiton, it would be morning. The buggy isn't closed, and everyone we passed would see us together. So with your guardian out scouring the roads, along with his family and servants, all it would take is one glimpse of your face beneath your cloak, and there would be a scandal and no way to hush it up privately. We would either have to marry, or, if you choose to spout your little tale about my ravishing you—"

"No, I wouldn't do that." It had been a bluff and a feeble one at that.

"The point is, it's too late to take you anywhere without creating a scandal." He stared grimly at her. "Your only choice is to go home on your own and tell them you spent the night in the woods. And you seem determined not to do that."

Lord, but he was stubborn. Fine. Then she would pretend to do what he wanted and walk to Honiton on her own. "Very well, what if I *do* agree to go home? Will you let me leave?"

"Of course," he said, his eyes searching her face. "And I'll follow at a discreet distance to make sure you reach there safely."

She blanched. "There's no need for you to bother. I know the way—"

He let out a frustrated laugh. "You're still just trying to make a run to Honiton on foot. Very well, you force me to go looking for your family."

As he turned for the door, she saw all her plans slipping away. "Blast you, just let me go!" She grabbed his arm to stay him. "Don't think about what could happen to me. Just forget that you ever saw me, and let me leave."

When he stiffened, she whispered, "*That* could be the trade, you know." Desperate to make him agree, she slipped her hand down to cup him through his drawers. "I pleasure you, and you let me walk out of here alone."

His sudden, ragged breath told her that she'd caught his full attention. So did the heavy weight of him thickening beneath her fingers.

"I'm not going to let you use your body to buy off my conscience," he ground out. He grabbed her hand as if to pull it away, paused, then entwined his fingers with hers.

When he continued, his voice was a tortured rasp. "But since I can't reasonably start asking questions in town for a couple of hours . . ." He pressed her hand back against his groin. "And since you're hell-bent on exploring what well-bred virgins aren't supposed to explore, I'd be willing to agree to a different trade."

He had that look in his eyes again, the one that tempted her to strip off her clothes and throw herself at him. "Wh-what?" she whispered.

"Pleasure for pleasure." He curved her fingers about his thick arousal. "You pleasure me." Taking her by surprise, he slid aside the front of her makeshift gown, then slipped his other hand beneath to brush the curls between her legs. "And I pleasure you. That, sweeting, is the only trade I would accept."

Pure shock, then alarm held her still. What he was suggesting was unthinkable. Dangerous! She'd touched herself down there furtively, in the dark of the night, never daring to dream of a man doing it. It was one thing for her to do things to *him*, but if he did things to her, too, who knew what might happen?

Even now, the teasing caresses of his fingers were affecting her, making desire pool and swirl in her belly. As his eyes turned a smoky black, her mouth went dry. Oh yes, this was dangerous indeed.

But it could be another way to persuade him to help her. Another form of flirtation, of tempting him and teasing him into not betraying her to her uncle. She should do it for *that* reason.

Surely she could control her own desires. Yes, she did have a shameless urge to feel him touch her down there, to fondle her like in those naughty pictures, but she would keep it in its place. She would.

"All right," she said, before she could regret the words.

He looked surprised, then his eyes narrowed. "Don't think it will change anything." With their hands still resting where hands should never rest, he stared into her face, his gaze searing her. "Because it won't."

"I know," she lied.

His feverish gaze dropped to her lips, then lower. "I must be mad. I have no right to— But I swear, if I don't at least get to taste you, feel you . . ."

"Yes," she whispered. "Please . . ."

With a groan, he pressed her back against the wall and kissed her, so fiercely, so deeply, she could hardly breathe. A shiver of need pulsed down low in her belly that grew more insistent when he drew his hand from between her legs to unbutton his drawers.

He guided her hand inside them, folding her fingers around the incredibly warm, rigid length of him. He stopped kissing her to murmur, "Grip it, sweeting, yes. Now tug on it, like you're tugging off a boot." When she clasped it tentatively, he commanded, "Harder. Up and down."

She did as he bade, and he gasped. Laying his forehead against hers, he said, "You are so sweet . . . oh God . . . such a sweet little temptress . . ." Releasing her hand to continue its motion, he brought his own hand up to where the silk was knotted at her breasts. "And speaking of tugging things off . . ."

One sharp pull and the silk was loose, baring her body entirely to his darkly covetous gaze. "You have a body made for pleasuring," he said raggedly as his gaze drifted down to her breasts, then lower to the chain that hung low on her belly. "A body made for jewels."

Tucking his thumb in the chain, he held her fast so he could bend his head and seize her bare nipple in his mouth. Her naked breast. With his hot mouth. She thought she'd die right there.

"Good Lord, Colin . . ." It was an amazing feeling, having his mouth suck her and his tongue flick her and his teeth tug her nipple as if it were his to devour, his to tease and fondle.

Except that it wasn't his, nor did he ever want it to be. That humiliating truth nearly made her end their fondling. Until his hand dropped back to between her legs so he could stroke her, delicately, then more firmly, making her moan and thrust herself shamelessly against him.

"That's it, my beauty," he murmured. "Your *yoni* is wet and eager for me. Part your legs more. Let me give it what it wants." She followed his instructions in a daze of need, aching for the touching never to end.

Then he slid a finger inside her and she started. Murmuring soothing words, he brushed kisses over her face, one of his hands caressing her breast while the other delved between her legs.

"You're so tight." He nuzzled her forehead, her tangled hair, the pulse beating madly at her temple. "So lovely and soft and welcoming . . ."

Now a pulse began to beat somewhere lower as his fingers, first one, then two, worked and rubbed and drove her absolutely mad. Like the beating of a drum, her blood thrummed down there, the insistent rhythm rising with his every caress.

"Faster," he choked out. "Stroke me faster, sweeting."

She did, and he did, too, their hands moving in a frenzy until they were both panting, straining, seeking . . . until the pleasure built and the need built and it all exploded in a fever of delicious excess that tore a cry from her throat.

He muffled it with his mouth as he pumped against her hand one last time before groaning against her lips.

Seconds later, she felt something wet and sticky spill over her hand.

For a few seconds they stood there rapt, their breaths frantic and their muscles taut. The pulsing in her veins died away as if to hide from the inexorable approach of dawn. Gray light now brightened the intimate darkness of his dressing room, shaming the feeble candles that still burned.

He drew back, the soft yearning in his face momentarily giving her hope that he might feel the same connection to her that she couldn't help feeling to him. Then a shutter came down over his features, chilling her soul.

"You should sleep now," he murmured. Dropping his gaze, he pulled her hand from his drawers and wiped it clean with the fabric of his banyan robe.

"Colin—"

"I have to go, Eliza. It's as I told you—this changes nothing."

Curse him for his stubbornness! How could he be so cold after what they'd shared? She caught his chin, forcing his head up until his gaze met hers. "Liar. You want me. I know you do. And not just in your bed, either."

His gaze pierced her, hot and intense and angry. "I wanted Rashmi, too. And all that got me was pain and trouble."

"Rashmi was your wife?" she asked, wanting but fearing to know the rest.

"Yes. She was much like you: stubborn, tart-tongued . . . beautiful. Ours was an arranged marriage, but when our families paraded her before me, I thought I'd die if I couldn't possess her."

Dragging Eliza's hand from his face, he stepped away. "I paid for my foolish desire every day of our marriage. It was a constant quarrel, in bed and out, with her always determined to get her way. She hated that I worked for the English government, she hated my cousin, she hated socializing with the snobbish English in Calcutta. I knew why she hated it—unlike *my* English father, hers had refused to marry her Indian mother, so she was very bitter about her bastardy. But I got tired of listening to it. I never had a moment's peace."

He concentrated on buttoning his drawers. "After our last quarrel, she flounced off alone to visit her mother in Poona." His hands stilled on the buttons. "I let her go, tired of fighting with her, tired of her sharp words, tired of trying to protect her from herself. And when I did go after her, I arrived just in time to watch her die."

"Oh, Colin . . ." Eliza whispered.

His head shot up to reveal an expression so full of impotent rage that it made her heart ache. "So I am *not* going to choose a wife as heedlessly as I did last time. No more fractious females for me, no matter how sweet and tempting their attractions. I've learned my lesson. This time I want a steady, responsible wife."

"I see," she choked out. Now painfully conscious of her nakedness, she bent to pick up the silk and hold it to her breasts to shield her body. "You want a docile wife, who will never gainsay you or have opinions of her own or—"

"I want peace. And I'd never find it with you."

She clutched the silk to her chest, fighting back tears. "You're right," she whispered. "Because I'd never accept such a tepid marriage. I want the passion, the drama, the thrill of knowing a man intimately enough to quarrel with him over the important things. I want love. And from what I hear, love is never peaceful."

"No." He stared at her a long moment. "But now you understand why—"

"Yes," she said, not wanting to hear any more of his half-insults.

She understood, all right. He wanted to ease the guilt he felt over his wife's passing, and he thought to do it by never feeling anything again. By handing her over to her uncle without a care for what happened to her.

Tears stung her eyes. Fine. Then she did not want *him*. Because she could never settle for that kind of careful marriage.

Abruptly, he turned and strode for the door. "I'm going to lock you in and order the servants not to enter my room. I suggest that you don your old clothes again. Because when I return I'll have your guardian with me, and I'll dump you in his arms, naked or no, and wash my hands of you, no matter what the consequences."

And with those horrible words still ringing in her ears, he left.

Six

Liar.

Colin ground his teeth as he drove the cabriolet toward Brookmoor two hours later. She'd called him a liar, and she'd been right.

He'd tried so hard to hide how badly he wanted her. The whole time she'd been flashing his erotic prints at him and tempting him with talk of the jeweled chain beneath her seductive costume, he'd been torn between laughter and the urge to throttle her. And that was before her sweetly innocent offer to pleasure him had sent his desire for her soaring into a frenzy.

He should never have suggested that stupid trade—pleasure for pleasure. But like some green cadet, he'd thought that touching her and kissing her and bringing her to ecstasy would somehow quell his need for her.

Idiot. All it had done was whet his appetite.

And banish hers.

No, the words he'd spoken afterward had done *that*. She'd clearly taken them to heart—when he'd gone to bring her breakfast and take his leave, she'd been wearing her male attire again and sitting pensively, reading his "dull" books. She'd spoken to him curtly, barely sparing him a glance.

It had struck him harder than he'd expected. He

rather liked her fierce determination, her teasing remarks . . . her attempts to seduce him. The possibility
that he might actually have crushed her spirit gnawed
at him.

Damn her, he did not want this! He did not want
her. After four years of torturing himself over his wife's
death, he'd finally reached the point where guilt didn't
plague him night and day. And then Eliza had come
along to torment him.

Well, he'd be damned if he'd let her draw him into
her gothic play. He would find her guardian and tell
him to come take her home. And even if the man tried
to shame him into marrying her, he would stand firm.
He would not be manipulated by some English hoyden.

Who kissed like an angel and didn't back down
even when he attempted to frighten her. Who thought
he was a gentleman despite his parentage and his
glowering. Who made him yearn for long-forgotten in-
timacies and the warmth of a wife's embrace—

Swearing under his breath, he urged the horses on.

His next few hours were spent introducing himself
to the townspeople: at a linen draper's shop, at the
apothecary's, even at the rectory. To his shock, although his appearance startled some, his title
smoothed his way toward acceptance, especially since
he was careful to place an order for Chaunceston Hall
at every shop where he stopped.

Unfortunately, his title didn't gain him answers. He
wasn't entirely surprised no one mentioned a runaway.
Eliza's guardian would have hushed that up to save
her reputation. What did surprise him was that no one
seemed to know an Eliza at all.

And he'd had the perfect pretense for asking questions about her, too. He'd said that he'd met a young

woman from Brookmoor at his cousin's house in London and now wanted to pay a call on her, but could only remember her Christian name. It probably sounded suspicious, but it was the best he could do.

Still, no one knew her. As a last resort, he decided to try the livery, in case she'd attempted to steal a horse from there, too. As he approached, he caught the end of an argument.

The livery owner stood in the yard, venting his temper on a maid. "Tell Mr. High-and-Mighty Whitcomb that I can't keep the horses in their traces all day just because he *might* be going on a trip to Cornwall."

"He'll be leaving momentarily," the maid said with a haughty air. "As soon as his niece feels up to traveling."

"He said that an hour ago. And an hour before that, when he came here all in a dither to rent a horse so he could fetch the girl. Said she'd up and gone off for a walk and he had to find her."

Colin perked up his ears. Could it be?

"He still has *that* horse, too. And now you say the girl is feeling poorly from her walk? Well, he might let some chit from a girl's school lead him about by the nose, but I don't see why I should have to do it."

The maid sniffed. "Because he's the magistrate. And if you don't want him having you rousted from the tavern for drinking every Sunday, sir, then you'd best keep that rig ready to go."

Colin's heart began to pound. If the maid *was* talking about Eliza and her guardian *was* the magistrate, it explained a great deal.

The livery owner cursed under his breath. "Fine. It'll be here when he needs it." As she walked off, head held high, he grumbled, "If anybody should be rousted, it's Silas Whitcomb. Ought to stop shoving his head in a bottle and start paying his bills, that's what I say."

So the part about the drunken guardian had been true. God help him.

The maid had already set off briskly down the road, so Colin hurried to catch up to her. "Excuse me, miss," he said as he pulled his rig up beside her, "but I'm headed to the magistrate's myself. Might I offer you a ride?"

The servant eyed him with suspicion.

"The name's Monteith. I'm the new owner of Chaunceston Hall."

One furtive glance at the crest emblazoned on his rig, and she was suddenly all smiles. "I'd be most obliged, milord," she said with a quick curtsy.

After he helped her in, he set the horses off at a fast trot. "You'll have to direct me. I've only just arrived and don't know my way around."

"The road to Mr. Whitcomb's manor is just on the other end of the bridge that you passed coming into town, sir."

The bridge? That had been a good four miles from Chaunceston Hall. And Eliza had walked all that way? At night? Alone, in the dead of winter?

He shuddered. "I take it that your master is planning a trip."

"Aye, milord. Him and his niece. Soon as she . . . is feeling up to it."

He took a stab in the dark. "Actually, I'm glad she's unwell, or I might have missed her. That's why I'm headed to Mr. Whitcomb's: to pay a call on Eliza. I know her from London."

The servant's gaze swung sharply to him. "Eliza, is it? You must know Miss Crenshawe well then."

He let out a breath. Eliza Crenshawe. He had her

name at last. "Well enough to want to see her again," he said absently, his mind awhirl.

He had the magistrate's niece locked up in his dressing room. And instead of cursing her for getting him into this mess, all he could think was how panicked she must have felt when he'd threatened to carry her to the magistrate.

Yet she'd stood up to him and threatened him right back, even knowing how it would infuriate him. For a young miss from a girl's school, she was damned brave. He could see now why she'd thought she had no choice.

His arrival at her uncle's house only hammered his conscience more. What had once probably been a thriving estate had fallen into utter disarray: the fields lay fallow, the tenants' cottages needed repair, and the stables were deserted. No wonder she'd had to steal a horse.

Servants seemed scarce, too. The maid he'd met was the one to usher him into her master's untidy study. She was the one to go call her master, leaving Colin in a setting that Eliza would surely call "perfectly gothic."

Colin called it tragic. His blood chilled to think of Eliza arriving here fresh from Hampstead Heath and still mourning her father, only to be set down in this gin-soaked room with its discarded bottles and stench of an overflowing chamber pot. And if she'd told the truth about being struck by her guardian—

"You've come about Eliza?" said a voice from the doorway.

Colin whirled to face Silas Whitcomb, already prepared to loathe the man.

Yet Whitcomb didn't look like a slovenly brute of a drunk. Dressed in riding breeches and bearing a crop, he looked like any man would after riding the roads in search of his missing niece: pale, harried, and hollow-eyed. The idea of this spindly fellow striking anyone seemed ludicrous. Colin could probably crush the man's skeletal frame with one sharp blow.

"I am the girl's uncle." Whitcomb entered with measured steps, his eyes wary. "The servant tells me you are my new neighbor, the earl. So what business could you possibly have with my niece?"

Colin hesitated. Now was his chance to tell the man that he'd found Eliza in his stables. That if the magistrate wanted to preserve her reputation, he would come at once and whisk her home.

Yet something held him back. He couldn't give her over until he was sure she'd be safe.

Colin repeated his tale about meeting her in London. "I wanted to call on her, since she mentioned she'd be here for the holidays." As he approached Whitcomb he could smell the gin on him, which gave him pause. "But the servant said she's been taken ill. I do hope it's nothing serious."

"It's just a piddling cold. She'll be fine. Sorry that you had to come here for nothing, my lord." He turned to the door.

"If it's just a cold, then she should be able to receive visitors," Colin persisted. "May I see her?"

Whitcomb froze. "Why?"

"There is something I wish to discuss with her before she goes on the trip that your servant mentioned." He had to get the man talking about Eliza's suitor. "You see, she and I were much thrown together at my cousin's house, and I—"

"If you've come courting, sir," Whitcomb snapped as he whirled back around, "then you've come too late."

"What do you mean?"

"My niece is already betrothed. Indeed, we're off to join her fiancé as soon as she feels better."

So she'd been telling the truth about the marriage, too. His conscience fairly beat at him now.

"I don't know how that can be." Colin paused before speaking his next lie, but in for a penny, in for a pound. "Miss Crenshawe and I had something of an understanding when she left London."

Whitcomb ran a shaky hand through his hoary locks. "She had no right to make you any promises. She is betrothed, I tell you."

"She mentioned no betrothal."

"It was . . . rather sudden."

"Which is why I want to speak to her," he said in a steely tone, determined to get the truth out of the man.

"You can't, damn you!" With sudden, inexplicable violence, the man swung his crop in a wide arc that sent a nearby table lamp flying.

Colin caught his breath. "Why not?" he said, trying not to think of Eliza being struck by this ass.

Who was now bearing down on him with crop in hand. "I know what your sort wants, and you can't get it from her."

"My sort?" Colin said in an icy voice that most men knew to fear.

But drink apparently made Whitcomb reckless. "Spawn of an Indian witch. The duke got you a title, and now you think to plump up your purse with my niece's fortune. Only she doesn't have one anymore, so you're wasting your time."

Colin's eyes narrowed. "I don't need or want her fortune. I just want her. And I'm willing to give her a generous settlement."

"So is her betrothed."

This was odd. Why would Eliza's uncle refuse an

earl's interest in her if she was so poor? Despite Colin's mixed blood, he was perfectly eligible. "Who is my rival?"

"It's none of your concern."

"I'm making it my concern." Time to force the magistrate's hand. He strode toward the hall, calling out, "Eliza! Are you upstairs?"

"Stop that, you fool!" Her uncle grabbed him by the arm with surprising strength. "You don't want her, I tell you. She's a reckless little hoyden—"

"Indeed she is, but I happen to find that appealing. Eliza!"

"Now see here, my lord, there are things you don't know about my niece."

Colin froze, then turned to the man. "What do you mean?"

Whitcomb hesitated, then squared his shoulders. "I didn't want to tell you this, but you give me no choice. There's a perfectly good reason I must take another man's offer for her hand."

Eliza scowled up at the transom window for the fiftieth time and cursed her wide hips. She could never wriggle through that tiny space, even if the boxes *weren't* too flimsy to climb on.

Blast Colin. He'd certainly found her a neat little prison.

With a sigh, she turned back to his naughty prints. She'd unearthed them again, unable to resist the lurid fascination they held for her. How these people could contort themselves into such positions was beyond her. *She* could never do it.

Not that she would ever get the chance. Once Colin returned, she'd be hauled off to marry her uncle's friend.

The thought of it made her sink onto the floor in despair. First her uncle and now Colin. They would both rather ruin her life than be inconvenienced.

A sob rose in her throat that she stifled at once. She would not cry. Somehow she'd get through this. She *would*.

The sound of the outer door opening made her tense. Hurriedly she tried to whisk the prints away, but there were so many that Colin already had the dressing door open before she could finish.

She faced him defiantly. "So you're back, are you?"

"Yes." His gaze flicked to the prints. "Doing more exploring, I see."

A blush touched her cheeks. "Where's my guardian? Downstairs? I don't suppose you want him to know that you stashed me in your dressing—"

"He's not here. And I didn't tell him that *you* were." Colin held the door open, then gestured for her to come out. "But you and I have to talk, Miss Crenshawe."

She tensed. He knew her name now, so he knew everything. Wary of his mood, she followed him into his bedchamber.

"I met your uncle. Apparently your tale wasn't so gothic after all." He fixed her with an unsettling glance. "But according to him, you left out a few things."

She frowned. "What things? I told you that I don't know the suitor he chose."

"Jacob Minyard. He's a brewer in Cornwall, willing to marry you despite your lack of fortune." He paused, his gaze unreadable. "And virtue."

"Lack of virtue?" She cast him a perplexed glance. "I don't understand."

"Your uncle says that some scoundrel in London seduced you. That's why he has to marry you hastily to a stranger. Because no one else would have you."

She stared at him dumbfounded as the words pelted her like stones, hard and cruel, destroying her every hope for the future. "How dare he?" Tears welled in her eyes. "I expected him to lie, but *this*. . . . Blast him, why would Uncle Silas ruin my good name?"

"He's clearly desperate," Colin said evenly.

Her gaze shot to him as she dashed her tears away with one fist. "You believe him, don't you? You believe that I actually let a man . . . that I'm not—"

"No." His voice was softer now as he came toward her.

"You do!" More tears chafed her throat. "You already think me reckless and foolish, so why wouldn't you think—"

"Because you're not reckless like *that*." Grabbing her hand, he drew her to him. "I'll admit that at first I was half-tempted to believe him, given how you offered to pleasure me." When she tried to pull away, he wouldn't let her, enfolding her in his strong embrace. "But it made no sense that an unchaste woman wouldn't try to buy her freedom by offering to share my bed," he murmured into her hair. "Or that she'd behave so innocently when I kissed and touched her."

"After what I told you about my acting, you probably figured I was pretending," she said peevishly. He was holding her and nuzzling her hair and being awfully sweet, but she was afraid to trust that.

He chuckled. "How to play the innocent when being seduced isn't something you learn in a schoolgirl theatrical." Brushing a kiss on her forehead, he added, "And I had other reasons for doubting your uncle's claim. For one thing, why would he reveal your 'condition' to a man who'd come courting his niece?"

"Courting?" She drew back to gape at him.

"I couldn't get him to tell me anything, so I claimed I'd met you in London and now wanted to marry you. I even offered a substantial settlement." His eyes turned black and cold. "Not only did he refuse me, but that's when he claimed you were unchaste. To warn me off, he said. Which is ludicrous. He should have leaped at the chance to make a good match for his ruined niece. Why marry you to a brewer in Cornwall when he could marry you to an earl?"

"I don't know." She shook her head. "None of it makes sense."

He fixed her with an intense glance. "Tell me, sweeting, when your father's will was read, was there mention of your fortune?"

"Yes!" She chewed on her lower lip. "But after Uncle Silas fetched me from school, he said that the trustees had looked more deeply into Papa's finances and discovered hidden debts. They were forced to use my money to pay them. By the time he told me this, we'd already reached Brookmoor, and he said he meant to bring me to Cornwall."

"And marry you off hastily, before anyone could gainsay him. He was counting on browbeating you into it, I imagine."

"But why?"

"I suspect that your uncle is desperate for money, so he's trying to circumvent the law and your trustees. Minyard has probably agreed to give him a portion of your fortune in exchange for brokering the marriage. When Whitcomb fetched you from school, he thought you'd just go along, take his word for it about the money." Colin chucked her under the chin. "You're a schoolgirl, after all. Why would you question your legal guardian?"

She ducked her head. "And I'm not that pretty, so he probably thought I'd leap to have a husband."

"Which only shows what an idiot he is. Any fool can see that you could have your pick of the men."

With a toss of her head, she met his gaze squarely. "Yes, you certainly seemed eager to have me."

He winced. "I . . . probably shouldn't have said what I did this morning."

"It doesn't matter," she lied, turning away. "It's how you feel."

"But it doesn't change what we should do."

She whirled on him. "I don't care what lies my uncle tells the world about me, and I don't care how badly you want to be rid of me. I *shan't* marry some horrible Mr. Minyard, and I *shan't* let my uncle—"

"Of course not," he said firmly. "It's out of the question."

Slightly mollified, she crossed her arms over her chest. "So what solution do you propose?" She brightened. "*Now* will you bring me to London? I can go to the trustees—"

"And what if your uncle *isn't* lying about the money?"

She swallowed. "I—I'll take a job at the school, then."

"Which they'll happily give to a young miss who traveled with a man alone for two days?" When she opened her mouth to protest, he added, "Or who was seen being put on the coach by the Earl of Monteith? After having been missing for a night? If you thwart your uncle, he gains nothing by saving your reputation."

Blast him, why must he always be right? "Then I'm ruined."

"Not if you marry me."

She blinked, then shook her head. "It's very noble of you to offer, my lord, but I shan't marry a man who thinks me so unsuitable to be his wife."

"Eliza—"

"No!" She turned her back on him, her throat raw with frustration and anger at the horrible situation her uncle had put her in. "I don't have to marry anyone. I'll go to Mrs. Harris, and she'll help me find some way through—"

"While you live like a pariah, your reputation shattered, your future uncertain?" He slipped his arm about her waist and drew her back against him. "This is the best way to handle it, and you know it."

Tears trickled steadily down her cheeks. "I-I am *not* s-some p-poor, pathetic creature you have to r-rescue."

"No," he murmured. "You aren't. But you deserve better than ruination, and a possibly fruitless struggle against your legal guardian. If you marry me, he can't touch you. And even if he denies you your fortune because we eloped, I don't need it. The only way to keep you safe is for me to marry you."

"I don't care about staying safe. And I deserve a husband who wants me."

"I do want you." He kissed her hair. "You know I do."

"I don't mean that sort of wanting."

"It's better than *no* sort of wanting, isn't it? Which is what you're liable to have if your reputation is ruined beyond repair." When she hesitated, fighting the temptation he offered, his voice grew acid. "Or perhaps you simply don't want to marry a man who'd give you little brown-skinned children—"

"Don't be ridiculous." She turned to face him. A

lock of raven hair fell across his brow, lending him a vulnerable air that tugged at her heart. "You're a beautiful man who would give me beautiful children. If things were different, and you really wanted to marry me—"

"I do. I meant to take a wife once I was settled, so why shouldn't it be you?"

She eyed him askance. "Because only a few hours ago, you told me that you wanted a steady, responsible female, not a hoyden."

"I was wrong. I've changed my mind." His smile didn't quite hide the fact that he was lying. "And you're not a hoyden."

"But I'm not a steady female, either."

"It doesn't matter."

It did matter. She'd heard just how much it mattered last night.

"You might as well say yes, Eliza. Because I'll keep you locked up here until you do."

She rolled her eyes. "You wouldn't dare."

"No, you're right. If I kept you locked up, I'd never get any sleep *or* peace." His eyes gleamed at her. "So I guess we're off to the north in the cabriolet."

"The north?"

"Gretna Green. That *is* where I'd have to take you, isn't it, to marry you? Since you're under age?"

Him and his noble character. It was heartening that he'd marry her just to save her from her uncle, but she couldn't let him do it.

He was right about one thing, however. Even if she went to London alone, the trustees would never believe her over Uncle Silas, especially if there really was no money left. Drunken sot or not, he was a man, her guardian, and a magistrate.

One way or the other, she had to deal with Uncle

Silas. Better to do it now than later. "There's another choice," she said. "I can go back and reason with my uncle." Alone, so she could get Colin out of this mess once and for all.

Colin scowled. "No."

"This morning you said that was the only solution, and you were right."

"No," he said, seizing her by the arms. "You're never going near that ass again. And certainly not alone."

She laughed bitterly. "You can't stop me from doing as I please this time, my lord. We both know you won't assault me. You can't tie me up and carry me off in the open cabriolet. And if you attempt to imprison me again in the dressing room, I will scream until the servants let me out. It was one thing when I had a reputation to preserve, but now I have nothing to lose. So either you let me go and save yourself, or you let me take you down with me."

Snagging her about the waist, he drew her into his embrace. "Or you could let me give you a reason to stay." The smoldering heat in his eyes ignited an answering heat in her belly. "You could let me show you that our mutual desire is more than enough to sustain a marriage between us."

The fierce determination on his face made her despair. He would never let her go, would he? Now that he knew how badly she'd been wronged, he wouldn't rest until he "saved" her. Even though he disapproved of her as a wife.

It was only because he desired her. That guided his actions right now, but once his desire was sated, he would come to his senses.

Her eyes narrowed. Then his guard would be down, and she could escape.

But she'd be ruined.

She sighed. For all intents and purposes, she was already ruined. Uncle Silas had seen to that. At least this way, she'd have one night with Colin to last her for the rest of her days.

Because he would always be the only man for her. She knew it down deep, an ache in the center of her chest. It was madness, of course. She'd known him for barely one day, yet it seemed as if she'd known him for ages. Like her, he never quite belonged, never quite fit in. Which was precisely why she liked him.

There was nothing she could do to change how she felt about him—except leap without looking one more time, and take what he offered. At least for tonight.

"All right." She reached up to untie his cravat. "Give me a reason to stay."

Seven

*C*olin caught his breath as Eliza tugged his cravat free, then shoved his coat off. "I can give you at least ten reasons," he vowed, startling even himself with the intensity of his need.

"Ten?" she said, her eyebrows arching high.

"Or however many you need."

"Ten is plenty, my lord." She flattened her hands on his chest. "*If* they're very compelling."

So she meant to make this difficult, did she? He supposed he couldn't blame her. He'd done his best last night to discourage her from considering a marriage between them, and a woman with Eliza's pride wouldn't easily forget that.

But that didn't mean he would let her walk out of here to a life of ruin and spinsterhood. Not after that horrible, patently untrue claim of her uncle's. No wonder she'd been so stubborn—she really *hadn't* seen a way out. And now neither did he.

Except to marry her.

An errant thrill coursed through him, the same one that had seized him when he'd first decided that marriage was their only course. He'd been a long time without a wife. She might not be the perfect choice, but God, how he wanted her.

So he would have her. He'd simply be careful and

do things differently this time. He could still have his peaceful life if he took her firmly in hand.

But first he must convince her to stay.

"Here's Reason One." He brought his mouth down to hers. "You like kissing me."

He devoured her lips, starved for them after hours away from her. Flavored with butter and honey, her mouth was a feast of pleasures so heady that when she tangled her tongue with his readily, hungrily, it drove him out of his mind. And when she broke the kiss, he gave an audible moan.

"That is . . . quite a compelling reason," she murmured against his lips. "But you have nine more to go."

"Give me a chance," he rasped, trailing kisses down her throat while he removed her ridiculous coat and waistcoat, then dragged her shirt free of the breeches so he could slide his hands up beneath it to cup her heavy breasts. "Reason Two: You like having me touch you."

He thumbed her nipples, and her breath quickened. "Yes . . . that, too . . . is awfully convincing." She worked loose the buttons of his waistcoat and shirt. "But let's see what other reasons you might have to tempt me, shall we?"

After shoving his waistcoat off, she dragged off his shirt, then ran her hands over his bare chest with a clearly admiring smile.

"So what do you think?" he choked out as her questing fingers sent shivers of need down his spine. "Will this do for Reason Three?"

A minxish laugh bubbled out of her, as if she'd guessed his discomfort. "Not until I see the rest."

"You first," he bit out, reaching for her shirt.

She pushed his hands away. "I'm the one who requires reasons, remember?" she teased. "I have to see how you compare to those men in your naughty prints."

"I won't compare favorably if you give me no encouragement," he warned. "So if you want me to . . . er . . . rise to the occasion. . . ."

"All right," she said, a pretty blush staining her cheeks. "I'll go first." She unbuttoned her breeches and slid them off, but the hem of her long shirt fell to below her garters, veiling everything. "Although you already saw me naked."

"In the dark. Not in the light of day." When she fumbled with the buttons of her shirt, he growled, "Here, let me help."

Seizing the lapels, he ripped the shirt in half, sending the buttons flying.

She drew a sharp breath. "Was that really necessary?"

"God, yes." His blood pounding, he shoved the remnants of the shirt off her shoulders to bare her full breasts with their lovely brown nipples, her eloquent dimple of a navel that cried out for a ruby or an emerald, and the sweet, honey-brown curls that hid her pretty *yoni*.

Though not for long. "You're a work of art, Eliza," he rasped as he lowered his hand to part her curls.

"You've seen enough for now," she murmured, stepping back from him. "It's my turn to see what *you* look like, Colin."

Muttering a curse, he shed his clothes and boots with record speed, then stood still for her critical perusal. It unnerved him to be examined like a horse at Tattersall's, though his cock didn't seem to mind—it leaped to attention at once. "Well?" he snapped. "Reason Three?"

Her gaze was fixed on his cock in alarm. "I'm not sure."

"Not sure!"

"I-I was hoping your naughty pictures were an exaggeration. When I touched you, it didn't feel quite so . . . But if you mean to thrust *that* huge thing inside me . . ."

A frustrated laugh boiled out of him. "It will be fine, trust me." Clasping her about the waist, he drew her to him. "We'll see how you feel about it later. For now we won't count it as one of the ten."

"All right," she said, though she still looked hesitant. "But that means—"

"I know, more reasons. And here's one." He slid his hand down between her legs to find the dewy center of her pleasure. "You should stay with me because I know exactly how to excite you."

He rubbed her until her lovely eyes turned molten and her cheeks flushed. Only then did he indulge his urge to suck and lick her tantalizing breasts.

Squirming beneath his hand and mouth, she gripped his head tightly to her. "Yes, that is . . . a compelling reason . . . my lord."

He played with her, fingering her delicate flesh, teasing and taunting each breast in turn, reveling in her gasps of delight and her quivering body.

When he could endure no more, he straightened and backed her toward the bed. "I want you, Eliza," he said as he tumbled her down atop the coverlet.

Eagerly he covered her with his body, loving the feel of her beneath him, the look of her with her glorious hair spread across the pillows and her eyes wide in wonder.

"I want to be inside you so badly I ache with the need." Laying his cock in the cradle of her thighs, he slid it up and down her damp nether lips, moistening himself with her juices, preparing her and him. "My blood burns every time I think of having you, of making you mine. Is that not a compelling reason for marrying?"

Her face darkening, she looped her arms about his neck. "It would be more compelling if I didn't know that any woman would suffice."

"Not any woman." He scattered kisses over her neck and throat. "You're the first woman I've desired since my wife died." When she started, he added, "It's true. And believe me, there were women enough who wanted me—pretty women, eager women. None of them tempted me. Until you." He brushed his mouth over hers. "Surely that's a reason."

Her breath beat hot and fast against his lips. "A very compelling reason indeed."

He slowly entered her then, fighting for control, fighting the urge to drive hard and deep inside her heated flesh. The urge grew nearly overpowering the farther he pressed, for she was so incredibly tight . . . so velvety soft.

"You do know this will hurt," he warned against her mouth.

She jerked back to stare at him. "You really *didn't* believe my uncle's claim about me, did you?"

"Of course not." He inched farther inside her. "Not that it would have mattered if he *had* been telling the truth. It certainly gave him no right to steal from you or force you into marriage or strike you."

She cast him a tremulous smile so warm, it made his blood race. "Then that's Reasons Five and Six, Colin."

"Two of them?" he queried as he met the barrier of her innocence.

"One for believing me over him, and one for not caring."

Gazing into her soft eyes, he felt an alarming hitch in his chest. "And here's Reason Seven. I'm taking your innocence, sweeting. Now you *have* to marry me."

With a quick, hard thrust, he broke through. When she cried out and stiffened beneath him, he clutched her tightly to him, a fierce wave of possessiveness surging through him. She was his, now, *his*. It was strange how glad that made him.

He kissed her and gentled her, though his blood ran high just to be planted to the root inside her. At last she began to relax.

"All right?" he whispered.

"I-I think so."

"Just wait, sweeting," he promised as he began to move. "It gets better. You'll see."

"Better is good," she mumbled. "Because if it gets worse, I might have to take back one of my reasons for marrying you."

He laughed raggedly. "Can't have that, can we?"

That was the end of speech for him, for he was too intent on making it better for her, pleasuring her and fondling her where they were joined. He kissed her heady mouth, too, and ravished the hollow of her throat before moving on to suck and nip her tender little earlobe as his cock swelled inside her, dragging him inexorably toward release.

"Better?" he asked hoarsely, not sure how much longer he could bear the exquisite torture of being inside her.

"Much better . . . oh Colin . . . I've never . . . it feels . . ."

She was shimmying beneath him now like a dancer, her hips arching up to meet his, her breasts crushed to his chest as she kissed his chin, his jaw, his throat.

"That's it," he growled against her neck, his release bearing down on him with brutal swiftness. "Let it come, sweeting. Let it take you."

"Take me, yes . . . yes . . ."

Suddenly she was moaning and thrashing and digging her fingernails into his back, as her flesh convulsed about his cock like a hot fist. That sent him over the edge into oblivion, tearing a guttural cry from his throat.

And as he spilled his seed inside her, he felt that same peculiar hitch in his chest as before. God help him. Eliza had the power to catch hold of him somewhere down deep, and he mustn't let that happen.

Not if he wanted peace.

Eliza had never felt so contented as she felt now, lying in Colin's arms. She felt like a woman. *His* woman. As she gazed up at his face, the painful truth hit her: she loved him. Quite desperately.

Oh, how could that be? How could she fall in love in one short night?

She didn't know, but she had. She loved his determination to right her wrongs, his sense of justice, even his gruff temper. Most of all she loved how desperately he seemed to desire her, even if that was all he felt.

But perhaps it wasn't all. Surely a man who could make love to a woman with so much fervor felt *something* for her. Perhaps if she loved him enough, it would make up for all the things about her that he thought unsuitable in a wife. Perhaps she might even dare to stay.

"How do you feel?" he murmured, nuzzling her hair.

"Wonderful."

"That sounds like Reason Eight to me, sweeting."

She cast him a tender smile. "Very well, I'll count it as Reason Eight." When he looked rather smug, she couldn't resist teasing him. "But only if you explain something to me."

"And what is that?"

"What exactly *is* the congress of crow?"

He chuckled. "Precisely what the picture shows it to be: a woman pleasuring a man with her mouth while the man pleasures her with his."

"But what does it have to do with crows?"

"Damned if I know." Eyes gleaming, he laid his hand on her hip. "Though I'm sure we could puzzle it out eventually if we tried it a few times."

"Yes, let's try it," she said, then blushed at her shamelessness.

He laughed. "I believe, sweeting, that makes Reason Nine: I can show you how to do all the things in those naughty pictures that you're clearly dying to attempt."

"I am not," she said with a sniff, not wanting him to think her a brazen wanton. "And anyway, that still leaves you one reason short."

"I'm sure I can come up with another on the way to Gretna Green." He glanced to the window, where the afternoon sunlight filtered through the muslin curtains. "We should probably leave tonight—surely your uncle will have given up on riding the roads looking for you by then. We can go to Honiton in the cabriolet, then hire a coach to take us the rest of the way."

"That gives us a few hours to sleep." And for her to make her decision. Though she had half-made it already.

But before she leaped into marriage with him, she wanted to know some things. "Do you mean to stay in England forever?" She shifted to face him. "Or are you just here to assess your estate's value so you can sell it?"

He cast her a sharp glance. "Why? Afraid I'll be dragging you off to India?"

"I would *love* to go to India. It's been a fascination of mine ever since Papa brought me back silks from his trips when I was a girl."

A faint smile touched his lips. "I should have known gothic plays and erotic prints weren't your only interests." He grew pensive as he stroked her arm. "I may visit, but no, I don't mean to live there ever again."

"Don't you miss it?"

"Sometimes. I miss the food and the music." He drew the covers up over them with a rueful smile. "And I really miss the climate. But very little else."

"Have you no family? I mean, on your mother's side."

"My mother died when I was young, but by then most of her family had already cut her off." He cast her a bitter smile. "My countrymen are no more fond of mixed-blood marriages than yours. But her sister, my aunt, took me in and raised me. That's why I stayed as long as I did—to look after her."

A faraway look entered his eyes. "So when the duke invited me to return with him to England, I refused. My aunt was too sickly to travel, and I couldn't leave her. But once she died . . ." He shrugged. "There was nothing left for me in India. I'd never really belonged there anyway—I'd always had one foot in the English camp. Then when Foxmoor gained me the title, I figured why not? At least England didn't have warring tribes and sudden rebellions and bandits who—"

When he broke off with a shudder, she laid her hand on his stubbled cheek. "Your wife was killed by bandits, wasn't she?"

He nodded tersely. "Marathas. Hired to fight for the

leader of our province." His eyes glowed with sudden anger. "They murdered her because she was the wife of the aide-de-camp to the English governor-general. Because of me."

"You couldn't have anticipated that," she said softly. "It wasn't your fault."

"I should have stopped her. When I realized she'd defied me and run off to her mother's, I should have gone after her. I should have kept her safe."

Eliza rather liked his protective streak, but it had clearly made life difficult for him. "She didn't want to be safe. She wanted to be happy. And sometimes they don't go together."

"No," he choked out. "I don't think . . . I made her very happy."

And that was the source of his guilt, wasn't it? His fear that he'd driven his wife to be reckless. "Did you try to make her happy?"

He eyed her warily. "As best I could."

"Because it sounds to me as if she was incapable of happiness. Some people are. I have a friend at school like that—nothing ever pleases her." She cupped his cheek gently. "You can't stop chronically unhappy people from doing foolish things in their endless quest for happiness."

He swallowed convulsively. "I've never thought of it like that, but you're right. Rashmi had a seemingly endless supply of misery."

"She didn't blame you for it, did she?"

A surprised look crossed his face. "No. At the end she blamed herself. She died begging me to forgive her foolishness." As he released a ragged breath, tears rose in his eyes.

Eliza stroked his face, wishing she could take away his pain. "Then you mustn't blame yourself, either. You did the best you could. That's all a woman can ask of a man."

His face crumpled, then he caught her hand to his lips, kissing it fervently before he bent his head to take her mouth in a long, loving kiss. As tears dampened his cheeks, she clutched him to her.

Perhaps they *could* make a marriage of it, after all. At least she could give him this. A bit of comfort and an end to the past. "You came to England to forget her, I suppose," she whispered.

"To forget all of it," he rasped. "To find . . . I don't know—"

"Peace," she said, remembering his words.

He drew back and wiped his eyes. "Peace. Yes." He gave a self-deprecating laugh. "I know it sounds absurd to you, but—"

"It doesn't sound absurd at all." They lay there in a companionable silence for a while, before she ventured another question. "And you mean to find this peace in Brookmoor? Or will you sell Chaunceston Hall and go back to London to live?"

"London isn't for me, sweeting." He stroked her hair back from her face, clearly in control of his emotions again. "I didn't like Calcutta any better than Rashmi did, but that's where my position took me. I prefer the country—always did. I'm not much for balls and parties, with all those curious eyes on me, the whispering about my family, the incessant rude questions. . . . In the month I stayed at my cousin's house, there was a constant swirl of gossip wherever I went. I wanted to escape it."

"There will be a swirl of gossip about you here, too."

"Yes, at first." A cynical smile touched his lips. "But I figure that the title will go a long way toward smoothing my progress, as will my owning a large estate in the area. Here I have a better chance of being accepted, being part of a community, than I'd ever have in London."

Not if they eloped. Not once her uncle spread his lies. Her heart sank. If Colin were right about Uncle Silas's reason for marrying her off, then the man would be furious about losing his chance at her fortune. And desperation could make a man do mad things—like destroy the reputation of the foreigner who'd thwarted him.

"Is it so important to you to be part of the community of Brookmoor?" she whispered. "Surely anywhere you bought property could give you that."

"I don't actually have a choice. The land is entailed. I can't sell it." He brushed her forehead with his lips. "Besides, this estate has been my family's for generations. My grandfather may have tried to keep it from me, but according to the letter my cousin unearthed to prove my claim, my father wanted it to be mine. That means something to me. I want to carry on for him."

He idly wound a lock of her hair about his finger. "I want to belong somewhere. I want my children to belong, and their children, too. My best chance for having that happen is here. Why? Don't you want to live in Brookmoor?"

"Brookmoor is fine," she managed, though her heart was breaking.

If they eloped, there would be lots of the gossip he hated. Being magistrate, her uncle could make it sound however he wanted. He could paint Colin as blackly as he pleased. She knew very well what English towns were like—insular and suspicious of strangers, especially foreign ones who stole away their females.

Peace would be difficult for some time to come.

She couldn't do that to him; not after everything he'd endured with his wife and his grandfather's treachery. He deserved his "peace," his place to belong. By involving him, by letting him make love to her, she'd given him no choice, as surely as her uncle had given her no choice.

Mrs. Harris was right—leaping without looking *had* landed her in the briar bush. First, when she'd come here and dragged him unwillingly into her troubles. And second, when she'd shared his bed.

That wasn't right. And there was only one way to make it right. To go back; to stop the leaping right where it had begun.

So when next he murmured her name, she pretended to be asleep. And she kept pretending while he settled himself against her and began to doze.

While she waited for him to fall asleep, she considered what she must do. As soon as she had her plan firm, she slipped from the bed. Thankfully, he was as exhausted as she, for he slept through her getting dressed, borrowing one of his shirts to replace her ripped one. He didn't even rouse when she wrote letters for him to post for her, and a note meant for him.

Tempted to stay, aching to be his wife, she paused at the door to give him one last yearning glance. "I love you, Colin," she whispered.

But she'd had enough of arranged marriages. There would be no more of them—either for her *or* for him. She would see to that.

Eight

*S*omething insistent tugged Colin from sleep, nagging at his consciousness. As he awakened, the vestiges of a dream followed him: Eliza saying she loved him. It was only a dream, yet its sweetness tantalized him. Opening his eyes, he turned toward her . . .

She wasn't there.

He tried not to panic as he scanned the room. She was probably just looking for the necessary or a chamber pot. "Eliza!" he called out.

No answer. He glanced at the window. She couldn't have gone far—it was still light. Then he saw the clock. Seven. But how could that be? It was winter, and the sun set early—

Heart pounding, he leaped from the bed and rushed to the window. Oh God, it was dawn, not sunset! He'd slept for twelve hours at least. So how long had she been gone? Confound it all, where *was* she?

He started for the dressing room, then neared his writing table and froze. There was a letter atop it addressed to him. Trying to still the frantic rush of his pulse, he picked it up. Beside it lay two others, one addressed to his cousin and another to Mrs. Harris.

He opened the one meant for him and read:

Dearest Colin,

I have decided to return to my uncle's. I would be most grateful if you could send by express the other letters I have left for you. I intend to stand firm against my uncle and refuse to marry Mr. Minyard until my friends come to my aid. I know it won't be long. If I remain resolved, Uncle Silas will surely see the wisdom of not bullying me. So do not worry.

Had she lost her damned mind? She meant to tangle with her drunken uncle alone? The woman must be mad! And how was he *not* to worry, damn it! If her uncle had struck her once, he could easily do it again. She would risk that? Was she *that* desperate to escape him?

He read on, his heart in his throat:

Thank you for your generous offer of marriage, but as you put it yesterday, I cannot in all good conscience accept. You were right—you do not need another reckless female for a wife. I know your offer was meant to save me from ruin, but it is too great a sacrifice.

If we elope, you will never have your peace. Magistrates, even drunken ones, wield much power in England, and you deserve better than to have your character assaulted and your life turned upside down. You are responsible for many people, so you must think of them, too. Without me, you can continue your plans for the estate unfettered.

Unfettered? *Unfettered,* damn her! How could she think he'd go merrily on with his life while she struggled to deal with her treacherous uncle? Did she really think he could find any sort of peace in that?

He read the next part:

> *It would be one thing if you loved me, but we both know that you don't.*

"We do *not* both know that!" he shouted to the empty room.

The words echoed in the depths of his heart.

God help him. He loved her. He did. He loved how she challenged him at great risk to herself, how she asked questions no one would ever ask, how she gave herself wholeheartedly once she decided she cared for a person. He loved that she was clever and resourceful.

And brave. Too brave for her own good.

A chill swept through him at the thought of what she might even now be enduring because of her unselfish act. He tossed the letter aside, dressed quickly, then found his pistol—God, she hadn't even bothered to take it—and loaded it. Then he strode for the door.

He opened it to find his servants conferring about whether to disturb him.

"My lord, are you all right?" his steward asked. "We heard shouting—"

"I'm fine. Have my horse saddled, will you?"

"Certainly, my lord, but . . . I did wonder . . . will you return in time for your meeting with the tenants? They are most anxious to meet their new landlord."

You are responsible for many people, so you must think of them, too.

Colin gazed around at his servants. Oh God, she was right—he wasn't the only person to consider in this. He really had no idea how much trouble her uncle could make for him. Did he have the right to risk not only his own future, but that of his tenants and his servants, even his future children? For love?

He wasn't even sure she loved him, after all. The final words of her letter had been cold and formal, not lover-like at all:

> *I hate to leave you now, though it is for the best.*
> *Do take care of yourself.*
>
> > Yours,
> > Eliza

Take care of himself. As if he were an acquaintance she'd met on the road.

And what if she'd lied about not caring he was half-Indian? What if she really *was* just another undisciplined female who didn't mind sharing his bed, but couldn't abide a marriage to him?

She'd chosen to leave him—he hadn't *made* her go. The wisest thing, the safest thing for his heart, was to let her have her way.

To hell with that.

What had being wise and safe gained him? He'd thought it wise to box up his wounded heart when Rashmi had died. But instead of bringing him peace, it had brought him loneliness.

Then Eliza had come along, and opened the box to let the light shine in on his heart so it could heal. She'd even dared to state what he'd known within an hour of meeting her: that he wanted her. And "not just in your bed," either.

Wise or safe didn't matter. He couldn't just let her go.

"Saddle a horse," he told the steward. "I'll be back as soon as I can, but I have to pay a visit to the magistrate." *I have to fetch the woman I love.*

*   *   *

Sitting in the bedchamber she'd used her first night at her uncle's, Eliza plotted how to handle him. Last night she'd sneaked into the house, raided the kitchen while he and the servant slept, and come up here. She'd been reeling from lack of sleep and the exhaustion of walking back, so that had been her first priority.

Thankfully, no one had discovered her, so she'd had a good night's sleep and dressed herself properly. But dawn had broken two hours ago, and she couldn't hide forever. She'd smuggled up only a day's food at most.

The longer she could stay undetected, the better, for it would give Colin time to post her letters.

Colin. Her heart lurched. No, she wouldn't think about him right now, or she'd lose her nerve and go running back to Chaunceston Hall.

The door swung open, and the servant who'd probably come to clean the room blinked at her. Eliza held her finger to her lips, but it was no use.

"Master, Master!" the servant was already crying. "The miss has returned! She's come home!"

Eliza groaned. So much for hiding.

She rose, determined to face her uncle with stoic indifference, but when he entered reeking of gin, with his graying hair disheveled and his cravat askew, her heart sank. How could she make him listen to her when he was in this condition?

"Go to the livery and order that rig brought here," he commanded the maid.

With a bob of her head, she hurried off.

"Where the devil have you been?" he growled at Eliza.

"I set off for London, but I was robbed yesterday. So I had to return."

He looked torn between concern over her misadventure and anger at her impudence. Anger won out. "Serves you right, being robbed. You're lucky they didn't murder you, too. And I hope it showed you a thing or two—like how lucky you are to have a suitor willing to overlook your wildness—"

"I'm not going to Cornwall," Eliza said stoutly. "I won't marry your friend."

His face darkened. "You'll marry who I say, and be glad of the chance."

"To have my inheritance stolen from me?"

"What do you mean?" he said hoarsely.

She swallowed. "I don't believe you about the money. I want to speak to Papa's trustees in London before I do anything so precipitous as to marry."

The blood drained from his face. "You dare to defy your guardian?" He stalked toward her. "I swear I will have your hide—"

"I posted letters to my friends in London." When that halted him, she added, "The Duchess of Foxmoor and Mrs. Harris. I told them everything. They'll come to my aid."

A look of sheer panic crossed his face. "Eliza, you don't know what you've done. You have to marry Minyard. You must or I'm finished!"

It clutched at her heart to see him so desperate. How far he'd fallen since she'd known him as a girl. "I'm sorry, Uncle Silas, but I can't."

His panic twisted instantly into rage. "You will write those friends of yours and tell them you were mistaken." He walked up to seize her by the shoulders. "I'll *make* you marry him, damn it!"

"Let go of her!" ordered Colin's voice from the door. "Or I swear I'll kill you!"

Releasing her, Uncle Silas whirled around.

Eliza's heart leaped. He'd come for her! She couldn't believe it. Oh, but he shouldn't have, blast him. Her uncle would destroy him, too.

"What are you doing here, Monteith?" her uncle snapped. "This is none of your concern. You stay out of it!"

"Come here, Eliza," Colin said.

When she tried to pass her uncle, he grabbed her. "She's my niece, and I'm not letting her—"

"Do you *want* to die?" Colin snapped, whipping out his pistol. "Let her go."

Her uncle blanched, but thankfully released her. As she hurried to Colin's side, Uncle Silas growled, "I'll have you charged with assaulting a magistrate."

"And I'll have you charged with fraud. It shouldn't take much to uncover your scheme with Mr. Minyard." When her uncle gaped at him, Colin added, his eyes deadly cold, "I told you yesterday—Eliza and I have an understanding. I mean to marry her. And nothing you say, no lie you tell me about her, will change that."

Oh, he was taking such wild chances.

"You dare to threaten *me*, sir?" her uncle snapped. "I swear I'll—"

"Let me reason with him, Uncle," she put in. "He doesn't know what he's saying."

"Damn it, Eliza, I know perfectly well—"

"Out here, my lord." She dragged Colin into the hall, then lowered her voice. "Have you lost your mind? Don't you realize what he could do to you?"

"I don't care."

"Oh, Colin, I can't let you—"

"I still haven't given you the tenth reason you should marry me." He fixed her with a darkly intent gaze. "I love you, Eliza."

The words poured over her like honey, so sweet she

was afraid to believe them. "You're only saying that because you're bent on saving me. You're just being the gentleman again."

"No! I swear I'm not." He gave a shaky laugh. "That's one thing I love about you—the way you think me so noble. Any other Englishwoman would take one look at me and assume I was a savage. But you pronounced me a gentleman within moments of meeting me, even after I drew a pistol on you. Do you know how rare that is, to be seen for what one is and not what one appears to be?"

As her heart began to soar, he caught her face in his hands. "And I see *you* now for what you are, too. I was wrong about you and Rashmi—you're nothing like her. She would never have done something as unselfish as you did today."

When she still didn't speak, her heart too full of joy for words, he added, "How could I not love you? You're the sun to my moon, the flame in my hearth—"

"Flame?" she choked out. "That doesn't sound entirely safe, my lord."

"I don't want safe. I want *you*. However I can get you. So if you think that in time you could come to love me—"

"I don't need time," she breathed. "I already love you so desperately that the thought of my uncle ruining your—"

He cut off her words with a sweet kiss that stole away any remaining objections. Colin was hers at last. And perhaps it was selfish of her, but she meant to keep him. No matter what trouble it caused.

"Lord Monteith!" said a sharp voice, making them break apart.

Blast, she'd forgotten about her uncle.

Colin drew her to his side, sliding his arm protectively about her waist. "I love her, and I'm marrying her, sir. There's naught you can do to stop me."

Uncle Silas looked like he'd swallowed nails. "You're not afraid of what I can do to you? I could make a great deal of trouble for you in England, you know."

A muscle ticked in Colin's jaw. "Then we'll go to India."

That seemed to take him aback. "You really aren't interested in the money."

"No, sir."

Her uncle paled. "And you, girl? You wish to marry this . . . this . . ."

"Yes, Uncle," she said hastily. "I love him, too."

His face fell. "Young love. The two of you sound like Nancy and me years ago." A heart-wrenching sigh left his lips. "Elope then, if you must. I won't stop you." He turned wearily toward the stairs, mumbling, "And now I'm ruined."

"Uncle Silas," she called out, "do you need money? Is that it?"

"Don't you dare offer that scoundrel money," Colin snapped.

Her uncle froze, then faced them with a haughty look. "Sometimes when a man is grieving and can't take care of his property, he gets into debt, sir. But that does not make him a scoundrel."

"When he tries to steal from his niece, it does," Colin shot back. "I know what it's like to grieve, but I also know that a real man pays his own debts. He doesn't push them onto the back of a young woman who needs him. Besides, we both know it has nothing to do with grief. You're so sunk in drink that you—"

"Colin," she chided when her uncle bristled, "*now* who's being reckless?" She glanced at her uncle. "You owe Mr. Minyard money, do you?"

He hesitated, then nodded. "He said he would seize everything I own to pay it, but he agreed to absolve me of the debt if I . . . I . . ."

"Gave him Eliza to marry," Colin snapped.

He hung his head. "Yes."

"How much do you owe?" Colin asked, to Eliza's shock.

Her uncle met Colin's gaze warily. "Why?"

Colin glanced down at Eliza, then back to her uncle. A sigh escaped his lips. "I propose a trade. I'd prefer not to elope—Eliza will suffer enough gossip by marrying me as it is. So if you'll approve the match and act as a guardian ought, perhaps I can help you repay your debt."

Uncle Silas shook his head. "Minyard won't accept it. He wanted her fortune, and if he can't have that, he wants the estate since it isn't entailed."

"He will settle for money and a schedule of repayment, if I bring my cousin into it," Colin said. "Especially if I point out the disadvantages to seizing the estate of the Earl of Monteith's relation. My title has got to be good for something."

The first sparks of hope leaped into her uncle's face until Colin added, "But there will be conditions."

"What conditions?"

"You must refrain from drink." When her uncle scowled, Colin added, "Every day that you do so, I'll send servants over to help you set this place to rights. We're neighbors now; we can help each other. But you must do your part."

Uncle Silas looked despairingly from Colin to her. "I don't know if I can."

"I remember when this house was filled with light and love and laughter," Eliza said softly. "It can be that way again, if you'll only try."

Her uncle uttered a weary sigh. "Very well. For you, girl, I shall do my best." He gestured to the stairs. "I suppose we should adjourn to my study to discuss the terms of the marriage and . . . the rest."

"Yes," Colin said and started for the stairs.

Eliza stayed him. "We'll be there in a moment, Uncle." As he nodded and continued down, she turned to Colin. "Thank you for helping him, but why—"

"You pointed out that many people depend on me. Well, people depend on *him*, too. You, for one. His tenants, and that poor servant. Not to mention the residents of Brookmoor. If their magistrate is ruined, what does it do to them?" He cupped her cheek. "Some people may be incapable of happiness, but does that mean we shouldn't try to help them find it?"

"No, it doesn't." The ferocity of her love for him stole her breath. "Trying to reform my uncle won't make for a very peaceful life for you, I daresay."

"Probably not." His eyes glittered with mischief. "But I'd never accept a life as tepid as that. I want the passion, the drama, the thrill of knowing my relations intimately enough to quarrel with them over the important things."

As she laughed, he sobered. "I want love. And from what I hear, love isn't always peaceful."

"No, it isn't." Sometimes it was a briar bush. And sometimes no matter how long you looked, you couldn't see the roses in the briars. But if you'd done your looking, and your instincts served you well, sometimes it was all right to leap.

"But fortunately for you, my love," she said as she lifted her mouth to his, "I think peace is vastly overrated."

After Midnight

Liz Carlyle

To Claudia Dain with thanks for all the years of friendship, commiseration, and wise counsel.

Prologue

THE END

The heavy *tock-tock-tock* of the schoolroom clock was deafening in the expectant silence. It was over at last. The books, the tennis racquets, the ribbons and the sketchpads; all the bits of flotsam from a moderately happy girlhood had been carefully packed away. Her trunks sat now in the carriage drive. Waiting.

The woman who stood by the window studying the traveling coach below turned abruptly, a muted smile upon her face. "You came to me a hellion, Martinique," said Mrs. Harris, her hands extended. "May I trust you do not leave me the same way?"

Martinique dropped her gaze. "*Oui, madame,*" she answered. "I am the perfect English miss now."

Mrs. Harris slipped a long, flawlessly manicured finger beneath Martinique's chin. "Liar," she said with a glint of humor in her eye. "Ah, but a lovely liar, all the same."

Returning her gaze to the woolen roses on Mrs. Harris's carpet, Martinique tried not to grin. "Perhaps Lord Rothewell will be well served if I am both a hellion and a liar," she observed. "Perhaps he shall soon rethink his notion of carting me away, and marrying me off to the first willing suitor he can find."

"Martinique!" said Mrs. Harris in a voice of gentle admonishment. "You cannot stay at school forever, much as we both might prefer it. Your uncle merely wishes you to be happy."

"He wishes me off his hands," Martinique returned. "Which is the reason he sent me to you in the first place, *madame*. In the West Indies, I was not wanted. Nor am I wanted now."

Mrs. Harris shook her head. "I cannot believe that true, my dear," she said quietly. "Baron Rothewell has provided a life of luxury for you."

Martinique's eyes flared wide. "It is quite true," she answered. "He is ashamed of me. And whatever he has done, it was done out of guilt."

Mrs. Harris took Martinique's hand and gave it an encouraging squeeze. "Were that so, my dear, he would hardly journey four thousand miles merely to marry you off," she said. "No, he is coming to see the job properly done. And, given the tone of the many letters he has written me over the years, there is no one better suited to look after your interests."

Martinique tried not to smile. "Was he an ogre to you, too, *madame*?"

Mrs. Harris hesitated an instant too long.

Martinique did smile then. "Yes, you took the razor's edge of Lord Rothewell's tongue once or twice, I do not doubt," she said. "I am sorry, *madame*, if he was cruel to you."

"Cruel is too harsh a word, Martinique," she replied. "And I beg you to have a care with your own little razor. One marvels that you and Baron Rothewell share no blood."

Martinique's face fell. "My apologies, *madame*."

"Martinique, my dear, you have been with me longer than any of my other girls," Mrs. Harris gently pressed. "And you have stayed past an age when most of them are long gone and well-married. This past year, you have shown yourself a fine young teacher, too. And yet in all this time, you have learnt to govern neither your tongue nor your temper."

"Alas, I have been a trial to you, *madame*." Martinique heaved a theatrical sigh. "I shall unburden you forthwith, and fling myself into the bed of some dull, decrepit old nobleman."

At that, Mrs. Harris laughed. "I rather pity England's population of dull, decrepit noblemen," she remarked. "I am not at all sure they are expecting you. And proper young ladies do not speak of gentlemen's beds, my dear. But you knew that, did you not? You are tormenting me again."

Her pupil winked. "*Oui, madame*. I know. Indeed, I know many things a young English lady ought not."

"And I thank you for not sharing them with your classmates," said Mrs. Harris with a sigh. "Martinique, dear child, you are an old soul, and wise beyond your years—or perhaps experienced is the word I want? No, that is not quite right, either."

Martinique laughed. "It is my shady past, is it not, *madame*?" she said. "I have seen just a little too much of the world, perhaps?"

Mrs. Harris sighed again, but did not correct her. "Well, on to more wholesome topics, my dear. Where do you go from here? Will you be staying in London?"

"For a time," she answered. "Aunt Xanthia and I are to have new wardrobes."

"How lovely," said Mrs. Harris. "Your uncle's letter did say you were to go away for the holidays."

Martinique wrinkled her nose. "We are to spend December in Lincolnshire with Rothewell's cousin," she confessed. "Lady Sharpe. Do you know her?"

Mrs. Harris shook her head.

Martinique shrugged. "Nor do I," she said. "But it does not signify. After the new year, we'll return to London to await the Season. Rothewell and Aunt Xanthia have bought a house—in Berkeley Square, of course. Sugar and shipping must turn pretty profits nowadays."

"Martinique." Mrs. Harris frowned. "A lady never discusses her family's finances in public."

Martinique grinned. "But we are not in public, *madame*," she returned. "And it is hardly a secret that my family is made of new money."

Mrs. Harris's frown deepened.

Martinique looked suitably chastised. *"Oui, madame,"* she said gravely. "You may trust me to be on my best behavior when I enter society. I should sooner die than reflect badly on your school. For six years, this place has been my home, and you, my family. I am ever mindful of that."

Mrs. Harris clasped both her hands, and squeezed them reassuringly. "Thank you, my dear," she said. "It has been a joy to have you here, and to see you grow into such a lovely young lady. The other girls have come to value you, Martinique. And now, my last lesson to you is: *learn to value yourself.*"

Martinique held her gaze steadily. "What do you mean, *madame*?"

Mrs. Harris looked quite serious now. "No more jests about your family," she answered. "No more self-abasing humor. Unscrupulous men will seek to take advantage if they sense even a hint of uncertainty. Hold up your head, and always act the wellborn lady, no matter—"

"But *madame,* I am not wellborn," said Martinique stridently. "I am just the daughter of a beautiful French courtes—"

Mrs. Harris laid a finger to Martinique's lips. "You are the adopted daughter of the late Baron Rothewell," she said. "And you are the ward of the current baron. It is an old and very noble title. Be certain of your worth, and everyone else will follow. Dear child, your exotic beauty will turn heads, and your pretty French accent will charm every man you meet. Moreover, your family is rich, and you are a great heiress, so—"

"*Madame,* you just told me I mustn't speak of money," Martinique interjected.

"Oh, you shan't need to," said Mrs. Harris a little grimly. "All of society will know it within two days of your arrival in London."

"How can they, if one dares not speak of it?"

Mrs. Harris gave a wry smile. "Martinique, pray do not play the naïve young miss with me," she said. "You are nineteen now, and as you so recently pointed out, far more worldly than a lady of that age ought to be. Now, before we go down, tell me about your aunt. Shall I like her? Is she like her brother, Lord Rothewell?"

Martinique blinked uncertainly. "I—I hardly know," she confessed. "I remember Aunt Xanthia as being very slender, and quite pretty. And she was always kind to *Maman.*"

"She has written you faithfully every month," Mrs. Harris reminded her. "In all that time, has she said nothing to hint at her feelings or interests? She is young, is she not?"

"I daresay." Martinique shrugged. "But she has never seemed so to me."

"My dear, she cannot be above thirty," said Mrs.

Harris. "A good deal less, I imagine. Perhaps she, too, has come from Barbados to marry?"

Martinique laughed. "Oh, I do not think so," she answered. "In that regard, she *is* like her brother. They think only of work and of business and of—well, of that dreadful thing we mustn't speak of—money. *Mais oui*, I shall be quite happy to see her again."

Mrs. Harris had drifted back to the window. Her head was bent, her eyes again fixed on the glossy black traveling coach below. "Well, it is time, Martinique," she said quietly. "All of your things have been loaded."

"Have they?" Martinique's voice was deceptively calm.

Mrs. Harris crossed the room again, her steps swift, and enfolded Martinique in her arms. "Ah, my dear child!" she whispered against her cheek. "Go, and be happy. Be happy, but be wise. Remember all that I have taught you—especially that part about valuing yourself." She set the girl away and stared hard into her eyes.

"*Oui, madame*," whispered Martinique, choking back a little wave of fear. "I can put this off no longer, can I?"

Mrs. Harris shook her head sadly. "No, my dear. We dare not keep Lord Rothewell waiting."

"*Très bien*," said Martinique. "Let us go, *madame*, and beard the lion in your den."

Lady Sharpe was a diligent, dutiful sort of woman who, after twelve years of marriage, had learnt the value of the Bard's good advice to assume a virtue, if you have it not. Fortunately for Lady Sharpe—and his lordship—she possessed most wifely qualities in abundance. Charity, honesty, humility and thrift; all came to her quite naturally. Patience, however . . . oh, well. Lady Sharpe consoled herself that no one was perfect.

Unlike most wives, it was not her husband who tried her temper. Now, his *family* . . . well, her many virtues forbade her to speak openly in that regard. Nonetheless, after so many years of having her invented patience sorely pressed, she had almost acquired the virtue in truth—thus proving the wisdom of Shakespeare's adage. Sometimes, life was just a matter of faking it.

On this particular day, the October sun was bright over Lincolnshire, the afternoon quite unseasonably warm; the perfect occasion for a long, solitary ride in the country. Regrettably, Lady Sharpe was obliged to spend her afternoon entertaining her husband's self-indulgent half-sister, who suffered from a perpetual case of the sulks, complicated by a recent outbreak of terminal ennui. Christine was, as she complained to anyone who would listen, being Slowly Bored to Death.

With a swift glance over her shoulder, Lady Sharpe nudged her mount around a puddle, keeping to the grassy verge of the bridle path. Zeus had already thrown up mud once this afternoon, spattering Christine's hems and setting her to screeching.

"Lud, another puddle," complained her sister-in-law from behind. "Pamela, *do* please mind the mud. Jenks scolds so when she has to brush it from my habit."

Lady Sharpe glanced back again. Christine's maid dared not raise so much as a peep of protest, and they both knew it. But her sister-in-law was smiling that tight, perfect smile again, and batting her beautiful eyes almost innocently.

Patience. Patience. Patience.

"Would you care to take the lead, Christine?" Lady

Sharpe sweetly suggested. "I should be pleased to rein Zeus back."

Christine's mouth made a little pout. "You know how I get lost in the country," she said, shifting uncomfortably in her sidesaddle. "Really, Pamela, do you not think it perfectly odious to be stuck in Lincolnshire? Why can't Reggie take us to Town?"

Lady Sharpe suppressed her sigh of exasperation. Her husband stayed in the country because he was needed. The last of the harvest was but a few weeks in, and the coming month had to be spent preparing the estate for winter. But Reggie's sister had no conception of duty. Her late husband had been a pampered younger son who lived on an allowance—or at least his creditors' expectation of one.

"There is no one *in* Town this time of year, Christine," said Lady Sharpe soothingly. "Really, my dear, I think you must find something with which to amuse yourself."

They had reached the foot of the hill now. Lady Sharpe eyed the roiling brook, which was swollen by the unseasonable rain, and wondered how best to cross it.

Christine was oblivious. "A dinner party, then, Pamela?" she wheedled, sounding less than half of her thirty-odd years. "Or a ball? Do let's have a little *something* before I go raving mad."

Lady Sharpe pursed her lips. "Perhaps when Rothewell arrives in a few weeks' time."

"Yes, speaking of raving mad," said Christine in a sour undertone.

Lady Sharpe ignored her, and gently urged her mount into the water.

"Really, Pamela, you know nothing of these so-called cousins, save for Rothewell's reputation,"

Christine went on. "You have not seen them since you were children. And then there is *that girl.*" This last was said in a tone which implied Lord Rothewell was bringing along a festering case of the plague. "She is no relation to you at all. The chit was adopted by Rothewell's brother—and then *he* had the audacity to die! It is not at all the same thing as blood kin."

"It is quite the same thing," said Lady Sharpe calmly. "She was just a child when Cousin Luke married her mother. And if he thought enough of the girl to give her his name, then that is the end of it."

"Well," said Christine, dropping her tone to one of dark suggestion. "I have heard *things.*"

"Have you indeed?" asked Lady Sharpe sternly. "Then I beg you will not repeat them."

They had crossed the rushing stream, water up to their horses' knees, without a shriek of complaint from Christine. "Reggie cannot be pleased that they are to spend a month beneath his roof," she remarked instead.

"Reggie is perfectly happy to share his home," countered Lady Sharpe, nudging her horse left so that they might follow the stream to the old millpond below. "Like me, Reggie knows his family duty, and he does it regardless of his personal wishes."

"Well!" The subtle jab was not lost on Christine. "I am sorry to be a burden to y—"

Behind her, Lady Sharpe heard a sharp intake of breath. She turned around to see Christine's gloved fingers pressed to her lips, her eyes wide as she stared down the course of the rushing stream. Lady Sharpe let her gaze follow, all the way down the brook, to the millpond below.

Good Lord in heaven!

In a patch of autumn sun lay a man; a very young,

very handsome man in a shocking state of dishabille. Well, that was not quite accurate. He was naked. Almost. He lay back, reclining onto his elbows, bare to the waist, with the fall of his trousers flopped open to reveal a trail of fine, dark hair which disappeared into . . . well, somewhere. His feet were bare, and if the brazen scoundrel possessed a pair of drawers, one could see no evidence of them.

For an instant, Lady Sharpe squeezed her eyes shut. Then, unable to stop herself, she opened one eye, and let it run over the half-naked specimen of raw masculine beauty. She took in the broad, bare shoulders, the high, aristocratic forehead, the arms layered with muscle and taut with tendons, and the eyes, so suggestively closed, as if his upturned face soaked up pure ecstasy instead of warm autumn sunlight.

"Suddenly," said Christine in a low, throaty voice, "I am not nearly so bored in the country."

Lady Sharpe well knew that tone. "Christine!" she warned. "Christine, do not you *dare*."

But of course, Christine dared. "I beg your pardon!" she cried, nudging her horse toward him. "Sir, I do beg your pardon!"

"Shout a bit louder, Christine," suggested Lady Sharpe sourly. "He cannot hear you over the rushing water."

Christine's head whipped around for an instant, a dark, daring look in her eyes. "Why, I daresay you are right, Pam," she agreed. "Sir! Sir! I fear you are trespassing."

The young man must have caught a flash of Christine's red habit through the bare branches. He turned to watch her approach, a shock of heavy black hair falling forward to shadow his face as his mouth curled into a lazy, almost suggestive smile. Then he rose with a languid grace, hitched up his trousers, and padded barefoot across the clearing to snatch a white linen shirt which dangled from a nearby branch.

Lady Sharpe followed her sister-in-law, half-afraid of what might happen should she not.

Christine reined her horse in along the edge of the clearing, and stared down at the dark young man as he dragged the shirt over his head. "Sir, I fear you are trespassing," she said in her husky voice. "I must warn you that the penalties for such a thing can be quite . . . *stiff.*"

"Ah," he said, his shameless grin intact. "Are you the local constable come to mete out my punishment?"

Christine leaned forward in the saddle, and smiled. "I am Mrs. Ambrose," she said. "But since you appear to be a very forward young man, you may call me Christine."

The grin deepened, but it did not reach his eyes, which were still flat and dark. He was not, Lady Sharpe realized, so very young after all. His body looked to be a very virile twenty-five, yes. But his eyes, oh, they were old. The shirt was clinging damply to his flesh now, and his dark, heavy hair looked rather unnaturally so. Lady Sharpe realized in some shock that the man had been swimming—*swimming!*—in October. He must be quite mad.

Lady Sharpe urged her horse nearer. "Have a care, sir, in that millpond," she warned. "The stream is quite fast just now, and the current runs deep. Indeed, I am not at all sure my husband would approve."

He turned his attention to her, his eyes sweeping over her with a certain dark efficiency. She had the feeling he summed up all his adversaries just so; one swift, all-seeing gaze. Just then, something in his face shifted, and Lady Sharpe felt a sudden stab of recognition.

He approached, and extended his hand upward. "Lady Sharpe," he said, his voice softening unexpectedly. "You . . . you do not remember me?"

"Oh, my God!" said Lady Sharpe, leaning down to take his hand. *"Justin?"*

He gave a muted smile. "In the flesh, ma'am," he agreed. "Damp though it may be."

Lady Sharpe shook her head. "I . . . why, I had no idea you had come home," she said. "No idea at all! What in heaven's name are you doing, swimming in October?"

Now that he had stepped near, his bloodshot eyes were unmistakable, as was his heavy shadow of beard. "Afraid I had rather a long night," he answered. "And the hair of the dog which bit me did not seem quite the thing this morning."

"I hope you will not catch your death instead," she murmured. "Good Lord, Justin. You look so very different."

"I am different," he said quietly.

Lady Sharpe managed to smile. "I meant only that you look so much older," she clarified. "And . . . well, I remember you as such a willowy young man. Sharpe thought that perhaps you meant to remain in Paris. But I forget—you are St. Vrain now. You have obligations."

Beside her, Christine cleared her throat sharply. St. Vrain let his hand slip from Lady Sharpe's glove. "I beg your pardon," she said. "How rude I am. This is Sharpe's sister, Mrs. Ambrose. Christine, this is Lord St. Vrain, our near neighbor who owns the land beyond the millpond. Have the two of you never met?"

"No," said Christine softly. "And more's the pity."

St. Vrain let his eyes run down her. "A pleasure, Mrs. Ambrose," he said, the almost taunting smile slowly curling his mouth again. "I begin to believe I lingered too long in Paris. You and Mr. Ambrose are visiting your brother?"

Christine returned the smile. "I am a widow," she said. "I just put off my black, and I am making my home with Reggie and Pamela for a while."

"How fortunate they are," he said. "But I am sorry for your loss, Mrs. Ambrose."

Lady Sharpe reined her mount back a step. "As we are sorry for yours, my lord," she interjected. "Sharpe sent our condolences. I hope that you received his letter?"

St. Vrain inclined his head. "It would have been hard to miss, ma'am," he murmured. "As one might imagine, there was no surfeit of sympathy notes on my desk."

Lady Sharpe's unease was deepening. She did not like the hardened edge time had given St. Vrain, and she liked even less the avaricious look on her sister-in-law's face. She touched her crop to her hat brim, and wheeled Zeus around. "We ought to go, Christine," she said. "I am sure Lord St. Vrain will wish to dress."

"Yet another pity," said Christine, not quite sotto voce.

Her face coloring furiously, Lady Sharpe tried to ignore Christine. "We must bid you good day, my lord," she said. "All of us at Highwood welcome you home. It has been too long."

Christine cast one last, lingering look over her shoulder, even as she wheeled her mount back toward the stream. "Good day, my lord," she purred. "I do hope you don't take pneumonia."

St. Vrain's shameless grin returned. "I've always been a hard one to kill, Mrs. Ambrose," he remarked. "Or so my enemies say. Good day to you. I shall look forward to receiving my punishment—at your earliest convenience."

The ladies rode side by side as they went back up the brook. "Really, Christine," fumed Lady Sharpe when her temper eased slightly. "How *could* you?"

"How could I what?" Christine smiled like a cat with at least one paw in the cream pot. "Ignore your good advice? Never!"

"*My* advice?" echoed Lady Sharpe. "Whatever can you mean?"

Christine lifted one thin, arched eyebrow. "Did you not just say that I should find something with which to amuse myself?" she asked. "Well, I have found it."

Patience fled. "Oh, for God's sake, Christine!" she snapped. "*Not* St. Vrain."

Christine lifted her chin. "Why not St. Vrain?" she returned. "He is quite wickedly handsome."

"He is a troubled man," warned Lady Sharpe. Then the devil gigged her just a bit. "Besides, my dear, you will not show to good advantage on his arm. He is so *much* younger than you."

Christine laughed. "Oh, younger in years, perhaps," she said. "But not in his soul."

Lady Sharpe could not argue with that. She resorted to begging. "Christine, please. I implore you."

Christine stuck out her lower lip. "Must you always spoil my fun, Pam? St. Vrain will make for a pleasant diversion. Indeed, Reggie should invite him to dine with us tonight."

Lady Sharpe pursed her lips. "I am not at all sure Reggie will oblige you this time, Christine," she warned. "St. Vrain is not received."

"Not received?" Christine sounded intrigued. "But did you not just say he and Reggie corresponded?"

"The man's father died," said Lady Sharpe flatly. "Reggie sent a letter of condolence. What else, pray, was he to do when the father lived but a stone's throw from us, and St. Vrain was his heir, much as his father might have wished otherwise?"

Christine's eyes lit with an unholy glee. "Oh, Lord!" she said. "You are speaking of the young man who ran away with his stepmother, are you not? What a tawdry little scandal that was!"

"Yes, quite."

"Well, that is reassuring," said Christine, rather too cheerfully.

Lady Sharpe looked at her askance. "What, pray, is reassuring about it?"

Christine lifted one delicate shoulder. "Well, at least we know he has a penchant for older women."

One

A ROOM WITH A VIEW

*L*ord Rothewell's heavy traveling coach lurched
right, turning onto the stone bridge which arched
over the languid River Witham and drawing ever nearer
the estate of Highwood. The baron himself seemed
oblivious to the sway of the carriage. His gaze seemed
eternally fixed on the baize account book over which he
had been poring since they had taken luncheon at an inn
north of Sleaford.

An account book, or a brandy glass, thought Martinique.
In the six weeks since their dispassionate reunion, she
had seen her guardian with little else in hand.

Beside her, Aunt Xanthia gave a little shiver. "Dear
God, does the sun never warm this wretched place?"

At last, Rothewell looked up. "This *is* warm, Zee," he
said coolly. "Or as warm as it ever gets in December. Life
in the West Indies has thinned your blood, that is all."

Martinique covered her aunt's gloved hand with her
own. "You shall grow accustomed to it, Xanthia," she
assured her, giving her aunt's stiff fingers a squeeze. "In
a few weeks' time, you will not think it cold at all."

Xanthia smiled wanly. "Already I long for Barbados."
She turned to her brother. "How much further, Kieran?"

Again, Rothewell looked up, his expression detached. "Another two miles, by Pamela's instruction," he said. "There will be a good fire, Zee. You will be warm soon enough."

But Aunt Xanthia still looked fretful. "Really, Kieran," she said, "do you remember these people at all? I feel most awkward."

"I remember Pamela," he said. "We played together as toddlers. And she came out to Barbados once with Aunt Olivia. Do you not recall it?"

Aunt Xanthia shook her head. "I should rather not think of our childhood."

Rothewell tore his gaze away, and turned his attention to the pastoral scenery beyond the carriage window. Martinique did the same. Already she knew this conversation was at an end. The Nevilles were well-practiced in the art of the unspoken; a family of quiet rage and restrained grief, or so she had often thought. Or perhaps it was just English despair. All she knew with certainty was that she, with her Creole temper and Gallic passion, would ever be a stranger to them.

She focused instead on the gently rolling countryside. Even in December, this land looked rich. A pity one could not grow cane here. Despite her bitterness at having been sent away, Martinique had learned to love England. She longed for Barbados, yes. She particularly longed for the memories of her mother. But they seemed to fade with time and distance, no matter how hard she tried to hold on to them.

It was almost as if her aunt read her mind. Xanthia cleared her throat a little sharply. When her brother did not notice, she gave his knee a little jostle. He looked up from his account book, his brows drawn together. "We are almost there," said Xanthia. "Was there not something you wished to do before we arrived?"

"Ah, yes." Rothewell's expression seemed to darken, as if that were possible. But he reached into the floor of the carriage, and took up the strange leather case which had sat there every day since their departure from London. He settled it on his knee, and slid a hand almost lovingly over the top, as if to brush away the dust, though there was none.

"Your aunt and I brought this from Bridgetown," he said, his eyes suddenly soft. Yet he was gazing not at her, but at the case. "Xanthia thought it was time you had it."

He passed it across the carriage, and set it gently in Martinique's lap. The thing was rather like a small dressing case. Curious, Martinique drew open one of the drawers. A long strand of pink-white pearls lay nestled in a bed of blue velvet. A second drawer revealed an ornate emerald pendant with a matching pair of long, elaborately fashioned earbobs.

"Those are still too old for you," Aunt Xanthia warned. "But the pearls and some of the other things you may wear now, if you wish."

Stunned, Martinique lifted the lid. Compartments of brooches and earbobs winked back at her. One of them, a simple gold pin set with seed pearls, was instantly familiar. "*Maman*," she whispered on a sudden surge of longing. "These are hers, are they not?"

Xanthia set one hand over hers. "Some were gifts from your natural father before . . . well, before she came to Barbados. But most of the pieces my brother Luke bought her after they were married. You were too young to remember."

"And now they are mine?"

Xanthia nodded. Martinique looked across the carriage at Rothewell, but already his gaze had returned to the window. Tears pressed hotly against her eyes, and an almost overwhelming swell of grief and gratitude tugged at her heart. And yet there was pain, too. Pain, and a deep sense of inadequacy. Just as her birth father had never wanted her, Rothewell had not wanted her. Perhaps her stepfather had not really wanted her, either? Perhaps he had been merely kind, to please her mother? It was her deepest, most secret fear.

But unlike his dead brother, Rothewell's disdain was apparent, and Martinique wished desperately to know *why*. Why was she unlovable? What was wrong with her? But if Rothewell noticed her distress, one could not discern it. He might as well have handed her a pair of old shoes. "My lord?" she said. "Do *you* wish me to have them?"

He turned again from the window, and without truly looking at her, gave a small, dismissive gesture with the back of his hand. "If it pleases you," he said. "But if there are pieces you do not care for, we can sell them."

Sell them? *Sell her mother's jewels?* Martinique should rather have sold Rothewell—not that anyone in their right mind would have wanted him. Or would they? Mrs. Harris always said there was no accounting for taste. Martinique let her eyes run over her guardian's figure, which was, admittedly, imposing and muscular. He was tall, too, with long-fingered, well-callused hands and shoulders which looked strong and work-hardened. And to her shock, he was *young*.

Martinique had been sent away on her thirteenth birthday, scarcely six months after her parents' deaths. Then, she had believed Rothewell old and obdurate. Only now did she realize he was still a very young man. Rothewell was dark: his hair, his eyes, and yes, even his complexion. The years of hard work in the Bajan sun had left him with skin far darker than her own, and a set of fine lines at the corners of his eyes. But the darkest thing about her guardian was his personality. No, despite his wealth, no one was apt to want Rothewell.

But on that score, apparently, she was to be proven wrong.

"Kieran!" Martinique heard the call ring out even before their coach drew to a halt.

She looked out to see a young woman coming swiftly down the front steps of a fine brick mansion. She looked a little past thirty, with smiling eyes and a wide, good-humored mouth.

"Cousin Pamela," Rothewell murmured to his sister. Then he pushed open the door, and stepped out.

The lady rushed forward to take his hand before he had a chance to help Xanthia from the carriage. Soon, however, they all stood on the graveled carriage drive, and Lady Sharpe was hugging Xanthia.

"Just look at you!" She set her away, eyes shining. "I am sure, Zee, that you scarcely remember me. But I remember you."

Xanthia returned the smile. "It is such a pleasure to be here."

Lady Sharpe turned her attention to Martinique, and extended her hand. "And Martinique, welcome. Cousin Luke wrote often of you, and with great affection."

Just then, there was a sharp *clack clack* of wood on stone. Martinique looked up to see an elderly woman coming down the elegant front steps, a gold-knobbed stick in her hand. She was a tall, big-boned woman, her shoulders barely stooped with age.

"Aunt Olivia." Rothewell went up the steps to take her elbow.

She shook him off almost irritably. "I can go down a dozen stairs without help, Kieran," she bristled. "Good Lord, boy, what the devil's happened to your skin?"

Lady Sharpe hastened forward. "Kieran is not mollycoddling, Mother," she scolded. "He is being a gentleman—a gentleman whom you've not yet cowed. Now come greet Xanthia, and meet Martinique."

"Well, little Xanthia," said the old woman, offering her wrinkled cheek to be kissed. "You grew up, girl—and you have your mother's lovely eyes."

"Thank you, Aunt Olivia," said Xanthia.

The old woman turned a beady eye on Martinique. "And so you're Luke's adopted chit, eh?" she said. "Come, child, and let me have a look at you."

Martinique stepped forward, but at that moment, a striking woman with pale blond hair came out of the house. She was clinging to the arm of a dark, dashing gentleman who could only have been described as beautiful, for the word *handsome* did not do him justice. Across the distance, his gaze caught Martinique's, and for an instant, her breath hitched. He looked not at Rothewell, nor at Xanthia, but directly at *her*, mesmerizing her with his intense, dark eyes.

Then the blond woman spoke, severing the strange spell. "Heavens, Pamela!" she said, abandoning her attractive companion to hasten down the steps. "Surely this is not Rothewell?"

Lady Sharpe blushed, and swiftly introduced her husband's half-sister, Mrs. Ambrose. "Christine is making her home with us at present," she explained. "And this is our neighbor, Lord St. Vrain."

The dark young man came down the steps with a polished grace, and bowed deeply. "It is my great pleasure to make your acquaintance," he said in a rich, soft baritone. But as he straightened, his eyes met Martinique's again, and inexplicably, a frisson of sensual awareness ran down her spine.

But Mrs. Ambrose had eyes only for Rothewell. "My lord, I have heard so much of you from dear Pamela," she cooed, slipping her arm through his. "Come, let us all go into the house for refreshment. You must tell me all about the exotic life you lead in the West Indies. Have you slaves? Are they frightfully dangerous? I have always wished to go there, you know. And to Boston as well. Perhaps I shall do both, and pay you a call one day."

"Boston and Barbados are some two thousand miles apart, Christine," said Lady Sharpe.

Mrs. Ambrose, however, was already halfway up the steps. "Are they indeed?" she said, glancing almost dismissively over her shoulder. "Why, it could not have been but an inch or two on Reggie's atlas."

The old woman's face had taken on an almost disdainful expression. "Come along, Xanthia," she said, starting up the steps, her cane busily clacking. "You, too, girl. Christine's going to embarrass herself. You shan't wish to miss it."

Once inside, however, Lady Sharpe gently overruled Mrs. Ambrose, and insisted upon seeing her guests to their rooms so that they might freshen up. "Mother, Christine, will the two of you please take St. Vrain into the drawing room and ring for tea whilst I get everyone settled? And where is Reggie? Faversham, kindly go and fetch Lord Sharpe, if you please. And tell Miss Pendle to bring the children down."

The butler hastened away to do his mistress's bidding, and St. Vrain offered the old woman his arm. Together, they vanished up the elegantly curving staircase. But Mrs. Ambrose was still clinging like a vine to Rothewell.

"Lord Rothewell is to have the blue suite which overlooks the lake," said Lady Sharpe to one of the footmen who was balancing a trunk neatly on one shoulder. "I recall, Kieran, how much you like a water view."

Aunt Xanthia leaned nearer to her cousin. "Would it be frightfully difficult, Pamela, for Martinique and I to room near one another?" she asked. "We are like giddy schoolgirls getting reacquainted."

Xanthia was just being kind. Martinique was finding this first foray into society a little daunting, and Xanthia was playing the mother hen. Lady Sharpe seemed to understand at once. "Actually, we have a pair of connecting bedchambers," she said, her brows knotting. "But Christine already occupies one."

Xanthia squeezed her hand. "We shall be fine anywhere, then."

"No, wait." Lady Sharpe laid a hand on Xanthia's arm, and looked past her. "Christine, my dear, would you mind awfully changing bedchambers? I should like to put Xanthia and Martinique together."

Mrs. Ambrose looked irritated. "Pamela, where shall Jenks sleep?" she asked. "I have been putting her in the adjoining room, in case I get one of my headaches at night."

Rothewell stepped forward. "I do not need the suite," he said. "Why do you not have it, Mrs. Ambrose? Surely there is another bedchamber with a view of the lake?"

"Yes, the room to the left of the suite has a fine view," said Lady Sharpe. "It is frightfully small—but it does have a pretty balcony."

"Ah, a place to smoke my cheroots," murmured Rothewell.

Mrs. Ambrose cast another look at Rothewell. "*Next* to the suite?" she said, her eyes alight with sudden mischief. "I must have Jenks move my things straightaway. If, of course, you really do not mind our being neighbors, my lord?"

Rothewell finally smiled. "Nothing would please me more."

The footmen were sent scurrying off to deliver luggage hither and yon, and within the hour, the family was again reassembled, this time in a long, sunny withdrawing room hung with some two dozen portraits. The children, Louisa and Judith, were brought in for introductions just as Lord Sharpe joined them, still in his boots and breeches. He was a large, affable gentleman with laughing eyes and a vanishing hairline. He kissed his daughters with unabashed affection, then bowed low over Martinique's hand, declaring himself delighted.

"My dear," he said to his wife, "Rothewell has given you an easy task. Bringing this exotic beauty out come spring will be no chore for you. But I shall likely die of exhaustion from beating back the suitors from our door."

Everyone laughed, save for Martinique, who felt her cheeks flame, and St. Vrain, who had propped himself languidly by one of the long, deep windows, his eyes moving over the crowd like quicksilver. Martinique wondered why he was there. To amuse Mrs. Ambrose, no doubt. There was a certain wariness in Lady Sharpe's gaze each time she glanced at the young man.

Though she, too, kept cutting odd, dark looks in the direction of St. Vrain, Mrs. Ambrose had clearly laid claim to Rothewell. He did not seem entirely displeased by her attentions. Oblivious to it all, Great-Aunt Olivia pounced at once upon Xanthia, peppering her with questions about her marital plans—or lack thereof.

Xanthia gave a muted smile. "I thank you, Aunt Olivia, for your concern, but my time is devoted to our shipping concerns just now."

"Nonsense!" said Olivia, rapping her cane on the floor. "Women have no business *in* business, my girl."

"Things are done differently in Barbados, Aunt."

"Not that differently, I'll wager," said Olivia with

asperity. "Let Kieran tend to such things, and get on with your life. You are already on the shelf—and covered with a layer of dust."

Aunt Xanthia looked embarrassed. "Kieran runs our plantations," she explained, dropping her voice. "I see to the shipping. After Luke died, there simply was no one else." She cast a glance in Martinique's direction. "Though perhaps someday Martinique will take an interest? She is, after all, a part-owner."

Olivia reared back in her chair. "But the girl is to go to Town and find a husband," she said, thumping her stick on the floor. "Rothewell says she is to stay in England permanently."

Xanthia cast a sidelong look in Rothewell's direction. "That shall be Martinique's decision," she said quietly. "My brother does not own the whole of Barbados, much as he might think otherwise. But as to our shipping concerns, we are soon to open a London office. Eventually, we shall move Neville Shipping altogether."

The old woman's hand still clutched her walking stick as if she might snatch it up and flail someone at any moment. "Shipping! Sugar!" she grumbled. "I should rather know why Rothewell has let his estate in Cheshire go to hell. I hear he has never even laid eyes on it."

"It is let," Xanthia countered. "The tenant is very responsible."

Martinique slipped from her chair, and began to drift around the room. Estate matters did not interest her, nor did the portraits which covered the far wall of Lady Sharpe's drawing room. Nonetheless, she feigned a burning desire to study each in detail, thus distancing herself from the family which still felt so very foreign to her.

So the family business—at least one of them—was moving to London. How odd. The Neville shipping empire was vast. Though her stepfather had begun it with just two dilapidated schooners, Neville's merchantmen and sleek, modern clippers now plied the world's oceans from the West Indies to France and England, as well as India and Africa, and most points in between.

Neville Shipping had been started, her stepfather used to joke, by Martinique's mother, Annemarie. The original ships had been a parting gift from her wealthy French lover—Martinique's father—upon his decision to take a wife: a pale, pretty Parisian girl of flawless breeding. Annemarie's remaining in the French West Indies was out of the question. So, with the understanding that she would never again darken his door, he gave his mistress a fistful of francs, the titles to two of his oldest vessels, and a good, swift shove off the dock onto a Barbados-bound mail packet. And that was that.

Still, it had ended well enough. Martinique's mother had ended up with a handsome younger man—one who loved her enough to marry her. Martinique had ended up with an unusual Christian name, a fine old English surname, and a stepfather whom she'd worshiped. And as to her birth father—well, *he* had ended up in insolvent debtor's court. His pretty French bride had soon bankrupted him, and his ships were sold off to satisfy his salivating creditors. Luke Neville had picked over the fleet, taking only the best to join the dozen his family owned by then. And that, Martinique decided, was a fine definition of justice.

"She was handsome in her youth, was she not?"

The low, rich voice came out of nowhere, sending a strange shiver down Martinique's spine. "I—I beg your pardon?" She turned to see that Lord St. Vrain stood at her side.

"Your great-aunt Olivia," he said quietly. "I am reliably informed that the portrait you are so intently study-ing is hers, painted some weeks after her marriage."

"*Vraiment, monsieur?*" Martinique managed. "To be sure, I did not recognize her."

"Nor did I," he confessed. "I am shocked the artist caught her without that infernal stick."

Martinique struggled to keep from laughing. "Does she never let go of it?"

"Not that I have seen." He cast a speciously wary glance in Great-Aunt Olivia's direction. "And I have been hanging about here for the last six weeks or so. She has even brandished it at me once or twice."

Martinique grinned. "Yes, you look the type who might warrant an occasional caning," she said. "Has Mrs. Ambrose thrown you over for my uncle, do you think?"

For an instant, his eyes widened, and then he, too, was compelled to suppress a burst of laughter. "I cannot say," he finally answered. "My prospects look grim at present, do they not?

"She does seem to have shifted her interest," said Martinique. "Are you poor, *monsieur?*"

"Am I *poor?*" he echoed incredulously. "Oh, yes, I take your point! No, my dear child. I am quite astonish-ingly rich—but alas, not very biddable. Oh, Lord. Christine has poor Rothewell by the arm again. It looks as though they are headed toward the solarium."

"Oh, she shall be back soon enough," she reassured him. "Rothewell is intractable, too—and often unpleas-ant in the bargain."

He turned to look at her, his dark eyes dancing. "Good God, poor Sharpe was sadly mistaken," he said in a low undertone. "Pamela is going to have a devil of a time with you. Do they really mean to marry you off?"

"They think so." Martinique lifted one shoulder. "But

I think I should be better pleased to work in the shipping business with Aunt Xanthia."

He cocked one slashing black eyebrow. "In *business*?" he echoed. "They really must do things differently in the islands."

"West Indian society has fewer strictures, *oui*."

His clear blue eyes held hers pensively. "I thought every young lady wished to marry," he finally said. "Do you not?"

Again, the shrug. "If I fell desperately in love, perhaps," she said. "But otherwise? It seems unnecessary."

"I do not think the English nobility are permitted either love or desperation," he said dryly.

"My parents fell deeply in love," she answered. "And I begin to believe, *monsieur*, that I, too, shall hold out for such depth of emotion."

"Your mother was French, I understand?"

Martinique smiled faintly. "Mostly, yes."

He smiled. "Half French, and half English," he mused, studying her. "A remarkable combination."

She gave another light laugh. She wished he were not quite so handsome, as it was more than a little unsettling. "*Non, monsieur*," she corrected. "I was the late Lord Rothewell's stepdaughter. There is not a drop of English blood in me."

"Ah." His dark, slashing eyebrows went up again. "I see."

St. Vrain studied the lovely breath of spring who stood before him. It had been a long time since he had conversed with anyone who seemed so full of life—or innocence. And she wished to fall in love. How quaint the notion seemed to him now. Thank God it was not his obligation to disabuse the girl of her dreams. Life, and Lord Rothewell, would likely do so soon enough.

As if by unspoken agreement, they had begun to

stroll around the room. No one had seemed to notice her absence from the older ladies' conversation. "You have been away at school until recently, I collect?"

"Oui, monsieur." She was clutching her hands at the small of her back as they strolled, looking quite perfectly at ease with him, more fool she. "I was six years at Mrs. Harris's."

"Mrs. Harris?" he said. "Ought I to know her?"

Martinique cocked her head and smiled. "The *ton* calls it Mrs. Harris's School for Heiresses," she said. "The place is infamous. Where have you been hiding, St. Vrain?"

"In Paris," he said matter-of-factly. "What, pray, is so infamous about it?"

"It is the school where the very wealthiest of England's nouveau riche girls are sent, so that they might learn how to feint and parry with society's rakes, rogues and fortune hunters."

Against his better judgment, his smile deepened to a grin, and then to a laugh. "Good God, you are jesting, are you not?"

"Oh, no, *monsieur*," she said solemnly. "By the way, are you a rake? Or a rogue?"

"I beg your pardon?"

The chit grinned at him. "Well, you say you are quite rich. So you cannot be a fortune hunter."

She was perfectly sincere. "Is every man who seeks your company one of the three?"

"So Mrs. Harris would have us believe."

Impulsively, he reached down and took her hand. "I wish I could say she was wrong, my dear," he answered, giving her fingers a reassuring squeeze. "But I fear she may have the right of it, no matter how cynical the sentiment."

Somehow, they had stopped walking. Miss Neville

looked up at him from beneath a sweep of dark lashes, and something in his stomach twisted unexpectedly. "You . . . you are quite beautiful, my dear." The words came out more urgent than he had intended. "I think that you really must heed your Mrs. Harris. And I— well, I ought not be alone with you."

"We are not alone." Her gaze was warm and steady as she studied him. "I wonder, *monsieur*, if we mightn't be kindred spirits, you and I."

"What do you mean?"

Again she gave that charming, Gallic shrug. "Are you not weary of being sought out for your beauty and your wealth?" she suggested. "Do you not wish that just once, you might attract the attentions of someone who wanted . . . *nothing*? Or who wanted, perhaps, to know the depth of your thinking and the turn of your mind?"

St. Vrain winced. "I am a man, my dear child," he said. "We have few deep thoughts, and are pretty well-satisfied to be wanted for any reason whatsoever—*if* the lady is lovely enough."

"Is Mrs. Ambrose lovely enough?"

"She is a beautiful ornament for a man's arm," he replied. "But I am not fool enough to mistake Mrs. Ambrose's attentions for anything other what they are: a sign of boredom, and a manifestation, perhaps, of her lingering grief."

"Grief?"

"She is newly widowed," he said quietly. "You are very young, Miss Neville. You cannot know what it is to lose one's companion too soon. It . . . does things. It disorders the mind. You . . . well, you blame yourself. And sometimes you will seize upon any diversion, any distraction, in order to forget it."

"Ah," she said. "You have known great unhappiness, I think."

"Who has not?" he asked rhetorically.

She managed to smile. "Let us speak of something more pleasant," she suggested. "Tell me of Paris; of what it is like to live there. I long so desperately to see it."

"Then you must find a handsome man, *chéri*, and charm him into taking you."

"Yes." She hesitated. "Yes, perhaps I shall."

A moment of awkwardness ensued, but he bridged it smoothly. "Then I shall give you the loan of my little house, Miss Neville," he said. "It is small, but idyllic—quite perfect for a wedding trip, I think. So if you go to London, and find that husband after all—"

A rustle of silk cut him off. "Why, there you are, St. Vrain!"

Lady Sharpe drew up beside him, her expression one of mild alarm. Ah, he understood too well that look. He was here on her sufferance. His presence at Highwood might be tolerated at tea or at dinner—or even in Christine's bed, so long as it was discreetly done. But it would not be tolerated at all, were he to go about cornering the family's pretty virgins.

He stepped away, wondering what had compelled him to cling to the chit's hand. He ought to be bloody grateful for Lady Sharpe's interruption.

"I was just telling Miss Neville what little I knew of these portraits," he said with a dismissive bow. "She has a keen interest in genealogy, but alas, I cannot recall all the names. Would you be so kind?"

Then, without looking at the girl again, he turned on his heel and left.

Dinner that evening was a pleasant affair, and Martinique found Lord Sharpe a most welcoming host. Afterward, Great-Aunt Olivia retired for the evening. Martinique envied the old woman her bed; the last leg of the journey from London had been wearying. But when Cousin Pamela suggested a game of whist, Martinique smiled and joined everyone in the parlor, declaring that she would watch—if, she silently added, she could keep her eyes from the intriguing Lord St. Vrain.

Mrs. Ambrose also declined a place at the table. St. Vrain seemed content to sip his brandy by the roaring hearth and observe the play as well. Despite an occasional glance in his direction, Martinique kept her distance. She had sensed Cousin Pamela's displeasure at their tête-à-tête in the drawing room.

She was tempted, of course, to continue flirting with him. It was a little dull at Highwood after the intellectual stimulation of Mrs. Harris's. Moreover, St. Vrain was charming, and almost disturbingly attractive. But even more dangerous than that, he seemed so *real* to her. There was a depth and a darkness to him which she yearned to understand. And there was something in his glittering gaze which set her pulse to fluttering, and left a strange, empty yearning in the pit of her stomach.

Martinique knew that emotion for what it was—desire—though she'd little experience with it. Her mother had been well-schooled in the art of creating it; of fanning its flames, of making heads turn. Even as a child, Martinique had been aware of her mother's mysterious allure. Had the skill somehow passed, unbidden and unspoken, from mother to daughter? Martinique rather doubted it. Nonetheless, desire was a basic human emotion. To ignore its importance might mean a life of unhappiness.

And now Rothewell would likely try to force her into an arranged marriage, just to be rid of her. To marry a man she did not desire would be foolish. Yet to court disaster by flirting with a man of St. Vrain's ilk would be more foolish still, no matter how many little shivers he sent down her spine. Better to leave that sort of gentleman to women of Mrs. Ambrose's experience. Martinique turned in her chair to face the gaming table, and did not look at him again.

The card game progressed amidst a great deal of laughter and good-natured teasing. A tray of coffee was brought, more candles lit and the fires stoked by the footmen. Eventually, St. Vrain excused himself. At once, Mrs. Ambrose stood, and went slinking from the room, winding her way past the furnishings like a cat after a mouse, and she looked in an ill humor.

With St. Vrain gone, Martinique glanced around for something with which to entertain herself, and spied the door to Lord Sharpe's library. During their brief tour of Highwood, Pamela had encouraged them to make use of it at their leisure. Well, she was very much at leisure now. There was nothing beautiful left to look at, surreptitiously or otherwise, and the card game was no longer enough to keep her awake.

Inside the library, a low fire had been lit, and a branch of candles sat on a side table nearby, casting a soft, flickering glow over one corner of the expansive room. Martinique lit a single candle, and drifted along the shelves until she found a book of botanical sketches. She returned with it to the hearth, and curled up in a worn but comfortable high-backed chair which faced the fire.

It was, in fact, just a little too comfortable. One yawn after another, she made it as far as page twenty-two—*crataegus laevigata*, the smooth hawthorn—before succumbing to the soft embrace of the old leather. She could not have drowsed for more than five minutes, however, when she was bestirred by the sound of the door at the far end of the room.

"In here, Justin," said a female voice. "I must speak to you."

Martinique jerked upright, almost sending her book to the floor.

"We ought to return to the parlor, Christine," said a deep, familiar voice. "What do you want?"

"To talk to you," Mrs. Ambrose said peevishly. "But you are in a vile mood."

"Am I?" asked St. Vrain quietly. "Tell me, my dear, did you enjoy rubbing your new conquest in my face tonight? It won't work, you know."

"I can't think what you mean."

"Lord Rothewell," he said. "You were flirting with him all through dinner."

"Yes? And why shouldn't I?"

"Why, indeed," murmured St. Vrain.

"You have tired of me, Justin." The words were sharp. "You are not the least bit jealous. Why can you not just admit it?"

"Do not be ridiculous, my dear," he said. "I have known you but six weeks."

"Yes, and already you are unfaithful!"

A long silence held sway. "Unfaithful?" he echoed. "My dear girl, you mistake me. I am not interested in . . . anything of a permanent nature. I thought you understood."

"Indeed, I understand that I have been used," she hissed. "Six weeks, and already you pay no attention to me."

"You mean I do not dance attendance on you," he corrected. "And I do not bow to your every whim. But were I to do so, Christine, *you* should soon grow tired of *me*."

"So that is your paltry excuse for her? Burn in hell, Justin!"

He paused for a heartbeat. "I thought you understood how the game was played, my dear," he finally said. "But if you do not—if, in fact, you seek a husband—then yes, you'd best sink your claws into Rothewell. Perhaps you can bring him up to scratch."

"I don't want Rothewell." Her voice was lethally soft. "I wanted *you*. Were you fool enough—or arrogant enough—to think I would not learn of your little doxy down in the village?"

"Oh, for pity's sake!" St. Vrain made a sound of exasperation. "That tavern maid? What does she matter to you, Christine?"

There was the rustle of silk, as if Mrs. Ambrose moved toward him in haste. "Stop bedding her, Justin." The words were dark with warning. "You are making me a laughingstock. I shan't have it, do you hear? Stop bedding that—that *woman,* and come to me tonight."

"Christine, my dear, that would be unwise."

The smacking sound of flesh on flesh rang out. *She had slapped him!*

"Come to me tonight, Justin." Her voice was taking on a shrill, desperate edge. "I demand it. And stop seeing that little whore, or I swear to God that I . . . I shall tell Reggie you forced your attentions on me."

"Christine, have you any notion how pathetic you sound?" he said coldly. "You are beautiful. Do not behave as if you are desperate."

A wracking sob echoed in the silence. "Oh, God!" she cried. "Oh, what is to become of me? You—you have just been using me, Justin. A poor, lonely widow, and you knew just how to manipulate me, didn't you?" And then she was crying in earnest; a great gulping, gasping, guilt-inducing fit of the vapors.

Mrs. Ambrose, Martinique decided, was frightfully talented.

It took a half-dozen such sobs before he broke. "Oh, God, Christine!" St. Vrain sounded resigned. "Oh, Christine, come here. I cannot bear to see a woman cry!"

There was the rustle and crush of silk, and the low rumble of St. Vrain's voice, muffled against something; her hair, perhaps. Then the sobs receded, and the words turned to soft, conciliatory murmurs. Dear God, had the poor man fallen for it?

The murmurs had turned affectionate now. Martinique wondered if he was going to kiss her. In her mind, she could imagine it. Not Mrs. Ambrose, but St. Vrain, and his sinfully beautiful mouth.

Good Lord! She was pathetic, too. And she should have made her presence known long ago. Suddenly, their footsteps sounded, moving across the room. There was the sound of one last embrace, a few hushed words of agreement, then the door clicked softly shut.

St. Vrain, it seemed, had just been bested.

Two

Room for Confusion

St. Vrain's evening should have ended at midnight, when the last of Lord Sharpe's houseguests gave in to their fatigue. The pretty virgin had long since followed her great-aunt Olivia up to bed, and after her little scene in the library, Christine had not bothered to return to the parlor. When the rest of the party surrendered amidst suppressed yawns and cheerful plans for the morrow, St. Vrain found himself eager to be gone.

He bowed low over Miss Xanthia Neville's hand, and bid her brother a polite good evening. Like St. Vrain himself, Lord Rothewell had spent the last of the evening drinking, perhaps a little too deeply. On parting, he shot St. Vrain a look of dark, barely veiled suspicion. St. Vrain wondered at the cause. Surely not Christine? No. No, it was his little tête-à-tête in the drawing room with the man's niece, more likely. Already, St. Vrain regretted that little indiscretion. He wondered what had come over him. Boredom, he supposed.

Sharpe saw him to the door, and offered to call for his mount, but St. Vrain refused the gesture. It had become his habit to fetch his horse from the stables himself—and in his own good time. Swallowed up by the gloom, he strolled the length of Sharpe's front portico, then set a brisk pace along the west wing of the house. At the end, however, he hesitated.

Damn Christine for getting under his skin. He did not welcome a quarrel with the woman, but he welcomed her machinations even less. He wished he had not allowed her tears to lead him into promises he'd no wish to keep. But he *had* promised. And so St. Vrain plunged his hand into his coat pocket and withdrew the key she had pressed into his palm weeks ago.

It was a simple matter to let himself in through the servants' door which gave onto the west gardens, and slip up Highwood's back stairs. With a sense of mild self-loathing, he hesitated at her door. He was not afraid of Christine's threats. But her tears—ah, they had struck at his heart. A maiden in distress had always been his worst weakness, and the source of most of his life's troubles, too.

He opened the door, and stepped into the pitch-black room. Christine, it seemed, had drifted off while awaiting him. In the gloom, her breathing was deep and slow. So much for her burning ardor.

His pride a little humbled, St. Vrain turned the lock, and began to undress, slowly folding his clothes across the armchair which sat near her bed as he'd done a dozen times before. Her body was warm and willing when he slipped beneath her bedcovers. She turned to him at once, enfolding her lithe form against his with a submissive sound. Whatever wrath she had possessed earlier seemed to have melted into a sweet, eager ardor which was irresistible, if a little unusual.

His interest in Christine quite thoroughly rekindled, St. Vrain covered her mouth with his, and thrust his tongue deep on the first stroke. She opened to him, and lifted her hips just enough to brush the length of his rapidly hardening cock. It was a delightful, almost innocent gesture, and it left him inexplicably aroused. Over and over, he plumbed the depths of her mouth, which tasted not like the evening's madeira he was accustomed to, but spicy-sweet, like tart spring apples. As if to entice him, she slid the smooth arch of her foot slowly up his ankle while one of her small, warm hands stroked the curve of his hip. It was hardly a carnal caress, but a bolt of raw lust suddenly shot through him, fierce and quivering. His ballocks drew taut with need, and for an instant, his breath came short and fast. *Good God.*

St. Vrain had meant this to be just a sympathy fuck. Something quick and hot, but meant only to assuage Christine's vanity. So why was he now tempted to linger? Unwilling to consider it too deeply, St. Vrain intensified the kiss, and plunged his fingers into her hair, which lay like a soft, silken curtain across the pillow. Beneath his hungry mouth, she gave a soft moan; a hint of a return to full consciousness. He almost wished she would not fully wake, but instead let him take her slowly and sweetly as she lingered on that perfect, magical edge where inhibition did not exist, and desire came fully and freely.

Unable to resist the temptation, St. Vrain eased one hand down the turn of her calf, and slithered her nightgown up inch by inch until the treasure he sought was unveiled. Throwing one leg almost possessively over her, he slid a forefinger into her warm thatch of curls, and eased it back and forth in the slick, silky heat. As he had hoped, a second soft moan escaped her mouth. The weight of his cock twitched insistently against her thigh. And suddenly, she went rigid as a board in his embrace.

He pressed his mouth hotly to her ear. "Shush, love," he murmured. "Don't fight it. Just relax for me."

She did not relax. "Good Lord!" It was a horrified whisper. "*St. Vrain?*"

There had been all too many of those dreadful, life-altering moments in St. Vrain's misbegotten life; moments when a man realized that one little word, or one seemingly insignificant action, had just damned him to an unalterable path. This was definitely one of them.

"*Oh, holy God,*" he whispered. "*Miss . . . Miss Neville?*"

The lithe, slender woman in his arms drew back. "St. Vrain?" she repeated.

He should have bolted from the bed, but instead, he let his brow fall forward to touch hers. "Dear Lord," he whispered. "Miss Neville."

"Yes, it is I," she said. "I believe we have established that." Her brisk words were belied by her breathing, which was now rapid and quite shallow.

"Miss Neville," he said again. "I am afraid that I—well, I find myself just . . . quite . . . utterly . . . speechless."

"Try," she whispered. "Search your mind, St. Vrain, and try to find the words which will explain to me just what it is you are doing in my bed, with your hand on my—"

He jerked the hand away as if she'd burst into flame. "Dear God!" he said. "My apologies."

"Your *apologies*?" she said incredulously.

"My *deepest* and most *profound* apologies," he clarified. "And as to what I am doing here, as best I can make it out, I am destroying any possibility of your future happiness."

She shifted her weight uncertainly. "How on earth did you get in?"

"A key," he choked. "I—I have a key."

"Ah," she answered dryly. "I wonder where you got it."

He did not catch the sarcasm. "Miss Neville," he whispered. "I find myself in the quite awkward position of—of being honored—quite *deeply* honored—to ask for your hand in marriage."

There was a long moment of silence. "Would you be so kind, my lord, as to light the lamp by the bed?"

He rolled to the edge of the mattress, and set his feet on Christine's carpet—or the carpet he wished quite fervently *was* Christine's. What the devil had happened? He was not *that* damned drunk.

"St. Vrain, the lamp, if you please."

He reached for the lamp, then hesitated. "I am not decent."

"It is rather late for modesty, is it not?" said Miss Neville. "You have stripped yourself naked, crawled into my bed, and offered me, amongst other things, marriage. Perhaps I should like to have a better look at my bargain before I make you my answer?"

"Miss Neville!"

She laughed a little weakly. "Oh, for God's sake, St. Vrain, just light the bloody lamp," she said. "Then we must make out what the devil we are to do."

"Oh, I know what we are to do," he muttered, fumbling awkwardly in the dark.

When at last he managed to light the wick, the lamp bathed the room in muted, flickering light. Miss Neville rose onto one elbow, and set a warm hand in the center of his bare back. "No one knows you are with me, my lord," she whispered over his shoulder. "And it is perfectly clear how you came to be here. Mrs. Ambrose forgot to tell you we had exchanged rooms, did she not?"

"She was a little agitated this evening," he admitted.

He shifted so that he might face her, pulling the sheet strategically across his thighs as he turned. Her black hair cascaded over one shoulder, a luxurious mass of silken curls. She looked up at him, her eyes still warm, and a little dreamy. The tension in the room leapt, and the silence stretched into infinity as they held one another's gaze.

"My lord," she finally whispered, "you no more wish to be saddled with me than I with you."

He could not help himself. With a hand which shook, St. Vrain reached out and cupped the turn of her cheek in his palm. "You are a beautiful woman, Miss Neville." His voice had gone slightly raspy. "And a passionate one as well. There are far worse fates which might befall a man than having you in his bed every night."

Beneath his hand, he felt her shiver. Her lashes dropped shut, fanning darkly across her cheeks, and he wished quite suddenly to kiss her again.

"And you are very beautiful," she whispered. "That was the word which first sprang to my mind the moment I saw you. *Beautiful.* I do not wonder that women find you desirable. But I do not wish to marry you, my lord. I wish to wed for love and for passion."

"Then I must accept your answer," he said, his voice uneasy. "But love and passion are not everything, Miss Neville. You would have found pleasure in my bed, if nothing else."

She looked up at him, her eyes wide. "Oh, I do not doubt *that* for a moment." The words were throaty, and not at all innocent. "May I ask, my lord, what your intentions are regarding Mrs. Ambrose?"

For an instant, he frowned. "My relationship with Mrs. Ambrose is at an end," he said. "Tonight has taught me that, if nothing else."

Miss Neville surprised him then by stroking her

warm hand down his arm. Then gradually, as if the world itself moved in slow motion, she leaned into him, and set her lips to the turn of his shoulder. "Then show me," she murmured against his skin.

"*Show* you?"

"Show me what it would be like to spend each night in your bed."

He let go of the sheet, and half-turned around. "What are you asking, my dear?"

She lifted her mouth from his shoulder, and looked at him with a gaze which was open and honest, yet smoldering with feminine desire. "I want you to finish what you started," she whispered. "The harm, whatever it is, is done."

He cut his gaze away. "I fear that is hardly the case."

Miss Neville brushed her lips over his. "You desire me, St. Vrain," she whispered against his mouth. "And I am not that innocent."

The fire he'd been trying to bank burst to full flame again. "God yes, I desire you," he rasped.

Martinique looked down as the sheet went slithering from St. Vrain's thighs, revealing the truth of his arousal. She felt mesmerized. Enchanted. She wanted to touch it. To touch . . . *him*. Everywhere. There was no fear, and very little caution, in her heart. And to have him on her, around her, inside her body—dear God, the clarity of such visions shocked her.

She had awakened to a dream. A fantasy. And a simmering desire she had never fully known—a desire, perhaps, she had never allowed herself to feel. But St. Vrain's skilled touch had inflamed her, and exposed to her a truth she had long suspected. A fire burned inside her; a passion like her mother's. A passion which, mere moments ago, had been consuming her. And St. Vrain was the cause.

He had closed his eyes. "You . . . are a virgin?"

"Not really."

His eyes snapped open, and his hands went to her shoulders, grasping them harshly as if he might shake the truth from her. "There are but two answers to that question, my dear," he gritted. *"Give me one of them!"*

"Yes," she answered. "Yes, I am a virgin, St. Vrain. But I am not a fool. I do not wish to marry like some silly English miss. I have other options for my life."

"Your innocence," he whispered. "It is precious."

"Not to me," she said. "It is a hindrance, like this . . . this awful yearning your touch engenders. Besides, one does not need to be a virgin to marry, unless one means to live a dull, conventional life."

For a moment, he hesitated. His hands, still gripping her shoulders, trembled so hard she felt it deep in her bones. And then something inside him gave away. His fingers went to the tie of her nightdress, fumbling awkwardly. He pushed the fabric from her shoulders, and night air breezed across her skin.

The gown slithered further, slipping down to drape off her elbows, baring her breasts. It should have felt embarrassing. Awkward. But St. Vrain's eyes burned with desire as they drifted over her, and it was nothing but gratifying. And all she felt was that sweet, hot ribbon of desire, twisting through her body again, drawing her to him.

"You are beautiful beyond words, Miss Neville," he whispered. "Skin like warm honey—and the taste of your lips, the scent of your hair—it is maddening."

She held out her arms. "Taste me," she pleaded. "Touch me again. Make me feel as I did when I awoke in your arms."

He clasped her face between hands which were

broad and a little rough, then kissed her again with his lips and his tongue, bearing her back into the softness of the bed. He dragged his weight over her, pinning her beneath his body, gently nudging her legs apart. She let her hands roam over him; over his wide, solid shoulders, down the strong length of his back, and further still. In the madness and the heat, he somehow drew off her nightdress. His chest was broad, and dusted with dark hair which teased at her nipples.

In minutes, she was burning; reaching out for him, and breathlessly pleading for something she knew only St. Vrain could give. Martinique sensed she was in the hands of a true master, and whatever the price, it would be worth it.

He urged her legs wider with the strength of his thigh. His mouth was on her breast, suckling her a little roughly. Her nipples drew into hard, aching peaks. As his hands roamed over her, he nipped and nibbled with his teeth, his breath came in harsh rasps until she cried out, drowning in pleasure and something which felt like pain, but was not. Instead, it was an exquisite torment.

"Good God, I must have you," he whispered, his mouth moving over her face—not in delicate kisses, but open and hot. Almost worshipful.

Acting on instinct, Martinique set one foot against the mattress, and curled her other leg about his waist. "Come to me," she begged, drawing him to her. "Come inside me. Make me . . . make me *feel*."

Despite his obvious arousal, she could sense his hesitation. "I will hurt you," he rasped. "I—I don't know how much."

"I want it," she pleaded. "Let me feel it—the pleasure and pain—I want it all. Can you understand?"

Again, he hesitated, his gaze roaming over her face as if to be sure. "God, what a damned fool I am!" he said. But already, the hard, weight of his erection brushed her flesh, grazing that hot, sweet spot he had tormented with his hand.

She cried out on a gasp. "Please. Yes. Oh, *please*."

A fraction of an inch. Then another. Martinique felt her body stretch unbearably. And then St. Vrain closed his eyes, and thrust. Her flesh tore, the discomfort acute but quick. Martinique cried out, and St. Vrain froze, his face a mask of agony.

She held him to her, her nails digging into the hard muscles of his buttocks. "Do not dare," she warned. "Just . . . move a little. Yes. Oh, God, yes. Like . . . *that*."

But to her undying frustration, he went perfectly still. "Easy, my love," he crooned, his breath warm against the turn of her neck. "Let me go slowly. Let me do a proper job of this."

She lifted her hips a fraction, and felt her flesh pull exquisitely against his hardness, making her shudder. "I cannot wait," she begged.

His mouth found hers, and his kiss was long and sweet. "You will have to wait, love," he teased. "You are quite firmly in my clutches."

Martinique thrashed almost feverishly. "Please, St. Vrain," she begged. "I want . . . I want—"

This time the kiss was rough and demanding. "I know what you want," he rasped when he drew his tongue from her mouth. "Be still, you maddening wench."

Trembling, she did as he ordered. For a long moment, he held perfectly still, his strong arms braced above her shoulders, his head thrown slightly back so that the dark hair fell away from his face, and the beads of perspiration slid down the sinews of his throat.

When at last he began to move, it was with a slow, exquisite rhythm. A rhythm of complete control, every stroke a perfect torment. His motions were skilled, his touch exquisite. He covered her mouth with his, and plunged inside with his tongue, over and over. She felt her body sheen with perspiration, felt her hips strain and strain for something she craved yet could not quite comprehend.

St. Vrain understood. He shifted his strokes, higher and a little harder. "Yes, yes, my love," he cooed. "Just let yourself come to me. Yes, like that. Like . . . that. Oh, God. You are—you are—*perfection*."

Beneath him, she arched hard, lifting her hips to his. For long moments they moved together in a timeless, instinctive rhythm, their sighs and moans soft in the night. Martinique ached for him, wanted to be joined to him, in every possible way, not just the physical but the metaphysical, too. She heard a voice chanting— pleading—in the darkness, and realized that it was hers. Stroke upon stroke, she strained for that ephemeral ribbon of pleasure, rising to him, begging him with her body and her breathless words.

And then something inside her shattered like glass. A thousand silvery splinters shot pleasure through her being, and the white-hot flame of desire consumed her. Dimly, she saw St. Vrain, his face taut with agony and joy. He thrust once more into her body, joining his soul to hers, and then he cried out and was lost with her in the splintering light.

Martinique drowsed for a time, hovering in that gossamer netherworld which only sated lovers inhabit. St. Vrain's arms were about her, rough and strong, his face buried in her hair. She was suddenly, fiercely, glad she had given herself to him. And when she shifted her weight, he rolled onto his side, drawing her firmly against him, her back to the wide, warm wall of his chest. Then he circled one arm about her waist, called her his love, and slipped into a deep, steady sleep. And for a few, fleeting moments, Martinique's life was at last perfection.

Martinique could not be perfectly certain how long she drowsed in St. Vrain's embrace. A quarter-hour, perhaps. The door, when it opened, swung quickly on well-oiled hinges, casting a breeze which made her shiver. Martinique woke to the glare of a lifted candle, and a sharp, horrified gasp.

Behind her, St. Vrain rolled up onto his elbow, and softly cursed.

Aunt Xanthia stood framed in the connecting doorway, her fingertips pressed to her mouth. Her lifted, trembling candle was quite unnecessary. They had forgotten to put out the lamp.

"Oh, Martinique!" Her aunt's voice quivered with rage. "St. Vrain, *what* is the meaning of this? Sir, how *dare* you?"

St. Vrain had turned to drag the cover to better cover Martinique's nakedness, and was murmuring soothingly. It was only then that Martinique noticed the figure in the shadows behind her aunt. Mrs. Ambrose stepped into the room, her hair down, her wrapper tucked primly about her.

"My dear Miss Neville, I fear I was not mistaken after all," she said, clutching at Aunt Xanthia's arm. "Would to God that I had been!"

"No, ma'am. You were not mistaken." Xanthia really was shaking now. "St. Vrain, get out. Get out, you bastard, and await my brother's displeasure. I pray God he sends you on a short trip to hell."

"Aunt Xanthia, please!" Martinique moved as if to

leap from the bed, but St. Vrain set a strong, restraining hand on her arm.

"It is all right, my dear," he murmured. "It will be all right."

But Martinique was barely listening. "You—you are quite mistaken," she cried. "St. Vrain is just—he was just . . . oh, please, Xanthia! Oh, God, *please* do not mention this to Rothewell."

Mrs. Ambrose swished around Xanthia, her expression one of grim satisfaction. "Poor, poor child," she said quietly. "As I said, I heard her cry out quite plaintively as I passed by."

"I have not hurt her," said St. Vrain quietly. "I have not, and I shall not. Now, if the two of you will kindly get out, I shall dress and say a few words to Miss . . . to Martinique."

Mrs. Ambrose cut one last glance down at St. Vrain, then set a hand on Xanthia's shoulder. "I shall leave you now," she said. "The ruin of an innocent is always such a tragedy. Please let me know, my dear, if I can be of further assistance."

"Oh, I think you've given quite enough assistance already, Christine," snapped St. Vrain. "Now, Miss Neville, I am about to climb out of this bed. And since I am indeed stark naked, I strongly suggest you avert your eyes."

Aunt Xanthia's cheeks flamed, and she spun about. Mrs. Ambrose and her satisfied smile slipped out the door. St. Vrain paused long enough to give Martinique a swift, strong hug. "Buck up, my girl," he whispered in rapid, flawless French. "It won't be so bad as all that, I swear it."

But the full horror of what she had just done to him was settling over Martinique, and tears had begun to swim in her eyes. "Rothewell shall kill you, St. Vrain," she replied in French, her voice cracking on his name. "He shall kill you, and I shan't be able to bear it."

He kissed her cheek, not once but twice. "He cannot kill me, my dear," said St. Vrain. "Not until we are wed, at the very least."

"Get out of my niece's room, St. Vrain!" Aunt Xanthia's voice was grim. "Get out, or by God, I shall throw you out, and your clothes after—*if* you are lucky."

She sounded as if she might well try. With one last, swift kiss, St. Vrain slipped from the bed, and dressed in haste. Had Martinique not been terrified for his life, the sight would have been worthy of applause. His expression might have been strained, but his trim, lithe body was magnificent, especially his slender waist, and the taut turn of his buttocks, with their sculpted dips where muscle and tendon met. She wanted desperately to reach out, and stroke her fingertips along his—

Good God, what was she thinking? Her life was in tatters.

When he was more or less decent, and his magnificent backside had vanished beneath the layers of drawers and breeches, St. Vrain threw his neckcloth over one shoulder, and headed for the door. "I shall wait upon your brother at two o'clock, Miss Neville," he said, his hand on the knob. "If that will suit?"

"Rothewell shall receive you," said Xanthia, her voice stiff and cold. "And I strongly suggest, my lord, that you put your affairs in order before coming."

"Do you indeed, Miss Neville?" St. Vrain murmured. "Shall I bring a brace of pistols then, and simply save myself the suspense?"

Aunt Xanthia spun around, her face a mask of rage. "Don't trouble yourself!" she snapped. "My brother is barely a gentleman at all. He will likely throttle you

with his bare hands. Now good night to you, St. Vrain.
I hope you are at least a little bit ashamed of the ruin
you have wrought."

He hesitated at the open door. "More than you will
ever know, Miss Neville," he said quietly. "More than
you will ever know."

Three

THE BETROTHAL KISS

$\mathcal{L}$ady Sharpe's tidy breakfast parlor was heavy with an awful silence. The three occupants had long since given up any pretense of eating, or of even drinking so much as a cup of coffee. Indeed, Lord Rothewell had already smashed one of Lady Sharpe's delicate Sèvres teacups to bits, crushing it like an eggshell in his massive fist.

He now roamed around the room like a caged lion, alternately dragging one hand through his hair and pounding his fist on whatever piece of furniture he happened to be passing by.

"Stop it, Kieran," his sister ordered. "Stop, and show me your palm. Have you cut it?"

"To hell with my palm," he growled. "To hell with everything."

"Oh, Kieran!" Lady Sharpe quite literally wrung her hands. "Oh, I never dreamt! I am so sorry! And to think—beneath my very roof!"

"This is not your fault, Pamela." Xanthia caught Lady Sharpe by the arm. "It is Martinique's fault, at least in part, for she says so. I cannot imagine . . . dear God, I really *cannot* think what made her do such a thing!"

Rothewell stopped pacing, and pinned the ladies with his harsh, golden glower. "Her mother made her do it," he gritted. "Good God, Zee, how many times must we have this discussion? Can you not see it? The girl is the very image of Annemarie."

"Annemarie was hardly the femme fatale you wish to think her," said Xanthia angrily. "But no matter. What's to be done about it now, Kieran? Would you marry the girl off to a scoundrel? And is he to have no punishment whatsoever?"

"Oh, I shall deal with St. Vrain," Rothewell snapped. "Damn it all, I wish Luke yet lived. Then he would have to deal with this bloody mess he has got us into."

"We all wish Luke were alive," snapped his sister. "But he is not, therefore—"

The slam of the door cut her off. "No, he is not," said Martinique, her voice decidedly bitter. "And no one rues that fact more than I. But a dead man can hardly be blamed for my ill judgment. And if my step-father has so burdened you with me, Rothewell, by all means, unburden yourself forthwith. Indeed, I wish you would."

Xanthia flew across the room to her. "Martinique, for God's sake, be still!"

But tears were streaming down Martinique's face now. "You hate me, do you not, Rothewell?" she whispered. "And you hated my mother, too. You were ashamed of her. Ashamed of her skin, ashamed of what she had been—and you are ashamed that I am a *sangmêlé*."

"Be still, damn you!" Rothewell's voice was grim. "You know nothing of my feelings. *Nothing*, damn it, do you hear me?"

"Well, rid yourself of me! But do not do it by forcing

me on some poor devil who has done nothing more than warm my bed—and at my insistence, too."

"I've had quite enough of this." Rothewell stalked across the room toward her. "You'll keep a civil tongue in your mouth, miss."

Xanthia slipped strategically between them. "She has not been uncivil," she said curtly. "Martinique, what is this nonsense about your insistence?"

"I keep telling you, Xanthia!" she cried. "It is not St. Vrain's fault."

"He looked a willing participant to me," said Xanthia grimly.

"But he only came into my room by accident," Martinique pleaded. "You see, he—he thought it was . . . well, someone else's room. More than that, I cannot say."

Another awful hush fell across the parlor. "Oh, dear God!" said Lady Sharpe, falling into a chair. "Christine! Oh, how stupid she is!"

Rothewell's face went white. Xanthia lifted an unsteady hand and set her palm to her forehead.

"Too late, he realized who I was," Martinique went on, her voice calming. "I—I shan't tell you the rest of it! It is no one's business but mine. I am nineteen years of age, Rothewell. I do not wish a come-out. I do not wish your patronage or your advice or your protection. And I certainly do not wish a husband. Indeed, I shan't have one. If you want to be rid of me, give me a reasonable allowance, and let me go."

"Go?" he roared. "Go where, for God's sake?"

"To . . . well, to Paris!" she declared, seizing upon the notion. "After all, I am mostly French. I shall find myself a little house, and live a quiet life, and leave you to yours, where you will not have to stand the sight of me. That should suit us both very well indeed."

Lord Rothewell lifted his arm, and pointed squarely at Xanthia. "Get . . . her . . . *out*," he said. "*Now*."

The notion of Paris faded. Martinique looked upon her uncle's trembling visage, and suddenly, she was deeply afraid. His arm was drawn taut, as if he really might backhand her. When Aunt Xanthia put an arm around her and urged her from the room, Martinique did not hesitate.

"Oh, dear God!" she heard Lady Sharpe say again. "Oh, that careless, careless Christine! This time, I really think I shall strangle her!"

By two o'clock that afternoon, the Earl of St. Vrain was holding a significantly less charitable a view of Mrs. Ambrose and her carelessness, which, he had concluded, was nonexistent. His encounter with Miss Neville had been planned, he was increasingly certain. In the mortification of the moment, he had been unable to spare Christine a thought. Now, however, he was beginning to grasp the method of her revenge. But what the hell he was to do about it now thoroughly escaped him.

He certainly need not wed Miss Neville, he acknowledged as he dismounted at Highwood's stables. Lord Rothewell, for all his bluster, could not force his hand. Besides, St. Vrain had weathered worse scandals. Christine had chosen her victim poorly in that regard.

Or had she? There was, St. Vrain supposed, some slight streak of honor yet left in him; some small part of his heart which still wrenched at a lady's distress. He did not look lightly upon the ruination of a young girl who had done no more than make for a handy pawn in Christine's spite. And all this over a tavern maid! A tavern maid who, by God, he had never so much as touched, despite her many blatant invitations. Perhaps her wounded pride had started the rumors? St. Vrain did not know, and scarcely cared. He had not been about to defend himself to Christine.

Since Georgina's death all those years ago, St. Vrain had drowned himself in a life of hedonistic pleasure— sensual pleasure, for the most part. As a young man in the boudoirs of Paris, he had learnt his lessons well, with women far more skilled, and far more predatory, than Christine could ever hope to be. They had numbed him, even as they had tormented and then pleasured him, honing his skills to a razor's edge. He had pledged fidelity to none; and indeed, none had expected it.

When he neared the west portico of Highwood, St. Vrain looked up to see Lord Sharpe standing at one of the windows, observing his approach. The gentleman moved as if to lift his hand in greeting, but so lamely it might have been made of lead. Now *that* was a meeting he surely dreaded. He had owed Sharpe better than this, by God.

But strangely, St. Vrain did not dread the altercation with Miss Neville's uncle. Unease never reared its head, even as the footman took his hat and coat, or as they strode down the long central hall of Highwood. Baron Rothewell, the servant informed him, awaited Lord St. Vrain in the library.

He stood behind a wide walnut desk with his back to St. Vrain, his hands clutched tightly behind his back as if restraining himself from violence. He was a hulking giant of a man, blocking out much of the wintry sunlight with his wide, rigid shoulders. He did not turn from the window until the footman had pulled the door shut again.

Rothewell did not mince words. "I gather, sir, that

my niece is no longer a virgin," he said. "And that I have you to thank for it."

"She is not," said St. Vrain quietly. "I regret it, Rothewell, but I shan't lie about it."

The baron's visage blazed. "I ought to horsewhip you until you puke, you lascivious, self-absorbed bastard," he said.

St. Vrain took a step toward him. "You are more than welcome to try," he calmly returned. "But better men than you have failed at it. And I cannot see how it will help your niece."

"It won't do a damned thing for her," Rothewell conceded. "But I'll feel vastly better satisfied to draw your blood."

St. Vrain smiled. "I begin to think I should like to see you try," he said quietly. "But at present, I am more concerned with Miss Neville's welfare, as I suggest you might be."

Rothewell's fist came crashing down on the desk. "Damn you, don't you dare tell me how to manage my family!"

"You act as if she *isn't* your family," said St. Vrain quietly. "Indeed, you act as if she is tainted merchandise with which you must now be saddled. The truth is quite different. And the truth is, I made a mistake entering the poor girl's room. But it was only that. A mistake."

"And yet you stayed when the truth became known."

St. Vrain hesitated.

"Why?" demanded Lord Rothewell.

Because she begged me? Because she is the most inherently sensual creature I have ever known? Because I desired her so much it made my heart clench?

No, those were not the answers the baron sought—

true though they might have been. "I am not at liberty to answer that question, Rothewell," he finally said. "I am not sure I fully understand what happened."

The muscle in the man's jaw twitched. "Well, understand this, St. Vrain—*you have an appointment with the parson*," he bit out. "It can be your wedding. Or it can be your funeral. I scarcely give a damn."

"You think me unwilling, sir?" said St. Vrain. "Your niece is lovely, and possessed of every feminine grace. I would account myself fortunate to be bound to her, but . . ."

"Good God, man, spit it out!" said Rothewell. "What lame excuse do you mean to seize upon?"

"None, save the lady's reluctance," said St. Vrain. "I offered to marry her long before your sister turned up with all her indignation blazing. Miss Neville refused me. And frankly, I do not think she means to change her mind."

"Then by God, I shall change it for her," Rothewell growled. "Trust me, the chit will be on her knees begging you before this day is done."

His words sent a cold chill down St. Vrain's spine. And the bastard meant them, too. The resolve was plain in his eyes. St. Vrain allowed no emotion to taint his words.

"I shall convince her," he responded, coming swiftly to his feet. "Leave this business to me, Rothewell. This was my doing, and I shall see to the undoing of it."

The baron made a growling noise in the back of his throat, but the massive fist relaxed, and some of the rage, if not the hatred, went out of him. "Very well," he snapped. "But there will be no more talk of what the chit will or will not do, St. Vrain. I want a wedding by Christmas. Either you see to it—or *I shall*."

*   *   *

St. Vrain found her in Highwood's west garden, strolling along the formal tiers of roses, now bare and long dormant. Spindly, naked tree branches clattered above his head, while beneath his feet, the wintry grass was stiff and all but dead. In the garden which rolled out beyond him, nothing bloomed. But Miss Neville was the beauty of May personified. Her warm skin and dark, luxuriant hair were the perfect foil for the rich colors she so wisely wore. Indeed, she looked like no debutante, no virgin, he had ever known. Moreover, there was a sensual sort of self-awareness in her being which simply astonished him—and, unfortunately, enthralled him, too.

For a time, St. Vrain simply watched her from the fringe of trees. If she were cold, or even frightened, one could not discern it. Her head was unbowed beneath the hood of her woolen cloak, her brow unfurrowed by worry. Her narrow shoulders did not hunch against the wind. Indeed, her chin was still up, and her wide brown eyes were clear, if a little dreamy. Perhaps she was dreaming of that love and passion she so determinedly wished to have. She might not settle for less. Yes, Lord Rothewell had found himself a worthy opponent if he wished to do battle.

But Rothewell would not lose, of course. She would. That was how the world worked. And so it fell to St. Vrain to convince her; to save her from her uncle's wrath. He owed her that, at the very least. A marriage to him was otherwise not much of a favor. He was wealthy, but so was she. He was all but unknown to society, having passed the whole of his adult life in shame and exile on the Continent, whereas her life, and all the benefit which polite society might offer, was yet before her. Those who knew him, for the most part, did not receive him. Only his former acquaintance with Lord Sharpe, bolstered by Christine's wheedling, had given him entrée to Highwood.

Miss Neville—*Martinique*—turned and paced the length of the garden, this time away from him. How pretty she was, from every angle. Dear God. She would not have lasted a fortnight on the marriage market come the spring, unless she'd wished to. But his lack of self-control was destined to cheat her of that opportunity. He had ruined his own life, and now he was about to ruin hers, he feared.

Ah, well. It was not the marriage he would have wished for, either. Once upon a time, when life was still a fairy tale, he had been determined to wed Georgina; to make her life happy again. They had only to wait, he had promised her, until his father was dead. Then they would find a priest or a parson somewhere in Europe who was willing enough, or dishonest enough, to do the job of sealing their illicit union.

But there had been no marriage. Georgina had died long before her husband; died in childbed, as it happened, in a futile attempt to bear their forbidden child. And St. Vrain's blind, youthful love for her had died long before that. He had quickly come to see Georgina for what she was: neither good nor evil, but merely weak and self-absorbed. And he had come to see the unvarnished truth of what they had done. But there had been no going back; no way to undo the horror of what he had done to his own father, and perhaps to Georgina, too. And there had been no future, either.

Until now. Now he was staring at his future—and strangely, it did not appall him as much as it perhaps should have done. He desired Martinique, yes. But it was more than that. She brought a light and a vibrancy to his existence; things he had believed lost to him. And there was an element of comfort in being with her. A peacefulness which settled over him, and made him feel that there was a future yet before him. He had returned to England with no thought of what he would do with the rest of his life, save for rebuilding the estate, and ensuring the welfare of his retainers. And now he was faced with . . . what? A tragedy? An opportunity? He hardly knew. A little roughly, he cleared his throat, and set off across the garden.

Martinique turned at once, her eyes flaring wide. In a few quick steps, she closed the distance between them, catching his hands in hers. "*Ma foi*, but you have survived it!" she said, and none too speciously, either. "I feared the worst, but—oh, never mind that! Are you off the hook, St. Vrain? Please say yes."

St. Vrain smiled warmly. "Yes," he lied. "I think perhaps I might be."

She sagged with relief. "Thank heavens," she whispered. "But what does *might* mean?"

He still held her hands in his, her gloved fingers wrapped tightly within his own. They felt light and warm and almost comfortingly familiar. But how foolish that was. "Miss Neville, I wonder—"

"Yes? Go on."

He looked at her, narrowing his eyes against the stark, wintry sun. She was damned pretty, with those long black lashes fringing her wide, worried eyes. "Well, I wonder if I am altogether pleased about it."

She drew a little away from him. "Oh, my lord, but you must be!"

He drew her back. "It was wrong, what we did, my dear," he said quietly. "What your uncle suggests is not entirely inappro—"

"*Suggests?*" Martinique cut him off, her tone bitter.

"Rothewell never suggested anything in the whole of his life. He orders. Others obey."

St. Vrain smiled faintly. "Well, in this case, we might," he went on. "Because I do think, my dear, that you ought to marry me."

Martinique was watching him assessingly. "But surely, St. Vrain, you've no wish to marry," she said. "And surely not to me."

Surprisingly, the notion was growing on him. "Why not you?" he murmured. "You are intelligent, you are beautiful, and you are a deeply sensual woman. Have you any notion, I wonder, how rare that is? But all that aside, I need a wife, I suppose. I have my estate to think of, and since I am eight-and-twenty now—"

"Only that?" she interjected.

Again, the faint smile. "Do I look prematurely decrepit, my dear?" he answered. "Please, do not spare my vanity."

"Well, you look like a man who has seen a vast deal of life in his twenty-eight years," she said. "As to your vanity, you are quite shockingly handsome, as I am sure you must know. And kindly do not lie, and say you do *not* know it, for that would be a waste of everyone's time."

"And did I mention, my dear, your plain speaking?" he went on. "Such honesty would doubtless be refreshing in a wife."

"Oh, perhaps it is refreshing now, *mon ami*," she warned. "But in a dozen years, you'll find it vastly annoying."

She might be right, he inwardly acknowledged. But there was no backing away from it now. He gave her hands another reassuring squeeze. "Why do you not at least tell your uncle you will agree to a betrothal?"

"What difference would that make?"

He smiled faintly. "Walk with me, Miss Neville," he said. "There is a little orchard just beyond the garden."

"*Très bien.*" She took his arm.

"It is like this, Miss Neville," he began when they were no longer within earshot of the house. "A betrothal is not binding upon you. And this is, after all, Lincolnshire, which might as well be the backside of the moon so far as the London gossips are concerned."

"And what is the advantage to me?" she asked sharply. "Or to *you*, come to that?"

"A betrothal will quiet your uncle's anger, and it will give you time to get to know me," he answered, a little disconcerted by the light, warm hand on his arm. "As to me, well, I shall have the benefit of a beautiful lady's companionship for a time. And I shall be welcomed here at Highwood, instead of turned off like a leper."

At that, some of her color seemed to drain. "Do you mean . . . are you saying that . . . that if I refuse you, you will be turned away from Highwood? And that I shan't see you ever again?"

He cut a swift, appraising glance at her. "My dear Miss Neville, use your head," he murmured as they strolled deeper into the orchard. "In Lord Sharpe's eyes, I have violated you beneath his very roof; violated his trust and his hospitality. Can there be a worse insult to an old acquaintance?"

Miss Neville jerked to a halt, and set her hand to her forehead as if she felt faint, though she certainly did not look it. "*Mon Dieu*, I did not think what I might be getting you into last night!" she whispered. "I—I was thinking only of—of . . ." Her words fell weakly away.

He grinned at her. "Of what, my dear?"

Her color returned in a bright pink flush. "Of my own desires." Her voice dropped to a sultry whisper.

"Of the way you made me feel. Your touch. Your mouth. Your—well, never mind that! But I—I just wanted you—so much so, that one awful moment, I was willing to risk my future. But I was never willing to risk yours! Please, St. Vrain, you must know that."

He took her hands in his, and stared at the ground beneath her feet for a long moment. "Miss Neville, I hardly had a future to risk," he said. "My reputation is less than pristine here in England. Had I chosen to wed, my bride would have been some—"

"But that is just it," she interjected. "You would *not* have wed. Admit it, St. Vrain. Men like you may have their choice amongst many women, at any time. And a wicked reputation but deepens their fascination."

So she had already heard of his reputation. And she certainly was not naive, he admitted as they silently resumed their stroll. She was right, too. After Georgina, he had thought never to marry. So why was he here now, half-hoping she would say *yes*?

Because he wanted to make love to her again. Wanted her more desperately than he had ever wanted Georgina. Even now, just looking at the rise and fall of her breasts as her breath came with a nervous rapidity, he could remember how delightfully she had trembled beneath him last night, and the stirring of desire in his heart and in his loins began anew. He wondered vaguely if one last romp on the mattress would put the chit firmly from his mind. And what if it did not? What would that mean?

The path through the orchard was just gravel now. Abruptly, she stopped beside one of the gnarled apple trees, and leaned back against it as if she were inestimably weary. Only now did she begin to look defeated.

"Miss Neville," he pressed. "What is your answer? If it is no, I cannot in good conscience linger here, further distressing Lord Sharpe."

She flicked a quick, sarcastic look up at him. "You have no such compunction regarding my uncle?"

"Rothewell does not look as if his sensibilities are easily wounded."

She licked her lips uncertainly. "They are not," she said quietly. "He . . . he hates me, you know. He is just fobbing me off on you, St. Vrain. Be careful. He is dangerous."

He did not try to argue with her; she might well be right on all counts. "Why do you think he hates you, my dear?"

Again she cut a quick glance up at him, this time warily. "He resented my mother's marriage to his elder brother," she said. He won't have her name spoken within his hearing."

He held her gaze gently. "Why did he resent her?"

Fleetingly, she hesitated. "I do not know," she admitted. "I assume he felt she was not good enough for his fine old English family."

"You said she was French," he mused. "Was *that* his objection?"

"No, it was more." She paused for a heartbeat. "I wish to tell you something, St. Vrain. Something I would insist on telling any gentleman who—well, who proposed any sort of relationship with me."

Her words seemed carefully chosen. "By all means, go on."

"My mother was not of noble birth," she continued. "Indeed, she was not even of legitimate birth—as *I* am not of legitimate birth." She paused, and held his gaze with a challenge in her eye. "My mother was a famous courtesan, St. Vrain. And—and a *sangmêlé*. Do you know what that is?"

"I know what a courtesan is," he said quietly. "What is the meaning of the other?"

"Something like an octoroon, as the English would call it." Miss Neville's tone was emotionless now. "Her blood was mixed, and her ancestry uncertain. She grew up on Martinique. Do you know it?"

"In the West Indies," he said vaguely. "But the French part, not the British."

"Précisément," she said. "She lived there in poverty until a rich Frenchman saw her carrying a basket of cane from the fields, and fell in love with her."

"Was she a slave?"

"She might as well have been. The Frenchman made her his mistress, and gave her little say in the matter. She was just fourteen years old, St. Vrain. Can you imagine it?"

"No," he whispered. "What a difficult life she must have had."

"The sad truth is, St. Vrain, it was a far better life than being poor and working the fields," she said bitterly. "My mother did what she had to do to survive. She sold her beauty to escape poverty. For eight years, she serviced the Frenchman. And in return, he made her into the perfect woman. Elegant, well-dressed and impeccably mannered."

St. Vrain suppressed a shudder. "Eight years?"

"A lifetime, *oui.* Or so it must have felt. But eventually, he decided to marry, and we were sent away."

"You . . . you are his daughter?"

"Oui," she said simply. "He gave *Maman* a little money and some property. In Barbados, she met Lord Rothewell—not this one, but his brother." Here, she lifted her chin a little stubbornly, and looked him in the

eye. "He fell in love with *Maman*. She loved him, too, and nothing could keep them apart. Eventually, he offered her marriage, and a name for me."

St. Vrain rather doubted the courtship had been the fairy tale Miss Neville believed, but he had no wish to distress her by arguing the point. "And it was a happy marriage?"

"Ecstatically." Her voice had grown quiet. "And I was happy, too—until they died."

"They died young," he murmured. "How?"

Her gaze softened, and went distant. "There was a rebellion," she answered. "A slave revolt. The cane fields were set afire, and their carriage became trapped in the flames. The lanes are so narrow. So treacherous. They could not turn in time. It was . . . horrible."

"Dear God."

She drew an unsteady breath. "My stepfather's will appointed his brother my guardian."

"I am so sorry for your loss," he said softly. "I am sorry, too, if Rothewell is indeed ashamed of you."

"Do you doubt it?" she whispered.

St. Vrain was no longer sure what he thought. There had been something deeper than dislike firing Rothewell's temper, he could have sworn. "Well, it hardly matters now," he said. "I think your ancestry concerns you a vast deal more than it does me."

"You wish this betrothal to go on, then?"

"Nothing you have said alters my argument," he answered.

She pushed herself a little away from the old apple tree and gazed at him with an odd look in her eye. "Then I will agree, St. Vrain, but on one condition."

She had been honest with him so far. He crossed his arms over his chest, and nodded. "Go on."

Again, the tongue darted out to touch the corner of

her mouth almost nervously. "I wish . . . I wish to strike a bargain with you," she answered. "I wish you to make love to me again."

"Good Lord! *Before* we wed?"

"We do not mean to wed at all, St. Vrain," she said. "*Do* we?"

He shook his head, then shrugged. "I'm damned if I know," he said. "Something tells me we ought."

"That is just your upper-class British morality speaking," she said. "Think of it as the French might. I wish to learn how to make love properly. And I wish *you* to teach me. Somehow, I do not think you will mind. Besides, you . . . well, you have that look."

St. Vrain hated to tell her just how little she needed to learn. "What look?"

Her lashes dropped almost shut, and suddenly, he wanted to push her back against the apple tree and kiss her senseless. "*You* know," she said huskily. "That soft, somnolent thing you do with your eyes the first time you look at a woman? It's as if you are offering her an apple in the Garden of Eden."

He could only stare at her, and wonder what the devil he was getting himself into.

"Well, *are* you?"

"Am I what?"

"Are you offering?"

He fisted his hands at his sides, and prayed for strength. "Absolutely not," he said firmly. "We are going to your uncle now, and announce a betrothal. And if we decide we suit, we shall marry. Then, my dear, we can negotiate those lessons."

"But it is said, St. Vrain, that in courtship, a man ought to put his best foot forward," she murmured, dipping her chin with a mocking modesty.

"But it is not my foot we are discussing, is it?"

She smiled. "No, it definitely is not."

His patience—not to mention his resistance—was at an end. He took her arm and hitched her firmly against him. "We are going inside now," he managed. "And we are going straight into the library, where you are going to tell Rothewell that we are to be married."

"Oh, if we are to so much as pretend a betrothal, *mon cher*, then you must learn not to bully, but to persuade." Her voice had gone husky again. "Now, do you still have that key?"

Good God. He had not a prayer. "Yes. I have the key."

She laid her hand on his arm, and drew it slowly down. "Then may I see you? Soon?" She was so close, her whisper brushed his cheek. "Already, I long to be with you again. I ache for the pleasure which only you, *mon cher*, can give me. I crave the warmth and strength of your taut, virile body, and the chance to touch and to stroke your—"

"Good God almighty!" St. Vrain swallowed hard.

Her look of longing broke suddenly into a grin. "And that, St. Vrain, is the difference between bullying and persuading," she said. "Now, *are* you persuaded."

"Yes, blast you," he managed. "Now, are we betrothed?"

"*Mais oui*, my beloved," she said demurely. They had gone but another five paces, however, when she slowed. "But you are forgetting something, are you not, St. Vrain?"

"Justin," he said a little grimly. "You will call me Justin. And what, pray, have I forgotten?"

She stuck out her lip, humor dancing in her eyes. "We have just become betrothed," she said. "I believe you are now allowed to kiss me."

"Wench!" he said.

But kiss her he did. He kissed until she was sense-less, with his arms wrapped almost desperately around her, tipping her head back until the hood of her cloak fell away. Until her lithe, warm body was pressed head-to-toe against him, and her mouth was open and urgent beneath his. Over and over he delved into the maddening temptation of her mouth, one hand urgently roaming beneath the shelter of her cloak, stroking the fullness of her breast, the elegant turn of her waist, and lower still, to the fine swell of her hip. And then somehow, the reality of just where they were returned to him, and he managed to set her away.

They came apart frustrated, unsatiated, and gasp-ing.

"Mon Dieu!" she said, a strange mix of lust and laughter in her eyes. "I believe, *mon cher*, this betrothal is going to prove interesting indeed."

Four

A WORD OF WARNING

*D*inner at Highwood that evening was a tense, nearly silent affair. Justin was noticeably absent, and Mrs. Ambrose's pale beauty had frozen into an expression which could only be described as embittered satisfaction. Rothewell said nothing, other than to gravely announce Martinique's betrothal and toast her happiness. The glasses were obligingly raised, but the sharp *chink* of crystal rang hollow in the stillness of the room.

In the days which followed, Justin resumed his visits, but only for dinner. He fell into the role of devoted suitor with disconcerting ease, but to Martinique's frustration, they were never alone. She could share nothing of substance with him; certainly she could not remind him of their bargain. Worse, his proximity served only to drive her physical yearning to a near fever pitch. When they strolled about the drawing room together, his long-fingered, elegant hand would clasp hers protectively, and his eyes would heat almost adoringly.

She was not alone in noticing it. Over the course of a few days, Mrs. Ambrose's embittered satisfaction slowly faded to something less benign. One evening after dinner, they retired as usual to the parlor, but no one suggested cards. Instead, Lady Sharpe went to the pianoforte, and began to hammer out a series of lively tunes, as if doing so might dispel the pall which hung over her family. Great-Aunt Olivia withdrew a bag of darning, and thrust a fistful of stockings at Xanthia. Eventually, Lord Sharpe invited the gentlemen onto the terrace for a cheroot.

Too anxious to sit, Martinique rose and began to examine the walls. This room was hung with landscapes, but again, they could not hold her interest. She was becoming quite obsessed with Justin. And not just because his touch inflamed her, though it certainly did. No, there was something more to the man, something hidden and almost unknowable behind the subtle mockery of his heavy-lidded eyes.

Suddenly, she felt a warmth hovering at her elbow. Martinique turned to see Christine Ambrose by her side. For an instant, her earlier mortification returned, but she stiffened her spine, and fought it off. *"Bonsoir,* Mrs. Ambrose."

"Congratulations, Miss Neville," she murmured. "You really have brought one of Lincolnshire's wealthiest bachelors to the point. I confess, I did not believe he would wear the parson's noose so willingly." Her eyes were dark with something akin to malice.

"Merci, madame," said Martinique stiffly. "I am sure it will all turn out for the best."

Mrs. Ambrose flashed a thin smile. "Yes, well, you are hardly the first to hope so."

"Pardon? The first to hope what?"

"The first woman to hope that being seduced by St. Vrain might turn out for the best," she murmured.

"Indeed?" said Martinique coolly. "But he is, after all, a man. And men are always a gamble, are they not? I think one must take one's chances."

Mrs. Ambrose's eyes glittered dangerously. "How very French of you," she purred. "I do not think the last young lady he seduced came away feeling quite so sanguine about the *affaire*."

"He has left a veritable trail of them, I collect?" Martinique forced herself to smile. "Well, if the passion falters, at least there will always be his great fortune to console me."

Mrs. Ambrose lips curled in disdain. "You are so very young and inexperienced, my dear," she said, her voice unmistakably catty. "I hope you can satisfy such a man. If not—well, he will always have his little whore down in the village."

"*Ça alors!*" Martinique pressed her fingertips to her chest. "Has he yet another?"

The sarcasm sailed over Mrs. Ambrose. "And then, of course, there is his stepmother."

"*Mon Dieu!*" Martinique gave an exaggerated lift of her eyebrows. "His stepmother, too?"

"Ah, did no one warn you?" Mrs. Ambrose's eyes darkened malevolently. "He seduced her under his father's nose. He is still desperately in love with her, I daresay."

"Mrs. Ambrose, I fear I learnt love's hard lessons at my mother's knee," she returned. "A woman cannot let a little competition ruin her life, or she is nothing."

"That is all very well, Miss Neville, but it is rather hard to compete with a dead woman."

A dead woman? "I shall manage well enough," she said, feigning confidence. "After all, *toujours de l'audace!*"

"I'm sorry?" Mrs. Ambrose stared at her. "*Toujours de l'audace?*"

"Audacity always pays." Martinique paused to wink.

Mrs. Ambrose was looking a tad unwell now.

Martinique patted her consolingly on the shoulder. "I believe Cousin Pamela has finished with the pianoforte," she said. "Why do you not have a go? I shall turn the pages for you."

Mrs. Ambrose seemed incapable of answering. She made her way from the room, looking a good deal less like a cat on the hunt, and more like a woman scorned. Martinique watched her go in grim satisfaction, but the emotion was short-lived. She had hidden it well enough, but Mrs. Ambrose's remarks had stung her. They should not have. She herself had said that St. Vrain looked like a man with a past. She could hardly blame him if it were thrown in her face.

Worse still, she had allowed her pride to back her into a damnable corner. *She had no intention of marrying St. Vrain!* Why, then, had she thrown down the gauntlet so thoroughly? The last laugh—and the last look of feigned pity—would be Mrs. Ambrose's when Martinique announced that she meant to cry off. *Toujours de l'audace*, indeed!

Unthinkingly, Martinique had wandered to the window, and now stood watching her reflection in the glass. Before her, the evening's chill radiated from the panes; as cold as her heart would be when the day came to release St. Vrain from his promise. For the truth was, she suddenly realized, she really did not wish to release him. Her bold words meant nothing next to his touch.

Perhaps she should just give in to her weak knees and flip-flopping stomach. Perhaps she should simply admit that she'd let herself fall in love. Yes, it was much too late, she feared, for Mrs. Ambrose's warnings. But could Justin ever love her back? Or would his part of the bargain end up like Rothewell's? Would she be nothing to him but a duty, as she had always been to her father, her uncle, and perhaps even her stepfather? Dear God, that she could not bear.

There was something wrong with her. Something which made her unlovable. An inadequacy she could not quite grasp. During those first awful months following her parents' deaths, she had felt it most keenly. The shortcomings. The inferiority. Her utter failure to make Rothewell love her, or to even make him wish to spend an hour in her company. It had been the same with her birth father, too. She had been an inconvenience.

Martinique dropped her gaze from the cold glass, but at that instant, a gentle touch brushed her elbow. "Martinique, are you well?" murmured Aunt Xanthia.

"Well enough." She flashed a somewhat watery smile. "Just . . . sorry, that is all. So very sorry for all the trouble I've caused."

"I think you take too much of this responsibility upon yourself."

"No," she said firmly. "No, Xanthia. I do not. That is the very worst of it."

Aunt Xanthia colored faintly. "Martinique, will it—" She cleared her throat, and began again. "Will it be quite dreadful for you? Do you think you will be unable to bear . . . the, er, duties of a marriage?"

Martinique tried not to smile. "It could never be dreadful, Zee," she answered. "Not with the right man." But she was wrong. It *could* be dreadful—if the right man did not really want her.

"I am sorry your mother is gone," said Xanthia quietly. "I fear I am not the best person to advise you in matters of the heart."

"But this is not a matter of the heart." Martinique tried not to look bitter. "It is a matter of expediency.

Rothewell was looking for a way to be rid of me, and I have foolishly given it to him."

Xanthia's hand grasped her upper arm. "It is *not* like that, Martinique," she whispered. "You do not know what you are saying. Kieran takes his responsibilities quite seriously—you more so than any."

This time, Martinique's smile was bitter. "But that is the very point, Xanthia," she said quietly. "That is all I am to him. Just a responsibility."

"Martinique, I wish I could explain . . ."

Again, she shook her head. "It little matters." Swiftly, she changed the subject. "They say St. Vrain had an *affaire* with his stepmother. Is it true? Did he?"

Her aunt's blush deepened. "Amongst others, I collect," she admitted. "They ran away together. It seems there was a dreadful scandal. We learnt the whole of it but recently."

"Was no one going to tell me?"

Xanthia nodded. "Kieran was considering it," she admitted.

Martinique pushed her shoulders back. "I wish that he had done," she said quietly. "Mrs. Ambrose enjoyed catching me unawares."

"Oh!" said Xanthia quietly. "Oh, how monstrous!"

Martinique turned to go, but almost bumped into Justin as he returned from the terrace. He caught her lightly by the elbows, his steady blue gaze searching her face. "Martinique, my dear, what is it? Has someone upset you?"

Martinique pursed her lips, and shook her head. "Come to me tonight, Justin," she whispered. "I cannot bear this . . . this awful distance. I—I need you. Please."

And without waiting for his answer, she slipped from his grasp, and made her way upstairs to bed.

*   *   *

He came in darkness, long after the house lay still. He slipped into her room like a whispered sigh, and drew near the bed at once. She sensed his presence with a lover's certainty, and came awake, though she had long since stopped expecting him.

"Justin?" she murmured, sitting up to push the hair from her face. "Oh, Justin, I am *so* glad to see you."

Tonight she had deliberately left the draperies wide to the moonlight. She watched in the gloom as he settled himself onto the bed. He gathered her into his arms, pressing his cheek to hers. "Good God, I must be mad!" he said. "What of your aunt? Is she sleeping?"

"Quite soundly, as always," Martinique replied. "She would have known nothing last time, were it not for Mrs. Ambrose's meddling."

Justin's head was on her shoulder now, his breath warm against the turn of her neck. "I needed to see you, Martinique," he whispered. "I—I meant to stay away. But I confess, I could not."

"And you did promise," she reminded him. "You do not strike me as the sort of man who goes back on his word."

"Never," he said quietly. "Not even, perhaps, when I ought."

Despite the gloom, her lashes fell shut, and she turned her face to his. He kissed her as she had known he would, long and languorously, with one hand cupping the turn of her face.

"Take off your clothes," she said breathlessly when they broke the kiss. "Please, Justin."

He hesitated. "You are sure?" he whispered. "We can just talk. I . . . I would not mind that, Martinique. To just lie with you and talk to you."

Her hand slipped beneath the lapel of his coat, and eased it gently off his shoulder. "I would mind," she answered. "Make love to me, Justin. And then, yes, we will talk. We need to talk."

In minutes, he was sliding beneath the bedcovers, dragging his naked body over hers. His weight bore her down into the softness of the feather mattress, and sent that warm, sweet twist of need through her body.

Eyes open wide, he kissed her again, lingering more tenderly this time. "You once spoke of lessons, my love," he whispered, brushing his lips over her left eyebrow. "What is it you wish to learn?"

Martinique hesitated. "I wish to learn to please you—and to please myself."

He gave a little laugh. "Ah, sweet, they are one in the same."

"Then teach me . . . teach me the most erotic thing you know."

"A woman who knows what she wants is the very definition of erotic, my love," he answered. "And there are many ways to find pleasure."

"Besides . . . besides what we did before?"

In the gloom, she felt his eyes hold hers. "Besides that, yes. Did you not know?"

She felt heat flood her face. "I was not sure," she confessed. "Show me."

He kissed her again, thrusting deep inside her mouth with a new intensity. When his mouth at last left hers, he rolled a little to one side, and stroked his hand up the smoothness of her thigh. "Open your legs for me, love."

She did it willingly, exhaling sharply when he stroked his fingers through her thatch of dark curls. He stroked again, deeper, until his fingertip found her secret place and left her trembling.

"*Ohhh.*" Martinique let her left leg fall wantonly to one side, and let her head tip back into the pillow.

"Beautiful," he said on a groan. "Have you never touched yourself like this?"

She felt a moment of embarrassment. "Not . . . not like this," she whispered.

"You are a sensual woman, Martinique," he said, gently teasing her with his fingertips. "There is no shame in desire."

"Well, it did not—" She paused to swallow hard. "It did not feel quite like this."

He gave a soft chuckle. "Here, let me show you." To her shock, he gently lifted her hand, and guided it between her legs. She felt the hard nub of her arousal, and gasped at the pleasure. "Yes, back and forth, love. Just like that."

Martinique did as he commanded, closing her eyes as she felt her own slickness grow beneath her fingertips. Justin made a deep, guttural sound of appreciation. "Good Lord, you are beautiful," he choked.

His words served only to exhilarate her, and she became quickly lost in her own arousal. She was already gasping for breath when his hand reached out, stilling hers. Wordlessly, he pushed her thighs wide, and shifted himself between her legs. She gasped again when he set his lips to her belly, then spread her flesh wide with his long, elegant fingers. But when he set his mouth where her fingers had been, she cried out softly.

Instead of cautioning her to silence, Justin plunged his tongue deep into the folds of her flesh, lightly licking at the core of her arousal. The trembling turned to a bone-deep quake which forced her to grasp his shoulders.

Justin made a sound of satisfaction in the back of his throat. "You like that, love?"

"I—I—I do not know," she lied. "I think . . . that it could be quite dangerous."

"Dangerous?" he murmured, just before stroking her again.

Martinique could not get her breath. "I fear a woman could die of pleasure from it."

"Then may you die a thousand deaths, my love," he said. *"Le petit mort.* And may tonight be but the first."

Oh, she was going to die of it! He lapped at her with delicate, teasing strokes until she was helpless. Justin watched her every move as he tormented her, his eyes burning into her despite the gloom. Martinique felt her own wetness slicking her body, and felt the edge of pleasure draw nigh. Within moments, her hips arched high and her entire body began to shake.

"Ohh, ohh," she chanted. And then her world shook, splintered and came apart.

She returned to herself to find Justin cradling her to him. "Oh, Martinique," he whispered into her hair. "So perfect. So lovely."

He slid his body up her length, and she felt the heat of his erection sear her. Uncertainly, she licked her lips. "I want you," she managed. "I still want you. Justin, please?"

He rolled himself fully atop her, urging her deep into the mattress. "Is this what you crave, love?" he murmured. One hand settled at her waist, the other slid lower to cradle the swell of her buttocks. "Do you want me inside you?"

Martinique let her head tip back into the softness of the feather bolster. *"Yes,"* she moaned. Her hands went to his broad shoulders, and involuntarily, her body arched to his. "Yes, Justin. Now."

With a little grunt, Justin lifted her hips and let the warm weight of his cock slide into the heated flesh between her legs. She was already slick with need. Carefully spreading her hips, he pushed himself into her body, parting the eager folds of her flesh, then easing deeper and deeper on slow but insistent strokes.

Too slow. Not enough. Insistently, she reached out to him, her nails digging into his shoulders. "Oh, Justin! Please!"

In response, Justin braced his weight and thrust in another inch. She could feel himself trying to gentle his motions. But she did not want gentle. She wanted him. All of him. Instinctively, she curled one leg about his waist, and drew him down until they lay belly to belly, chest to chest. Her head swam with his familiar scent, and her hips strained for that last sweet inch. "Justin, *please*," she said again.

"Shush, love," he whispered gently. "Let your body grow accustomed to me. I've no wish to hurt you."

"You aren't," she choked. "You could never hurt me, Justin."

In the gloom, she felt his mouth moving over her cheek, down the length of her neck, teasing lightly at her skin as he drew in her scent through nostrils flared wide. Until he found her breast again. His lips drew the taut peak into the heat of his mouth, slowly suckling her as he began to move inside her.

In his arms, she still shuddered with anticipation, her hands coming up to slide through the glorious mass of his hair. "Oh, Justin," she pleaded. "Yes. Yes. Don't stop."

He kissed her again, deeply and passionately, and she could taste the sheen of salt on his skin. "I won't stop," he said softly. "I want to make you tremble beneath me, Martinique. Always. Forever. Just give yourself over to me."

She very much feared she already had. Her head moved restlessly on the pillow as she rose to take his strokes, which were harder and more intense now.

In the soft moonlight, they thrust and moved together, nothing breaking the stillness of the room save for the sounds of their sighs and the soft creak of the bed beneath them. Martinique felt her body quicken as she hungrily drew in the scent of sweat and arousal. She needed more. Yearned for . . . something. That trembling that began in her bones and sent her over the edge of madness.

Her nails dug deeper into his flesh as Justin thrust and thrust in that sweet, timeless rhythm. She urged herself higher. Urged him deeper. "My greedy girl," he rasped. "Go slowly and drive me to madness again."

"It's too late, Justin," she choked. "I—I feel . . ."

"What do you feel, love?" he crooned. "Tell me."

"Us, Justin," she panted. "I . . . I feel us. Together. And it's perfect."

She hung on the edge of desperation now, his strokes a torment of pleasure. That beautiful moment was just beyond her grasp as the fire built and spiraled, consuming them as one. And then the silvery edge slid nearer. She met one more hard, perfect thrust, and threw herself into the fire, toward that almost unattainable pleasure, and was lost in it, sobbing.

Justin awoke to a nightmare; one of the old, familiar ones which generally sent him bolting for a brandy bottle. He rolled up on one elbow, his eyes adjusting to the slant of moonlight which cut across the bed. *It was Paris again.* The bleak little house in rue de Birague. But when he fought his way from the fog, he found himself entwined in a pair of warm, slender arms, and fell back onto the bed again.

Martinique. Thank God. Sweet, new memories returned to him on a breathless rush, washing away the old. He sensed rather than saw that her eyes were open. Her hand came up to settle reassuringly on his cheek. "What is her name, *mon cher*?"

He looked away. "Obvious, is it?"

"*Oui*, to me," she said.

For a long moment, he hesitated. "Georgina," he finally answered. "Her name was Georgina."

Martinique set her lips to the turn of his shoulder. "Was?"

"She died."

"Ah." There was a wealth of meaning in the word. "The stepmother. I comprehend."

He turned again to look at her. "Do you?" he answered. "I wish to God I did."

Martinique had begun to toy with a strand of his hair, which had grown too long. "Was she your reason for staying in France for so long?"

"I took her there, yes," he admitted. "We had a little house in *le Marais* where we lived for two years."

"Only two years, *mon cher*? And then she died. How very sad. Why did you not come home?"

He shook his head, and felt his hair scrub against Martinique's pillow. "I was too ashamed," he confessed. "She died in childbed, you know. It was a just punishment for us both, I sometimes think. But I already knew that I could never come home. Not so long as my father lived."

"Justin, how did it happen?" she asked, as if she struggled to understand.

He smiled without humor. "Oh, as those sorts of things usually happen," he said. "A misplaced sense of the romantic. I mistook my father for a dragon, and my stepmother for a maiden in distress. Unfortunately, the truth—as with most of life—was not so cleanly cut."

"Did . . . did she love you?"

He propped one arm behind his head, and swallowed hard. "She was in love with the notion, certainly," he answered. "She was a romantic. Father wed her when she was but seventeen. I was sixteen, and still at Oxford. We . . . we became friends, I suppose, for we were of an age, and I was often at home. But when I left school two years later, I realized how truly unhappy she was."

"Ah," said Martinique. "It was an arranged marriage?"

He nodded. "Georgina was a beauty, but she hadn't a sou to her name," he said. "Father was lonely, and so he went to London for the Season to find a wife. But I do not think that a middle-aged recluse was quite what she had in mind."

Martinique looked at him knowingly. "Ah, but your father had plump pockets!"

"Just so," he agreed. "And he spoke with her family, who were poor as church mice, and it was settled. Georgina consoled herself that she would be a countess. But she did not realize, I think, that Father did not really care for London, and loathed entertaining. Or that he lived only for his hay, his horses and his hounds. And she certainly did not understand what a pinch-penny he was."

"So she developed a sense of the dramatic?" Martinique suggested. "He became an ogre, I daresay. He did not understand her needs. He became cruel and abusive until she was driven to madness? To suicide, even, *n'est-ce pas*? And only you, Justin, could save her."

He looked at her in wonderment. "How did you know?"

Martinique lifted one shoulder. "I am French," she reminded him. "No one understands *la production dramatique* better than us. And I am a woman, *mon cher*. Even in death, we rarely fool one another."

He felt some of the tension flood out of him. "I was the only fool," he whispered. "My father was a hard man. I knew that. Perhaps . . . yes, perhaps he was cruel. But it was not my place to interfere."

"No, it was Georgina's father's place," said Martinique. "If the worst of her allegations were true."

"And yet I never once thought of that," he admitted. "I was a young blade full of impatience and fury, besotted by her frail beauty and persuaded that my father was a monstrous beast. She cried herself sick every night. She begged me to save her, to take her away. And so I did."

"Yes. You slew her dragon."

He flashed a bitter smile. "Pathetic, was it not?" he murmured. "I betrayed my father, without even giving him the chance to defend himself. To this day I do not know if I hurt him deeply, or if he simply hated me. I did not even touch Georgina until many weeks had passed, and it became clear that we had been thoroughly disowned; that it was just the two of us, alone against the world."

"*Mon dieu*, had you any money?" asked Martinique. "How did you live?"

He snorted. "By my wits, at first," he said. "But I soon became quite the *joueur invétéré* in the gaming salons of Paris—a predator, really. And I had a little jewelry left me by my mother, which was to go to my wife. I sold all but one piece to buy the house in *le Marais*. As I told you once, I have it still, though the place seems bleak to me now."

"Is it?"

"No, it is very old and quite beautiful," he admitted. "Exquisite, really. But I do not wish to live in it, and yet I cannot bear to sell it."

Martinique seemed to consider it for a long moment. "I think, *mon cher,* that I understand."

His face fell forward into his hands. "Good God, how could you possibly?" he rasped. "What I did was a sin against God's law, Martinique. It is . . . unforgivable."

She stroked one hand down his hair. "No, not to me," she answered. "I know too well that blurry line between right and wrong; between moral and immoral. Sometimes we do what we think we must do in order to survive—or to help someone else survive."

He lifted his head and looked at her, his eyes stark with pain and with hope. "If you understand that awful truth, Martinique, then I am the most fortunate of men," he said. "I daresay you have been warned away from me—and in great detail, too. The old gossip always precedes me. I cannot escape it."

"I heard some of it, *oui,*" she answered. "But much of it, I did not need to hear. You are a good and honorable man, Justin. Nothing you have said changes that."

The hope in his eyes warmed. "Martinique," he whispered. "Oh, Martinique, I know I have an unworthy past. But I have paid for my sins, I pray. And now, this understanding between us—it troubles me. I want—no, I *need* to make our betrothal real."

"Why?"

"It seems so wrong now," he answered. "There has already been too much deception in my life. And yes, I have known you but a fortnight, but I already know, Martinique, that . . . that I love you. You have given my blighted future a ray of hope. Will you do it? Will you be terribly imprudent, and marry me, despite who I am?"

She shook her head. "I cannot, Justin, and it has nothing to do with you," she whispered. "Do you think I give a snap for the women in your past? It has to do with me. What if you wake up one day, Justin, to find that I am a millstone about your neck just as your stepmother was?"

"Martinique!" he said, embracing her tightly. "It will never be like that for us. You are not Georgina. You are strong and sensible. You are true to yourself. And I am no longer a foolish boy. I know, Martinique, what love is—because I have learnt quite thoroughly what it is not."

"But you do not know me," she whispered hollowly. "People change, I think. Or . . . circumstances change. Something does. You will grow tired of me."

"No, I shan't," he argued. "I love you. And I knew it so swiftly and certainly it left my head spinning. Do you believe, Martinique, in love at first sight?"

She opened her mouth to protest, but he covered her mouth with his, and kissed her senseless again. Somewhere in the depths of the house, a clock tolled four. Reluctantly, he drew himself back an inch.

"I had best leave you now," he said quietly. "But I mean to return, and to bring you a gift. Slip away, love, and meet me in the orchard later. Make me no firm answer until then. Please?"

Somehow, she managed to nod. "Yes, all right," she finally agreed. "In the orchard. I—I shall be there."

THE BEGINNING

$\mathcal{M}$artinique lay sleepless through what was left of the morning, then sent her breakfast tray away without lifting the cover. Instead, she wriggled back in the depths of the bed, and pulled the woolen coverlet to her chin. She fancied she could still smell Justin's scent on the linen sheets, and it comforted her in a moment of dreadful indecision.

Justin loved her. He had loved her almost at first sight. And she loved him; not just in that breathless, heart-fluttering way, but with a quiet confidence. He was a strong, broad-shouldered man, literally and figuratively. He would be the sort of husband one could laugh with, and yet rely upon throughout life's inevitable joys and hardships. She was fortunate indeed to have found him so soon. And now she was willing to refuse him? Truly, she must be mad. Martinique threw back the coverlet, and began to pace the room.

Be certain of your worth, and everyone else will follow, Mrs. Harris had said.

Wise words, to be sure. But how did one apply them to one's own life? Perhaps by insisting upon having what one deserved? She was a *good* person. Did she not deserve love, and to be loved in return? But perhaps more important than that, didn't she deserve to be dealt with honestly, and with respect?

She knew then what she must do. And in knowing it, something in her heart seemed to fall into place. The dread was quashed, and in its place came a firm resolve. Martinique rang the bell for her maid, then went to the wardrobe and drew out her best walking dress.

She found him in alone in the library, a copy of the *Times* spread out on the desk, along with the ever-present stacks of files and ledgers piled neatly to his left, a cup of coffee at his elbow. She rapped lightly on the door frame, but did not await his permission, and shut the door behind her.

Rothewell noticed, glancing up at once, his swift, dark gaze taking in her face and the hands clasped somewhat apprehensively before her. Remembering Mrs. Harris's advice, she dropped her arms to her sides, and pushed her shoulders firmly back.

"Martinique," he murmured. "Good morning."

"Good morning, my lord." She held his gaze firmly. "I wish a moment of your time."

He gave her another assessing glance, and motioned languidly at one of the chairs before the desk. "By all means," he said. "But if you are here to protest your betro—"

"I am here to protest nothing," she interjected, taking the proffered chair. "With all respect, sir, my days of arguing with you are done."

There was a flicker of some nameless emotion in his eyes. "I am pleased indeed to hear it."

"I have decided that I am going to take charge of my own decisions," she said gently. "And that I shall decide about this betrothal, amongst other things."

"Martinique, I am your guardian," he said, his voice cool. "I am responsible for your decisions."

"Yes, my lord, but I am nineteen years old," she said. "In less than six years, I will come into my inheritance. I will be a part-owner in Neville Shipping, with all the attendant rights and responsibilities. But I am old enough now to be my own person, and to make my own choices, for good or ill."

"And speaking of ill choices, Martinique, you made a most regrettable one a fortnight past," he said tightly. "But setting even that misjudgment aside, the fact remains that you *are* a female. You require a husband."

"Xanthia has no husband," Martinique countered. "She makes her own decisions—and many of the business decisions, too."

"That is hardly the same thing," he said. "Xanthia's situation is . . . unusual."

Martinique lifted one shoulder. "I shan't debate that," she answered. "I did not come here to quibble over Xanthia."

"Then what, pray, did you come to quibble over?" asked Rothewell coolly.

She watched him carefully; she did not for one instant underestimate his resolve or his ruthlessness. "I wish to know, my lord, why you sent me away," she said in a clear, quiet voice. "Moreover, I wish to know why I may not now return home. And kindly do not pretty up your answer with hollow words like *duty* and *responsibility*. I have long since given up any hope of pleasing you, or of being loved by you. Now I wish only to have the truth from you."

To his credit, he neither flinched nor hesitated. "It little matters whether you please me or whether I love you, Martinique." His voice was dangerously calm. "Just as it little matters what you think of me. Love has nothing to do with life. I was given the task of ensuring your safety, and that I have done to the best of my ability."

Her safety? It was an odd choice of words. "But why was I sent away, my lord?" she said again. "Did you hate me so much you could not bear the sight of me? Pray speak plainly, sir, for I am beyond being hurt by it. If I am to go forward in life, I would first seek to understand the past."

At that, his face seemed to soften, not to gentleness, or even to affection, but to an almost inestimable weariness. And for the first time, she wondered just what this guardianship had cost him.

"No one wishes to understand the past more than I, Martinique," he said quietly. "After your stepfather's death, it was left to me to sort out the pieces, and to do what I thought best. And that is what I did. I found you a place at one of the world's most preeminent schools. I have followed closely your academic progress and your welfare. I have paid every penny of your expenses, and provided you with life's every luxury. What more would you have had me do?"

"But why force me from the only home I had known, my lord?" she pressed. "Why send me thousands of miles away when I could have stayed with you and Xanthia? And why to England? Can you not understand that this was a foreign country to me? This was not my home, Rothewell. It was yours. But it was not *mine.*"

"Your remaining in Barbados was out of the question." The words were firm and cold. "And that situation is unchanged."

Martinique was resolute. "Why, sir? I demand to know."

She watched his knuckles go white, and realized

that the pen in his fingers was about to splinter. "You *demand*?" His lip curled into a sneer. "For God's sake, Martinique, have you no notion what Barbados is like now? It is no longer safe for any white slave owner—and it certainly is not safe for someone like you."

"Someone . . . like *me*," she echoed. "Of mixed race, do you mean?"

"That is precisely what I mean," he snapped. "There has been a seething resentment in the air since the rebellion, and it only grows worse. The planters mistrust their slaves, and with good reason. The slaves mistrust their masters—with even better reason. And people like you are caught in the middle. Martinique, you are a beautiful young woman—a very, very rich and beautiful young woman of mixed blood and uncertain ancestry. Do you think the high sticklers amongst white aristocracy welcome that? And do you think the slaves are any happier? Your mother never made a secret of her lineage, though I now think that perhaps she should have done, for all our sakes."

"But . . . but her death was an accident, was it not?" whispered Martinique. "The rebels set the cane fields afire. *Didn't* they?"

Rothewell looked grim indeed. "At the time, we thought it most unlikely," he answered. "That carriage was trapped like a rat in a burning cane field—and yet there was not another such fire set within miles of it. The rebellion might simply have made for a convenient excuse."

A long moment of silence held sway over the room. "You . . . you think it was someone else," she said quietly. "And not an accident."

"I do not *know*," he said harshly. "I did my damnedest to uncover the truth, but learnt little. And when I could not be sure, Martinique, I sent you away."

"It is true that many of the other planters never liked *Maman*." Martinique's voice was growing strident. "Their wives never welcomed her into their society. Everyone felt she married above her class and her blood. I sensed it."

"Many amongst the planter aristocracy did not approve," Rothewell acknowledged. "Society is rife with small-minded people, Martinique, and you would do well to remember it. We feared for your safety. You stood to inherit all Luke's wealth, save for the actual barony here in England."

"Mon Dieu!" The thought horrified her.

He tossed down the pen as if disgusted. "On the other hand, it is just as likely someone wanted me dead."

"You, my lord? Why?"

He gave a twisted smile. "I have a way of making enemies," he said. "And it was supposed to have been me in the carriage that night, not my brother. But— well, let's just say I was in no condition to attend a dinner party. On the other hand, perhaps it really *was* the rebels. Perhaps they envied your mother and wished her ill. Or perhaps they did not mean to trap the carriage, or to kill anyone. We will never know. That is why I do not want you back on the island."

"I—I see."

But Rothewell's expression had turned inward, and his jaw was set into that familiar harsh line. She could sense that he was regretting his candor. He was a man who kept his own counsel, and that would likely never change. Nonetheless, she had learned the truth—or a part of it. Martinique was not fool enough to believe she would ever have the whole of Rothewell's story.

She left him staring broodingly into his cold coffee, leaving the library door open as she went. She was not even sure he was aware she had departed.

Xanthia, however, had got wind of the untouched breakfast tray, and bustled into Martinique's bed-chamber almost as soon as she returned. "Dorothy says you did not eat," she said worriedly. "What is wrong, my dear? Are you unwell?"

Martinique sat down in the chair beside her bed, and let her shoulders fall again. "I am well enough," she said. "Well enough for a girl who has managed to bollix up her entire life in a fortnight."

Xanthia settled on the edge of the mattress, and clasped her hands in her lap. "Have we done the wrong thing, Kieran and I?" she asked, as if to herself. "We did not know, you see, the whole of St. Vrain's past. I could speak to Kieran. I can make him listen."

Martinique shook her head. "I have already spoken to him," she answered. "Besides, it is not Justin's past, Xanthia, which troubles me."

Xanthia reached out and clasped Martinique's hand in her own warm, capable ones. "Can you not learn to love him, my dear? Is it quite out of the question?"

At that, tears began to press hotly at the backs of her eyes. "Oh, Zee!" she said. "I *do* love him. Can you not see? That is the very problem."

"Is it?" Xanthia looked confused. "Does St. Vrain believe he cannot love you? Most men marry for much less than that, you know."

Martinique gave a bitter laugh. "He says that it was love at first sight," she said. "He says he scarce deserves me, and that I have given him hope for a happy future."

"Then I fail to see the problem, my dear," she said briskly. "Surely you would not refuse this marriage merely to spite Rothewell?"

Martinique dropped her eyes, and shook her head. "It is not that," she whispered. "It is not spite. It is just that . . . well, Zee, what is it that is so wrong with me? Why does Rothewell hate me so? Why doesn't *he* want me? I—I need to understand."

"Oh, Martinique!" Her voice was weary now. "Those are such complicated questions."

"But how can I go forward in life if I don't know what I did wrong in the past?" she cried. "What if Justin tires of me, too, and wishes to send me away? Is it my ancestry? Is it my blood? I went to Rothewell, and I asked him these things, but all he would tell me was that he was not sure who had killed my parents. But there is something more lurking there, tainting all that goes on between us. I feel it. I always have."

Xanthia rose and paced across the room to the bank of windows which overlooked the lake. With one finger, she pulled back the drapery as if absorbed by the scene, but Martinique knew that she gazed not at the present, but at the past. "Kieran never tired of you, Martinique," she finally said, letting the drapery drop as she turned around. "He sent you away, my dear, because he had to."

"Oh, yes!" said Martinique sarcastically. "He feared for my safety."

Xanthia's gaze turned inward again. "That much is true," she said quietly. "The rebellion was barely quashed, and we were all afraid. All the time. Of everything. Many men sent their wives and children away. If there is more to the story, my dear, it is Kieran's to tell. Not mine. But you must trust me when I say he does not hate you. You are family now, and to Kieran, that means everything."

"But he holds me at such a distance, Xanthia," Martinique whispered. "Both literally and figuratively. I think it must be my heritage. I think he is ashamed of me."

"Oh, no," said Xanthia firmly. "Oh, no my dear. That is simply not true. Where ever did you get such a notion?"

"I do not know," Martinique admitted.

Xanthia fell silent for a long moment. In the passageway beyond, a door creaked and a tray rattled with dishes. There was the coo of a dove on the windowsill, and below, the clatter of the gardners unloading shovels and rakes. And still Xanthia hesitated. "Kieran is difficult to understand," she finally said. "His past has been . . . well riddled with disappointments, I daresay."

"Because you were orphans?" asked Martinique. "Is that it?"

Slowly, Xanthia nodded. "Yes, in part," she admitted. "And like many of us, Kieran has made some bad choices—choices with which he must now live."

Martinique hung her head. "He told me that it should have been him in the carriage the night my parents died," she confessed. "Is that the sort of thing you mean?"

Again, Xanthia paused. "Yes, I suppose," she said, still standing at the window. "Nonetheless, his problems are not yours, my dear. You cannot afford to entangle your emotions with his. You must live your own life. Promise me, Martinique, that you will do that? Otherwise, you make a mockery of all that Luke worked to give you."

"I . . . I suppose you are right." And it was a good point, Martinique conceded.

Suddenly, Xanthia spun around. "And you—*you*, Martinique, are the *very image* of Annemarie," she said out of nowhere. "Can you understand that, my dear? Kieran cannot but look at you and remember in the next breath that it should have been him in that carriage, not your mother. Not our brother. It is such a stark reminder."

"I—I never really thought of it that way."

Rothewell felt guilty? Perhaps that was it, in part. Xanthia, of all people, had no reason to lie. Martinique's stepfather had loved her dearly. Perhaps that—and his acceptance of her—was what she should cling to.

Rothewell did not hate her.

He had sent her away not because he was appalled by her, but because he wished to keep her safe. Was it true? Perhaps. Perhaps in part. *Confused and conflicted*, Xanthia had said. But it ran deeper even than that, Martinique suspected. Rothewell was a profoundly unhappy man. Should his unhappiness continue to blight her future? Should she give up this one chance—this one perfect chance at love—simply because a bitter man could not sort out his own emotions? And should she punish another man for it?

No. No, she should not.

She came off the bed and onto her feet in one motion.

She saw him the moment he crossed over the hill, and watched him as he strode down, his eyes narrowed against the morning sun. Today Justin was dressed for the hunting field, in a long, drab duster and tall brown boots, with a fowling gun laid loosely in the crook of one arm. As he waded toward her through the tall grass, the duster swirled round his boots while a white-and-liver spaniel dashed madly about his legs.

At the edge of the orchard, he lifted his hat in greeting. "Why, Miss Neville, what a pleasant surprise!" he said. "It looks as though you've caught me poaching in Sharpe's orchard."

She had hitched up her skirts, and was hastening toward him. "And just what are you hunting, sir?" she asked primly.

He let his eyes run over her, then caught her against him with his free arm. "The ivory-breasted bird of paradise," he whispered, lips pressed to her ear. "And I've just caught *mine*."

She pushed back far enough to see his eyes, which were dancing with laughter, yet tinged with hope. "I think perhaps you have," she answered.

He held her gaze with his melting dark eyes, then let the fowling gun slide into the grass. He caught her full against him, and kissed her deeply, his hands roaming circumspectly beneath her cloak.

At last, they broke apart, their breathing audible in the still of the morning. "Oh, Justin!" she said at last. "What if everything you thought was true was not? Or—or was only half-true? Or was not the whole of it?"

He threw back his head and laughed. "Oh, Martinique, we never know the whole of anything," he answered. "And most of the time, we do not know the truth. But you were speaking of something specific, I think?" He paused to kiss her on the nose. "Tell me what it is that has you in such a flurry."

She set her hands against the broad wall of his chest, and let her fingers curl into the wool of his lapels. He smelled of citrus and soap, and of the wonderful scent he'd left on her bedsheets last night. "Oh, never mind that just now!" she said. "It will wait, will it not? It will wait forever. Now, you were to bring me a present?"

Again, he laughed, and thrust one hand into his coat pocket. The laugher, she realized, made him look like a different man. Not innocent, no. Never that. But carefree; like a man newly unburdened, perhaps.

"Ah!" he said, extracting a drawn velvet bag. With great care, he loosened the cord, and shook the contents free. It was a ring. A grand oval sapphire mounted in a setting of ornately carved gold, and flanked with two diamonds nearly as large.

"Mon Dieu!" she exclaimed. "Justin, that is worth a fortune."

"Yes," he said quietly. "It is."

He lifted her hand and slid it onto her finger. Martinique held out her hand to the sun, and the facets seemed to catch fire. "Oh," she breathed. "Oh, Justin. I cannot wear this."

"I am afraid, my dear, that I must insist," he said, smiling. "It was my maternal grandmother's wedding ring, and her grandmother's before that, and . . . oh, Lord, I do not know how many fingers wore it, Martinique, before it came to you. But it *has* come to you, and it is said to bring great happiness to every wife who wears it, and I could not forgive myself, my love, if I brought anything less than great happiness to you."

For a long moment, she studied the ring, marveling at what it was likely worth. Then slowly, she curled her fingers into a fist, and looked up at him. "You kept it," she said quietly. "The one thing you did not sell, even when you were all but penniless."

His smile was a little bitter. "That one ring alone would have bought me my little house in *le Marais.* But I dared not sell it. It was meant for my wife. And it became, eventually, a—a sort of symbol of hope."

"Your hope?"

"My only hope of someday finding the right woman, and of ensuring her happiness."

"Oh, Justin," she said, holding his gaze. "You do not need a ring, my love. You need nothing save yourself to make me happy."

The last of the clouds lifted from his expression. "So you will do it, then?" he asked. "You will marry me, Martinique?"

She held out the ring again, and studied it coyly. "A Christmas wedding, I think," she said musingly. "Then a New Year—and a new life—in Paris."

He laughed, and his eyes widened. "In *Paris*?"

Martinique smiled up at him. "We have old fears and old memories to sweep away, you and I," she said. "What better way than for us to begin than in Paris?"

"Why not?" He was slowing nodding. "What better way indeed?"

Martinique twined her arms round his neck. "And after all," she said, "you once promised me the loan of your little house in *le Marais* for my wedding trip, you will recall. And you are a man who never goes back on his word."

He chuckled quietly and leaned into her. "Well, then, Lady St. Vrain-to-be," he said, touching his nose to hers. "Here are three more words to be kept: I love you. And if I am not much mistaken, the key to that house is in my other pocket."

THE MERCHANT'S GIFT

Julia London

For my mother, who taught us that it did not matter what side of the tracks a person came from, but whether they were polite and if their clothes were clean and neatly pressed. My clothes are clean and neatly pressed, Mom.

One

*O*n a warm August afternoon, an ornate post chaise painted black with gold trim and topped with gold feather plumes thundered into Leeds on the strength of four grays that each stood sixteen hands high.

The coach was returning from London en route to a stately mansion, only recently completed, that boasted twelve chimneys on the banks of the River Aire. Mr. George Holcomb, the owner of Heslington Park, was fond of pointing out to anyone who was kind enough to listen that his home had more chimneys than any other house in Yorkshire.

Generally speaking, Mr. Holcomb was fond of speaking of his wealth at every opportunity. After all, he'd come by it honestly (an enormous number of sheep) and, at least in his estimation, he'd come by it rather brilliantly, for he'd foreseen a growing market for English wool and wool products in America. As a result of his foresight, Mr. Holcomb now enjoyed one of the largest wool production operations in all of Yorkshire. He had risen from obscurity to be considered the wealthiest of the gentry in the region.

His success meant that his youngest child and only daughter, Grace, would have a dowry that would attract only the best suitors. That she would be afforded the opportunity to enter London society and rub elbows with aristocrats and then marry an aristocrat. And on that happy day, George Holcomb would receive the recognition he so richly deserved from the members of the most elite society.

He was so keen to see that happen that he made application on Grace's behalf to Mrs. Harris's School for Young Ladies, a renowned finishing school for young heiresses. Grace was accepted, and upon her graduation two years past, she had entered the London social scene with a presentation at court to rival all others.

Her debut had been so spectacular—a full ball, an orchestra of twelve, and French champagne served in crystal flutes—that Holcomb was certain she would receive an offer within a month's time.

Not only did Grace not receive an offer within a month's time, she did not receive even a *hint* of an offer her entire first Season.

Her father could not fathom why. Grace was handsome; not too fat or too thin. Her hair was a pleasing shade of auburn, the same as his own, and her eyes the russet color of autumn leaves. Her mien was bright and pleasant, she showed no symptoms of a nervous disposition, and there was the added incentive of his enormous wealth. What more could a man desire in a bride?

When Mr. Holcomb questioned Grace upon her return from London—and he'd done so endlessly, reminding her that she had cost him a fair sum in gowns and slippers and other flummery in the process—she had assured him that her manners were impeccable and she'd not offended anyone of which she was aware.

Yet Mr. Holcomb was not convinced and sent Grace back to Mrs. Harris in advance of the next social season so that she might reacquaint herself with her lessons in etiquette. Grace was always happy to see Mrs. Harris, a wise woman who understood the difficulties a young heiress of common birth faced when entering the marriage mart of high society. Unlike Grace's father, Mrs. Harris was never cross or impatient. In fact, Mrs. Harris saw no reason to mention to anyone other than Grace the horrible faux pas Grace had made last Season.

It was very innocent, really. When she'd been introduced to Lord Billingsley, a viscount who would one day be earl, she had proudly told him her father's occupation when asked. Lord Billingsley had seemed quite impressed and had asked her lots of questions about sheep, which she took as a sign of his interest in her. In her determination to secure a match, Grace had thought it perfectly acceptable behavior to make a gift of a cap—made with Holcomb wool, naturally—to Lord Billingsley at a garden tea one afternoon.

He'd laughed with delight when she'd presented it to him, and he'd professed to being grateful to the wool industry for all the socks and caps it produced. How was she to know he was being snide? How could she have possibly known he was laughing at her behind her back, or that some people began to talk of the shepherdess from Leeds?

When Mrs. Harris had told Grace the truth, she'd been very kind, and had used it as an opportunity to review some fundamentals: Be polite, but a bit mysterious. Be demure, but forthright. Be clever, but circumspect, and so on and so forth.

Needless to say, as the end of her second Season came and went, Grace still had not received an offer.

And now Grace was in the post chaise being hurtled toward an audience with her father much as a boulder might be hurtled into the sea, and she dreaded it more and more with every passing mile. By the time they reached Leeds, she could scarcely stand the coach another moment. She needed to walk, to think, to rehearse what she'd say. When the coach slowed for traffic, she was eternally grateful, for even a moment's delay was preferable to what awaited her at Heslington Park.

As the coach groaned to a near stop, she quickly shifted forward to peer out the window. They were in the heart of the Yorkshire textile market in the center of Leeds. Mule-drawn carts piled high with cloths of various colors and fabrics, to be traded at the various Cloth Halls, clogged the city square, along with vendors vying for space and the attention of wealthy merchants. Men hurried back and forth carrying bolts of beautifully colored fabrics between the halls.

If there was one thing Grace had learned to appreciate, it was that fine cloth could be made into a finer gown. "Betty," she said, reaching across to her maid and her traveling companion, "I've in mind a new gown. Tell the driver to let us off here."

A few minutes later, she was inside the Cloth Hall, Betty trailing behind as she examined several stalls of rich silks, brilliant satins, and soft brocades.

"Here you are, madam, blue silk made only in the Cotswolds," one merchant called out to her.

Grace turned and saw the bolt he held up. It was indeed a beautiful blue silk, changing hue with the light, and she instantly moved forward to where the merchant had unfurled a long strip of it for her inspection. "T'would make a lovely gown for a grand lady," he said.

She glanced up to ask the merchant the price, but her eye caught sight of a broad back and broader shoulders just behind him. On top of one of those broad shoulders were stacked several bolts of thick gray wool, the type used for servants' gowns.

But it was not the cloth that caught Grace's eye; it was the shape of the man's back, evident through a lawn shirt that tapered into a pair of buckskins that fit his lean hips and thighs admirably well. She knew that back and those hips—she'd admired them more than once in the last few years. They belonged to Mr. Barrett Adlaine, a man who'd built a small but thriving textile mill on the left bank of the River Aire, started with the inheritance he'd received when his father, a cloth trader, had died. The Holcomb market pens were very close to Mr. Adlaine's mill, and he'd bought sheep from her father on several occasions.

There was a time, when Grace was a child—before her father had become so wealthy—that she, her two older brothers, and the Adlaine boys had played together in the Cloth Halls. Mr. Adlaine had become an ambitious man, a hard worker . . . and extremely virile.

Grace meant to look away, to return her attention to the blue silk where it belonged, but Mr. Adlaine chose that moment to turn around, and for a moment in that crowded and noisy hall, their gazes met, and Grace lost her train of thought.

He was just as handsome as she recalled, his jaw square, his eyes a blustery blue, his lips spread in an irrepressible smile. His dark blond hair, tied in a queue at the nape of his neck, was a bit longer than what was fashionable in London. He shifted his weight to one hip, put his free hand on his waist and brazenly winked at her. *Winked* at her, as if they were intimate friends instead of the mere acquaintances that they were now.

Grace instantly felt herself color, but she did not look away. If anything, her smile turned a bit brighter.

"How many bolts shall I wrap for you, miss?" the merchant asked.

"Will you take the cloth, miss?" Betty asked.

"What?" Grace said, startled, and looked at Betty, who was peering curiously at her.

"The cloth, miss. Will you purchase it?"

"Yes, yes," she said instantly. "Two bolts," she told the merchant, and glanced behind him again. Mr. Adlaine was gone.

With a small sigh, she put the cloth to her father's name and sent Betty to fetch a footman to carry it back to the coach. She turned away from the merchant, and almost collided with Mr. Adlaine, who was now standing before her.

"Miss Holcomb?"

His sudden appearance flustered her almost as much as his blue eyes. She felt the blood ripple in her veins. "Oh. Mr. Adlaine," she said coolly as she surreptitiously glanced around. "How do you do?"

He looked around, too, but without the slightest bit of discretion. "Very well, thank you." He still held the bolts of cloth as if they weighed nothing, as if they were a bird on his shoulder. "You must be returned from London."

She blinked. "London?"

"London . . . rather large town on the banks of the Thames?" he reminded her with a lopsided grin.

That smile caused her body to tingle violently, and Grace had to struggle to remember that he was not the sort of man she had been raised to admire. "I beg your pardon, sir, but I wasn't aware that my itinerary was so widely known."

"Oh, I think your itinerary is hardly known at all," he assured her with another knee-melting smile. "But your father mentioned to me this morning that you were due to arrive today."

"Ah," she said, mildly deflated. For a fleeting moment, she had imagined him making polite inquiries as to when she might return.

"Did you enjoy your stay?" he asked.

"Of course," she said, shifting her gaze to her silk again, uncomfortably aware of his body. "I am often in London, you know. One must be in London if one is to be in society."

"By that I suppose you mean *high* society."

"Of course," she said with a bit of a frown. What else would she mean?

"How wonderful for you."

"Well," she said, tracing an invisible line down the silk. "There are so many soirées and assemblies to attend that it's positively exhausting keeping order of one's social engagements."

"That sounds frightfully *taxing*," he said, his brows furrowed with concern. "I can only hope that you had some assistance."

"No," she said, shaking her head. "I had to do it entirely on my own."

"A *tragedy*."

She realized then that he was teasing her and she blushed as she fidgeted with the cross at her neck . . . until she recalled Mrs. Harris's admonishment against fidgeting, and dropped her hand. "Unless you have actually *been* to London, Mr. Adlaine, you cannot imagine the hubbub." She glanced at him sidelong. "Have you ever been to London?"

"I certainly cannot claim to be quite the traveler *you* are, Miss Holcomb," he said. "I've only been to London a dozen times, and my social engagements were too few— and, I daresay, too common—to warrant any assistance."

"Ah. Well." Now she felt incredibly foolish—of *course* he'd been to London! It wasn't as if it was across the ocean and impossible to reach! "Naturally, I received quite a lot of invitations because I was presented at court." Really, *that* made no sense either, but Mr. Adlaine had always had a way of making her feel a bit tongue-tied.

"I am certain you had far more invitations than my humble beginnings could *ever* entice," he said dramatically, but his eyes were shimmering with amusement. He shifted the bolts on his shoulder and moved a step closer to Grace. She instantly stepped back—she meant nothing by it, of course, it was really only a habit, but she could see in his eyes that he believed he repulsed her.

His gaze flicked over the length of her. "Beg your pardon," he said, his smile gone. "I will take my leave of you with the hope that you will not find Leeds too tiresome after experiencing *high* society in London."

That wasn't what she'd meant to convey at all, but Betty and a footman had reached Grace, and she couldn't think how to extract herself from the little hole she'd dug herself. "Thank you," she said, and pointed the footman to the bolts of silk cloth she'd purchased. "Good day, Mr. Adlaine."

"Good day, Miss Holcomb," he said, and, shifting the bolts of cloth on his shoulder, he walked away.

As he left, Grace noticed Betty was staring after him with big round eyes, practically drooling. "For goodness sake, Betty!" Grace exclaimed, nudging her. "He's not a Christmas goose!"

"No, miss. He's not in the least," Betty said softly, and jumped a little when Grace abruptly moved her along.

Two

$\mathcal{G}$race's first day back in the bosom of her family
turned out to be as miserable as she'd anticipated. Her father paced the hearth, his lanky stride
eating up the carpet as he verbally reviewed his suspicions as to why she hadn't received an offer of marriage, while her brothers, Frederick and Stephen, sat
idly by, both of them visibly bored by the proceed-
ings.

Her mother, as usual, was silent and very solicitous
of her husband, rarely speaking except to agree with
him.

That left Grace to fend for herself. "I swear to you,
Papa, I did nothing wrong," she said for the hundredth
time since arriving home.

"But Gracie, love—surely you will agree that *something* is amiss, or else you would have received an
offer. Just this morning, your mother was told that her
cousin's daughter, who has been out only one Season,
has gained an offer."

Grace looked at her mother.

"It's quite true," she said. "Mary is marrying a
baron."

"By your own admission, Gracie," her oldest
brother, Frederick, chimed in behind a yawn, "three
young ladies who attended Mrs. Harris's school re-

ceived offers this Season. Add those three to the four
who received offers last year, and you have seven of
Mrs. Harris's charges who have received offers. How
do you account for it?"

"I *don't* account for it," she said briskly, chafing at her
brother's remark. When they were children, her brothers
had treated her as an equal. But as soon as she'd
sprouted a bosom, they had started to act like men who
had a say in her life. "I am not in the habit of tallying the
number of offers made to graduates of Mrs. Harris's
school, nor am I privy to their unique situations."

"Don't you want to marry, Gracie?" her father
asked.

The question surprised her. Of *course* she wanted
to marry. She wanted to have children and to be mistress of her own house, and to know a man's kiss
whenever she wanted. But she wouldn't encourage
the interest of a man merely because he was of noble
birth. She'd encouraged Lord Billingsley, and look
what had happened. She'd encouraged Lord Warren,
as well, until Mrs. Harris confided in her that he was
perhaps too fond of his drink. She had encouraged
both men for the wrong reasons. Now she knew better and believed that she should at least *esteem* her future husband.

"Well? Do you?" her father demanded, and four
pairs of Holcomb eyes turned to her.

"Yes, of course I do," she said. "But I—"

"And don't you want to marry well, to a man of
means and importance whose connections will help
better your family?"

"Of *course*—"

"Then why haven't you encouraged a proper
courtship with a young aristocrat? Mrs. Wells tells me
you have had callers."

She was really beginning to despise Mrs. Wells, the chaperone her father had hired to stay with Grace in London. She'd believed her to be a kind, grandmotherly woman until she had discovered Mrs. Wells was reporting her every word and deed to her father. Then she'd really begun to dislike the old bag.

"They were merely friends."

"*Friends!*" he bellowed. "On my word, there is no such beast as *friend* between a man and a woman, Grace! If you'd given one of those fellows the least bit of encouragement, you might have had your offer!"

"Perhaps it is her hair," Stephen said thoughtfully, playfully studying Grace through his mother's lorgnette. "I don't care for the color."

"I don't mind it in the least," Frederick said.

"For God's sake, it is not the color of her *hair*," Papa said irritably. "It is something much more than that. It must be in the way she presents herself," he said, eyeing her critically.

"It is because we are in *trade*," Grace exclaimed with great exasperation.

A collective gasp went up from the other four Holcombs; they all gaped at her.

"I can see no point in tiptoeing around it," she defiantly continued. "We all know that there are certain influential members of the *haute ton* who believe that it is vulgar to be engaged in business of any sort."

"*Vulgar?*" her father echoed, his face turning red. "*Pray tell,*" he bellowed, "to what lofty *occupation* does this certain influential lot of fops and dandies subscribe? A man's occupation is irrelevant once he has achieved a certain amount of success, which *I* have achieved. And titled men of leisure appreciate the sort of dowry I might put on you. This situation, Gracie, rests on *your* shoulders."

She could feel herself color and looked helplessly at her mother.

"He's quite right, darling," her mother said. "And it makes me rather ill to think of all the money we have paid Mrs. Harris, and yet you *still* do not conduct yourself in a proper manner. I let you run with the boys too long, I fear."

"But I—"

"I've got it!" Freddie said, jabbing a finger high in the air. "Everyone is in the country just now, are they not?"

"Yes?" Stephen asked, having discarded the lorgnette.

"We should have a soirée. A country dance as it were, and we should invite nobles from the region and see for ourselves what keeps Grace from gaining an offer."

"Oh dear God, *no!*" Grace started, but she was interrupted by the enthusiastic agreement of her father.

"An excellent suggestion, Freddie!" he exclaimed, clapping his oldest son on the shoulder.

"Papa, please!" Grace cried. "It's hunting season, not the time for balls and routs!"

"A capital idea!" Stephen exclaimed, perking up. "We must combine it with a weekend of hunting that culminates in a ball! We've more than enough game to support it, sir."

"Yes, of course!" her father gleefully replied. "A ball is just the thing!"

It wasn't the thing at all, but as the three of them were already busily planning their grand ball, Grace realized there was nothing she could do to stop them. With a sigh of resignation, she slumped back in her chair.

Three

The hunting season was a fortnight old when George Holcomb hosted a weekend of shooting and a ball at Heslington Park. It was attended by the region's most notable persons, including an earl and some lesser lords, as well as wealthy merchants with whom Holcomb had the pleasure of doing business.

Included in that number was Mr. Barrett Adlaine, who, Grace had surreptitiously observed, looked even more splendid when dressed in proper clothing. He wore a coat of dark navy superfine, and a patterned waistcoat embroidered with gold thread. His thick hair was brushed over his collar, and his neckcloth was tied in an intricate and handsome knot, which rather surprised Grace—she supposed only men with valets possessed such artfully tied neckcloths.

She had not found an opportunity to speak to him—her father had kept her quite occupied by introducing her to the earl, and then two barons, a baronet, and a man who had been knighted recently for his work on the canal between Leeds and Liverpool. Moreover, she had worn beautiful satin slippers that matched the blue silk gown she'd commissioned using the cloth she'd purchased in Leeds, but they were a smidgen too tight. Her feet were paining her, so any thought of promenading by Mr. Adlaine with the goal of attracting his attention was out of the question.

Not that he would have noticed her, Grace thought absently as she observed him across the crowded ballroom. He'd been engaged alternately with Miss Davies or Miss Moorhouse all night, dancing with one and then the other, and in between, several of the married women in the crowd.

He danced quite well, actually—very graceful for a man so tall and muscular and not part of society. She'd have thought his lack of experience in the ballrooms of proper society might make him a bit ungainly, but he was not in the least so. He seemed to enjoy himself thoroughly. Every time Grace glanced at him—not that she *meant* to glance at him, but her gaze just kept falling on him, inadvertently, of course—he was smiling and laughing and being altogether too charming.

She was watching him escort a smiling Mrs. Huddersfield onto the dance floor when her father suddenly appeared before her, interrupting her view. "Grace," he said, his expression radiant, "may I present Lord Prescott."

Lord Prescott, whom she knew to be a widower and, from the look of it, older than her father, smiled proudly. Grace pasted a smile on her face and sank into a curtsy as she extended her hand. "How do you do, my lord."

"Very well, Miss Holcomb," he said, taking her hand and bringing it to his thin lips. "Your father did not do your handsome looks justice in describing them to me."

"Oh," she said and gave her father a look. "Perhaps he'd forgotten, as he's had me in London for quite a long time."

"Apparently not long enough," her father responded with a meaningful look.

"Perhaps you will do me the honor of standing up

with me and relating your experience in London?" Lord Prescott asked.

She did not want to dance with him, she did not want to touch him, and furthermore, she should have known better than to wear these blasted shoes to a ball. But she could feel her father's eyes boring into her at that very moment and said, "Of course, my lord," as politely as she could and tried very hard to look pleased by the invitation.

Judging by the menacing look her father gave her, she didn't succeed completely on that front.

Lord Prescott led her onto the dance floor, and as they began to dance, Grace began to talk, chattering on about her debut—taking particular care to note the expense— then how many assemblies she'd attended in London, and how many hats and gowns she'd purchased. Judging by how often her father railed about her mother's spending, she hoped it would put the man off. And indeed, when the danced ended, Lord Prescott seemed a little dazed. Grace quickly curtsied. "Thank you, sir—"

"Miss Holcomb," Lord Prescott said, stepping toward her and preventing her escape. "If you will allow—"

"Miss Holcomb?"

She had been saved! Grace instantly turned from Lord Prescott to see who was her benefactor, and felt her heart jump a bit at the sight of the dashing Mr. Adlaine before her. "Mr. Adlaine!" she exclaimed buoyantly.

"I do beg your pardon," he said with a warm smile as he shifted his gaze to Lord Prescott, "but I fear if I do not request a spot on your dance card now, I shall miss the opportunity." He glanced at Grace. "May I have the pleasure of the next dance, Miss Holcomb?"

"I would be *delighted*, sir," she said, and glanced at Lord Prescott.

Lord Prescott pressed his lips together and bowed. "Please excuse me," he muttered, and with another look at Mr. Adlaine, he walked on.

Grace closed her eyes and sighed softly. When she opened them again, Mr. Adlaine was smiling at her, his blue eyes full of amusement.

"You have done me an enormous service, sir," she said, putting her hand in the palm he presented to her.

"Have I indeed?"

"*Yes*," she said as he began to lead her to the dance floor. "You cannot imagine what trials I must endure!"

"I confess I cannot. You must enlighten me."

"Well," she said airily as she curtsied and he bowed, "there is first the trial of having to smile and pretend to enjoy the attention of any man in search of a wife."

"I assure you, Miss Holcomb, I am not in search of a wife," he said as he slipped his hand around to her back. "Unless, of course, you are suggesting—"

"Oh no, I hardly meant *that*," she said quickly as he led her into the dance, but instantly realized how *that* sounded. "It's just that I am expected to marry well." *Oh, dear God, she was doing it again!* She certainly hadn't meant to say *that* either! What was it about Mr. Adlaine that kept her all at sixes and sevens?

But Mr. Adlaine appeared to take no offense. "As we all are," he said, smiling down at her with such lovely blue eyes that she felt she could almost swim in them.

Of course they were *all* expected to marry as well as possible, but he was not subjected to a father who was determined to see him married *exceedingly* well. "I daresay no one is expected to marry quite as well as me," she said with a sardonic laugh.

"Yes, of course, for the king of England is already married, and infamously so."

Now he was laughing at her. "I *mean*, sir—to put it rather bluntly—that my father has spent quite a lot of money to present me in London. His expectations are higher than most."

"Ah," Mr. Adlaine said, his gaze drifting languidly to her bosom. "And does your father expect anything else from you, other than to bring him a prize stag?"

"I beg your pardon?"

Mr. Adlaine smiled. "It all sounds rather mercenary, Miss Holcomb. You make it sound as if you are being sent into the upper echelons of society to bring home the prized stag."

She hadn't quite thought of it like that, but it was a rather apt description. At the moment, however, she preferred to think of how lovely it was to dance with him . . . so strong and graceful, wasn't he . . . only he was looking at her as if he expected a response.

"Would you argue that my father should not send me to London?" she asked pertly. "For if he didn't send me there, he would surely be combing Leeds for a suitable offer, and that, I believe, is the same thing, is it not?"

"Not at all," he said amicably. "For I don't think you'd have much hope of cornering a stag in Leeds. Perhaps a sheep—but not a stag." He gave her a lop-sided smile. "But you don't sound the least inclined to consider the sheep, which, I might add, is rather ironic given your own humble beginnings."

"Really, Mr. Adlaine, you are willfully misunderstanding me," Grace said, affronted. "I am merely saying that my father would like me to marry to the best of my ability."

"Then I suppose the only question is whether or not you believe marrying well means marrying for an improved situation? Or for love?"

He looked at her pointedly, and Grace could feel herself color. "One might aspire to marry for an improved situation *and* love."

"*Hmm,*" he said, and suddenly and effortlessly twirled her to the right. "It is possible, but not probable if the size of a man's purse is first and foremost in one's mind."

Grace's eyes narrowed. She did not like what he was implying. "You mistake my family's intentions," she insisted as he twirled her around again, but he merely chuckled at her displeasure. "Ours is not the consideration of a man's purse, sir, but his position in society."

"Aha. So you seek a *titled* man," he cheerfully surmised.

Blast it all, he had a way of twisting her words around to make her sound positively awful, and really, dancing with him, feeling his arm around her waist, the firm grip of his big hand around hers, his leg against hers when they twirled about, made her head even foggier. He had a way of making her feel light as a feather in his arms.

"No, of *course* not," she said, remembering their conversation. "In fact, I do not *seek* anyone. My *father* seeks."

"And *you* are merely burdened by the attention of too many gentlemen. I must set your mind at ease, then, Miss Holcomb. You have my vow that I will not burden you with my attention."

"*Oh,*" she exclaimed, frustrated that she could feel her cheeks coloring again. "Mr. Adlaine, you misunderstand me completely! It's just that I was dancing with Lord Prescott, with whom my father made a point of pairing me, and that . . . that is really all I meant by it."

Mr. Adlaine twirled her to the left, then squinted at the crowd on the side of the dance floor. Grace followed his gaze, saw that he was peering at Lord Prescott, who was, regrettably, watching her. "I see your dilemma," he said, frowning a little. "I wonder if I should save you from him? Perhaps lead you off onto the terrace? Hide you behind a potted plant?" He looked at her thoughtfully, as if he was debating it.

She looked at him hopefully, silently willing him to do precisely that.

"I don't know if I should," he said. "Lord Prescott seems to fit the criteria you have laid out."

"No!" she exclaimed.

"No?" He smiled down at her. "He is a lord and a wealthy one at that. By all accounts he was quite fond of his wife, may she rest in peace—"

"He is too *old*," she whispered hotly.

"Ah, you require a youthful suitor," Mr. Adlaine said, nodding. "We must add that to your very long list."

"Mr. Adlaine!"

He laughed. "Do not fear, Miss Holcomb. You will have both your wishes tonight. I shall rescue you, but I will not, under any circumstance, *burden* you with my attention."

Oh, but he was making this difficult! "Splendid!" she said pertly. "You are indeed a gentleman."

He laughed again. "That is very high praise indeed, from a woman so ardently admired."

Grace glared at him for good measure, but in the end, he proved to be a gentleman. As the dance drew to a close, he did indeed maneuver them to one of four sets of French doors leading onto the terrace, and put his hand on her arm and led her out.

On the terrace, he gave her a playful nudge toward the stairs that led down into the gardens, which were lit with rush torches. "Your escape, Miss Holcomb," he said, and bowed low.

"*Thank* you," she said, and hurried down the steps to the rose garden and an arbor she knew very well, her face flaming. Their exchange while dancing was precisely the sort of conversation for which she had no talent.

Grace sat on the wrought-iron bench. She suddenly remembered her feet, which, interestingly, she had quite forgotten while she was dancing with Mr. Adlaine. From her vantage point, she could just make out the bottom steps leading up to the terrace. No one could see her here. She wouldn't remain here for long—frankly, she was afraid to be away for *too* long, for if she did not present herself well tonight, her father would resort to measures too drastic to even contemplate.

She'd rest only a moment, just long enough to avoid Lord Prescott and to relieve her poor feet from bondage. She kicked off her slippers and sighed with relief.

In truth, she did not care for such large balls. She'd been to so many in London and never once had she felt as if she truly belonged—she was forever "the shepherd's daughter," an oddity, someone who was remembered for her common roots rather than her accomplishments. It was bad enough, apparently, to be a merchant's daughter . . . but sheep seemed to be particularly offensive to the *haute ton*. At so many events she attended, she felt as if she were on display, much like a roasted pig was displayed on the Christmas dinner table before her father started carving bits of meat off of it.

The sound of footsteps on the stone steps startled her, and she made a move to grab her shoes just as Mr. Adlaine ducked his head and stepped beneath the arbor. He glanced around. "I don't suspect you'll find any stags here."

"Mr. Adlaine!" Grace cried. He was impertinent, coming down here uninvited and making note of her bare feet, as he was doing at that moment. "If you don't mind, sir—"

"Not in the least. I'd take them off too, were I you, and put them safely away," he said, nodding at the offending shoes next to her on the bench. "There are enough beads on them to string a rather grand necklace."

Momentarily distracted, Grace glanced at the shoes—but she had no moment to reply, for Mr. Adlaine suddenly squatted down before her and held out his hand. "Let's have one, then."

"What?" she asked, looking at the broad palm of his hand. "My shoe?"

"Not your shoe. Your *foot*."

Grace blinked at his outstretched hand. "You cannot mean—"

"I can and I do. I happen to be quite renowned for my ability to massage feet."

"By whom?" she asked suspiciously.

He cocked a brow. "Give me your foot, Miss Holcomb, and I shall count you among my most ardent admirers." She looked again at his palm, the callus below his ring finger, the blunt cut of his nails, and felt a delicious sensation rifle through her body.

He followed her gaze and smiled charmingly. "They are clean, I assure you."

"Of course!" she cried, perhaps a little too violently. "I didn't mean—"

"We are wasting precious time, Miss Holcomb. I swore I'd pay not the slightest bit of attention to you, but the gentleman in me cannot bear to see you hobbled."

Grace glanced at the steps behind him and instantly shook her head as visions of her father coming down those steps marched across her mind's eye.

He gestured impatiently for her foot again. "You will not endure the remainder of the ball if you do not allow me to help you . . . and besides," he said, his voice dropping low, "they've all gone to supper."

"Oh." She was, she realized, alarmingly titillated by the prospect of his hands on her feet.

"Come," he said, slipping his hand around her ankle. "On my honor I will not compromise your virtue. I mean only to give you relief."

She couldn't help but look again at the stairs. She couldn't hear a blessed thing on the terrace above, as they had indeed all gone to supper. With a tentative smile, she allowed him to lift her heel up onto his thigh, which felt as hard as granite. With both hands, he began to massage her foot.

Grace instantly closed her eyes and sagged against the back of the bench. "Dear God, it's *heavenly,*" she murmured.

He chuckled low. "Remarkable for a laborer's hands if I do say so myself." He worked on her foot for a few moments before putting it down and taking up the other one.

Grace opened her eyes. "You're sinful, Mr. Adlaine. I shall not possibly be able to return to dancing now, much less look you in the eye when we next meet."

He grinned, his blue eyes piercing hers as he worked her toes. "I have no doubt you will manage to do both quite beautifully, and without the slightest hint of having fallen off your pedestal. If I may, Miss Holcomb," he continued, before she could voice her dudgeon at that remark, "have you ever considered what *you* might like to accomplish, as opposed to what your parents or society wishes you to accomplish?"

It was an odd and a rather weighty question under the circumstances, for his attention to her feet had turned her to mush. "I . . . I don't know," she answered honestly.

He dropped his gaze to her feet again. "Maybe you should think on it."

"I am not free to choose," she said lazily, admiring his long dark lashes fanned against his cheeks. "Regardless of what I may want, I may only have a life that is prescribed for me."

He glanced up again, eyeing her thoughtfully. "Do you truly believe that?"

Of course she did. But Mr. Adlaine did not understand the pressures society put on a family like hers.

"I believe that if you had a vision of what you truly desired to make you happy, you would find a way to accomplish it." His hand moved to her ankle, and up, to her calf. "And I think if you did, it would bring you immeasurable joy."

His massage of her leg was giving her immeasurable joy, but nevertheless, she insisted, "There is joy in my life, Mr. Adlaine."

"Indeed?" he drawled, looking at her skeptically as he moved his hand to her knee. "It's not entirely evident. In fact, Miss Holcomb, you seem a little . . . inflexible."

He was quite serious. She wanted to argue, but there was something in his gaze that stopped her, and his touch had turned to more of a caress. He gave her a smoldering smile, as if he knew that his touch had heated her blood.

Grace instinctively removed her leg from his grasp. "Thank you. I am much improved."

She avoided his gaze as she shoved her feet back into her shoes. When she glanced up at him again, he offered his hand to help her stand, his gaze boldly on hers, silently daring her to look away. She could no more look away than she could speak. She put her hand in his and stood. But her feet objected, and she swayed a little. Mr. Adlaine caught her with a steadying hand to her waist and held her there. His eyes were gleaming with an emotion that Grace understood, and she could not seem to move, could scarcely even breathe.

Mr. Adlaine's hand remained on her waist, and it occurred to her that she seemed to have no defenses against him, not when he was massaging her foot, not when he was touching her, not when he was looking at her with a gaze so deep as this. When he lifted his other hand and caressed her temple, Grace did not move—if anything, she shifted closer, drawn to him, completely mesmerized and titillated by what she thought he intended—what she *hoped* he intended.

His gaze flicked across her face, down her body, and up to her lips again. "Shall a miller teach you how to enjoy life?" he mused as he leaned toward her, his head dangerously close to hers, his warm breath tickling her cheek and his musky scent wrapping around her. "Or do you enjoy all those entitled men sniffing about your skirts?"

Grace could only watch as his lips descended to hers, could only feel the heat within her erupt into a full conflagration when his lips touched hers. She heard herself sigh faintly, felt herself falling toward him as if in a dream.

His hand snaked around her waist, possessively pulling her closer and pressing her body into his. The fire in Grace was suddenly raging, consuming her body and all rational thought. He cupped her cheek, his fingers splaying across her chin, angling her head, sliding down to her neck and collarbone, his thumb on the cross she always wore around her neck. Her hands gripped his muscular shoulders and she was acutely aware of the heat of his mouth on hers, his tongue probing her lips and caressing them deliciously, the iron-clad feel of his arms around her, and the feeling of lightning that struck through her veins as he kissed her so thoroughly.

She'd never felt anything like it, had never felt her heart beat so rapidly or her skin heat so quickly with only a touch. The realization that she'd never been kissed so seductively jolted her into awareness; her mistake filtered into her brain and she suddenly cried out against Mr. Adlaine's mouth while at the same time she pushed his shoulders with both hands and stepped back.

He appeared to be not the least bothered by it—he ran a palm over his head and smiled lazily. "Miss Holcomb?"

"I cannot condescend to *this*," she cried fearfully. "Dear God, what on *earth* am I doing?"

"Miss Holcomb—"

"I pray you, sir, please, do not speak!" she cried, holding up a hand. "This is . . . this is wholly and completely insupportable! I have surely lost my foolish mind!"

"Insupportable," he echoed, placing a hand on his trim waist.

She could not take her eyes from the lips that had turned her to fire. "I beg your pardon, sir, for *ever* having given you even the *slightest* indication that I . . . that I—"

"Please do not distress yourself, Miss Holcomb," he said calmly. "Sometimes, these things just . . . happen."

"Things like this do not just happen to *me*! Surely you understand that were anyone to see us, were anyone to *know*, my chances for a good match would be ruined—utterly and completely ruined!" An image of her father came to mind and she blanched. "Dear God," she said, and suddenly ran past Mr. Adlaine, forgetting how her feet had pained her, and scurried up the stairs to the terrace, and around to the servants' entrance, lest anyone see her and Mr. Adlaine appearing from the gardens.

As she hurried through the kitchen, the cook gaped at her wide-eyed. "Miss Holcomb!"

"Do not mention this to anyone, Nettie!" she cried as she hurried by. She raced around to the front of the house, pausing only to collect her wits and make certain she was in order before forcing herself to walk serenely into the dining room. Her father was near the door, of course, and the moment he saw her, he strode forward. "Where have you been?" he hissed.

"The retiring room, Papa," she said, hoping madly she didn't look as flushed as she felt.

Her father looked at her accusingly, but led her to her seat—next to Lord Prescott, of course, who proceeded to explain his worth to her. As she tried to navigate her way through that conversation, she saw Mr. Adlaine wander in, moving like a lion, casually perusing a herd of gazelles. He made a point of walking past her table, pausing to smile wickedly at her over Mrs. Bonifield's head as he sauntered by.

There it was again, that feeling of fire.

Grace did not see Mr. Adlaine after that.

But she felt him.

Lord God, she felt him long after the guests had left and she was in bed, felt every muscle in his shoulders, felt every inch of his lips, every sinew in his arms that had held her so securely to him.

Four

$\mathcal{M}$r. Barrett Adlaine could not account for what had come over him. He was not the sort of man to boldly kiss a young woman in the shadow of her father, particularly without the slightest hint of invitation. But he'd been quite unable to resist Grace Holcomb.

Frankly, he wasn't entirely certain why he was so taken with her. She was too pompous, really . . . but something had moved him. Perhaps it was her delicate feet, or the smooth skin of her leg, or the way her cheeks flushed when he teased her about marrying well.

Or perhaps Grace Holcomb's appeal was more simple than that. She was a very handsome woman—a pretty face, soft curves, satin skin, and shining hair— and he was a very basic man. In truth, he'd admired her since she'd come of age. As a child, he recalled that she was forever hanging from trees or throwing rocks with her brothers, but it seemed as if overnight one summer she'd changed, turning into a pretty, vibrant young woman.

Still, he did not know how he could forget himself so completely, and he could not disagree with her assessment—his actions could very well have plunged them into scandal. Yet Barrett could not help but take issue with the ardent way she had announced his kiss so wholly insupportable.

In spite of the fact that it *was* insupportable, her remark had left him feeling perturbed these last two weeks, unable to think clearly in the course of his day. The same question kept creeping into his head, over and over: did she find *him* so terribly insupportable?

Granted, he didn't possess a lofty title, but he was a man who had a thriving business, one that he hoped would one day rival her father's. He was well respected around Yorkshire. His father had been well known and liked in the Cloth Halls, just as his brother was now. His connections could not be linked to the *haute ton* of London—save one old friend, Lord Dewer—but in Leeds, he counted the most revered citizens among his close acquaintances.

Frankly, Miss Holcomb could do far worse than him.

In fact, Miss Holcomb had a glaring tendency, Barrett decided, to favor title and fortune over a man's character. If that was what she wanted for herself, so be it, but *he* could not esteem a woman who valued lineage and material wealth above natural compatibility and esteem. And the superior way she had of looking at him, as if she were the bloody queen of England, and he her lowly knave!

It took all of a fortnight to rid himself completely of all the bothersome thoughts about Miss Holcomb—and he was not helped in his endeavor by the frequent memory of that kiss. Of her shiny hair and glimmering brown eyes, for that matter. But he did, at last, put her out of his mind.

Until he saw her again.

The local justice of the peace, Mr. Thomas Dumont, hosted an assembly celebrating his son's purchase of a commission into the Royal Cavalry.

Barrett hadn't thought of Miss Holcomb attending, but when she appeared with her parents and two brothers, he felt his damnably traitorous heart skip a beat. She was a vision of beauty in a gold satin gown that, at least to his untrained eye, perfectly complemented her auburn hair, done up in curls and held together by a long strand of pearls. The gown showed her fine figure at its best, and on her feet, he couldn't help notice, she wore a pair of gold satin high-heeled shoes, adorned with tiny little seed pearls. And around the smooth column of her neck, against milky white skin, a simple gold cross.

Miss Holcomb didn't notice him at first. As her mother and brothers conversed with Mrs. Dumont, she moved around the room on the arm of her father, greeting various persons of note. When her father paused to greet Sir Giles, she happened to turn just so and saw Barrett standing there, gripping a glass of ale so tightly that it was a wonder it didn't shatter. She smiled—a lovely wreath of a smile, and he felt his heart take wing.

"Miss Holcomb," he said, bowing over the hand she held out to him.

"Mr. Adlaine, how good to see you."

"Adlaine!" Mr. Holcomb boomed, turning from Sir Giles. "I am surprised to see you looking so well. I saw you up to your elbows in sheep dung earlier today!"

Barrett swallowed uncomfortably at that image and glanced at Miss Holcomb, who was, he thought, smiling with amusement. So much for her fear of ever looking him in the eye. "An intolerable situation, sir. I removed myself as soon as I was able."

"It's good you've come away from the mill, sir," Mr. Holcomb said jovially. "I've oft remarked that you'll work yourself into an early grave." He took Barrett's hand and shook it vigorously. "By Jove, if hard work was capable of giving harm, you'd be dead," he blustered loudly. "Good to see you well, Adlaine. Come along, Gracie. There is someone I should like you to meet."

Grace Holcomb smiled at Barrett as her father marched her away, glancing back at him over her shoulder and giving him a tiny, helpless shrug. With that tiny shrug, all his ill feelings about her began to flit, one by one, out of his fool head.

But Mr. Holcomb kept a tight rein on his daughter that evening—Barrett couldn't get near her to speak to her. When supper was served, he was seated as far from her as was possible and next to Miss Ellington, whom he had long known to be a particular admirer of his. As Miss Ellington chatted about her delicate palate, which did not, apparently, digest haddock particularly well, he stole glimpses of Grace Holcomb. Lord Prescott was seated across from her; Mr. Grant, on her right, and both were quite attentive to her, and she to them.

After supper, the women removed themselves and the men enjoyed their cigars and brandy. Then the men joined the ladies again in a salon where two card tables had been set up, one for loo, one for whist.

"Miss Holcomb," Barrett heard Mr. Dumont say behind him, "will you partake in cards?"

He half-turned and looked at Grace.

"I've never been very good at loo, sir," she said. "It goes far too quickly for my tastes. But I do enjoy whist."

"Then we must have you play," he said.

"But I haven't a partner!" she exclaimed laughingly. "And I pray you, please do not suggest my brother Freddie, for he is frightfully impatient with the game."

Barrett turned fully around and bowed. "If you will allow it, Miss Holcomb, I should be pleased to partner with you."

"Oh!" She glanced across the room at her father. "Are

you quite certain, Mr. Adlaine? I should not like to force a partnership if there is someone else you might prefer."

"How could I possibly prefer anyone else?" he asked gallantly.

"There you have it, Miss Holcomb. You cannot refuse a man who speaks so ardently in your favor," Mr. Dumont said.

"I surely cannot," she said, and put her delicate hand on the arm Barrett offered.

They were paired with Mr. and Mrs. Crabtree, who had been married for many years and had several children. Mr. Crabtree was a rotund man with woolyworm eyebrows. Mrs. Crabtree was likewise rotund with curls as large as sausages bobbing about her ears. One might have hoped that their many years together had endeared them to one another, but that hardly seemed to be the case. Mr. Crabtree commended every card Grace laid, but found fault with everything his wife managed to do. Mrs. Crabtree huffed and puffed at Mr. Crabtree when she wasn't regaling Barrett with her husband's many faults.

"Good God, Harriet!" Mr. Crabtree exclaimed after Mrs. Crabtree had misplayed a card and Grace had taken the round, "do you *intend* for us to lose?"

"Will you *please* stop blustering so!" Mrs. Crabtree admonished. "You are not the only one among us to have played a few hands of whist in his lifetime, Mr. Crabtree—I am quite well aware of what I am doing!"

He rolled his eyes and looked at Grace. "Take care, child, of whom you marry, lest you be subjected to a disagreeable partner when you sit for cards."

"You needn't worry about Miss Holcomb," Barrett said. "She is destined to marry quite well."

Over the top of her cards, Grace gave him a withering look.

"But of *course*," Mrs. Crabtree said as she squinted at her hand. "Miss Holcomb shall marry a *great* man, for her father will never consent to anything less." She looked at Grace over the top of her cards. "You will never have cause for concern over money, my dear."

"I—" Grace started, but Mrs. Crabtree had not quite finished.

"Your father is very keen to see you married well, Miss Holcomb, and if there is a man in Yorkshire who will see it through, it is Mr. George Holcomb, mark me."

"If the character mark of a great man is determined by the size of his fortune, than Miss Holcomb must go to London, for I do not believe a *great* fortune can be found in Leeds," Barrett said, and looked at Grace, silently challenging her to disagree.

"No, of course not, not in *Leeds*," Mrs. Crabtree adamantly agreed. "Only Lord Prescott has the sort of fortune Mr. Holcomb envisions, I am sure."

"You are both far more informed of the particulars than am I," Grace said demurely, her eyes narrowed on Barrett.

"My wife is hardly privy to what Mr. Holcomb envisions," Mr. Crabtree groused, and looked at Grace. "You must forgive her, Miss Holcomb. She has far too active an imagination."

No one spoke. They played another round, which Mr. Crabtree trumped. "And what of you, Mr. Adlaine?" he said as he swept the pile of cards into a stack. "I've heard quite a lot of speculation as to when *you* will marry."

That surprised Barrett; he'd never mentioned marriage to anyone and certainly had not thought of it until very recently—he'd been too busy building his livelihood.

"Oh yes, all the unmarried ladies have their eye on a

prize such as *you*, Mr. Adlaine," Mrs. Crabtree echoed, and glanced coyly at him.

"Take my advice, sir, and don't waste your youth making your fortune, for the more you make of it, the more your future wife will spend," Mr. Crabtree said.

"On my word, I don't think of it," Barrett said, and with a subtle wink for Grace he added, "After all, I am but a man from Leeds without a very great fortune at all."

"Oh, Mr. Adlaine, there is *much* more to recommend you!" Mrs. Crabtree said, smiling sympathetically at him.

Grace snorted as she laid a card that trumped Mrs. Crabtree's, then said sweetly, "A man is not defined by his fortune alone, Mr. Adlaine. His greatness also lies in his bearing and education and the good opinion of his peers."

Barrett hid a derisive laugh behind a cough, then lifted a dubious brow.

Likewise, Grace lifted a brow over glittering brown eyes.

"I will tell you a great man who has neither fortune nor peers," Mr. Crabtree said thoughtfully. "Reverend Sloan. He has neither fortune nor peer in his part of Yorkshire, yet he is a great man."

"It must certainly derive from his bearing and education then," Barrett said low.

"Yes, well, wherever he derives it, he is not worthy of *your* consideration for matrimony, Miss Holcomb," Mrs. Crabtree said imperiously.

"Dear God," Mr. Crabtree sighed wearily. "You have not only expressed Miss Holcomb's desire to marry as if it were your own, now you have determined who she may marry!"

"I am no stranger to the desires of a young woman,

Mr. Crabtree," Mrs. Crabtree insisted. "It has not been so very long that *I* was a young and unmarried woman."

"It has been far longer for me," Mr. Crabtree muttered.

"I claim no particular desire to marry at once," Grace protested sweetly. "I would much rather have a partner who paid close attention to the card I have played than a very *great* fortune." She looked at Barrett pointedly. He, in turn, looked at the cards that had been played this round.

"You have trumped my card without a care, sir."

"On the contrary, Miss Holcomb," he said politely. "You played a queen of hearts. The king of hearts has not been laid in five rounds and, therefore, the odds were very good that Mr. or Mrs. Crabtree had that king. I was protecting your hand."

"And there you are, Mr. Adlaine, unappreciated for your ability to protect and defend a lady in every conceivable way," Mr. Crabtree sighed as he studied his hand. "You might as well be married."

"Oh, Mr. Crabtree! You've neither defended nor protected me in twenty years!" Mrs. Crabtree snapped as she laid her card.

Barrett looked across the table at Grace, who smiled prettily as she pulled a card from her hand and let go, so that it flitted to the table.

"Dear Lord, Mr. Adlaine, she has invited you to trump her again," Mr. Crabtree said, bemused.

And as Mrs. Crabtree squinted at the cards that had been played, Grace continued to smile pertly. Barrett thought he'd never seen a more mischievous or lovelier smile and felt his heart surrender to her as he trumped her yet again.

Mr. Crabtree was right. Perhaps it was time he married.

Five

G race thought of little else but Mr. Adlaine the following week—the way he'd sat so casually across from her at the whist table, watching her. Or the way a lock of his darkly golden hair dipped over one blue eye and the way his lips curved up in the corners and ended in twin dimples with his quiet smile. Or the way he held his cards in hands that were twice as broad as hers and looked as if they could break a person in two . . . *or caress her leg* . . .

The memory gave her another delightful shiver, and she privately lamented that he was merely a textile merchant, not an earl. Or a baron. Not even a baronet.

But her greatest regret was that she would return to London soon and likely would not see Mr. Adlaine again until after she'd received a viable offer of marriage. In that, her father was quite determined, particularly after she had, in a fit of tears, refused to even entertain the notion of marrying Lord Prescott.

Two days past, Papa had announced that he would send Grace back to London and Mrs. Wells, where she was to first call on Mrs. Harris and be "refreshed" in her training. Then, she was to take advantage of the Christmas season and, Grace presumed, what her father believed were scads of aristocratic bachelors moping about London in desperate want of a debutante's hand.

"I'll not have an argument, Gracie," Papa had said sternly when she'd weakly protested, knowing full well it would do no good. "You'll be two and twenty in three months' time. If we are to make a good match, we must do so before you grow too old."

"I hardly think two and twenty is too *old*, Papa."

"You are to London," he'd said firmly. "And you will listen very carefully to Mrs. Harris's instructions and you will follow them to the letter, miss. Do I make myself perfectly clear?"

"You are *always* perfectly clear," she'd said petulantly. But she was not, thankfully, completely without her powers of persuasion. Her father agreed to allow her to remain at Heslington a fortnight more, until Michaelmas, before the weather typically began to turn cold and rainy.

Two days before she was to depart for London, Grace accepted Freddie's invitation to have a drive about the countryside one afternoon. "The weather is fine, Gracie," her brother had said, eager to test his new cabriolet. "We'll not see many more days like this, I'd wager."

He was right—the day was unseasonably warm and gloriously sunny. They drove around the lake their father had stocked with pike and trout, and around the newly built pavilion that would house an orchestra of twelve next summer when the Holcombs hosted a summer day of games for the local gentry on the east lawn. And when they had toured the park thoroughly behind two young and eager horses, Freddie drove to the road that went down to the River Aire, and sent the horses running.

They would have driven all the way to the end of

the road where the Holcomb pens were located, had not a flock of wayward sheep blocked the road and caused Freddie to pull up so sharply that the carriage brake locked up. "Dammit!" Freddie cursed, and jumped down to have a look. "Bloody hell, but that doesn't look good at all," he muttered.

Ahead about a quarter of a mile was the Adlaine textile mill. As Freddie crawled beneath the carriage, muttering under his breath, Grace wondered if Barrett was at the mill. She imagined him in his office, working diligently over his accounts. She looked at Freddie—or rather, Freddie's legs—and abruptly climbed down the other side of the carriage. She squatted down, peeked beneath the carriage. "I'm going to stretch my legs a bit."

"Well for God's sake, don't wander too far. Papa will have my head if there's even a hint of dung on your hem," he groused as he inspected the brake.

For a man who'd made a fortune from sheep, her father did have a rather strong aversion to them.

Grace walked on, through sheep that scattered like a school of fish. As she neared the mill, she could see the front pens were teeming with them. It appeared that a flock had been brought in for shearing. Several men were working them, moving them through a small chute into a barn to be shorn, and out another chute into a pen where they bawled loudly for having lost their fleece.

Grace passed through a gate into an enclosed yard at the entrance to the mill, but as she reached the office door and lifted her hand to knock, he appeared around the corner of the mill. *Adlaine.*

She caught a breath in her throat—she had never seen him like this. He was wearing a shirt open to the waist, the down of chest hair glistening with the sweat that had stained his shirt. His hair was in a queue, and his shirt tucked into a pair of filthy buckskins. His boots, covered in mud and dung, rose up to his knees, and his damp, bare forearms—forearms that seemed as thick as Grace's legs—were wrapped securely around the four legs of a sheep he held securely across his shoulders.

He glanced up at the same moment Grace turned toward him, and a look of horror passed over his features. The sheep he held was bleating fiercely, struggling to free itself, but Mr. Adlaine held it as if it were a cat.

"Mr. Adlaine!"

"Miss Holcomb," he responded, his voice tight. He suddenly remembered the sheep and put it down. The poor thing bolted, bleating madly, as Adlaine wiped his hands on his thighs. "Is there something amiss?" he asked. "Is your father—"

"No, he is well," she said, unable to tear her gaze away. Despite his manner of dress, she found him to be a most stirring sight.

"Are you all right?" he asked, jolting Grace back to the present.

"Oh! Yes, thank you, I am well. Ah . . ." She glanced over her shoulder, to the road. "Freddie and I were driving, and something went wrong with the brake. I thought . . ." She gestured vaguely behind her. "I thought I would take the opportunity to tell you that some of your sheep have escaped."

"Ah," he said, nodding. "I believe Mr. Terrence is rounding them up."

"Oh. We, ah . . . we were just out for a drive," she repeated, feeling very self-conscious and foolish. "Freddie thought I might enjoy a drive before I leave for London—"

Mr. Adlaine suddenly looked up and pushed a loose strand of hair behind his ear. "To London?"

"For Christmas," she said, taking a step backward. A sheep suddenly appeared from her left, darting into the space between her and Mr. Adlaine. "My, ah . . . my father thought I would enjoy the season more were I in London."

Mr. Adlaine put a hand to his nape and rubbed it for a moment. "May I inquire as to when you are leaving?"

"Monday morning," she said, taking two more steps back. *This was madness, absolute madness!* What was she doing here? He must think her terribly forward to come here alone—or worse, *silly*.

Two more sheep trotted in between them, but Mr. Adlaine did not seem to notice; he pressed his lips together and nodded, his blue eyes full of . . . of regret? Of disappointment? Whatever it was, it confused Grace and made her feel as if she had treaded onto ice. She took another abrupt step backward and bumped up against a sheep. Suddenly, a dozen or more sheep darted between her and Mr. Adlaine, crowding into the small, fenced space, looking for an escape as even more filed in behind them.

Startled by the sheep, Grace stepped back, but almost stepped on a sheep and stumbled. Suddenly sheep were everywhere, the stupid beasts pushing at her and into the space even though there was no place to go. Just beyond the fence, there were rolling hills and a cloudless blue sky, but in the small space where Grace stood, she could hear nothing but the angry bleating of the sheep, could smell nothing but damp wool.

"Oh God," she gasped, and tried to turn around to find an escape, but it was difficult to turn at all in the midst of so many sheep. "Oh dear *God*, aren't there *pens*?" she exclaimed as she stepped on another and stumbled again.

A pair of strong hands grabbed her from behind, righting her. "Yes," he said calmly into her ear. "But you left the gate open."

"Please!" she cried helplessly, falling back against Mr. Adlaine's hard wall of a chest, "I can't bear it—I must get out of here!"

Mr. Adlaine unexpectedly bent down and swept her up in his arms. Grace cried out with surprise, but threw her arms around his neck to keep from falling into that sea of sheep. She looked up at Mr. Adlaine, who gave her a reassuring smile as he carried her past the sheep, nudging them out of his way with a well-placed boot.

His strong arms holding her securely aloft, she could feel the curve of hard muscle in his arms and shoulders as he moved with her. She could feel the extraordinary strength in his body, but more than that, she was aware of the expression in his eyes. His gaze was full of a hunger no man had ever cast at her before, and she realized that the fluttering in her belly was just that—her hunger for him.

When they reached the fence, he carefully put her down on the other side, letting her body brush against his as he lowered her legs. Grace's hands slid slowly from his neck and down the hard plane of his chest. She no longer heard or saw the bleating sheep, for all she could focus on was Mr. Adlaine.

His hands remained on her arms, his eyes moving over her face—her mouth, her hair, her eyes. With the back of his hand, he carefully brushed her cheek.

Grace unthinkingly lifted her hand to the place he had touched, certain there was a mark, for she could feel it burning even though his hand had drifted to her shoulder.

His gaze fell to her lips and Grace drew a steadying breath. Mr. Adlaine's grip on her arm tightened slightly and he bent his head.

He meant to kiss her.

He meant to kiss her!

The properly trained debutante in her mind told her to step away, but her heart told her something entirely different. She was only scarcely aware that she was lifting her face to his, preparing to be kissed . . . but from the corner of her eye, she saw Mr. Terrence and his dogs as they rounded the corner, sending a dozen sheep to the pens.

Her cowardly heart panicked. "Well," she blurted, shifting away. She was quite flustered, uncertain of what she should do or say. So she smiled. Far too brightly. "Thank you. It would seem Mr. Terrence has found the rest of the villains."

It felt as if moments passed before Mr. Adlaine could tear his gaze from her eyes and look in the direction she indicated. But when he saw Mr. Terrence, his hand fell away from her arm. "It would seem that he has," he said, and reluctantly stepped back. His gaze swept over her once more, the hunger still in his eyes. "I wish you Godspeed in your journey, Miss Holcomb." He lifted his hand as if he meant to touch her again, but it fell to the railing as Mr. Terrence passed. He waited for the man to walk farther away, his lips pressed together, as if there was something he would say. But with another glance at Mr. Terrence, he seemed to think better of it and said, "Good day, Miss Holcomb."

"Good day, Mr. Adlaine," she responded softly, and watched as he turned and strode across the yard and through the herd of sheep as if he were walking through tall grass, parting them easily, before turning the corner of the mill and disappearing from her view.

It felt a little as if she'd arrived too late at an important affair only to find the doors shut and locked. Feeling a little light-headed, Grace self-consciously glanced about before retreating quickly to Freddie's carriage.

Freddie had repaired the locked brake and was ready to return to Heslington. On the way home, he reviewed all the problems with the brake, but Grace didn't hear him because her head was swimming in confusion. In her mind's eye, she saw an image of Mr. Adlaine, a sheep tossed across his shoulders, his masculine form astonishingly evident in the buckskins and lawn shirt. And then she saw him leaning over the fence toward her, about to kiss her. These were memories that would haunt her for the rest of her life, she was certain.

Six

*O*n a wet and dreary Michaelmas afternoon, Grace was standing at the large floor-to-ceiling windows in the family salon, looking out over a rain-soaked landscape. She had been standing for a quarter of an hour, dreading her return to London and the life as an outsider in a society that would not have her.

She could not help but think of Lord Billingsley, and his public ridicule of her, or how Miss Elizabeth Robertson, whom Grace had thought was her friend, had commented in a room full of gentlemen that she could smell sheep. Grace had been mortified to the tips of her toes.

How could it possibly be any different this time? Her friend, Ava Broderick, the Marchioness of Middleton, said it was merely that Grace had met a lot of fops and dandies thus far, and not the sort of gentlemen worthy of her consideration.

She was mulling that over when her eye caught a movement on the road.

She straightened up and peered out the thick, rain-streaked glass pane. A rider was coming toward the house, bent over his horse's neck, his hat pulled down low over his eyes, his long brown cloak flapping behind him.

She knew instantly who it was and, startled, she abruptly turned from the window.

He was coming for her, to see her.

She glanced up: her family was seated around a roaring fire—her mother was sewing, her father with his nose in a newspaper. Freddie was writing someone, and Stephen was asleep on the settee. Grace did not want to see Mr. Adlaine with an audience, so with her heart pounding, she very calmly walked across the room.

"Gracie?" she heard her father call out as she quickly closed the door behind her.

She ran down the carpeted corridor to the grand staircase, then down to the marble foyer. As no one had knocked, there was no footman about, and she moved to the door, opening it just as Mr. Adlaine swung off his horse and wrapped the reins around a post.

He saw her in the doorway and with a look of great surprise, he jogged up the steps, stopping under the portico to remove his dripping hat.

"Mr. Adlaine," she said, trying very hard to keep from laughing with elation.

He bowed low. "Miss Holcomb."

"Do come in, sir," she said, stepping back.

He swept inside, unfastened the clasp of his cloak at his throat and removed it from his shoulders, draping it over one arm.

"Allow me," she said, and took the rain-soaked garment, laid it across one of two upholstered armchairs beside a console. "Have you come to call on my father?" she asked coyly as he removed his gloves.

He glanced at her as he tossed the gloves and hat on top of his cloak, his gaze raking over her face. "I did not. I have come to call on you, Miss Holcomb."

Delight filled her to the point of bursting. "How good of you to call in such wretched weather," she said, stealing a quick glimpse over her shoulder. She was in luck—no footman, no butler, not even a chambermaid in sight. "My family . . . my family is engaged," she lied, "or I would invite you into the main salon. But perhaps the green drawing room . . ." Her voice trailed off as she gestured uncertainly to the corridor on the right that led to the green drawing room, seldom used by anyone in her family. "That is, if you wouldn't mind—"

"Is it this way?" he asked, and firmly put his hand on her elbow to steer her in that direction.

Grace smiled so widely that she thought she must be making a complete ninny of herself, not to mention her absolute recklessness in accepting a gentleman's call alone. She hadn't exactly thought through how she might accomplish this without her father finding out, but at present, she could think of nothing but Adlaine's hand on her elbow.

They walked quickly across the foyer and into the corridor, to the door of the green drawing room. Mr. Adlaine reached for the handle and turned it, then pushed the door open. "After you," he said low, and gave her a gentle push.

Once inside, she hurried across the room and pulled the heavy drapes open to let in a little gray light. She heard the door shut behind her, and she suppressed a shiver of anticipation. When she turned around, Mr. Adlaine's gaze devoured the length of her.

"I confess you caught me quite unawares at the mill," he said as he moved toward her. "And I further confess that I have come here with an entirely diabolical motive."

Grace drew a steadying breath. "Should I be alarmed?"

Some emotion flicked across his features. He boldly

reached up and stroked her cheek, then let his hand fall to her collarbone and the cross she wore. "Only if you are afraid of sheep." He removed his hand, reached in his coat pocket, and withdrew a small furry thing which he held out in the palm of his hand. Grace looked down; it was a toy, a miniature sheep made of wool, with the prized black face, tiny wooden legs, and a bit of horsehair to form the tail.

"It's a lamb!" she exclaimed with delight and took it from his hand.

"We make them at the mill for children in the parish. I thought you might like to have it near you in London as a remembrance of your friends in Leeds."

London. Grace's happiness was effectively doused. "How good of you. Thank you—I will treasure it," she said hesitantly as an image of a laughing Miss Robertson flashed across her mind's eye.

"As I will treasure the few hours I've had to enjoy your company."

"Oh," she said, surprised. "*Oh.* I am flattered, but I—"

"Hush," he said, his voice drifting over her like a silken drape as he pressed the palm of his hand against the side of her neck. "You've made it perfectly clear that you are saving yourself for an exceptional match. Yet I cannot conceal my desire for you any longer."

Grace caught a breath in her throat as he drew her close. He leaned forward, touched his lips to her forehead. "Not a moment longer," he whispered, and pressed his lips to the bridge of her nose.

Grace closed her eyes and lifted her face to him, unwilling to think of the consequences, not caring for anything other than his touch. When his lips brushed hers, they singed her. But then he kissed her fully, and Grace could feel every inch of her body begin the same sort of slow burn she'd experienced that night under the arbor. It was an incredibly alluring sensation—she felt almost weightless as he slipped an arm around her back and pulled her against his body.

He'd kissed her that night in the arbor, but she did not remember it like this, not so hot, so fiery, pushing her dangerously close to the edge of reason in her father's house. When his hand pressed against her breast and covered it, the slow burn quickly turned to liquid fire.

His hand brushed the bare flesh of her bosom; then his fingers dipped into the valley between her breasts. Something erupted inside her, and the desire that swelled so monstrously began to cloud her thoughts. She sagged against him as his hand slipped inside her bodice, to the flesh of her breast, to the tip, and a dizzying charge shocked through her.

"*Grace,*" he whispered against her skin, and pressed his lips to her neck, then to the hollow of her throat, and down further still, to the mound of her breast.

Grace did nothing to stop him, just closed her eyes and let her head fall back, relishing the thrill of his hands and mouth on her body, feeling the heat of it deep in her groin.

He straightened, pushed her back until she bumped up against a piece of furniture. In a cloudy daze, she felt herself falling onto the settee, her fall stopped by his strong arm. He took her head between both hands and wildly sought her mouth with his, filling her with his kiss, twisting her around so that he was on top of her on that settee.

Grace arched into him, craving more. He moved from her mouth to her bosom, and with one hand, freed her breast from the fabric and took it into his mouth.

Grace gasped wildly and pressed her breast against

him as he sucked and nibbled her, driving her to madness. Her sex was wet and her body aroused like a sleeping dragon that was now breathing fire. Her hands flitted across his temples, his shoulders, his neck. She thrust her fingers in his hair, squeezed her legs around him and fought the abandon inside her, the thing that didn't want him to stop, didn't want him to ever stop.

Her leg rose up on one side of him, and Mr. Adlaine ravaged her breast, teething the rigid nipple while his hand slid down to her bottom and kneaded her flesh, then down her leg, to the hem of her skirt, and beneath, his hand on her calf, then higher, to the apex of her legs.

She moaned when he touched her, put her hands on his shoulder and pulled him, unthinkingly, to her body.

Mr. Adlaine looked up at her with eyes as vast as the sky. "God help me, but I cannot resist you." He rose up and roughly caught her face between his hands, caressed her hair, and looked into her eyes before kissing her once more. "But I must resist you. I will not risk your dishonor." And then he stood, took her hand and pulled her up, watched as she fit her breast back into the bodice of her gown.

"Mr. Adlaine—"

"Barrett," he said earnestly.

"Barrett," she whispered. "I . . . I don't . . ." She had no idea what to say. Her body was still burning, her heart still throbbing in her chest. She lifted her gaze to his eyes and saw such desire there that she shivered.

"I must go before we are discovered," he said, yet he made no move to walk away. He put his hand to her neck, leaned down, and nipped her bottom lip. "I must go, yet I can scarcely force myself to walk away."

She grabbed his wrist, lifted her face to him once more. "Don't go," she whispered, hardly caring that it was impossible for him to stay.

But he had a wiser head, and with a long sigh, he kissed her once more. "Good-bye, Grace," he said, and took up her hand, turned it over, and kissed the soft inside of her wrist before backing away, still watching her, his gaze raking over her as he moved to the door.

When he reached it, he opened the door slowly, glanced out in the corridor, then stepped across the threshold and walked away.

Grace put her hand to her throat, felt her pulse beating like a thousand wings in her neck. She didn't think she could make her legs move, but then she heard the front door shut.

The spark he had ignited began to fade. She moved numbly to close the drapes, and as she glanced around the room, she put her hand to her throat, a small habit . . . and noticed that her necklace was gone. She searched the room but in the dim light, she could not find the cross.

The sound of voices in a distant corridor alarmed her. With the lamb tucked carefully in the folds of the skirts, she left the room without her cross, leaving it behind with the memory of a man she most certainly would have loved had her circumstance been any different.

Seven

After a month in London, Grace was no closer to gaining an offer than she had been last Season.

Mrs. Wells fretted endlessly about it, but Grace was much more tranquil. She thought it was perhaps because her heart was not fully engaged in the process of finding a match. After all, she'd thought of little else but Mr. Adlaine since that extraordinary and illicit farewell in her family's drawing room. She thought of it every day—dreamed of it, too—and always woke wanting more. She could still feel his hands on her, could still taste his mouth . . . and every other man seemed to pale in comparison.

Unfortunately, she had to put her feelings firmly behind her, for Mr. Adlaine could not possibly be part of her future.

And she was *trying* to forget him. In the last fortnight, she had attended two supper parties, one assembly, and a soirée. At every event she had done her best to be charming and bright. And she thought she had succeeded, too, until she had occasion to attend Mrs. Harris's tea just two days past.

Mrs. Harris had reminded them all that Christmas would be upon them shortly, and it was very easy to be caught up in the spirit of the season, but that they must have a care that they not forget themselves. At the conclusion of tea, she had handed each of the graduates a sealed letter to read when they arrived home.

Mrs. Harris had written Grace a lesson of sorts, to be applied during the Christmas season with an eye toward improving her social skills, which, she said, "would require careful consideration" in the new year.

Specifically, during tea, Mrs. Harris had reminded Grace that she had, at times, been a little too trusting of other people's intentions. Of course Grace knew to what she referred—the entire *ton* knew of the mistake she'd made with Lord Billingsley, for heaven's sake.

That being said, Mrs. Harris's lesson for her, in part, read:

While your trusting nature is an asset, Grace, you must also remember that if you trust others too quickly you might be perceived as naïve, and, therefore, pliable. I caution you about giving gifts to a gentleman or receiving gifts from gentlemen during the Christmas season unless you are quite certain of their intentions. A true gentleman will not offer a gift unless he means to declare his esteem, and therefore, he deserves your serious consideration. A young lady who offers a gentleman a gift is likewise declaring her esteem, and must be certain of the gentleman's feelings. In either instance, I hope you will take a moment to reflect on your intentions, as well as the gentleman's, and not allow yourself to be persuaded by false flattery.

Grace snorted as she read the letter. *She* would never make that wretched mistake again, and as far as any gentleman giving *her* a gift, well . . . the only gift she had received was the little lamb from Mr. Adlaine, and while she was very attached to the little thing, she could hardly count it as a declaration of his esteem. Besides, Mr. Adlaine was as unattainable to her as she was to him.

Fortunately, her friend Ava, the Marchioness of Middleton, had taken it upon herself to find Grace a suitable match, as Grace had no heart for it. Ava was very determined, and arrived one afternoon to find Grace moping about.

"That's a fine face to be wearing when you are to be my guest at Lady Purnam's assembly," she said, having flounced in and arranged herself on a settee.

"Lady Purnam's assembly?" Grace echoed, having heard nothing of it.

"Saturday evening. The old bat is *desperate* to see her niece married and hopes to get a jump on next Season's competition. I told her she was quite out of her mind, for most of the very good bachelors are in the country just now enjoying their guns and dogs. I would be there, too, were it not for my darling little Jonathan," she said, referring to her fourteen-month-old son.

Grace heard only the bit about all the very good bachelors being out of town. She could not imagine the ugliness of her father's disposition if she went home with no prospects once more. Perhaps she wouldn't go home at all. Perhaps she would remain in London until she was old and wrinkled and—

"Grace!" Ava cried, thwacking her on the knee with her hand. "Have you heard a word I've said?" At Grace's blank look, Ava rolled her eyes and scooted closer. "I *said*, dearest, that Sir William of Gosford is in town and will attend Lady Purnam's assembly."

Grace supposed she had heard that in the distant background, and nodded.

"You still do not take my meaning!" Ava complained. "Have you any idea who is Sir William?"

When Grace shook her head no, Ava cried, "Oh, you're *quite* hopeless! He is frightfully handsome and a very brave man—he fought at Waterloo, you know, and distinguished himself there very well indeed. He's been abroad this last year, but he has returned, and he is *quite* unmarried in spite of having five thousand pounds a year. I dare say there is not another bachelor of his consequence, and moreover, he is to be made Baron of Gosford this spring by order of the king."

"Baron?" Grace asked, perking up. That would meet one of her father's requirements, and certainly, five thousand pounds a year would meet the other. "He won't care for my family's occupation," she said solemnly.

"Nonsense," Ava said. "That's ridiculous. Mary Franklin's father was a tea merchant and *she* married an earl!"

"Tea is better than sheep."

"That's silly!" Ava cried. "A trade is a trade. Now Grace, you just haven't been introduced to the right nobleman as yet. Sir William is a perfect match."

"*Frightfully* handsome, did you say?" Grace asked, to which Ava beamed with conspiratorial pleasure.

Eight

$\mathcal{L}$ady Purnam's assembly was a glittering display of wealth, and her poor niece, fresh from Devonshire, stood about all evening with her eyes as wide as moons. Apparently, the girl had never been to London or a high-society assembly.

One might think Grace hadn't either, judging by the way Ava and Lady Purnam—the self-proclaimed matron of society—eyed her so critically in a small room off the foyer before allowing her to enter the ballroom. She was wearing the latest fashion from Paris—a green and white striped silk, embroidered with tiny rosebuds along the hem and sleeves that matched the embroidery on her shoes.

"It is a lovely gown," Lady Purnam said, frowning, "but far too much jewelry. Rather reminds one of the crown jewels. Here," she said, sticking out her hand. "The bracelet. And the earrings."

"My jewelry?" Grace echoed in dismay.

"It's really overdone," Lady Purnam said, and it was clear she would brook no argument. Grace reluctantly removed the offending pieces and watched as Lady Purnam slipped the items into Grace's reticule, then stood back and studied her again.

"Well?" asked Ava.

"Yes," Lady Purnam said with a nod. "I think we've

done it. Now dear," she said sternly to Grace, "you must remember that young ladies should not mention their father is in trade unless—"

"Lady Purnam!" Ava cried.

"What?" Lady Purnam asked, wide-eyed. "She really *shouldn't.*"

"Yes, madam, I am very much aware," Grace said with a sigh as Ava ushered her out.

But she had nothing to fear with Sir William. He was, just as Ava said he would be, quite charming. Tall, with dark hair and brown eyes, and an easy smile, he wore his Knight of the Garter badge proudly on his chest. Moreover, he seemed to be taken with Grace. "Had I known such a flower existed among the reeds in London, I should have returned even sooner," he said after Ava had encouraged the two of them to enjoy a glass of wine with each other.

"How poetic, sir," Grace said, beaming.

They talked at length—Sir William had just returned from Paris and had thoroughly enjoyed his stay. He asked her about her family and she told him what she could without mentioning any sort of trade, and he politely did not inquire.

When supper was served, Ava managed to have Grace seated with Sir William so that they might continue their conversation. She found Sir William to be exceedingly agreeable and a perfect gentleman. She detected no artifice in him, and thought that of all the men she'd met in London thus far, for the first time, she had a glimmer of hope for something more. Sir William seemed to enjoy her company, too, and Grace was certain that with a proper bit of courting, she could come to esteem him greatly.

When Ava came to fetch her so that they might leave for the evening—"I cannot bear to be away from my son for very long, Sir William," she said apologetically—he bowed gallantly over Ava's hand.

"I would never stand in the say of a mother's yearning," he said, and let go Ava's hand. "But I shall lose my good companion." He gave Grace a winsome smile. "I will only bear the loss if she will consent to allowing me to call on her in the very near future."

Grace tried to be demure about it, but Ava beamed a smile so broad that it was impossible for Sir William not to see how pleased she was.

"I should like that very much," Grace said, with a not-so-subtle kick of Ava's ankle.

"I shall meet you in the foyer," Ava said, with a sly smile for Grace. "I must first bid our hostess good night."

"I shall see you to the door, Miss Holcomb, if you will allow it," he said, offering his arm.

She happily allowed him. When they reached the foyer, he hesitated; his smile faded a little as he turned to look at her. "Miss Holcomb, if I may be so bold . . . I cannot recall a time I have enjoyed another's company so. I really must thank you for a resplendent evening."

She could feel herself coloring at his earnestness and smiled. "You are too kind. I, too, have had a pleasant evening."

"Splendid," he said, his winsome smile returning. "I'll fetch your cloak."

"Thank you. It's blue," she said, and watched him stride away, the smile still on her face. When he had disappeared into the cloak room, she sighed and turned toward the door—and her heart lurched in her chest.

Mr. Adlaine was standing there, watching her. *How could it be?* She was so surprised, so shocked, that she could not find her tongue. He, however, did not seem shocked in the least, and regarded her coolly.

"Mr. Adlaine!" she exclaimed. "You startled me!"

"I gathered as much," he said quietly.

She had in her mind that he had somehow entered the residence without invitation—how else could he *possibly* be at Lady Purnam's? She glanced over her shoulder to see if anyone else had seen him. "What are you doing here?" she whispered frantically.

He stepped forward to take her hand, and Grace stupidly, unthinkingly, stepped back, away from him, and saw the injury skate across his features.

His hand clenched at his side. "I am enjoying an assembly, of course. Perhaps not as well as you."

"What if Lady Purnam should see you?"

One dark brow rose. "Lady Purnam *has* seen me," he said. "Do you think you are the only one from Leeds capable of gaining an invitation?"

She opened her mouth, then shut it, as those words filtered into her frantic brain. He smiled, but it was not a particularly pleasant smile. "Apparently, you thought precisely that."

"No, I . . . I thought—" She didn't like his hard expression at all and swallowed uncomfortably. "I am just surprised to see you. I had not idea that you—"

"Lord Dewar!"

That was Ava calling out behind her, and Grace quickly turned away from Barrett Adlaine, her mind racing ahead to how she might possibly introduce him to Ava.

"Lord Dewar, I've not seen you in *ages*," Ava was saying happily to a tall man who stood to the left of Barrett.

"I've been in Scotland," he responded, just as Sir William returned, holding Grace's blue cloak.

"Lady Middleton, may I introduce my good friend, Mr. Barrett Adlaine," the man said, and gestured to Barrett, who stepped away from Grace.

"Mr. Adlaine, it is my pleasure." Ava smiled and extended her hand, which Barrett took.

"The pleasure is mine, my lady."

"Lord Dewar, have you met Miss Holcomb?" Ava asked, putting her hand on Grace's elbow.

"I have not."

Her face flaming, Grace curtsied. "A pleasure, my lord."

"Mr. Adlaine—"

"Happily, we are acquainted," Barrett said quickly, his eyes on Grace, his expression inscrutable. "We both hail from Leeds."

"Oh!" Ava exclaimed, looking at Grace, then at Barrett, then at Grace again. "What a lovely surprise! Now I know *two* people from Leeds. Then please allow me to introduce Sir William of Gosford, soon to be Lord Gosford."

"You will bore them with such detail, Lady Middleton," Sir William said easily as he greeted the two men.

"Surely *you* are not leaving, Lady Middleton. Adlaine and I have only just arrived," Lord Dewar said as Sir William moved to place Grace's cloak around her shoulders. Barrett's gaze darkened; Grace dropped her gaze to the floor.

With a laugh, Ava playfully tapped him on the arm. "You know very well that I am an old married lady now, sir, and one with a beautiful baby boy from whom I cannot be parted for long. Miss Holcomb and I must bid you adieu."

"A pity," Dewer said, and some other platitude that Grace did not hear, for her mind was completely muddled—one moment she'd been smiling at Sir William, thinking that perhaps something might come of their acquaintance, and the next she was trying to understand what Barrett Adlaine was doing here, in a fine salon in Mayfair, so far from his sheep and his mill and his . . . his *place*. And by invitation, no less!

She peeked up at him, but Barrett hardly spared her a glance at all—he looked past her.

"Grace? Shall we?" Ava asked, and Grace dragged her gaze from Barrett to Ava.

Sir William smiled easily and bowed again. "I shall see you soon, Miss Holcomb."

"Thank you." She shifted her gaze to Lord Dewer. "My lord." She looked at Barrett again, but he had stepped away, was speaking with another gentleman.

"Good evening kind sirs!" Ava trilled and stepped in behind Grace, pushing her along.

Together, they walked through the double-door entry, down the steps behind a footman who held a lantern up to light their path, and into the Middleton carriage. It wasn't until they were safely inside that Ava squealed and squeezed Grace's knee. "I cannot *bear* it another moment! What happened? He's quite lovely and handsome and you cannot leave out a *single* detail, or I shall be crushed!"

"Nothing happened!" Grace cried, horrified that her expression had shown so much. "Mr. Adlaine is from Leeds, and my father has some business with him, nothing more. I can hardly claim to know him even a little!"

Ava blinked. A slow grin spread her lips as she leaned back against the squabs and folded her arms. "I was speaking of Sir William, darling, not Mr. Adlaine. Apparently you have much *more* to tell."

Grace began to shake her head, but Ava laughed and sat up, putting her hands on Grace's knees. "Do not leave out a *single* detail, do you hear?" she demanded, and Grace groaned in resignation.

Nine

$\mathscr{B}$arrett awoke the next morning to a throbbing headache, brought on not by drink as he might have hoped, but by a sleepless night in which his dreams had burned with the image of Grace smiling at Sir William, her brown eyes sparkling with delight.

What had he expected, for Chrissakes?

Did she love Sir William?

When he'd seen them standing so closely together, smiling so intimately in that way lovers had of looking at one another, he'd felt as if he'd been kicked in the stomach and had the breath knocked clean from his lungs. He could not look away, could not help but gape and wonder if she loved Sir William.

How long had she known him? Was it an affair continued from the summer or something new altogether? What did they say? Did they whisper their declarations of esteem to each other?

Barrett could not help but wonder if Grace ever thought of him, the man who had kissed her, touched her, held her, adored her in Leeds?

He'd been a fool to come—she was clearly immune to the passion they'd ignited in Leeds. In fact, she'd seemed embarrassed to see him and fearful of her association with him, a lowly merchant from Leeds.

Yet it was nonetheless excruciating, for he'd thought of little else but Grace since she'd left Leeds. Of course he'd tried to convince himself that it was lunacy to pursue this—Grace had been quite clear that she was to marry a titled man with far greater riches than Barrett might ever hope to achieve—but he could not stop thinking of her, or the way her hair shimmered in the light, or the delicate curve of her neck into her shoulder, or her laugh. Or her *smile*.

He'd never been as captivated by a woman as he had been that rainy Michaelmas Day in her drawing room, enchanted and bewitched by her kiss and her smile, and desperately wanting more of her.

So desperately that he was enticed to leave his mill in his brother's hands so he could follow her to London with a hope of love. His brother had scoffed at his romantic notions. "Grace Holcomb?" he'd said, clearly surprised. "Are you mad?"

Yes, he was mad, mad enough to hope. And foolishly, he'd not counted on there being another man. How could he not have contemplated it? What man could look at Grace and not want her? She was vibrant and beautiful and witty and charming—of course she would have suitors in London, and he'd not be surprised if there were squads of them, giving Grace the dilemma of who to choose.

Barrett's only regret was that he hadn't spoken of his feelings for her that day in her drawing room, had let her leave for London without knowing. That mistake had cost him—dearly, perhaps. He'd let her get away and walk into the arms of another man who loved her.

He got up as the day dawned, splashed ice-cold water on his face. He had determined, after a sleepless night, that he would not disturb her further, but that he'd not make the same mistake twice—he would tell her how he felt before returning to Leeds.

Barrett arrived at fashionable Upper Seymour Street and stood across the square a moment to take in the house. Mr. Holcomb had bragged about leasing it, mentioning the stonework on the façade of the house—which included some very artful carvings of lions and whatnot that crawled about the corners and above the door. The house was as large as Holcomb claimed—big and garish, it took up half a city block and looked out over Portman Square.

But then again, Mr. Holcomb was not the sort of man to enjoy his wealth quietly.

As Barrett stood taking in the house, the front door suddenly opened, and Sir William stepped outside, donned his hat, jogged down the steps to the street, and struck out purposefully to the north.

Barrett watched his rival until he could no longer see him, then glanced back at the two great oak doors that served as the main entrance to the house. Determined to say his piece, he strode across the street, took the steps two and three at a time, lifted the knocker and let it fall twice.

A footman opened the door in a matter of moments, his livery so red that he reminded Barrett of a ripe tomato. He bowed low. "Good afternoon, sir," he said, and extended a heavy silver tray for his card.

"Mr. Adlaine calling for Miss Holcomb," he said, dropping his card into the tray.

"Very good, sir. If you would be so kind as to step inside."

He followed the footman into a foyer so large and deep that at first glance, it seemed more appropriate for a place of business than a residence. Barrett half-expected to see dozens of clerks emerging at any moment. The décor, however, was not business-like at all. The walls were painted a vibrant blue. Papier-mâché columns on the walls rose up and gave the illusion of supporting a domed ceiling on which was painted a scene of dozens of cherubs on clouds. Barrett had a fine business, was steadily building his fortune and his future . . . but he had nothing that could compete with this.

"If you please sir," the footman said from his right, startling Barrett. "Miss Holcomb will receive you in the yellow sitting room."

As he fell behind the footman, he reviewed in his mind precisely what he would say. At a polished oak door, the footman rapped softly and opened the door. "Mr. Adlaine," he said, bowing low, and stepped aside so that Barrett could enter.

As Barrett walked across the threshold, his gaze immediately went to Grace. She looked resplendent in a white frothy dress suitable for tea, her hair braided and hanging over one shoulder. She smiled beguilingly as he entered, and he thought, in that moment before her warden accosted him, that Grace was happy to see him.

In stark contrast, however, her warden, or chaperone, was not the least bit happy to see him. She stepped between him and Grace, her thin lips turned down with her displeasure, her thin hands clasped so tightly before her that he feared she might snap a bone. "You ought not to have come, sir!" she proclaimed. "No good can come of it, you must know!"

"I beg your pardon?"

"Mrs. Wells!" Grace exclaimed, her voice full of mortification. "Please allow me to at least *introduce* Mr. Adlaine!"

"No introduction is necessary," the woman said haughtily. "I know who he is and what he wants."

"I beg your pardon, madam, but how is that possible?" he asked, trying to be polite. "We have never met."

She peered up at him with little blue eyes. "Miss Holcomb informed me who you are."

He looked at Grace, whose cheeks were stained pink with embarrassment. "He is my *friend*, Mrs. Wells."

"Is he, indeed? Your friend all the way from Leeds at this time of year? Your father will be very displeased," Mrs. Wells said to Grace. "*Very* displeased."

"Why in God's name should he be displeased?" Barrett demanded. "I've a good relationship with the man—I've bought enough of his bloody sheep to at least warrant a call on his daughter while I am in London!"

"You seek above yourself, sir," the woman said.

"*Mrs. Wells!*" Grace exclaimed. "That is *quite* enough!" She hurried forward, put her hand on Barrett's arm. "Do come in, sir," she said, drawing his attention from her keeper. "I confess to being quite startled last evening—I had not known you were in London!"

"Yes," he said, with a wary look at Mrs. Wells, who looked as if she might possibly be brandishing a bludgeon behind her back. "I did not know I would be in London when last we met."

"Then you've come on business?" she asked, gesturing to a chair.

"Of a sort," he answered honestly, and focused his attention on Grace, who instantly warmed him with her smile.

Grace and Mrs. Wells sat. So did Barrett. As he'd not

made many formal calls on ladies in his life—actually, none—he felt uncomfortable and out of place, and chafed in the presence of Mrs. Wells, who continued to glare at him. He wanted to speak with Grace, to ask how she was, how she found London. If she loved Sir William, if she'd loved him for very long.

"How long do you intend to be in London?" Mrs. Wells asked.

"I am leaving on the morrow."

"*Oh,*" Grace said, her smile fading as Mrs. Wells smiled for the first time. "Where are you staying, Mr. Adlaine?" Grace asked.

"With my friend, Lord Dewar."

Mrs. Wells's thin brows rose almost to her hairline with her surprise. "*You* are acquainted with Lord Dewar?"

He really had the urge to roll the old crone in a carpet and toss her out the window. "We've been good friends since we were schoolmates," he said tightly.

"Indeed?" Mrs. Wells exclaimed and exchanged a glance with Grace. "Schooled with Lord Dewar!" She was, apparently, quite impressed and surprised by his connection.

"How have you found London?" Grace asked.

He looked at her big brown eyes, the tiny curls of auburn hair at her temples. He noticed she was fidgeting with the sash of her gown a little, and that she was not wearing the gold cross. "I despaired it would be dreadfully dull after the Season, but as it happens, there are still quite a few people in town," she added.

He nodded for lack of anything to say, and self-consciously put his hands on his knees.

Mrs. Wells looked at him expectantly, and he supposed it was his turn to say something trite. He glanced at the window, saw the sunshine that would soon fade with dusk. "The weather is unusually warm in town for this time of year," he said, his hands clenching his knees. He looked at Grace again. "Perhaps we might walk in the square and avail ourselves of the sun before it disappears."

"I would like that very much," Grace said, coming instantly to her feet, surprising him and, judging by the way her jaw slacked, Mrs. Wells, too.

"Miss Holcomb, I am not dressed to go out," Mrs. Wells protested.

"Then I shall ask a footman to attend us," Grace said, her eyes on Barrett.

He, too, quickly gained his feet.

"A footman! That is hardly proper!" Mrs. Wells protested.

"I'll just fetch a cloak," Grace said, ignoring her.

Barrett realized Grace was making an escape from Mrs. Wells, and for that, he was grateful. The old crone was clearly horrified that Grace meant to go out with him into the wild outdoors, chaperoned by a mere footman. "It was a pleasure to make your acquaintance," he said curtly, and walked to the door, reaching it just ahead of Grace.

"Oh, Grace, your father will be *most* unhappy!" Mrs. Wells cried as she, too, gained her feet.

"Don't be silly! Mr. Adlaine hardly means to kidnap me," Grace sang out, and fairly flew down the stairs, the tiny heels of her slippers clicking staccato against the marble.

In the foyer, Grace grabbed a cloak from a cloak tree and yanked a bellpull. Another man in the red tomato livery appeared, bowing low.

"Richard," she said breathlessly, "send Daniel out to the square to have a walkabout with Mr. Adlaine and myself, will you?"

"*Daniel*, miss?" the footman asked uncertainly.

"Yes, yes, Daniel!" she said, shooing him along. "And do please be quick about it!"

The footman bowed and walked quickly in the opposite direction. Barrett grabbed the cloak from Grace's hand and draped it over her shoulders just as Mrs. Wells appeared on the landing above them. She leaned over the railing and called down, "Miss Holcomb, please wait! I shall join you shortly—"

"That's quite all right, Mrs. Wells!" Grace called up just as an old footman, his wig askew, walked a little crookedly into the foyer.

"Daniel! Oh, Grace, that will not do!" Mrs. Wells cried upon seeing him. "That poor man can barely see or hear! He could be crushed by a carriage trying to cross the street!"

"I shall keep a vigilant eye on him!"

In the meantime, the old footman bowed so low that Barrett feared his wig would fall off, then rose and said, "I am at your service, Miss Holcomb."

"Thank you, Daniel," Grace said kindly. "We just mean to walk in the square, and Mrs. Wells is not dressed. Would you mind?"

The footman responded by lurching to the door and pulling it open. Grace grabbed a bonnet and she and Barrett followed him.

"*Miss Holcomb!*" Mrs. Wells shrieked behind them.

But they had escaped, had made it to the bottom of the steps and onto the street with the footman inching along behind them.

On the street, Grace lifted her face to the sun with a sigh of relief, then smiled brilliantly at Barrett. "I am so glad you have come, Mr. Adlaine. I have been desperate to be out of the house all day." She gave him a playful frown. "But I should be cross with you for not telling me you'd be in London."

"It was . . . unplanned," he said, and put his hand on her elbow to guide her across the street.

In the square, they slowed their pace so they wouldn't lose Daniel completely, and walked side by side toward a round arbor in the middle of the square. Barrett didn't know what to say now—his mind was racing through the various things he'd intended to say, all of which seemed inappropriate now.

"I am very pleased to see you," Grace said guardedly. "I hadn't expected it."

He smiled sparingly. "I had not . . ." He paused, searching for the right words. "Miss Holcomb . . . *Grace*," he said, despising how uncertain and boyish he seemed at the moment. He clasped his hands tightly behind his back. "I have thought quite a lot about you."

She smiled up at him. "And I you," she said, and shyly shifted her gaze to the path before them.

He sighed, feeling a bit beefheaded. He had never proclaimed his esteem or admiration for a woman, and wished he'd thought to bring something, a bouquet of flowers, perhaps. Anything to bolster his flagging confidence. He glanced over his shoulder, noticed that Daniel had taken a seat on a wrought-iron bench.

"If I may inquire," he said tentatively, shifting his gaze to Grace again. "Is Sir William a particular friend?"

Grace blinked. A moment passed before she shrugged a little and looked at the vines over which she was trailing her fingers. Barrett imagined her walking along the rose garden of his house—his very small manor house—trailing her fingers against the rose blooms.

"He is a friend," she said at last.

Neither of them spoke.

They were nearing the arbor, and as it was late in the day and a chill was settling around London, most people had gone indoors. With the exception of Daniel somewhere behind them and one or two men striding through the square, they were almost alone. They said nothing more until they reached the arbor, at which point Barrett quite lost his mind, or found his courage—he really had no idea which. "Grace," he said, stopping in the path. "There is something I must tell you."

"Is something wrong, Mr. Adlaine?" she asked, her gaze dropping to his lips.

"No," he said. "Not . . . *wrong*, precisely, but . . ." Really, he could scarcely think with her looking at his lips. "I came to London to see you," he admitted. "I've no other business in town but that."

Grace blinked. "Oh," she said, and suddenly flashed a lovely smile that spurred him on.

"I must be mad," he said, studying her face, soaking up her image to hold in his mind's eye. In the waning light of day, her skin had the rich luster of pearls. "I understand quite well that you have come to London with a purpose." Her lips . . . Barrett was assaulted with the memory of those lips. He impulsively reached out to touch the column of her neck. "Yes, I am quite mad, I fear."

"For wanting to see me?"

He smiled a little, caressed the hollow of her throat, the soft patch of skin where the cross should have been resting. "For wanting you at all."

She looked up at him with big brown eyes that reflected the desire he felt, desire he should not feel, desire that would not be sated. He should not touch her, should not kiss those lips, for it would only torture him. He should not gaze at her so longingly, or want to feel the weight of her bare breast in his hand. Yet he could not seem to drop his hand, to look away, to regain his senses. He was mesmerized by her, his heart and mind seized by her and this single moment beneath an arbor in a public square in the middle of London.

"If you are mad, then so must I be," she said, and leaned into him, placing her slender hand on his chest as she rose up on her toes, and brushed her lips against his, settling lightly on his bottom lip, scarcely touching him but clinging to him all at once.

Whether it was her boldness or the erotic simplicity of that kiss, it electrified Barrett. His male instincts rapidly took hold—he wrapped a strong arm around her waist, pulling her into his chest and returning her kiss with one that was more intense and urgent and filled with a man's longing.

His tongue swept boldly and possessively into her mouth, drinking her in. Grace's hands moved up around his neck; her tongue darted out to tangle with his. When he dragged his mouth to her ear, she kissed his eye, his temple; her hands ran down his arms, across his chest.

He heard her sigh, felt the grip of her fingers on his arm. With her body pressed against his, every delicious inch of it, he put his hand against the side of her breast, then over it, squeezing it, and Grace sighed long and deep, put her hand against his cheek, her fingers against his lips. "*Barrett,*" she whispered.

It took him a moment to regain his senses; he focused on the feel of her fingers as they drifted across his lips, forced himself to remember who and where he was, and forced himself to drop his hands.

Grace's eyes were closed, but she was smiling softly as her hand drifted away from him. When she at last opened her eyes, her smile turned brilliant. "I am happy you've come to London."

She could not possibly have been happier than he was at that moment. He reached for her hand, brought it to his mouth, kissed her knuckles, his gaze steady on hers. But then he heard a man clear his throat.

Daniel. They'd forgotten about Daniel. Barrett turned and saw the old man standing just outside the arbor, looking very uncomfortable.

"Oh," Grace said, withdrawing from Barrett and fidgeting with her cloak. "Thank you, Daniel," she muttered.

"We'd best return before you take cold," Barrett said.

"Very good, sir," Daniel said, and began walking back the way they had come.

Barrett glanced at Grace, who put a hand over her mouth to suppress her laughter, and as they walked back to the huge house on Upper Seymour Street, they laughed together like lovers.

Ten

*T*he next two weeks went by so quickly for Grace that the days and events blurred together. It was remarkable—after suffering through two Seasons in London with only a handful of gentleman callers, she was suddenly juggling two full courtships.

Mrs. Wells was enthralled with Sir William's attentions, which were, Grace had to admit, charmingly persuasive. He said all the proper things, was very solicitous of her, and was a perfect gentleman. Grace truly admired him; under any other circumstance, she could see herself married to him and presiding as mistress over Gosford Hall, which, her friend Ava had pointed out, was quite large and quite grand.

But while she admired Sir William, when she saw him, she did not experience the shock of excitement she felt each time she saw Barrett Adlaine. When she saw *him*, her world erupted in a cascade of stars.

Unfortunately, Grace did not see Barrett as often as she saw Sir William, for Mrs. Wells made sure invitations for tea or supper or walking in Hyde Park were extended to Sir William. She made equally sure none were extended to Mr. Adlaine.

Mrs. Wells worked tirelessly to keep Grace away from Mr. Adlaine, and had probably written numerous letters to her father relaying her diligent work on his behalf. But Grace was too clever for her keeper, and arranged, through written messages exchanged with the help of pliable servants—namely her maid, Betty—to meet Mr. Adlaine in public venues such as the zoo, museums, and once, Westminster Abbey.

If Barrett was offended by the fact he never received a proper invitation to her house, he gave no indication. And really, Grace preferred it this way, for she and Barrett saw a lot of London as a result. But it wasn't until word began to spread throughout the *ton* and *les on-dit* in the newspapers that Sir William intended to offer for Grace Holcomb (with commentary as to how shocking that was, given that Grace's father was in trade) that Grace confided in Ava.

At first, Ava was titillated by the prospect of two suitors: she was the last person to argue that a woman should not receive the attention of as many men as she might attract, for she'd gained quite a reputation for precisely that before her marriage. But as time went on, Ava seemed to lose her enthusiasm for the dual courtship.

"What do you mean to do?" Ava demanded one day upon seeing Grace's flushed cheeks and bright eyes. "You cannot allow Mr. Adlaine's courtship if you are to accept Sir William's offer!"

Grace shrugged. "Sir William has not offered, so therefore I see no reason I cannot accept the attentions of both men."

"But what shall you do when Sir William offers? For he *will* offer, Grace. It is all but assured."

Grace wondered how Ava could possibly be so certain that an offer was *assured*. "I don't know," she answered honestly as the very thought of having to give up Mr. Adlaine sobered her. "The truth is . . ." Her voice trailed off—did she even *know* the truth? She was fond of both men, but in vastly different ways.

"The truth is?" Ava prompted her.

Grace looked at her friend and groaned unhappily. "Heaven help me, Ava, but I don't know the truth! On the one hand, Sir William is everything for which my family has hoped. He's kind, he's a gentleman, and soon he will be made a lord. Yet on the other hand, there is Mr. Adlaine, who is . . . is witty," she said hesitantly. "And handsome. And *quite* strong, and really, he's very skilled with textile mills."

"*Mills?*" Ava repeated.

"Yes, mills! He's built one practically from the floor up, and it's very successful!"

"I'm certain that it is," Ava said with a frown. "But it is a *mill*, dearest."

At Grace's look of surprise, Ava sighed and shook her head. "Please don't misunderstand me, Grace. I think it a perfectly fine occupation . . . but your family has desired a match with a titled man who has no need of work to provide his living. Your Mr. Adlaine is the very opposite of that."

"I hardly need reminding," Grace said morosely. Honestly, there wasn't a day that passed she didn't think of it. She'd lost sleep from thinking of it.

"You are being unfair to both men," Ava continued.

With a roll of her eyes, Grace plucked at the upholstery and asked, "What is fair about making a match?"

But she understood Ava's point, and in fact, Ava had only spoken aloud a dilemma that had been playing deep in Grace's heart and mind.

That dilemma was not eased as Christmas neared. Sir William became more attentive and solicitous, and one afternoon, in her parlor with Mrs. Wells close by, pretending not to hang on every word—but almost falling off her seat as she strained to hear what was being said—Sir William said low, "There is something I should like to give you when we next meet."

"Oh?" Grace asked, raising a brow.

He smiled, put his hand over hers and squeezed affectionately. He never took liberties with her, never touched more than her hand. Barrett, however, touched her far more than was decent, but God help her, she enjoyed the caress of that man's hand—it stoked a fire in her, one that always seemed to burn dangerously out of control.

"It is a surprise. Would you allow me to call the day after the morrow before Montgomery's Christmas assembly?" Sir William asked, referring to the annual assembly Lord and Lady Montgomery hosted to usher in the Christmas season.

From the corner of her eye, Grace caught sight of Mrs. Wells turning partially toward them, the smile on her face bright with anticipation.

But a knot was forming in Grace's belly. "The Montgomery assembly?"

Sir William chuckled. "You are toying with me, Miss Holcomb. I know very well you have been invited. If you will allow it, I should be very pleased to escort you."

Something to give her? He desired to escort her? Why, that would certainly give the entire *ton* the impression that he intended to offer for her. Grace should have been elated. But she wasn't. She was mortified. Panicked. Feeling like a cornered fox with no place to run. "Oh," she said, trying very hard not to squirm. "How very kind."

Sir William looked a little surprised by her vague response. Mrs. Wells, however, turned fully toward Sir William with her ridiculous beaming grin and said, "She would be *delighted*, sir."

Sir William looked questioningly at Grace. "Of course, I am," she said instantly, forcing a smile. She hated herself for being so weak, for allowing her father, through Mrs. Wells, to dictate the course of her life for even a moment, much less for all the days to come. Yet she remained perfectly polite and docile, just as she had been trained from the cradle to do.

But inside, she was churning—her mind was racing, plotting how she might escape this room and these two smiling faces, how she might run as far and as fast as she could from what had been destined to be her fate since she could remember: marrying a man of wealth and title, all to legitimize her father's status.

Sir William seemed to notice her discomfort, because he politely squeezed her hand again. "Miss Holcomb?"

"I should be delighted," she said again. "But if you will excuse me, sir . . . I have a bit of a headache."

"Of course," he said instantly, and gained his feet. He was a gentleman and perfect for her, absolutely perfect. But as Grace walked out of the room, nothing felt even remotely perfect.

Eleven

$\mathcal{B}$arrett paced the floor of Dewar's salon the morning of the Montgomery assembly, anxiously awaiting a reply to the note he'd sent to Grace. Dewar, who had earlier proclaimed he'd never known Adlaine to be the sort easily smitten, laughed at his old friend behind the newspaper he was reading.

"What?" Barrett demanded.

Dewar lowered the paper. "Nothing at all . . . other than you quite remind me of a colt who can scarcely wait to be let out of his pen and given his head."

Barrett scowled and walked to the window, peering down the street for any sign of Betty, their courier of choice.

"One would think a man as anxious as you appear to be might give in to his feelings and ask for the woman's hand," Dewar added.

Barrett shot a look over his shoulder at Dewar, but he'd raised the paper again . . . although Barrett guessed, from the way the paper shook, that he was enjoying another laugh at his expense.

Damn Dewar. Damn the world. He couldn't help how he felt about Grace Holcomb. He couldn't help that he thought of nothing but her, went to sleep with her smile in his mind's eye and spent most of his waking moments remembering her scent, the satin feel of her skin, the way she laughed and walked and spoke.

Dewar was right, of course—a man this besotted should certainly offer, and there was nothing Barrett wanted more. Yet there was something that held him back, nothing more than a feeling, really—but a general malaise, a disquiet in him that arose from an uncertainty he could not seem to put down. He and Grace had not spoken of his intention. Her reason for being in London was quite clear to him, but surely, he thought, she had since changed her mind. How could she not? How could she not feel and want the same thing he did?

He caught sight of Betty trudging down the lane. He quit the room and his chuckling friend to meet her.

It was a cold and blustery afternoon, but nonetheless, Barrett strode through Cumberland Gate at Hyde Park, where Grace had agreed to meet him, and saw her standing to one side. He instantly felt his heart lift.

"You are blue," he said with alarm. "I should see you home."

"No, no," she said, smiling. "Let us walk. That shall warm me."

As they walked, they talked like old friends—sometimes it seemed to Barrett that he'd always known Grace, perhaps as well as he'd known himself. They took a path that wound around to a small rose garden, built around an old observatory tower that had been closed off to the public. There were no roses to admire—it was too cold for the blooms. But neither of them minded the chill or the lack of foliage, as long as they had one another's company.

As they wandered around, they came to the door of the old observation tower. Grace paused, tilted her head back, and looked up to the top, about five stories high. "Why is it closed, do you suppose?"

"A precaution, I would assume. It is an old structure and perhaps it is not sound."

Grace gave him a sidelong look. "Would you like to see London from the top of the world?"

He smiled conspiratorially. "Miss Holcomb, do you entice me to lawlessness?"

"Why, Mr. Adlaine, surely that is not *all* to which I entice you," she said, and with a saucy smile, she moved to the tower's door.

The door was locked, but Barrett was able to jiggle the lock with a stick and open it. Laughing like two mischievous children, they stepped inside the dark entry to the tower and closed the door. It was musty; cobwebs stretched between the stair bracings. The only light filtered in the small portal windows that followed the curving staircase up to the observation platform. At each floor, there was a small landing and two side-by-side portal windows. After Barrett had tested the stairs and proclaimed them sound, they walked up, pausing at each portal, their heads together, peering out.

At the second floor, Grace rose up on her toes and pressed her nose to the dingy window and looked out at the rose garden. "I think I see my house!" she exclaimed.

Barrett chuckled. "All of London can see your house. I have no doubt the masses frequently mistake it for the king's palace."

Grace laughed, turned around, and pressed her back up against the wall.

Her smile was so alluring that Barrett felt in danger of losing his head completely. After weeks of skirting about the fringes of his desire, he could no longer hold it in check. He impulsively put his palm to her cheek; his gaze dipped to her lips.

Grace took a quick breath and smiled.

He slipped a hand around her waist and pulled her against his body. Grace sighed and closed her eyes, and Barrett lost his reason.

He nipped and licked at her lips, but when he slid his tongue into her mouth, a harder desire began to possess him. She was warm and alive beneath his hands, her body responding to his touch, her hands moving up his arms, to his neck, his face.

He found the tie of her bonnet, and yanked it free, toppling the thing off her head at the same time he thrust his fingers into her auburn hair. She smelled like lilacs; her skin felt like rose petals. He moved his mouth to the lobe of her ear, then her neck, and the soft indentation of her throat, where he could feel her pulse beating wildly beneath his lips.

He continued to move, sliding down her bosom as his hand found her hip and his fingers dug into the flesh there. With his free hand, he dipped into her décolletage and lifted a breast to his mouth. Above him, Grace gasped with pleasure, fanning the flames that were beginning to engulf them.

Barrett rose up again, covered her mouth with his, her breast with his hand. Grace melted against him and cupped his face. He groaned with the ache to be inside her, the desire to own her, and the strength it took to restrain himself from doing just that. But he grabbed her by the waist and twirled her around, seating her on one of the steps leading up to the third floor, and going down on his knee, took her breast in his mouth again.

Above him, Grace plunged her fingers into his hair, then dropped her hands to his shoulders, gripping them. "You drive me mad with want," he said against her skin, his calloused fingers holding her breast reverently. "Would that you were mine, Grace." He caressed her leg, sliding his hand down to her ankle, and then carelessly flipping off her shoe.

Grace laughed. "I pray you, sir, do not lose my shoe! I'd have a devil of a time explaining that to Mrs. Wells."

"I shall buy you all the shoes in London," he said, as he moved his hand to her ankle and up, to her calf.

She was watching him, drawing a breath when he slid his hand up her calf, her eyelids fluttering when he moved his hand to the soft skin on the inside of her knee. "Dare I ask what you intend to do?"

He said nothing, just kept his gaze steady on hers as he moved his hand to her thigh. Grace's smile faded; she drew another, shaky breath, but she did not speak or look away.

Emboldened by her silence, Barrett moved his hand up further still, to the apex of her legs, his fingers on the slit of her drawers. Now Grace drew her bottom lip between her teeth.

"Do I frighten you?" he asked.

Grace slowly leaned back, bracing her elbows on the step at her back. "The only thing that frightens me is how easily I submit to your touch."

Oh God—nothing could stop him. He withdrew his hand and gathered the yards of wool that made her gown and pushed it up, over her knees, so that her drawers and stockings were revealed to him.

Her breathing began to come much faster, her chest lifting with each breath.

"I cannot bear to be near you and not touch you," he said, and with his gaze steady on hers, he slipped his fingers into the slit of her drawers to feel the springy curls that covered her sex.

"*Oh,*" she gasped.

He moved his fingers deeper, slipping into the wet folds. Her eyes widened, and then closed, and she let her head drop back, revealing her long neck to him. "I will surely go to hell," she muttered.

"Never." She was warm and wet; he stroked her dauntlessly, his fingers glancing against a most sensitive tip, sliding slow and long and back again. He could scarcely bear it, could feel his lust straining at his trousers, could feel the need in him throbbing through every vein.

When he could stand it no longer, he removed his hand from between her legs and reached for her waist at the same moment he grabbed for her drawers, wrenching them from her body, pushing them down to her knees.

"No," Grace said, weakly putting out her hand. "I *cannot*—"

"I want to give you pleasure," he said sternly, and pushed her drawers to her ankles. He lifted her foot and freed her of the drawers, the only barrier between his mouth and her sex.

Grace knew it, too—as Barrett moved her legs wider apart, she gave a small whimper, but his mind was intent on her body sprawled before him, the sight of her female flesh, the earthy scent that aroused him to madness. He stroked her bare thighs, delighting in her little hiss of breath as he did. Then he lowered his head.

"Oh no—*no*," Grace said, sitting up as he neared her, but when he touched his mouth to her, she moaned. "Oh God. Dear God."

He flicked his tongue against her; she gasped and moved forward, widening her legs. With a growl of pleasure, he began to explore her body intimately with his tongue and lips, feasting on her flesh.

When he drew the small pearl that was at the core of

her desire in between his teeth and lips, her fingers sank into his hair and she writhed beneath him, her body surging up to meet his mouth, then away, as if she feared the climax that would come. He had no intention of letting her escape it and greedily pushed her to the brink, almost losing himself as she fell headlong into it, crying out, her hands scraping the old stone walls, her legs squeezing him, her body bucking with pleasure.

And then she lay still, completely spent, her breathing labored. Barrett sat back on his heels, dragged the back of his hand across his mouth, then used her drawers to wipe her clean. Only then did Grace open her eyes and sit up. Her hair was a tangled mess. She stared at him for a long moment, her affection for him plain.

She smiled, a lazy, lopsided smile full of satisfaction. "You are *wicked*, Barrett Adlaine. However shall I explain myself to the world?"

He grinned. "I haven't yet begun to show you wicked, Grace Holcomb. And I don't give a damn how you explain yourself to the world." He sat on a step, his erection aching . . . but he was happy, as happy as he'd ever been in his life. Beside him, Grace was busy repairing herself, her cheeks pink with lustful delight.

"Grace," he said, taking her hand. "I have something for you."

She glanced up with a sheepish smile. "I think you have given me quite enough," she said with a little laugh, and playfully nudged him with her shoulder.

He laughed, but withdrew the small box from his pocket and held it out to her.

Instead of exclaiming with delight as he had supposed she might do, her face fell. She stopped in her attempt to repair her appearance and stared at the box. "I don't . . ."

"It is a Christmas gift," he said, thinking that perhaps she had misunderstood.

"A gift."

Barrett held it out to her, not understanding. "For *you*, Grace."

She tried to smile, but couldn't quite seem to master it, and he felt the first of several stabs of pain to his heart. She reluctantly took the box and opened it. "*Oh*," she breathed, her hand going to her throat where her cross had once hung. She looked up at him, her eyes wide with surprise. "How did you know?"

"That you lost your cross? I see everything about you, don't you know? Don't you know that I cannot take my eyes from you, that I cannot think of anything but you?"

She looked at the gold cross again, and tears welled in her eyes. "Barrett . . . it is *beautiful*."

He smiled, pleased that she liked it.

But when she shifted her gaze to him, her eyes were full of sadness—not joy. "I cannot accept it."

His heart plummeted, crashing headlong to the ground. "What? Why not?" he demanded roughly.

"Because," she said sadly, and closed the box, thrusting it back at him as tears slipped down her cheek. "To accept a gift would imply . . ." She stopped, closed her eyes and swallowed.

"Imply *what*?" he demanded.

"That there is more to our friendship than there can be."

Dumbfounded, Barrett didn't know which enraged him more—that she would call this a friendship after what had just happened between them? Or that, having spent the last few weeks courting her as earnestly as a dog courts his master for a walk, she would proclaim there to be nothing more?

His anger catapulted him from his seat on the steps to his feet, and he stood at the portal window, one hand on his waist, one pushing through his hair.

"Barrett, please don't be cross," she said behind him, but that small admonishment broke something inside of him.

He whirled around; she recoiled at the expression on his face. "Don't be *cross*?" he echoed angrily. "Will you at least do me the honor of telling me *why* there can be no more than our *friendship*?"

"You know why—"

"No, I do *not* know why!" he bellowed. "Everything has changed, Grace! I know what your father wants for you, but do you really want that for yourself? I know you don't—I know that you cannot have been so accepting of my affection and not understood my intent!"

Grace quickly gained her feet, stooping down to pick up her bonnet. "I should go."

She started past him, but Barrett grabbed her arm.

"Unhand me!" she gasped.

"I have adored you and courted you as ardently as a man can do!"

She struggled to free herself, but Barrett easily pushed her up against the wall and pinned her there. "Do me the honor of telling me *how* you can turn me away so easily, Miss Holcomb. Is my fortune so paltry? Is that it? I will give you everything—"

"*Stop*," she cried, the tears slipping from the corners of her eyes. She turned her head to the side and squeezed her eyes shut. "I beg you to stop!"

"I will *not* stop! Good God, Grace, do you not see my heart laid bare before you? Do you not understand how much I love you? Is it so much to ask that you at least do me the courtesy of trampling my heart for something more profound than a lack of fortune?"

She did not move, did not look at him.

"*Grace!*" he exclaimed, shaking her lightly. "Do you feel nothing for me? Are you in the habit of allowing men to court you without regard for their feelings?"

She suddenly cried out, a keening cry of grief as tears streaked down her cheeks. She shoved hard against him. "No, *no!*"

"Why have you so completely disregarded mine?"

"I haven't! God knows I haven't!"

"But you have!" he insisted angrily. "You *are.*"

"How could I?" she shrieked. "How could I disregard your feelings? I *love* you!"

Her response did nothing to satisfy him; if anything, it confused him more. He let go of her, stumbling back as she slid down the wall to her haunches, crying uncontrollably. Several moments passed as he tried to catch his breath, tried to lift his head from the fog of crippling disappointment. At last he reached into his breast pocket and withdrew a handkerchief, squatted down before her, and pressed it in her hand. "If you love me," he said hoarsely, almost choking on the words, the hope, the dream, "then why can we be no more than friends?"

"My father will *never* allow it!" she said as she dabbed at her eyes.

"How do you know unless we ask? I am a good man, Grace. Granted, I do not have the wealth your father has, but I work hard, and I—"

"Oh please!" she cried. "It is not the size of your fortune!" She looked at him, her eyes flashing with anger. "You are a *merchant,* Barrett! You are not a lord, nor have you any hope of becoming one. I have been groomed since I was a child to be the wife of a titled man, to move among the *ton.* Not to marry someone in *trade.*"

She said it as if to marry a merchant was to marry the lowest form of humanity, and it wounded him deeply. "Your *father* is in trade—"

"It is not the same," she said sharply. "His wealth has opened some doors."

Barrett was so stunned by the cold hard truth that he fell back. He didn't know exactly what he'd imagined, but he'd never imagined *this* from Grace. "What of love?" he asked. "Has that no meaning?"

"No," she said, and covered her eyes with the handkerchief.

With that, his heart shattered. He rose up to his full height. "I see," he said coldly. "A *merchant* or a man in *trade* may be allowed to adore you and bare his soul to you, but he is not worthy of your precious, wealthy hand. What a fool I have been. I thought it was your father who pushed this on you. But you *share* his opinion."

"*Barrett*—" she said, reaching for him.

He moved out of her reach. "Thank you for having enlightened me. I will not burden you again, Grace. I will leave on this evening's coach to Leeds." He dropped the necklace on the ground at her feet. "If you had given me a gift, I swear to you that I would have gotten down on my knees and thanked God that you thought enough of me to give it."

Sobs racked her body. "*Barrett!*" she cried again, but it was too late—he was moving down the steps, taking them two and three, fury filling the space in which his shattered heart had once beat.

Twelve

$\mathcal{T}$he wind had picked up as Grace made her way home, yet she scarcely felt the cold of it. She could have walked into the Thames until the water covered her head and not realized it, so sick at heart was she for what had happened with Barrett.

She had done the only thing she could do, had responded the only way she knew how. Mrs. Harris had been very specific about accepting gifts, and her father had been more than specific about what he expected of her.

Yet she could not bear the look on Barrett's face when she had refused his gift. She could not bear the pain in his expression, the wounded look in his eyes, particularly since she had felt it so acutely herself.

She would have liked nothing more than to have given herself completely to Barrett. But how could she make him understand that if she did, she would give up her family for it?

When she reached her home, the butler took her cloak and bonnet. Barrett's gift she held tightly in her hand; her drawers, she'd left behind. He politely ignored the state of her hair and her tearstained cheeks as he handed her a folded vellum. "Mrs. Wells has gone out," he said.

"Thank you," Grace whispered, and took the note to her chamber.

It was a lovely note from Sir William, relaying his eagerness to see her tomorrow afternoon, the sort of note to make a young woman swoon. But it only made Grace cry more. Had she met Sir William before this turn in London, she would be over the moon. But she hadn't—she had fallen hopelessly in love with a man in trade.

She did not come down for supper, preferring instead to cry herself to sleep, refusing to let Mrs. Wells in, even when she threatened to send for Grace's father. When she awoke the next morning, she cried again, and when she had cried herself dry, she rang for Betty. "Is there any note today?" she asked weakly as Betty poured water for her bath.

"No, miss," Betty said with a sympathetic smile.

Grace went about her toilet without conscious thought—all she could see or hear or think of was Barrett. By the time Sir William arrived, she had composed herself. With a serene countenance, she was prepared to accept his offer. Mrs. Wells, so thankful Grace had come out of her room, even allowed her to receive him alone, choosing to stay in the adjoining sitting room with the door open.

Sir William complimented her on her cream-colored velvet dress, saying she looked beautiful. She invited him to sit, and he sat next to her, inquiring about her health and her day. Her answers were polite but vague.

Then he took her hand in his and turned it over, looking at her palm before lifting it and kissing it. It was perhaps the most intimate thing he'd done since this courtship had begun.

It only made her think of the intimacy she had shared with Barrett . . . an act that still radiated hot through her now and made her blush.

"Miss Holcomb, I am quite certain you have recognized the high regard in which I hold you."

No, no, I don't want to hear this, please, I don't want to hear it . . .

He smiled, his eyes dropping to her bosom for the first time that Grace had ever noticed, and she suppressed a shudder of revulsion. She couldn't imagine his touch, couldn't imagine his kiss. She couldn't imagine anyone but Barrett.

"I have a gift for you," he said, raising his gaze again. "A small token of my esteem, as it were." He reached into his breast pocket and extracted a small package, wrapped in red silk cloth and tied with a red ribbon. He pressed it into her palm.

"Oh," Grace said, looking down at the package. "I . . . I don't know what to say."

"Say nothing, Grace," he said, using her given name for the first time. "I hope only that you enjoy it."

Her hands were shaking as she pulled the ribbon. Sir William chuckled at her clumsiness, mistaking it for maidenly jitters. She forced a smile and unfolded the silk cloth to see a very large round topaz, surrounded by a circle of diamonds, on a gold chain. "Oh my," she murmured.

"Egyptians say topaz was colored by the golden glow of the sun god. It reminded me of your eyes," Sir William said proudly. "If I may . . . you have lovely eyes."

The necklace was very expensive and very thoughtful. But looking at it, she realized the cross she wore around her neck meant so much more to her. Whatever his occupation, whatever his background, Barrett Adlaine loved her and she loved him. To marry for anything less than that—to marry for jewels and a title and a fortune—seemed insane at that moment.

"Is something wrong?" Sir William asked, his smile fading. "I thought you would find it pleasing—"

"Oh, I do," she said and looked up at him, feeling a strength she'd never felt in her life. "It is . . . it is lovely, sir. But I cannot accept it."

"What?" he said, clearly surprised as she placed the necklace into his hand.

"I cannot accept it, for to do so would imply that there is more to our friendship than there possibly can be."

He blinked with shock, glanced down at the necklace, then at Grace again. "Grace, do you realize what you are saying?" he asked quietly. "I have courted you properly for weeks. This is what everyone expects—it is what *I* expect."

She nodded. "It is what I expected as well, Sir William. And as much as I have come to value your good opinion and your friendship . . . I cannot love you. My heart belongs to another."

He reared back as if she had slapped him, his hand closing tightly into a balled fist around the necklace. "I am astounded," he said flatly. "I thought we understood one another."

"As did I. I cannot apologize enough to you, sir. I did what I thought was expected of me, but in truth, I was fighting my feelings. I had not realized until this moment how . . . how *ardently* I feel about another," she said, fingering the cross. "I never meant you harm, Sir William. I am very sorry if I have."

He said nothing; the silence in the room was deafening. "No," he said at last, his voice weary. "I am very disappointed. But I cannot fault you for being true to your feelings." He stood up, thrust the necklace into his pocket. "May I at least have the honor of knowing which gentleman has won your heart?"

Grace rose to her feet and said, "Mr. Barrett Adlaine of Leeds."

He gave her a curt nod. "Then there is nothing left but for me to wish you much happiness."

"Thank you," she said, and held her breath as he turned and left the room. *She had done it.* She had made her feelings known, had spoken for herself, had finally, for the first time in her life, considered her *own* wishes before the wishes of anyone else. Now all she had to do was find Barrett, beg his forgiveness, and hope that he would see her through the horrible day her father disowned her and tossed her out on the street.

She hurried to the foyer before the door had closed completely behind Sir William. "My cloak," she said low to a footman.

"Miss Holcomb?" Mrs. Wells called from top of the stairs, her voice full of excitement.

Grace closed her eyes and sent up a silent prayer that the footman would return with her cloak before Mrs. Wells could make it down the grand staircase.

"Miss Holcomb! Do you not hear me?" she called again. Fortunately, the footman had reentered the foyer with Grace's cloak. She rushed to meet him, grabbed the cloak, and turned and looked at Mrs. Wells.

"I refused him, Mrs. Wells. I hope my father does not fault you for it."

"*What?*" Mrs. Wells howled. "What on earth are you saying? Don't you dare step one foot out that door! *Miss Holcomb!* Don't you *dare* step out that door!" she shrieked as Grace ran to the door and out.

She had only moments, she felt certain, before a footman could be persuaded to detain her, and she thought frantically what to do. She had no idea where Lord Dewar resided, but she knew who might.

She walked as quickly as propriety would allow the four long blocks to Lady Middleton's house, chanting a prayer with each step that Ava was home.

Not only was Ava home, but she and her husband, the Marquis of Middleton, were standing in the courtyard of their palatial home, preparing to board a carriage when Grace came striding through the gates.

"Grace!" Ava said, smiling, obviously surprised. "What a pleasant surprise! I should think you'd be at the Montgomery assembly by now."

"My lord," Grace said, dipping a barely discernible curtsy to Lord Middleton before turning her attention to Ava. "Ava, where does Lord Dewar live?"

"What?" Ava asked laughingly.

"Lord Dewar. I'm quite serious, Ava. I *must* see Mr. Adlaine before he leaves for Leeds, and he is a guest of Lord Dewar!"

Ava's smiled faded. "But Grace, darling . . . you can't *possibly* call on him at Dewar's. It is the height of impropriety."

"I don't care a fig, Ava. Just tell me where he lives! Mr. Adlaine is leaving tonight, and I absolutely must speak with him!" she said frantically.

Ava looked at her husband, who stepped forward and put his hand on Grace's arm. "It would appear that Miss Holcomb is in need of assistance, my love," he said kindly. "We shall escort her to Dewar's."

"Thank you," Grace said, and moved to step into the carriage before she was invited. She didn't care how rudely she was behaving; she had no time to waste.

Naturally, on the ride to Dewar's, Ava extracted the whole ugly truth from Grace. The gift Barrett had given her, her refusal to accept it, Sir William's gift and her refusal to accept that one as well, her escape from Mrs. Wells. Ava exclaimed at every turn, and even Lord Middleton looked quite wrapped up in her tale.

Unfortunately, neither Mr. Adlaine nor Lord Dewar

was at home when Lord Middleton inquired, and the butler was not entirely sure where either of them had gone. That prompted quite a discussion in the carriage—Grace wanted to look for him, but Lord Middleton calmly put his foot down. He explained to Grace that while she thought her situation was rather dire, it did not compare to how dire it might become were she to knock on every door asking after a certain gentleman. It was best, he suggested, for her to either accompany them to the Montgomery assembly or return home.

With a vision of Mrs. Wells in mind, Grace opted for the assembly. But she could scarcely summon a smile.

"Poor Grace," Ava said as the carriage moved along toward Piccadilly, where the assembly would be held in a hall. "I cannot bear to see you so sad."

Sad, broken, dejected—frankly, Grace didn't want to live at that moment. "I love him," she said, her eyes welling with tears again. "I love him desperately, and I shall never love another, and I did *everything* quite wrong. I know you don't think him a proper match Ava, but—"

"Why on earth would you say so?" Ava exclaimed.

"You said I shouldn't allow him to court me!"

Ava reached across the carriage and squeezed Grace's hand. "I said you could not allow him to court you if you intended to accept Sir William's offer," she reminded her. "And I was right. But Grace . . . if you *love* Mr. Adlaine, then there really is no other choice, is there?"

Grace looked from Ava to her husband, who smiled at his wife. "I must agree with my wife, Miss Holcomb. She and I have learned this valuable lesson in a rather difficult way . . . haven't we, darling?"

Ava laughed and looked up at her husband with

such love and admiration that Grace's heart wrenched. "We have indeed, sir."

She would never know that sort of love, Grace thought miserably as the two of them smiled at one another. She'd never know what it felt like to look at a man and feel pride and love and know that she couldn't bear to be away from him. She would never know—

Her eye caught sight of a man's back. Tall and broad-shouldered, a bit of dark blond hair peeking out from beneath his hat, a bag in his hand. *"Stop!"* she shouted, startling the Middletons out of their wits. But Lord Middleton called up to stop, and the carriage shuddered to a halt, flinging Grace almost onto Ava's lap.

"What on earth?" Ava cried.

"He's there!" Grace cried, pointing out the window.

Ava instantly put her face to the window. "It's a public coach station," she said. "Darling, do go and stop him," she said to her husband, but Grace had already reached the door handle and had flung it open.

"Grace!" Ava cried.

Somewhere deep in Grace's mind was the notion that to run after a man would ruin her reputation, but she ignored Ava and jumped down, her need to apologize to Barrett far outweighing any rule of propriety. She was oblivious to the people at the station who gaped at her as if she were a madwoman. She didn't notice several ornate carriages across the street, lined up to release their riders at the public hall where the Montgomery affair would be hosted. She didn't hear Ava call, or see Lord Middleton vault after her for that matter—she saw nothing but Barrett's back moving toward the ticket window.

"Barrett!" she shouted. He turned halfway, looking

curiously about, but did not see her. *"Barrett!"* she shouted again, waving her arm.

He saw her then, his gaze traveling the length of her and up again, looking quite disgusted. Grace dodged through the crowd to reach him nonetheless, her heart pounding, her palms damp, and with absolutely no idea how she would say what she wanted to express.

He spoke first. "Grace," he said, shaking his head. "You shouldn't have come here."

"I had to."

"There is nothing left to say. Go back to your friends."

He turned as if he meant to walk away, and Grace unthinkingly grabbed his hand and held it tightly. "Don't go," she said. "Please—I . . . I should be taken to the Tower and flogged, I know, for I was *beastly* to you—"

"Yes," he said, nodding. "You were."

She swallowed. "I was arrogant and proud and following the course I thought I *should* follow, but you were right, it was my *father's* course, not mine, and I was wrong, I was so very wrong, and I love you, Barrett!"

"It is too late," he said firmly.

"No!" she cried, squeezing his hand. "You cannot say that! I have refused Sir William, I have told him that *you* are the man I love, and Barrett, it is true. I long to be with you," she said, closing her eyes, squeezing back the tears. "I have longed to be with you for ages, and now . . . now I have given up everything to be with you."

"Ah, come on then, let her have ye, lad!" a man shouted, and several people laughed.

"Grace." It was Lord Middleton behind her. He put his hands on her shoulders and tried to draw her away. "You are creating quite a scene."

"I don't care," she said tearfully, looking at Barrett. "I don't care if the whole of London sees me. Barrett . . . do you recall that you once told me that I should consider what *I* want, and envision it, for surely then I would find a way to attain it? Well, I've done it. *You* are my vision, Barrett Adlaine. So you *must* forgive me, because like you, I have now laid my heart and soul open to you and I won't be able to bear it if you leave me."

Barrett stared at her, his eyes unfathomable, his expression grim.

"It is none of my concern, sir, but . . . it sounds rather heartfelt to me," Lord Middleton said. "And I wager it sounded as heartfelt to these good people here and those who stand behind me."

Grace blinked and looked around. Everyone at the public station was watching them. She bent to one side and looked behind Lord Middleton. Just beyond Ava, who was standing with her hands clasped, smiling tearfully, there were a dozen guests of the Montgomery assembly, watching her curiously.

"Oh *Lord*," she moaned. She turned round again, closed her eyes, and sagged against Lord Middleton for a moment before opening her eyes and looking at Barrett, silently pleading with him.

The barest hint of a smile turned up one corner of his mouth. "She has indeed caused quite a stir," he said thoughtfully.

"*Barrett . . .*"

"I suppose I'd be made of stone if I could walk away from such a poetic display of emotion."

Her heart surged with hope.

He sighed, swept his hat off his head, thrust his hand through his hair, and slowly sank to one knee, right there, in the dirt, with people crowding around him to hear. He looked at her for a long moment, then smiled and threw his arms wide. "Marry me, Grace Holcomb."

With a cry of joy, she lurched out of Middleton's grasp and into Barrett's arms as a cheer went up from the crowd, followed by polite applause behind her, which was almost drowned out by Ava's blubbering that she'd never seen anything so endearing in all her life—with the exception of the time Phoebe, her sister, declared her love to a footman when she was twelve.

In the days that followed, the newspapers were full of the titillating news of Miss Grace Holcomb's scandalous public display of affection for a merchant from Leeds, and how she had turned her back on the incomparable Sir William. Many people said that they expected no less from the shepherdess, for really, good breeding came from good stock.

Others whispered that it had warmed their hearts to see the young woman entreat the man she loved so ardently.

Sir William, upon hearing the tale, set sail for Paris again.

Mrs. Harris, sickened by the scandal that surrounded poor Grace Holcomb, felt much better about the situation when she received a letter a few days later from Grace. *I shall forever be in your debt,* Grace wrote, *for had it not been for your wisdom, I most certainly would have accepted Sir William's gift as I thought I should do, instead of Mr. Adlaine's gift, which my heart yearned to do. Because of you, I shall marry the man I truly esteem above all others.*

Predictably, Mr. Holcomb disowned his daughter and vowed never to lay eyes on her again. Happily, that vow did not last, as he was granted a knighthood for his improvements to the sheep industry and thereby had his wish to hobnob among the Quality. And the arrival of his first grandchild—Charlotte—renewed his hope that he might marry his grandchildren into the ranks of the aristocracy one day.

Over the next ten years, the scandal surrounding Grace Holcomb died away and the Adlaine mill in Leeds grew into a thriving regional business. Mr. and Mrs. Adlaine built a large manor house on the banks of the River Aire and welcomed four more children into their lives.

And every year at Christmas, when Mr. Adlaine gave his wife a gift, she got down on her knees and thanked God that he'd thought enough of her to give it.

MISCHIEF'S HOLIDAY

Renee Bernard

To Geoff, who let mischief into his well-ordered
world when we met and proceeded to
demonstrate just what a hero really is.
I never knew love could be so wonderful.
Thank you.

One

M̄iss Martin,
*   Your enthusiastic and lively nature*
brightens the lives of those around you, but you
must apply yourself to better control and decorum.
I know it is your greatest desire to impress and
excel amongst your peers, but you must recall
yourself in each and every moment and mind your
surroundings. Think before you act, my dear, and I
am sure your better nature will assert itself.
*   So, of all the tasks I am assigning to my*
students for the holidays, yours is perhaps the
simplest and I fear the most daunting. Your goal is
to survive the holidays without incident and prove
to all that you have the restraint and manners of a
true lady.
*   Good luck, Miss Martin.*

*   Yours in sincere regard,*
*   Mrs. Charlotte Harris*

"Survive the holidays without incident," Alyssa Martin whispered, eyeing the elegant handwriting yet again. She bit her lower lip and slid the folded vellum into her reticule. At first glance, it appeared a very simple assignment. But with the sage experience of eighteen years of notable mischance, Miss Alyssa Martin was not fooled. No matter how hard she applied herself to the fine and graceful arts required of a proper young lady, she'd provided more mirth and mischief to the world than anyone had a right to claim. Her brow furrowed as she contemplated her task.

It wasn't as if she were an ungainly thing! Taller than most of the other girls at Mrs. Harris's School for Young Ladies, she'd been complimented for her lithe posture while learning dance figures and for her quick hands when tackling embroidery. She'd spent endless hours practicing stately strides and mastering the drills of the drawing and dining rooms until her head spun. No matter that she'd excelled in her academic studies—she shook her head. No, none of her dainty accomplishments lingered in any of her acquaintances' memories.

Instead, her classmates recalled with relish each wonderful misadventure and often begged her to retell them. She could hardly blame them. Who else had accidentally sewn herself to her chair cushion, mixed poison oak into the class floral arrangement or gotten trapped on the school's roof during a simple scavenger hunt? Alyssa had no illusions about her luck. In each instance, she would have sworn she was making brilliant choices. It was only afterward when chaos had been unleashed that she'd been forced to see her missteps. It was hard not to laugh at herself along with her friends, especially since pouting and self-pity just weren't in her nature.

Fear, however, was *not* out of her repertoire.

After all, she would be coming out soon, and society was notably less forgiving of wealthy young women from humble bloodlines who failed to keep up appearances. Her father had made a vast fortune in commerce and trade, but had started in relative obscurity. The infusion of new money was desirable to the realm's elite classes, but there was no end of people willing to publicly cut anyone for a perceived lack of refinement. If she was going to make the desirable match her father wanted, she would have to prove that she was the equal of any blue-blooded debutante or the titled quarry they sought.

Alyssa tucked a stray blond curl under her bonnet and sighed, making an effort to push her concerns aside as the carriage began to roll up more familiar lanes. Almost home, she smiled, cheered at the thought of being home after such a long absence. She'd missed her father, seeing him only on holiday breaks from school. But now she had finished her schooling and Mrs. Harris had sent her off with a final assignment and words of advice. Her debut was a few weeks away so there was still time to stave off the worst of her fears. Between public humiliation and the threat of romantic predators, Alyssa knew which she dreaded more. She had difficulty imagining that a man's kissing her hand and quoting poetry could be more painful than realizing she was wearing two mismatched slippers at the end of the day. The latter was a more likely disaster in her experience.

Mrs. Harris had advised her students continually against being swept away by love and blinded to practicalities. Her graduates proudly eschewed romantic nonsense. Alyssa had decided she would simply use the utmost caution when approaching the opposite sex. Now, if Cupid's test involved an inkwell and a misplaced bonnet, she'd have worried more. Alyssa laughed, her humor finally reasserting itself. "Survive the holidays without incident." She straightened her shoulders. "How difficult can it be?"

"God res' ye, murry gennelmen!" The slurred singing of her coach driver carried back on the wind and made her smile. Her father had sent the man instead of her usual driver, and she could only assume he'd fortified himself against the cold with a nip or two. He'd seemed a cheerful sort, but she hadn't expected a serenade of carols. Even off-key and with a notable lack of consonants, she was sure it was the spirit of the song that mattered most.

"'Member Chriz'a saber wuz born on Chrismuz day!" he crooned.

She tapped her foot and hummed quietly along with him; at least, until the carriage lurched and they hit a series of bumps that nearly jostled her clear off the cushioned seat. Perhaps the spirits *in* the singer were more of an issue. Before she could call out the window to suggest that they slow down, another shocking jolt convinced her that the problem involved more than velocity.

"Whoa! Ho, there!" The driver's voice was filled with alarm.

Alyssa gripped the seat and placed a hand against the windowsill to try to stay upright. "W-whoa, indeed," she moaned, suddenly aware that she was too terrified to muster a scream. Though it seemed that the coachman was doing enough yelling for both of them.

The world was a blur as the carriage lost contact with the ground and then came to a sudden halt. It took her a few seconds to confirm that aside from the alarming angle at which the carriage was resting and the odd sound of flowing water, she felt alert and well. Alyssa tested her limbs and managed to drop the window in the door, which was now slightly above her. Climbing up onto the seat, she peeked out from the opening. "Sir? Sir, are you injured?"

"Ye wait there, mish! I-I'll fetch help! D-don't fret, mish!" The driver's voice came from farther away than she'd anticipated.

Her jaw dropped as she leaned out the window and saw that somehow the horses and her inebriated driver had remained safely on the road, while she and the carriage had fallen down the embankment and landed almost sideways in the middle of a shallow creek. Before she could protest or suggest a more immediate extraction, the man walked off, his unsteady gait making the situation all the more ridiculous.

"Sir! Wait! Sir, you . . ." Alyssa bit her lower lip before finishing the sentence quietly for her ears only, "You appear to be going the wrong way. The village is east."

Well, so much for the holiday spirit!

She carefully climbed back down to locate her reticule. Eyeing her bag with its assignment tucked inside, she could only hope that a carriage rolling into a bit of water didn't count as an "incident" in Mrs. Harris's judgment. After all, a lady could hardly be blamed for such setbacks. Could she?

Thinking of Mrs. Harris instantly renewed her determination to stay mindful of her training. No matter what the situation, a true lady would keep a cool head. As she'd recently been lectured, a woman of breeding shone brightest where others lost their composure. Alyssa straightened her bonnet and slowly let out a breath. The creek didn't seem too deep, and if she avoided slipping and taking an icy bath, the worst part would be wet skirts, stockings and shoes. Incident or no, she would then treat the walk to the house as simple exercise.

Besides, she told herself with a sigh, the long walk would give her ample time to come up with a way to deflect her father's displeasure from her inebriated driver. It was the least a lady could do for an overly "merry gennelman."

The day was brisk and overcast, but the clouds had so far kept their moisture to themselves. Leland Yates was not ungrateful since his penchant for fresh air was not without risks. Leland was the sort of man who braved the worst rainstorms if it meant he could enjoy an hour or two of solitude. Society made him uneasy, and even the best of company could be a trial. He was a private soul and preferred a good book to the squawk and squeals of social gatherings. He hated the posturing and endless, ambitious wrangling that accompanied most elite circles in London. As a second son of a titled lord, Leland had made his own way in the world, determined to carve out a fortune with his wits and bare hands. Although other peers looked down on men who sullied their names with the pursuit of profit, Leland was proud of his accomplishments and refused to slide into a life of fashionable ease. He'd developed a talent for keeping to himself his scathing opinions about soft-headed men who couldn't fasten their own pants without assistance.

He had readily accepted Reid Martin's invitation for the holidays. He'd long admired the man's practical approach to business; Leland was sure that if nothing else, he would manage one or two sensible and profitable conversations during his visit. Martin had promised him that the gathering would be small, and the demands on his time would be minimal.

"Come, ride and relax, sir! Get away from London's dreary winter streets and if you wish, you may strive to rearrange the dust on the collection of leather-bound tomes my wife insisted on collecting," Martin had chuckled.

The lure of a quiet country Christmas was strong but Martin's hint at a well-stocked library made the invitation irresistible. After all, if there was one thing a man needed, it was his peace and—

Leland reined in his mount, startled at the sight of two matched stocking-footed horses still harnessed to a disconnected pole. The bar had broken neatly at the mounting braces from a carriage, and was caught on a low branch. An odd sound carried on the wind, and Leland feared he'd happened upon a terrible accident. He rode over quickly and then gaped in astonishment at the sight awaiting him.

The carriage sat upright in the middle of the creek bed. But the surprise entailed more than the vehicle's unusual location. Encumbered by a skirt and petticoats, a pair of delectable legs was kicking furiously, their owner entrapped in a carriage window. Apparently, the window had fallen and latched in place to pin her at the waist. The flash of stockings and shapely ankles and calves was distracting in the extreme, and Leland marveled how such a creature could have ended up in such a position. The view offered more than passing enjoyment, and while it didn't seem gentlemanly to linger in appreciation, he didn't think any man in long breeches could avoid the temptation to savor the display. It was clear this female was in need of assistance, but that was the only fact he could swear to.

He walked his horse carefully down the embankment. Rather than screaming for help, the sound of a muttered lecture of some sort drifted through the carriage's window. He wasn't sure, but he thought he heard something of a rallying speech, interspersed with grunts at her efforts to wriggle free. Was she talking to someone named Mrs. Harris?

He cleared his throat to soften the surprise of coming up behind her. "May I offer you a hand, miss?"

The kicking ceased abruptly and he detected one small squeak as his damsel in distress absorbed that she was no longer alone. "Oh! Oh, dear."

Leland's mouth fell open for an instant, surprised at the disappointment he heard in her small muffled exclamation. It was far from the relief he'd anticipated. "You'd prefer to wait for someone else?"

He was rewarded with a small groan and a feisty kick. "No."

"How in the world did you manage this?" He couldn't resist the question as he surveyed the luscious curves of her bottom and caught another glimpse of delicate ankles and her stockings with tiny ribbons.

"If you must know," a calm voice carried to him, as if they were discussing her choice in bonnets, "the door was stuck, and I thought the window a logical exit. And as I didn't want to land headfirst into the water . . . Well, I'm sure I'd have managed it if the carriage hadn't shifted and the window hadn't closed on me."

"I see."

He was treated to another small wriggle before a ragged sigh reached his ears and a more contrite damsel continued, "Have you ever wished you could be invisible?"

Leland urged his horse closer, shaking his head. "I would guess that this would be a terrible moment to have gotten your wish. That can hardly be a comfortable position."

"It isn't one I would recommend." She gave another frustrated shimmy of her hips. "Could you help me, please?"

"As you wish." It was naturally his intent all along to extract her, but for a fleeting instant, it occurred to him that this wasn't going to be the simple chivalrous act she might envision.

Sidling his mount closer, he was able to slide his leg underneath her pert bottom to shift her weight off of the windowsill. He'd hoped to increase her comfort, but his heart rate skyrocketed at the contact. Leland's throat closed at the surge of desire that worked through his frame. The soft swell of her round bottom against the hard muscle of his thigh was evocative enough to make him draw a quick breath as his cock stiffened. Her luscious curves beckoned his hands, but he refrained from touching her as she wriggled in protest. Even if she were some doxy, he'd prefer to negotiate an agreement before going too far.

"Sir! I'm not sure—"

"Don't worry," he said as he pulled the horse closer, ensuring her perch on his leg was steadier. "I'll have you out in no time."

The window itself had latched in place, so Leland reached around her hips and marveled at the way her body felt against his. By gaining a firm but gentle grip, he was able to use his free hand to release the latch and lift the frame. "I've got you."

Within seconds, she was freed and he had his arms full of feminine curves. She squeaked as if to protest, but didn't speak. He had to work to keep control of his mount and to keep from dropping her into the water. Leland could only repeat, "I've got you."

It was meant to offer comfort, but the possessive tone of his voice made him frown a bit. As he pulled her across his lap to nestle her against his chest, he noted that the promising view of his damsel's legs and bottom was amply matched by the rest of her. She was young and impossibly pretty, her face flushed and her bonnet askew over golden curls that tumbled down her back. The cut of her dress and coat was hardly provocative, giving him his first misgivings that chaperoned or not, she probably wasn't the easy gel he'd assumed. Still . . . a man could hope.

"Is there another passenger to look after?" he inquired without moving his mount. If he was drawing out the experience, Leland wasn't going to admit to a shred of guilt. It wasn't as if the gods were usually this generous and, in his opinion, only a fool would fail to enjoy the moment. "I could have sworn I overheard you addressing someone else inside. A Mrs. Harris?"

"No!" she corrected him quickly, her color deepening to a sweet pink that made him wonder how much of her body was susceptible to the fascinating change.

Where is your chaperone? For if ever a girl needed one, I think it's you, miss.

"Sir, this is . . . improper," she managed, her gloved hands clutching at his coat lapels for balance.

"I can put you down here," he offered nonchalantly. "But I'm afraid the water's colder than it looks."

She eyed him warily before replying, humor making her beautiful blue eyes sparkle. "Perhaps the shore would make for a better landing?"

"If you insist," he played along, urging the horse to return to the embankment. Reaching dry ground, he gingerly lowered her and then dismounted carefully to keep his coat closed to hide just how "improper" the situation had become. "I take it you are unharmed?"

"I'm . . . fine." She straightened her bonnet, and then rewarded him with a heart-stopping smile. "Well, *that* was an adventure."

"At the very least," he agreed.

She extended a gloved hand. "Thank you for rescuing me from my carriage."

He smiled at the formal gesture, taking her hand and bowing over it. "Allow me to introduce myself. I am—"

"Oh, no! Please . . ." She took back her hand, coloring a bit. "I'm not a rude person, really! It's just that . . . Well, if you introduce yourself then I shall have to introduce myself, and you will always associate my name with this embarrassing incident. It doesn't seem fair."

"Fair?"

"In the retelling, you will be the hero and I will forever be the dolt who got stuck in a carriage window," she explained with a sigh, then gave him another bone-melting smile. "It encourages a lady to lie to protect her reputation."

Leland wasn't sure how to respond. A lifetime of relying on his wits evaporated in the aftermath of her speech. He scrambled for an appropriate reply. Stranger still, instead of being insulted at her refusal to accept his introduction, he was amused. "But then you'll have a reputation for falsehoods. Is that not worse?"

She squared her shoulders, as if bracing herself for the firing line. "You're right. I'll simply have to admit to everything. Unless . . ."

"Unless?"

"Unless you would be kind enough to swear never to tell anyone what's happened here today. Then I wouldn't have to lie."

Leland shook his head. Whoever she was, she had an incredible talent for making a man's head swim. "I could, but it's not every day a man forgoes being proclaimed a hero."

She laughed. "Nonsense! Men can always invent opportunities to boast."

He struggled to keep a straight face at the "innocent wisdom of babes." "I'll have to suppress my instincts then. You have my personal oath not to disclose your predicament."

She nodded, the matter happily settled, and made a lovely curtsy. "Well, thank you for your discretion. Now if you'll excuse me, I really should be off."

"Wait." He refused to believe she was going to curtsy and simply walk away. "Where are you going? It's miles to the village and—"

"The weather should hold for a while, and I'm perfectly capable of walking the rest of the way." Her chin rose in determination. "Exercise can be very beneficial."

"As a gentleman, I can hardly ride away and leave you to walk, miss. At least take my horse." Frustration crept into his countenance. It was one thing to parry verbally with a member of the weaker sex. It was another matter to be completely disregarded.

She tilted her head, contemplating the reins he held out to her, and then crossed her arms. "I'm sorry if I've insulted you, as it wasn't my intention. I'm afraid that . . ." She took a deep breath before continuing, "Sir, I've promised not to cause any trouble over the holidays and I'm afraid that taking your horse will somehow make things worse."

It was the last thing in the world he'd expected her to say. "Worse?"

"I confess I'm not much of a rider. And since I've already embarrassed myself with one mishap and invisibility is, as you pointed out, not an option—I'd rather not tempt fate. And how would I return a horse to a stranger? I'll look like a horse thief to my family. So I'll just walk home and recover what tiny sliver of dignity I can muster before explaining to my father where my luggage is."

"But—"

"I won't tell anyone, if you won't."

"This is insane."

She sighed and smiled, her eyes flashing with humor. "I'm sure you'll thank me later for the reprieve."

"Miss!" Leland was not a man to be commanded by nonsensical directives. "There is a compromise to be made, which will no doubt protect your oath *and* your sliver of dignity."

She uncrossed her arms. "A compromise?"

"We can both ride until we get close to your home. Then if you wish, you can walk the remainder of the distance and arrive on foot with no one the wiser that you avoided an unnecessary hike."

"I—it is probably out of your way."

"That's irrelevant." He wasn't giving in. Whoever she was, she wasn't walking miles in the cold on her own. "I will know that you have been delivered safely without any further 'incidents.' And since you haven't supplied your name, and neither of us will mention the morning's events, I believe you have run out of excuses, miss."

Her lips parted, but she didn't offer a counterargument. Instead she tucked a stray curl back into her bonnet, a gesture that distracted him for a split second, before she finally answered. "As you wish."

She had no one to blame but herself. The ride was wreaking havoc on her senses. It was one thing to experience the shock of a strange man's hands extracting her person from a carriage window, spanning her hips and holding her waist in a way that made her head spin. Even ending up in his lap briefly had brought on an overwhelming rush of new sensations, but *this*! This was no brief storm. This was endless minutes, tucked between his thighs, the heat of his broad chest at her back, his arms around her waist keeping her snug against him. She'd been warned about men for so long, Alyssa was sure that this was Fate's merry way of driving the lesson home. He was too handsome to be roaming about the countryside rescuing women and chivalrously insisting on seeing them home. Why wasn't he escorting his wife, or his fiancée, or his lady friend? Her first impression of his dark and dashing looks refused to fade as she stole a few backward glances at him and sighed.

Beneath a plain riding hat, his hair was almost coal black and unfashionably reached his collar in the back. Nothing about his features seemed too sharp or too blunt, but instead he was a study in masculine lines and strength. His dark brown eyes were framed by elegant brows that gave him an aristocratic air, but there was nothing of the dandy in his clothing or manners, and Alyssa was left with a puzzle of a gentleman who could be anything from pauper to prince.

It had begun to snow and she didn't doubt that her plan to walk the remaining distance would have resulted in a miserable plight. Still, she thought, better to be numb with cold than overly aware of every inch of her body that was in contact with his. Layers of cloth offered a thin buffer, and she couldn't believe the betrayal of her own senses. She'd imagined a man's embrace as a vague and potentially cumbersome experience, but this! Each breath he expelled trailed along the back of her neck and beckoned her to lean back against him, to melt into a sinful and unfamiliar surrender. The humiliation of being found in the worst position imaginable had faded to a vague alarm that Mrs. Harris must have omitted some vital information in her warnings regarding the opposite sex.

Not that this man was any sort of rogue, nor would she ever see him again once she was released in the old grove near her father's estate, but she dearly hoped she was having an unusual reaction to him. If all men held such sway over a girl's heartbeat it was no wonder women had been dubbed the weaker sex. This was impossible!

She stiffened her back, wriggling to break his spell, to no avail. The movement made it worse. The friction of her petticoats and undergarments against her thighs was alien, as if her flesh had never before felt their touch. Damp heat seemed to be steaming from her body, and Alyssa's lips pursed at the desire to press harder against him and let this delicious sensation overtake all reason.

She bit the inside of her cheek to force her thoughts back into the realm of sanity. *Hanging upside down in carriage windows must affect a person's mind. Next time, I should insist on sitting still for a few minutes before climbing on a horse.*

A distraction would be helpful. The most obvious choice was conversation, but that was a challenge. She'd been such a brat to refuse to give him her name. She'd behaved unforgivably. Consoling herself with the certainty that she'd never encounter him again, she sighed and attempted to make amends. "I am very sorry to cause you all this trouble."

"It is hardly trouble, though I confess, you seem to have a talent for it." His voice was a surly rumble that vibrated through her, giving her goose bumps and setting off another delicious shiver down her spine.

There was no sense in denying the truth of his words. "You have no idea, sir."

"Are you warm enough?" he asked.

Warm enough? I cannot recall an August when I felt this warm. "Yes, thank you," she managed with only a small betraying wobble in her voice. Alyssa shifted again, and heard his sharp intake of breath. "Oh! Have I injured you, sir?"

"No!" His denial was instantaneous and firm, but one of his hands dropped from the reins to reach around her waist as if to hold her in place. "Just . . . be still for a moment."

She froze at the intimate touch of his hand against her stomach, but also at the revelation that his strange tone meant she might not be alone in her current plight. She stole another peek at his face and was instantly captured by his direct gaze. His look was intense and possessive and Alyssa lost the will to ward away the chaos her body clamored for. The expression in his dark brown eyes robbed her of speech and she held her breath.

He shook his head. "I may have underestimated your talent for trouble."

She turned her head forward and smiled. "In all fairness, you were honestly warned, sir." Alyssa spotted the first curve of the old grove and decided it was time to part ways with her benefactor. "I can walk from here."

"Here?" The question conveyed a bit of surprise, but she allowed that the man had every right to think her daft and ill-mannered.

"My home is not far at all," she assured him as he dismounted and then helped her down. "I hope I haven't caused you to lose your way to your own destination. That path will take you back to the main road, and from there, the village is just a few miles."

He gave her a strange enigmatic smile. "I'm sure I'll find it from here."

"Well, thank you again," she said, brushing out her coat, wishing she didn't miss his warmth at her back. She extended her hand. "I hope to meet you again one day under better circumstances."

He didn't look convinced at her sincerity, but took her hand graciously nonetheless. "I'm looking forward to it." He bowed briefly over her hand and released her as custom dictated.

She pulled her muffler tighter and turned to begin her brisk march home on unsteady legs. The aftereffects of his embrace lingered along with the faint scent of him. After several steps, she risked looking back and was a little surprised that he had already mounted and disappeared.

Well! She adjusted her bonnet. She could hardly blame him. What else had she expected? Another protest from him that a lady shouldn't walk alone in this weather? It wasn't as if she wanted him to follow her. Explaining her arrival on foot to her father and the servants was one thing, but to bring home a man? There wasn't a holiday assignment on earth that could have excused it!

No, this was better. She would be able to make a quiet approach to the house, and if her luck improved, the fuss over retrieving her luggage and the carriage would fade quickly and no one would ask how she'd gotten out of a creek by herself without soaking her skirts.

Several minutes later, the house came into view, and her steps quickened.

The worst of my holiday mishaps is officially behind me.

Two

W omen were trouble.

Leland had prided himself on keeping a safe distance from their scheming clutches. He'd spent long years focused on gaining his footing and personal fortune, determined to prove himself apart from his family's connections. A good marriage was the only socially approved means of acquiring wealth for a man in his position, but something in him had balked at the prospect. He'd seen other men, including his father, squander their fortunes and reputations over women who had rewarded them with only misery. Leland had long congratulated himself on not being as blind to the dangers as his peers.

At least, he had until today.

Clearly, this girl was trouble and any man with a shred of sense would know exactly what his course of action should be. But damned if he wasn't in a fog at the moment. She had asked him to release her at the edge of his host's property. Since his arrival a few days ago, he'd had ample time to familiarize himself with the property and he'd recognized the grove instantly. It was too much of a coincidence. She was evidently another holiday guest of Martin's.

There was no escaping her.

His damsel in distress would be arriving on foot and

he acknowledged a small curl of anticipation at seeing the shock on her face when they were formally introduced. She'd sworn him to secrecy, but he wondered if she would confess to the mishap with the carriage at the mere sight of him.

Leland frowned as a stable boy approached to take the reins so that he could dismount. Her reaction shouldn't matter to him, he reminded himself. But instead of looking forward to reacquainting himself with the classics in Mr. Martin's library, he was caught up in foolish daydreams about his host's mystery guest and how this afternoon's odd game would play out in the days to come. His thoughts turned to less innocent images of her round bottom nestled against him, of how light and warm she'd been in his arms, how her curves were firm and luscious. She'd fit against him so perfectly. It was hard to believe she'd been unaware of her power. Each prim little wriggle had pushed her bottom tighter against his arousal; he hadn't been able to decide if she were deliberately tormenting him or innocently adjusting her seat on the horse. In either case, it had been a torment he would happily have undergone for another thirty miles.

"Damn it," he growled as he walked toward the house. He was here for a simple holiday, a Christmas away from the gray soot and dreariness of London—not for a potentially dangerous liaison. She'd refused to give him her name, which meant she could be anyone with any number of connections that would squash this first inkling of interest.

Not that he planned to express interest! The last thing he needed was to find himself in a tangle with a woman who might even turn out to be his host's mistress.

No, she'd told him she'd sworn not to cause trouble over the holidays and he was the last man on earth who was going to challenge her vow. The wrinkle in his country holiday was officially behind him.

"My dearest! There you are." Reid Martin held out his hands to his only child as she descended the stairs. "They said you'd arrived on foot and I could hardly believe it. Tell me you didn't walk all the way from London!"

Alyssa rushed to him, blushing at his jest. "Father, don't be silly." She kissed him on his cheek and felt instantly warmed by his embrace. "The carriage broke down on the drive and I wasn't about to spend any part of my Christmas holiday sitting by the side of the lane."

"And where is Gilbert, your driver?" he asked, scowling. "If he left you unprotected by the side of the road, I shall see to him personally!"

She reached up to put a soothing hand on his cheek. "I insisted he go to the village for help, but then realized I was too close to home and to my dear father to wait. Don't be harsh with him. I was impatient and the walk was ever so short."

He released her, beaming with pride and affection. "Well, let's have a look at you then. What a beautiful lady you've become! I should hardly recognize you."

It was the same comment he made each time she returned from school, but it never failed to please her. Her mother had died when she was very young, and with her father's attention diverted to commerce, Alyssa had always done her best to prove that even without a mother's influence, she could become a lady. If her doting father heard reports of her mishaps at school, he never condemned her for them. Instead, he praised her spirited progress and cemented her determination not to disappoint him.

"I am taller," she conceded shyly.

"You are a vision of your dear mother"—he squeezed her hands—"and now I shall cease prattling for fear of turning maudlin. Are you refreshed enough to meet our guests?"

"Did you invite Mr. Turner again this year?" He was one of her father's oldest friends, an avowed curmudgeon, but Alyssa loved his tales of holidays past when her mother had graced the halls and played hostess.

He shook his head. "His health plagues him and I'm afraid he didn't feel up to the journey. But he sent his best wishes and made a point of asking after you."

"He is too kind." She took his arm as they headed toward the salon. "A full house this Christmas?"

"Not too crowded," he assured her. "Your cousin arrives the day after tomorrow, and the Cunninghams are already settled. Mrs. Wolfe has descended and brought her pugs! And then there is Mr. Yates."

"Mr. Yates?"

"I met him through my club and may possibly have business dealings with him in the future. I understand his family is wintering somewhere in southern Europe and Mr. Yates preferred to stay closer to home. I was able to convince him to join us for the holidays. No small feat, I can assure you!"

"Are we infamous then?"

"Ah, Mr. Yates is not one to make merry, I'm afraid. But I've promised him as much peace and quiet as can be managed, and so far, I think he has been content enough."

As they reached the salon doors, she braced herself. She was long used to her father's elderly, eccentric friends and grim business associates. "I will be as quiet as a church mouse, Father. Mr. Yates won't even know I'm here."

His look was skeptical but benign, and she urged him

through the doors before he could point out the obvious flaws in her pledge. Rounding the corner, she put on her best hostess smile.

"There she is! Oh, Reid, she will break countless hearts!" Mrs. Wolfe gushed, and crossed the room like a galleon at full sail. She was an old neighbor and family friend, who Alyssa tolerated for her father's sake. Mrs. Wolfe's large bosom was barely restrained as she leaned in to give Alyssa a kiss on the cheek. Pugs darted between their feet and Alyssa stepped back as soon as she could manage it.

The woman's improper use of her father's first name had not escaped her notice, but it wasn't the correct moment to press a point of etiquette. "You flatter me, Mrs. Wolfe. I'm so glad to see you here, and with your—beautiful little dogs." One of the little darlings had wriggled under her skirts, and Alyssa had the distinct impression that one of her ankles was under attack.

"They are dears, aren't they? I can't go anywhere without them." Mrs. Wolfe beamed, oblivious to the chaos.

Alyssa did her best to agree, glancing about the room for an ally. Mrs. Cunningham had deliberately stayed seated, wisely keeping her feet safely tucked under the settee. Mr. Cunningham rose to offer a polite bow, but also returned to the sanctuary of his seat at the earliest chance. They smiled from their perches, though Mr. Cunningham kept a close watch on the four-legged ambushers.

Her father cleared his throat before releasing Alyssa so that he could move further into the room and avoid stepping on one of Mrs. Wolfe's dears. "Energetic things . . ."

"Oh!" Another nip at her ankles, and Alyssa wished she'd had the forsight not to change out of her traveling boots into daintier shoes, which evidently drove pugs wild. "H-how many do you have now, Mrs. Wolfe?"

A subtle kick only made it more of a game, and still Mrs. Wolfe failed to notice Alyssa's dilemma. She was literally trapped just inside the doorway.

"Five," the lady said proudly, sweeping one of the culprits into the crook of her arm, then sailing toward a seat next to the fire. She glanced back at Alyssa. "Won't you join us? Mrs. Cunningham was just about to tell us of her eldest daughter's engagement."

"Congratulations, Mrs. Cunningham. Fern must be so excited." Alyssa shifted her weight, and tried to edge away from the pug's increasingly relentless teeth. The dog, however, apparently had determined that she was too tasty a prize to relinquish and planted himself in a maneuver worthy of a master strategist.

Her lifelong nemesis, gravity, entered the fray.

With one more attempt to neither crush the pug nor lose her footing, the inevitable occurred. With a small squeak of surprise, Alyssa found herself tumbling backward.

Instead of making an undignified landing, strong arms caught her from behind and a familiar voice rumbled in her ears. "Pardon me, miss."

"Binkley!" Mrs. Wolfe cried out, spotting at last the offending pug emerging from underneath Alyssa's skirts. "What a naughty boy!"

For a moment, Alyssa wasn't sure whom Mrs. Wolfe had called "Binkley"—the pug or her rescuer. The man was still holding her, politely waiting for her to steady herself, as shock and surprise worked against her recovery.

What was he doing here? Had Mrs. Wolfe just called him a naughty boy? What would the woman say if she could read my thoughts? If she knew that every time this man touches me I turn into a wanton?

She pulled away, painfully aware that her cheeks

were ablaze with embarrassment as she turned to face him. "Th-thank you, sir."

"Mr. Leland Yates," her father intervened jovially, "you have just met my daughter, Alyssa."

The man who had rescued her twice today bowed briefly, his expression unreadable. "Miss Martin, a pleasure."

She curtsied, wishing once again for invisibility. "Mr. Yates." Her breath caught in her throat as she took in his appearance. In his crisp and impeccably fashionable attire, he looked even more handsome than he had before.

"Join us, Mr. Yates," Mrs. Cunningham invited, gesturing to a vacant chair. "We've seen so little of you these past few days."

"I apologize if I've been reclusive. I fear I have no talent for drawing rooms and prefer the library." His hesitation was palpable.

"Ah, you've talents enough, sir!" Mrs. Wolfe cooed.

Alyssa glanced across the room, seeing nothing that would lure a man to remain there. Between Mrs. Wolfe and her pack of miniature black-faced marauders, the Cunninghamses' promised tales of their daughter's engagement and her own exposure as his host's rude offspring, what man would linger? One look at her father confirmed that he was at a bit of a loss to offer Mr. Yates an out in the wake of Mrs. Wolfe's enthusiastic coaxing. She had no choice but to attempt to rescue the man on her own.

"Mr. Yates's talents are not in debate," she said with a smile, as if they were all in accord. "But we can hardly compete with the quiet solace of the library, can we?"

There. A graceful opening to allow the man to slip out of the noose. She was sure that Mrs. Harris would have approved.

"The library provides a different kind of entertain-

ment, Miss Martin," he replied, his eyes flashing with
mischief. "But I would hate for your father's guests to
harbor the wrong impression of me."

To her amazement, he moved into the room, taking a
seat across from a delighted Mrs. Wolfe. The pugs eyed
him briefly, but made no effort to overrun him or taste
his footwear.

"Ah, this is much better!" Mrs. Wolfe beamed in triumph. "Now, we can all become better acquainted."

As all eyes seemed to focus on Mr. Leland Yates,
Alyssa took a seat on one of the window cushions, still in
shock at finding the man who'd witnessed her humiliation earlier that day in her father's house.

"Yes," he agreed, then patted one of the pugs. "Have
you known the Martins long, Mrs. Wolfe?"

She puffed up visibly with pride, happy to take center stage in the conversation. "For as long as my memory
can fashion history! I remember when Mr. Martin
bought this house to please his young bride, and I
remember his daughter's great adventures when she
was barely out of swaddling clothes."

"Really?" he responded innocently. "Miss Martin
does not give the appearance of being a great adven-
turer."

Alyssa's eyes widened as she realized he had just
deftly maneuvered himself out of the line of fire—and
thrown her into it. Her sympathy evaporated and she
silently vowed to kick him in the shins when the opportunity presented itself.

"Oh, yes!" Mrs. Wolfe gleefully continued. "Wicked
little thing! Don't let her demure appearance fool you!"
She turned toward their host. "She had more adventures
than any child I have ever known. Do you remember,
Mr. Martin? Climbing trees and scampering about like a
wild creature till I thought you'd resort to a cage for her."

"She was hardly a wild animal, Mrs. Wolfe!" her father protested gently.

"Ha! Caught her naked in the vicar's garden—"

"I was eight! I was not being wicked, and I most certainly was *not* naked!" Alyssa's composure scattered as she noted how closely everyone was following the scandalous turn of the conversation—especially Leland Yates. "I was chasing a rabbit and it had gone down into a hole. I took my dress off so that it wouldn't be spoiled. I had a slip on!"

Laughter erupted in the room and Mrs. Wolfe clapped her hands. "There, you see, Mr. Yates? One can never tell."

Mr. Yates shook his head. "I wouldn't be so sure."

Alyssa gasped. "*I* am sure, sir. I am absolutely sure my rabbit-chasing days are far behind me."

"I only meant that the story reveals a creative mind and apparently one with a unique way of approaching problems." His serious visage at last yielded a smile. "I didn't mean to imply that we should worry about your current modesties."

Alyssa crossed her arms, caught between the urge to box his ears or answer his smile with one of her own. The man was infuriating!

"My daughter is like no other," her father said in a tone full of protective pride, "And we will have no more tales." He walked over to her and put a comforting hand on her shoulder. "Even the most proper lady is allowed to keep her childhood mishaps to herself."

She put her hand over his, delighted by his defense. "Thank you, Father."

Mrs. Wolfe pouted, openly displeased at the jest ending too quickly, "Granted, Mr. Martin, but we meant no harm. Who is not entertained by pleasant reminiscences?"

Mrs. Cunningham, who was notoriously shy, intervened softly, "I am always entertained in your good company, Mrs. Wolfe."

"You are a dear!" Mrs. Wolfe gushed. "But then we are forgetting your own great news! I am sure Mr. Yates will be delighted to hear of your daughter's impending matrimony this summer to Mr. Bonner."

"Oh, perhaps we can spare the poor man!" Her father laughed. "No bachelor wishes to hear about impending matrimony."

"Few men not already netted can abide the subject," Mr. Cunningham agreed. He gave his wife a loving look, briefly touching her hand. "Wait till he has felt the sting of Cupid and met his own match; then he will cheerfully suffer stories of wedding trousseaus and household china."

Mr. Yates shook his head vigorously. "You mistake me for another man. I do not subscribe to a belief in cherubs with arrows and I do not seek a match."

"No man does!" Her father gave Mr. Cunningham a conspiratorial look. "But whether we look for them or not, they seem to happen nonetheless."

Mr. Yates shifted in his seat, "I fear I am outnumbered with none to take my side."

Alyssa bit her lower lip. She would have loved to chime in that he had every right to choose his own fate. But in light of her looming debut, Alyssa knew any comment she made would ring false. After all, a good marriage was considered the "ultimate prize" and to argue against it would only upset her father and alert him that his daughter had learned more than Latin at Mrs. Harris's school.

"Ah, you see! Miss Martin looks terribly disappointed, Mr. Yates." Mrs. Wolfe chuckled.

"You mistake my reaction," Alyssa said, unwilling to

let the misunderstanding go unchecked. "Envy is not disappointment, Mrs. Wolfe."

"You feel envious of our poor bachelor?" Mrs. Wolfe pressed merrily.

Alyssa's chin came up in defiance, terribly aware that every eye in the room was on her, so she did her best to convey carefree bravado. "Men have the luxury of doing what they will. I am simply envious of Mr. Yates's skills. After all, he seems sufficiently agile to avoid Cupid's arrow if he keeps a clear head about him. As for me, I can't seem to avoid tripping over a little dog."

Her remark ended the standoff as everyone broke into peals of laughter. All at her expense, but Alyssa paid the price without hesitation.

Alyssa studied her hands in her lap until the conversation shifted to less harrowing topics. Mr. Cunningham enquired after her father's new hounds and then Mrs. Wolfe compared the recent weather to the storms of the month past. When Alyssa was sure it was safe, she risked a glance upward.

The rise and fall of voices faded as she realized that Mr. Yates was looking directly at her. Not in judgment or even as if she were the brunt of a great jest, but instead his dark brown eyes seemed to study her intently. He looked as if he were trying to determine her secrets or decide a great question. Alyssa wasn't sure if she should be insulted or even allow such an intimate assessment. It would have been easy to duck her chin down and break her brazen acknowledgment of his scrutiny. But it would have been a cowardly choice, and something in her refused to yield.

I'm not afraid of you, Mr. Yates. And I've no worries of humiliating myself in front of you, as I have already handily accomplished that a few times over. So look your fill!

The fluttering in her stomach belied her courageous

thoughts, though. His attention unnerved her, as shimmering heat flashed through her and reminded her of their ride home together. No man had ever held her with such intimacy before; once again, she could feel his strong chest and shoulders at her back.

She blushed and gave up the battle, looking away to the relative safety of a shelf of curios. For the first time, Mrs. Harris's warnings returned—with more weight and substance. Apparently, men *could* be more trouble than mismatched slippers.

Dratted man. He had a bruised shin coming at the very least!

When she looked at Leland again, she saw he'd turned his attention to her father. Now she could study him unobtrusively. Dressed in dark colors, barely relieved by the solemn white of his cravat, he looked like a panther seated among them. His hair was in fashionable disarray, soot-black curls burnished with dark mahogany streaks. His features well formed and elegant. She liked the firm lines of his mouth and the tiny crease between his brows when Mrs. Wolfe said something particularly grating. Her father had described him as a man who didn't make merry, and she believed it. Though she suspected he hid a livelier sense of humor he didn't want others to see for some reason.

The thought made her smile. She would regard him as she did any of her father's associates. Allowing for his younger age, he was no different from previous male guests they had entertained. He would linger in male company, prefer talk of business and horses and cross her path with only a polite nod.

Now if she could just picture him with the gout, the illusion would be complete.

Three

*S*leep eluded her, and Alyssa finally gave up the struggle. Kicking off her bedcovers, she sighed, resolving to make the best use she could of the dark, quiet hours. She'd never been one to waste the gift of time granted by an occasional bout of insomnia—though this bout had a new unique twist. Her brain simply wouldn't stop replaying the sensations of her ride with Mr. Yates earlier in the day. It was an exhausting exercise, to say the least.

Donning her dressing gown and slippers, she made her way to the windows to admire the wintry scene outside. Frost covered everything in a subtle glittering layer that appeared and disappeared as clouds moved across the moon.

Home. She'd missed it during her months away, long absence adding appeal to every remembered detail of the house and its occupants. Now the return was just as sweet. Her belongings had been recovered that afternoon, and carriage and horses retrieved without great ado. But word of the accident and Gilbert's state had reached her father and he had pulled her aside after dinner to give her a tight hug and express his concern. Due to her pleading, her father had been lenient with poor Gilbert. Instead of unemployment, the driver had earned a month of mucking stalls for his merriment, and Alyssa was relieved. She leaned her head against the cool glass wishing she could worry her father less and please him more.

Pulling the sash of her dressing gown a little tighter, Alyssa decided that there was nothing more to be done than to put the day entirely behind her. She needed no candle to guide her as she found her way to the library. Reading a good book perched in her favorite reading chair was going to be a homecoming gift to herself. It would certainly clear her mind of the troublesome Mr. Y—

"Don't young ladies always have a dragon-like chaperone in tow?"

She froze as she entered the doorway and saw that the man in question already occupied her favorite chair though she replied readily enough. "Mrs. Hale wouldn't appreciate the description, if she were here. Unfortunately, her sister became ill and she went home to attend her for the holidays."

The panther rose from his chair by the lit fireplace. "Leaving you unprotected?"

She lifted her chin defiantly. "I'm not . . . unprotected."

His eyebrows rose as he looked about the room. "You brought one of the pugs with you?"

She smiled. "They *are* formidable. Am I in need of protection?"

He closed the book in his hand. "From the likes of me?"

"I . . . I mean . . ." she said haltingly. "You're not . . ."

"Dangerous?" he supplied with a wry grin.

The question sent an odd thrill down her spine. He had shed his coat and cravat, and wore a simple white linen shirt untucked over his elegant breeches. He stood before her in disheveled elegance, with his throat bare. She couldn't take her eyes off that newly exposed bit of flesh. She imagined she could see his pulse jump in the corded tension of his neck keeping pace with her own wildly beating heart. "You're a guest of my father's. He's not in the habit of inviting . . . dangerous men to the house."

"I see." His look was inscrutable, and made her skin feel flushed and warm. "You're sure of this?"

She forced herself not to take a step back. "You're deliberately pretending to be more fearsome than you are, sir. Earlier today, you very chivalrously rescued me—not the act of a villain. Besides, I hardly think murderous thugs lurk in libraries in the middle of the night reading . . ." She stepped forward to get a better look at the book he was holding. "Jonathan Swift?"

"I find pessimists amusing sometimes," he confessed easily, his expression unapologetic. "Perhaps they make me feel more cheerful by comparison."

"You aren't normally cheerful?"

"Hardly, but then we thugs have to keep up appearances."

Alyssa laughed. "I will keep that in mind."

"Well," he said, crossing his arms and shifting his weight; his eyes raked her up and down with evident appreciation, making Alyssa recall that she was not dressed for a debate on literature. "I must say it never occurred to me to consider my reading choices so . . . revealing."

"Oh," she exclaimed softly, embarrassment flooding through her. With all his talk of danger, she'd been picturing burglars and murderers, while he'd been hinting at the pitfalls of addressing a relative stranger alone in the middle of the night when wearing nightclothes. "Oh, dear."

"Exactly my thoughts." He nodded solemnly, but his dark brown eyes were lit with amusement.

She nervously touched the knot in her sash, "I . . . I should go. After all, I wasn't going to linger anyway. I'll just take an old favorite and be on my way." She crossed to the shelves and took a volume without even looking at it. Clutching it to her chest, she turned to him. "There then, I'll just bid you good night."

He left his own book on the chair and drew nearer, the firelight playing off his features. She simultaneously felt a curl of pleasure and a small spark of fear. It was as if every nerve ending in her body was suddenly attuned to him, and cared nothing for the rules of any hour.

He reached out to her, and Alyssa's breath caught in her throat. Surely he wouldn't—

His fingers curled around the book's spine, taking it from her easily. "*Lady Peabody's Guide to the Art of Flower Arrangement*?"

"I . . . I was having trouble sleeping," she countered.

"This should solve that problem." He held the book out to her. "An old favorite?"

She snatched the small volume back from him, wishing she'd had the luck to reach for a book on the art of shin kicking. "There are several amusing anecdotes." She looked up at him, another wave of awareness sweeping through her. He was close, but in a strange way, not close enough.

Go. Tell him good night and then just go. You're acting like a ninny.

Instead, she heard herself saying, "I should thank you for . . . keeping your word. You would have had an opportune moment earlier today in the salon to top Mrs. Wolfe's tales of my mishaps with one of your own."

"A gentleman is only as good as his word." His eyes darkened with a look that sent another silken coil of pleasure down her spine.

"Lucky for me that you are such a gentleman," she whispered.

He shook his head slowly, his smile in the firelight casting a spell that kept her in place as he drew closer. "Did I make that claim?"

"You . . ." Alyssa suddenly couldn't remember what he'd claimed earlier, much less why she was holding *Lady Peabody* as if it were a shield. "You did."

"Oh," he said with a nod, "then I suppose I must be." His hand ever so slowly reached out and captured the long, thick braid that trailed over her shoulder. "Still, it seems to me that I have too readily forgone the chance to boast of your rescue. Surely your father would have been pleased . . ."

"You wouldn't!"

"Well," he said, shrugging again, a casual gesture that diverted her attention away from his strong hand holding her braid. "I've been feeling guilty since I agreed to deceive your father, a man I hold in high regard and whose trust I have hopes of earning in business. My very livelihood and reputation are now in jeopardy, and I am entirely at your mercy. It hardly seems fair of you to ask such a thing, without . . ."

"Without?" She held her breath.

"Without payment," he supplied, his voice deep and soft, like a caress.

"You want money?!" she squeaked in shock.

His eyebrows arched in disbelief, his fingers temporarily ceasing their gentle play on her braid. "Miss Martin, you do have a way of saying the most surprising things."

"What kind of payment are you suggesting then?" she asked.

"I was thinking of a kiss."

For just a moment, she could have sworn that the space between them had diminished, that all the air in the library had become electrically charged. The sensation came too quickly for fear, and Alyssa marveled that even without really touching her he could evoke a fever-like heat in her blood.

His lips brushed hers for one fleeting moment, a feathery touch full of promise; but before she could marvel at the tender shock of it, his arms were around her, his hands splayed on her back, and first impressions fell away in a sweet blaze as his mouth claimed hers completely. Her lips parted at the onslaught of white-hot passion, and the discovery of his tongue and the sensations it elicited banished the world. His teeth grazed the pulsating flesh of her lower lip, and Alyssa's joints melted at the jolt of delicious pleasure. A daring she had never known overtook her as she in return sampled each texture and taste of him. Another sound escaped her, but it was far from a lady-like sigh. It was a small moan of need, uttered without thought as Alyssa arched against him, eager for more.

Without warning, he gently ended the kiss, his breath hurried as he slowly stepped back to hold her at arm's length. "Miss Martin . . ."

"Yes?" She held still, her own breathing ragged, struggling to focus on his face. A twinge of horror at her unbridled reaction to his kisses flooded her. *Oh, dear. I'm sure a lady would have had at least one fleeting thought about protesting. Did I disgust him by not doing so?*

He released her completely and bent down to retrieve the book she'd dropped, and she felt the intimacy of the moment slip away. "Your secrets are safe with me." He held out the slim volume and then made a slight bow, effectively ending their exchange. "I hope you enjoy Lady Peabody's excellent company."

She nodded, still somewhat dazed, and escaped in a flurry of lace. Instead of relief, she felt confused at the abrupt end of his kiss and at the realization that she was more than a little disappointed.

Disappointed? That he hadn't proven himself to be less of a gentleman? How is that possible? What would Mrs. Harris say? Something stern about minding her surroundings and applying herself to better decorum, no doubt. Oh, my word! I stood there in my nightclothes, engaged him in conversation and then . . . I let him . . .

She was sure she'd shocked the man. Hurrying back to her room, Alyssa could only be grateful that the sole witness to her most recent bit of lunacy was Lady Peabody and her flower arrangements!

Leland watched her go, taking a few moments to recover his composure.

Damn it!

He returned to his chair by the fire to pace in front of it in frustration. He'd come to the library to retreat from the apparitions of Alyssa Martin that were keeping him from his rest, only to find himself haunted in the flesh. She'd come upon him like a vision in ivory lace and green ribbons and all his stern philosophies had melted to drivel.

The small ornate clock over the mantel chimed the half hour, and he finally stopped his march. He hadn't intended to touch her, much less enter into a lively game of sensual blackmail. But it hadn't felt like a game. For the first time in his life, his own infallible reason hadn't stepped in to remind him of the dangerous consequences.

Her inexperience had been sweetly evident, but it hadn't been nearly as jarring as her innocent and unguarded reaction to his touch. But she was his host's daughter. He was a guest under their roof. It would be pure villainy to take advantage of Martin's invitation by seducing his daughter. She was also only weeks away from her social debut, and possessed a fortune that every eligible bachelor from eighteen to eighty would be vying for. A dry inner voice reminded him that she was exactly the kind of ripe prize his family expected him to secure.

All his vows of personal integrity and proclamations against such a marriage tasted like ashes in his mouth. If a gentleman was only as good as his word, then he was in a terrible tangle.

Four

"Sleep well?"

Alyssa blushed as she took her seat at the breakfast table. "Yes, thank you, Father."

He grinned merrily, unaware of her discomfort at the inquiry as he settled back into his meal. "I imagine there is no better rest to be had than your first night back home."

"Oh, yes!" she agreed, focusing on the eggs on her plate. She couldn't remember falling asleep the previous night, but odd heated dreams featuring Leland had chased her into the morning. As the sun had mercilessly driven her from bed, Alyssa had decided that kissing was hazardous to one's health. How could anyone survive for long without a good night's sleep?

"Ah!" her father hailed. "Mr. Yates! I was wondering if we'd see you this morning."

Alyssa managed not to drop her fork before composing her features into a smile. "Good morning, Mr. Yates."

"Good morning, Miss Martin." He took his place across from her, looking entirely too rested and handsome as far as Alyssa was concerned.

"I'm so glad to have you both here," Mr. Martin went on. "I have a bit of a favor to ask."

"What kind of favor?" Alyssa asked.

"Well." He set aside his kipper. "Mrs. Wolfe has invited me to accompany her for some shopping in the village. Apparently, there are a few more gifts and sundries she would like to purchase before Christmas, and I didn't wish to send her off alone."

"You are too thoughtful a host for that, sir," Leland noted

"And the . . . favor?" Alyssa pressed, a bit confused.

"I'm afraid I also promised to take Mr. Yates on a riding tour of the property this afternoon. I was thinking that since you would have enjoyed the outing as well, my dear, there's no reason you couldn't take my place." He gave her a hopeful look, like an expectant schoolboy begging a treat. "I wouldn't trouble you, but Mrs. Wolfe most insistent and I find I wouldn't mind a bit of holiday shopping."

Alyssa swallowed hard, not wishing to disappoint her father, but—to be alone with the man who made her bones turn to jelly? After *that* kiss? "I would love to, but I'm sure Mr. Yates would rather wait for you, Father. Perhaps tomorrow or—"

"The weather is too fine to waste and it may not hold much longer," Leland interjected, the very picture of innocence though his eyes sparkled with amusement at her reaction. "I'm sure the tour will be most enjoyable with such a pleasant guide. I confess I had been looking forward to the ride, sir, so it is most generous of you to volunteer your daughter."

"You see?" Her father reached across the table to take her hand. "No need to lose the day after all!"

"Should I ask Mrs. Cunningham to chaperone?" Mr. Yates offered, and Alyssa bit back a squeak of surprise. She'd hardly expected him to crusade for her protection. Before she could second the brilliant return to proper etiquette, her father waved a hand.

"She doesn't ride and, frankly, I hardly think a chaperone is required in these circumstances."

"What circumstances?" she asked, unable to stop the question.

Her father chuckled, eyeing them both benevolently. "I believe I can trust Mr. Yates well enough, especially as a man so openly reputed to avoid romantic entanglements. No, I have no concerns."

Alyssa wasn't sure whether to be flattered at his trust or a bit miffed that he was so wretchedly wrong. In any case, she could hardly argue without revealing too much of her own transgressions. She risked a look at Mr. Yates, and was rewarded with another of his heart-stopping smiles.

Leland turned to her father. "Thank you, sir."

It's a conspiracy! Well, I don't care. I'm not afraid of you and you can look as handsome as you please! Alyssa thought. She was sure of one thing. If she kept a good seat on her horse, he could hardly manage another one of those kisses. *I'll tie myself to the saddle if I have to!*

She spurred her mount forward, secretly pleased at the docile little mare and her sweet manners. To his credit, Mr. Yates didn't seem to mind the leisurely pace his livelier horse was forced to match. The weather had cleared, though a few patches of winter white lingered in the hollows and shaded groves. She loved the rolling hills and admired her father for keeping the remnants of the old-growth forest, which had been thinned over the years by previous tenants and farmers. As a child, she'd always imagined that the trees were ancient friends and great manses for the fairies and sprites her nanny had told her of. Now the landscape's beauty was stark and undeniable. As they covered the estate's terrain, winding along a riding path through the grove, Alyssa was grateful to have her own horse—though the sight of Leland's thighs in tight deerskin riding breeches was enough to stir her blood. She glanced over at him, determined to redirect her thoughts. "Tell me more about yourself, Mr. Yates."

He arched his eyebrows. "Where should I begin, Miss Martin?"

"Any of the usual points would suffice," she suggested with a smile. "Your family? Your home? Perhaps you could tell me about your business?"

He laughed. "And bore you to tears?"

"I doubt you are so dull."

He shrugged. "Only if your standards for excitement are exceedingly low."

"You are deliberately being mysterious!" She tossed out the accusation, laughing.

"Gentlemen aren't allowed their secrets? Only ladies, then?" he countered.

"Aha! Then you *do* claim to be a gentleman!"

He smiled enigmatically. "I try."

"You, sir, are a rogue—and I am not fooled by you in the slightest." She lifted her chin, a surge of confidence fueling her saucy words.

"Thank God," he said. "But how do you know that I am a rogue?"

She blushed. "Well . . . I know the signs."

"Really?" His skepticism was palpable and it urged her on.

"I'll have you know that I am well-informed about scoundrels."

"Well informed. I see. And the signs?"

"Scoundrels are handsome and charming, with easy flirtatious manners that make them very affable. A scoundrel ignores the rules of good society, but he's like a chameleon, fitting in anywhere, often welcome in all sorts of circles."

"Sounds like a frightening fellow," he interjected, his expression somber though his eyes betrayed his merriment. "Definitely to be avoided."

She frowned, realizing now that everything she'd said seemed a compliment to the dratted man. "Scoundrels lack credibility," she added sternly.

"So, a man of mystery would be . . ."

"A gentleman need never prevaricate." Alyssa nodded in triumph, pleased to have her argument come to a witty turn.

"Well"—Leland leaned over as if disclosing a confidence—"that will certainly narrow your search for a husband. I take it you're looking for a very honest man who is ugly, a complete bore, but with good references and lofty introductions. And of course, as a strict adherent to the rules, he should indicate no interest in your person beyond tentative attempts to hold or—dare I say it—kiss your hand?"

Her mouth dropped open in astonishment. Her description of a scoundrel hadn't seemed laughable when she'd spoken, but its opposite was beyond preposterous. Still, this was hardly a debate she could concede. "You are deliberately twisting my meaning! And deliberately trying to get me flummoxed!"

In a spark of spirit, she spurred her trusty mare off the path, intending to make a point of putting some distance between them. But instead of a flashy show of independence, fate once again intervened. Her mind was on the infuriating Leland Yates and not on her chosen direction. The density of the grove of trees didn't invite or allow the haughty gallop she'd envisioned and disaster set in within a few paces. Low branches formed a stubborn web of snares; barren twigs and branches tangled in Alyssa's bonnet and curls and arrested her forward progress. The pain was startling, but the humiliation of getting stuck well within view of Mr. Yates was worse.

She reached up to try to free herself, but only managed to make the mare sidestep from her struggles. "Whoa, girl!"

"Miss Martin?" Leland's voice carried from the safety of the path.

"Yes, Mr. Yates?" Alyssa responded calmly, determined to brazen it out and salvage what pride she could. *At least I kept my seat in the saddle.*

"May I offer you a hand?"

Her heart skipped a beat at the familiar words. Twice in as many days, she'd managed to get herself stuck—and once again it was the delectable Mr. Yates on hand to rescue her.

"I . . . I appear to be imitating Absalom."

She heard him approach, the sound of his horse's hooves muted by the soft ground.

"Just remain still." His voice was soothing, to keep the mare from spooking at his encroachment. His approach was slow, as he navigated the low branches and wove his way around the worst of it to reach her. At last, he drew his horse alongside hers. His expression was concerned, but also reassuring. "Just stay as still as you can, Miss Martin, and we'll have you free in no time."

She started to nod, but winced at the tug on her hair. "I suppose you're going to remind me that invisibility isn't an option?"

He smiled. "It hadn't occurred to me. But let's see to you first and then we can return to the debate." He reached over and gently began to assess the damage. Alyssa held her breath as he ever so slowly snapped some twigs and then eased her riding hat from her head. It caught on another sharp branch, but he carefully made the effort to save her fashionable accessory. He studied it briefly, before tucking it behind him.

"Was that the worst of it?" she asked cautiously, mesmerized by his gentleness.

"Almost," he reassured her. Removing his gloves, he leaned in again. This time, his eyes locked with hers and Alyssa almost dropped the reins of her mount. He was impossibly close, and suddenly she wanted nothing more than to experience his kisses again.

"If you took the reins and held her still, I'm sure I could manage the rest myself," she offered.

He shook his head. "Patience, my beauty."

Her lips parted to chastise him for the ill-timed compliment, but his touch silenced her protest. He began unpinning her hair with gentle hands, untangling long tresses from the rough twigs, making her gasp at the sensation of his fingers brushing over her bare face and neck and working through the silken strands.

"Ouch," she whispered, as one stubborn branch refused to relinquish its grip.

He lowered his hand and stroked her cheek, his fingers trailing down her jaw to her neck. His touch was pure sin. "Stay still."

A command easier to give than to follow, Mr. Yates! Dratted man! He's deliberately torturing me!

Only the snap of wood and the cadence of their breathing echoed in the grove as Leland freed her, teasing her with each restrained caress and stroke.

At last, her hair was completely undone, a golden cascade of rambunctious curls down her back. The effect was intoxicating. To have a man disarm her with such slow, tender precision—it was something she had never imagined. A lady would never allow such liberties. She felt naked and vulnerable with her hair down, hating the heat that flooded her cheeks, staining them a telltale pink.

"You . . ." Words abandoned her as she saw the flash of desire in his eyes.

In one fluid movement, he pulled her from her saddle onto his lap. She struggled against him in surprise, but he was much stronger than she. "You shouldn't—"

His lips descended, following a sensual trail along one side of her face and down the column of her throat.

"Oh, my . . ." she murmered, gripping his coat lapels and reveling in his attentions and offering more of herself to him. The grove spun around as the world narrowed to hold only the two of them. With one of his hands entwined in her hair, he moved to take control. Her jacket buttons gave way, and his hand skimmed over her collarbones to graze the pearl buttons of her blouse—a whisper-light touch that explored the barriers between his skin and hers and sent bolts of heat down her spine to pool between her legs.

His lips abandoned the pulse at her throat and, at last, found her lips. This kiss had no tender start, but instead betrayed his hunger—and hers. Hard, demanding kisses enflamed her and Alyssa could only cling to him and savor the fiery-sweet taste of his mouth. Her lips felt swollen and soft against his, and she groaned as his tongue tasted each sensitive curve and pulse of hers. When his hand moved over the pert swell of her breast, his thumb teasing its peak through layers of silk, the coil of need within her tightened into a pleasure that was almost painful.

Oh, dear. A lady wouldn't . . . Oh, my! But she couldn't seem to dredge up even the faintest bit of resistance to his touch. Instead, she wanted the pearl buttons torn away and the heat of his hands on her. Her eyes fluttered open, astonished at her own desires.

He growled in response as she arched her back to instinctively beg for more. He pulled her closer and shifted back to settle her more tightly between his legs. "What a siren, you are . . ."

His words emboldened her and she daringly made her own tentative trail of kisses down his throat, to find the same sensitive spot on his throat and drive him on. Instinctively she grazed her teeth over the pulse, and was instantly rewarded as he tightened his hold, his hand moving against the buttons of her blouse. The smooth pearls gave way easily, and the ties of her chemise and corset yielded just as quickly.

The touch of his bare fingers against the ripe curve of her breast sent a shiver of raw need through her. His mouth caught hers again, drinking in her gasps and sighs as her nipple hardened against his touch, the circular teasing dance of his fingers matched by his tongue and sweeping her into a spiral of ecstasy. His mouth trailed away from her lips to sample the taut coral point, and Alyssa was sure that there was no sensation more wicked and sweet than the soft friction of his hot tongue against her swollen nipple.

This. This was beyond . . . anything . . . how in the world . . . Coherent thought eluded her, and Alyssa almost sobbed at the aching want that whipped through her. His hand left her back and traced the outline of her outer thigh through her riding skirt, and she trembled. *If he meant to . . .* she had no real idea where the dance was going but every nerve in her body seemed to thrill at this exploration. She wriggled tighter against his hard thighs, setting off another cascade of tension and heat. He slid her skirt up slowly, his fingers finding the firm warm flesh of her thigh above her stocking, shifting the ribbons to tease the skin just beyond his touch. Slowly his hand moved upward, and Alyssa wondered if a person could die from wicked rapture alone.

And then he abruptly stopped, his eyes wide as he raised his head.

"D-did I . . . hurt you?" she asked confused.

He shook his head and then smiled. "Hat pin."

"Hat pin?"

He reached around his back and offered up her now slightly crumpled riding hat from where he had tucked it behind him. Their embrace had dislodged it, and he had suffered an ignoble poke in his backside.

"So much for trying to be a gentleman," he said, shaking his head. Firmly but gently, he began to retie her undergarments, calmly restoring everything that he'd so feverishly undone.

It was all she could do to catch her breath as his fingers touched her bare skin. "I don't know what to say." She was sure that no etiquette book had ever touched on this particular situation. Her face burned with embarrassment at the liberties she'd allowed him—of the liberties she'd have begged him to take.

He was looking at her again with an intensity and hunger that made her tremble in his arms. "Let's get you back to the road and safely home. You'll have the ride to compose a good lecture to give me, and I promise I'll absorb whatever punishments you see fit."

She nodded, a mischievous smile giving her away. "A good plan."

"For now, turn your face toward my shoulder. I'd hate to see it scratched." Cradling her protectively, he led her mare back through the grove to the groomed path on which they'd been riding.

Alyssa was grateful for the reprieve, praying that the color in her cheeks would recede now that she wasn't looking into his eyes. Once back on the lane, they dismounted.

She nervously finished buttoning her blouse at her throat, brushed at her skirt and closed her riding coat, wishing some of that lecture would compose itself. *A lady would have come up with a scorching reprimand by now. Oh, dear.* "Well, shall we head back?"

"Not just yet." He reached in his pocket and held out the handful of hairpins he'd retrieved during her rescue. "You may want these first."

She took them with a shaky laugh. "Ah, yes! Harder to explain than losing a carriage."

"I would offer to help, but . . ." A lingering flash of desire in his eyes eloquently made his excuses. It definitely wasn't wise to test their resolve by allowing him to touch her again.

"No," she readily agreed. "I . . . I can manage. Just hold my bonnet for me, please."

She had never before done the simple task while a man looked on. After their heated exchange, it seemed silly to ask him to look away while she arranged her hair. But the intimacy of the moment was unavoidable. Nervously, she tried to distract him from his open admiration of her efforts. "You have a twig in your hair, sir."

He found it easily and pulled it roughly from a dark curl at the nape of his neck. "Thank you."

She smiled, envious of his ease. "You . . . have quite a talent for rescuing me, Mr. Yates. I should thank you again, though I believe it is your turn to render payment."

His look was pure amazement. "Are you asking me for a kiss?"

"No!" She blushed, wishing she'd regained more of her scattered wits. "I was thinking you could . . . answer at least one or two questions about yourself. I'm willing . . . to risk boredom."

He shook his head and then began to laugh. A true, hearty laugh that altered his countenance completely and made her heart soar. The serious Mr. Yates was anything but grim at the moment, and it pleased her to watch him try to catch his breath from laughing so hard. "How is it that I can never predict what you're going to say or do, Miss Martin?"

She finished pinning a braid along the crown of her head, and arranged the rest of her curls as she replied cheerfully, "I'm not sure. I think I'm very predictable. I'm fairly sure it's the rest of the world that is determined to remain indecipherable."

"Well, one thing is certain." He handed over her bonnet for the final touch. "It's impossible to become bored in your presence, Miss Martin."

Alyssa secured her bonnet with a shy smile. *I could say the same for you, sir. Dratted man.*

"You're impossibly tall!" Violet squealed with delight upon her arrival later that afternoon, pulling Alyssa into a rib-crushing hug on the house's front steps. "You swore you wouldn't grow!"

"I was twelve," Alyssa gasped, smiling over her cousin's shoulder. "You cannot hope to hold me to that oath."

They both laughed and Alyssa released her to take in Violet's changed appearance as well. It had been years since they'd seen each other. Violet had always been more petite with a delicate exotic beauty that Alyssa had envied. Now it seemed that Cousin Violet in full bloom didn't disappoint. Every shining brunette curl was in place, framing porcelain perfect features, and her brown eyes were as brilliant as Alyssa remembered.

She shook her head in astonishment, "Violet, instead of looking weary and wilted, you look as fresh as if you'd just taken a turn around the village."

"Nonsense! You're sweet to say such things." Violet shrugged off the compliment, removed her bonnet and preceded Alyssa into the house. "My parents send their warmest regards and, of course, wanted me to express their regrets that they couldn't partake of your father's hospitality this Christmas."

"We were so looking forward to their company."

"Oh, please! They are as dear to me as anyone ever could be," Violet cut her off with merry enthusiasm. "But trust me, between Mother's smelling salts and Father's propensity for shouting everything, since he won't admit that he can't hear well, they are an imposition extraordinaire!"

Alyssa kept from answering, not sure how to argue that she'd always loved her aunt's and uncle's quirks. Perhaps because they made her own quirks seem more normal.

Violet continued as they made their way to the guest room that had been prepared for her arrival. "I cannot wait to hear more about your time at school. Your letters were so entertaining, but I refuse to believe you shared all the best details!"

Alyssa couldn't contradict her. She would never commit all her infamous mishaps to paper. "I shall make up a few to please you, then. But only if you tell me how you are enjoying being 'out.'"

"Oh, it's ever so much more fun!" They reached the room and Violet pulled her to a small settee for their tête-à-tête. "Just the excitement of your first dance is magic. And of course, the ability to engage in private conversation with unmarried men without fear of judgment."

"Oh, yes," Alyssa answered innocently. She was not unaware of the rules she'd broken with Mr. Yates. She'd just decided that the rules never seemed to apply to the odd circumstances that kept throwing her into his arms.

"You'll see!" Violet assured her with the supreme confidence of a young woman with a full year's experience of being out in society.

Alyssa tried to muster the required enthusiasm. "I can hardly wait."

"You have nothing to worry about cousin," Violet said, reaching over to pat her hand, as if in consolation. "You are not ugly after all, and once word of your fortune is known, you'll have your choice of suitors."

Alyssa shook her head and attempted a smile. Violet was never one to mince words. "Let's talk about something else."

Violet shrugged. "Tell me. Are there many guests? Do you expect more for the gathering on Christmas Eve?"

"A few more for the party. You're the last of the houseguests to arrive, though it's not a terribly full house. The Cunninghams have come, though their daughter Fern is staying in London with friends. Mrs. Wolfe—you might remember her from your last visit—has brought her entire pack of pugs. And . . . there is Mr. Yates."

"Mr. Yates?"

"A business associate of my father's," Alyssa supplied, willing to allow Violet to make her own assumptions.

"Oh," she said with a pout. "I hate to give offense, but I do wish my uncle would invite someone young and personable."

Alyssa had to bite the inside of her mouth to keep a

straight face. "Yes, well. His friends are his own, and nothing to do with us."

The footmen arrived with Violet's trunks and the maids began unpacking. Their privacy lost for the moment, Alyssa left her cousin to oversee the settling of her things and to allow her to bathe and change after her journey. Her conscience nibbled a bit at the deception regarding Mr. Yates, but there was nothing to be done now. Violet would see for herself how "young and personable" he was, and Alyssa wondered if she could plead ignorance—as if she'd never noticed how handsome he was.

Or as if I were hoping Violet wouldn't.

Nonsense! Alyssa corrected herself, determined not to allow her good sense to abandon her completely. If the man was handsome, it was not a point that should concern her. Girls who were not officially out were, by rule, supposed to be happily ignorant of any and all characteristics that a man like Mr. Yates might possess.

And if Violet was in the more liberated position to make an inventory of his every delectable feature—it shouldn't make a bit of a difference.

When Alyssa entered her own room, her eyes rested on the bound leather volume at her bedside. Lady Peabody mocked her silently, as if to note that out or not out, the dowager botanist hadn't missed that for most of the previous night she'd just lain awake and uselessly tried not to think about Mr. Yates's eyes.

She sighed again, and sank into a chair by the fire. There was no fighting the inevitable. Mr. Yates would meet her lovely cousin who never got stuck in carriage windows, trapped by trees or chased rabbits and that would be that. He would bestow his heart-stopping kisses on Violet, and there was nothing she could say.

At least if he is paying attention to Violet, he will be ig-

noring me, and maybe I can get a good night's sleep—with
or without dusty old Lady Peabody's help.

The inevitable was longer in coming than Alyssa
anticipated. Mr. Yates sent his regrets for dinner that
evening, eating in his room and working on business
correspondence. Alyssa expected to feel some relief,
since she wasn't sure she could look at the man without blushing like a fool.

The following day, Violet was a welcome distraction
from Mrs. Wolfe and her pugs. The cousins escaped to
the solarium amidst the potted palms and plants,
where Violet could regale her younger friend with exciting stories of her first social season.

"The dancing is the best part," Violet assured her. "I
even wore out several dancing slippers, if you can
imagine!"

"In one evening?" Alyssa asked, deliberately over-
playing her ignorance in the hope that Violet would
laugh and change the wretched subject.

The tactic failed.

"Over a few nights, silly! Not that they are made to
last, mind you. There is something thrilling about sac-
rificing a fashionable and lovely scrap of silk and ribbons for the pleasure of the dancing."

"Or is that so the shoe sellers can make more
money?"

Violet gasped in shock. "Alyssa! You mustn't say
such vulgar things! Commerce is hardly the subject of
a lady's conversation."

"I fail to see how a practical grasp of the shoe trade
is repulsive." Alyssa bit her lower lip and decided that
the point wasn't worth the battle. "But I'm sure you're
right. I'll try to keep your advice in mind."

Violet's expression softened and she took Alyssa's

hand. "You'll be fine. Besides, you're lucky. You could paint yourself blue and set fire to your hair and still manage to catch a husband."

"And how would I be able to manage that?"

"Your dowry, silly!" Violet released her hand. "You'll be forgiven anything."

"How comforting." *If a discussion of commerce is vulgar, then how is the trade of my fortune and my future any less offensive?*

"Oh, don't be so dour. After all, you have many advantages that other girls would die for, and when it comes to marriage—"

"Ah, here you are, dearlings!" Mrs. Wolfe interrupted. "I told your father you would be as thick as thieves."

"Forgive me for keeping her to myself, Mrs. Wolfe," Violet said, undaunted by the intrusion. "We were making plans for the party Christmas eve!"

Alyssa's squeak of shock at the lie was easily lost to Mrs. Wolfe's louder endorsement. "How delightful! What sort of plans?"

Alyssa was ill prepared to respond. "I . . . *umm* . . ." *So much for a clever improvisation.* As the world's worst liar, all she could do was hope that Violet would do better.

"An entertainment!"

"What kind of entertainment?" Mrs. Wolfe pressed, openly intrigued. "A game?"

"A little musicale." Violet reached down to pat one of the pugs. "Alyssa has a lovely voice and we thought it would make a lovely surprise for her father."

One of the pugs barked, and Mrs. Wolfe laughed at the canine's endorsement. "Delightful! Well, if it is a secret, naturally, I shall say nothing. Come, Binkley, let us leave the ladies to their plans and schemes."

Once Mrs. Wolfe was safely out of earshot, Alyssa couldn't stop herself. "Why did you tell her that story? A musical performance? Are you serious?"

"A small pageant! Your father will be delighted, and I'm sure you'll look adorable. You *can* sing, can't you?"

Alyssa's mouth dropped open; she was dumbfounded by the looming disaster. "Somewhat, but not—"

"Perfect!" Violet was the epitome of calm. "Your father won't expect much and I have a wonderful idea for our costumes. It will make such a lovely impression during our song. I'll play the piano and it will be a bit of a duet."

"Costumes?"

"Come now! You are officially the hostess and are expected to lead the evening's festivities."

"Yes, but for simple games, or to make sure the mulled wine doesn't run low. I'm not sure I—"

Violet raised an eyebrow, her look one of pure challenge. "Don't tell me you're shy."

"Shy isn't the word I would have chosen. I'm not . . . a performer." It was a vast understatement, but Alyssa wasn't ready to admit defeat.

"But I'll be performing, too. It's not as if I've thrown you to the wolves to face them alone, cousin."

That's what it feels like. "Of course you're not. You just caught me by surprise."

Violet giggled. "It will be fun!"

"Fun," Alyssa echoed tonelessly. The party was two nights away. Until that moment, she'd been only mildly nervous about the gathering. She'd been looking forward to a lively evening of Yuletide festivities. But now, she was wondering if a head cold might be her only escape.

Violet sighed dramatically. "I'd meant to tell you my

idea before. Mrs. Wolfe's sudden appearance reminded me of it. Besides, I didn't want her to know we were talking about marriage. She might have turned matchmaker! After all, doesn't she have a nephew or two lurking in the Cotswolds?"

"Just one," Alyssa said, shuddering at the thought.

"Odds are he resembles a pug!" Violet whispered conspiratorially and they both laughed.

Alyssa stood. "Come, I should see what my father wanted."

"Rescue from Mrs. Wolfe, no doubt!" Violet stood gracefully to follow her.

"Violet, please! They are old friends and nothing more. She is hardly . . . pursuing him."

"I meant nothing by it. My mother has always contended that he should have remarried long ago. It's a mystery why he hasn't."

"No mystery." Alyssa turned back to her cousin. "My parents loved each other very much. Once you've known that kind of love, you can hardly expect to marry for anything less."

"Anything less?" Violet was openly skeptical. "I wouldn't have guessed you were such a romantic."

"I'm not a romantic!"

"So you'd consider it wrong to marry for anything less than a great love?"

Alyssa crossed her arms defensively. "We were speaking of my father."

"And now let us speak of you."

How to get out of the tangle? "The topic is hardly interesting. I'm not foolish enough to expect any man to melt into a puddle when I enter a room."

"What do you expect?"

The question was so simple, but it shook her a bit. Mrs. Harris had made it very clear how treacherous the social landscape could be and that love was more often the guise of cruel fortune hunters than of warm-hearted heroes. But she'd seen the love of her parents and secretly hoped for a miracle of her own. It had only been in the last year or two that she'd decided that between the threat of fortune hunters and loveless marriages, she would prefer to just keep house for her father and turn into a happily eccentric spinster. Mrs. Harris had the right of it. Better to live independently than forfeit everything for the wrong man.

"I expect, through no fault of my own, to be a delightful disaster this summer. I'm sure I'll meet a lot of interesting people and then when it's all over, I think I will have an amusing journal to mull over for some time."

"Umm . . ." Violet appeared to have been struck speechless.

Emboldened, Alyssa went on. "As for the love of my life, trust me, Violet, I have no illusions. He won't discover me unless he trips over me, and even then, I'm sure he'll simply enjoy telling his friends about a funny young woman he once bumped into."

"Unless he's sworn to secrecy," Leland's voice came from behind her and Alyssa froze.

"Mr. Yates!" Alyssa whirled around to face him, "I thought you were riding."

"The weather drove me in." He didn't look pleased.

Violet poked her in the back and Alyssa knew the moment was upon her. "Allow me to introduce you to my cousin, Violet Horner. She just arrived yesterday in the late afternoon."

Violet executed a perfect curtsy, her features flushing demurely to show off her lovely coloring, and Alyssa's stomach churned with dread. They would make a beautiful pair, her cousin's beauty the foil against his darker coloring. "Mr. Yates."

"Miss Horner." He managed a stiff bow, then stood back. "I hope your journey was tolerable."

"I was ahead of the weather and very lucky, sir."

"Yes, well . . . if you'll excuse me. I have some additional business to attend to before dinner." He bowed again and then moved past them down the hallway.

It was only when the echo of his steps had faded that Violet found her voice. "Oh, my!"

"My thoughts exactly," Alyssa whispered too quietly for Violet to hear.

"Why you wicked creature! I was expecting some teetering old thing!"

Alyssa shrugged. "Isn't he?"

Violet punched her playfully in the shoulder, "You know very well he isn't!"

"I suppose," she conceded, gathering her skirts to continue her way to her father's study.

"So what do you know of him?" Violet caught up quickly, taking her elbow.

Another good question. "Just what I told you before. He is a business associate of my father's. I believe they met at his club." At Violet's unsatisfied expression, she cast about for anything neutral to add. "And he's . . . very industrious and hard-working."

"Is he unmarried? Is he always that serious? Is he rich? And what was that jest about secrecy?"

Alyssa stopped, freeing herself from her cousin's grasp. "Unmarried; yes; I'm sure I don't know and as to his fortune, I never thought to ask. Violet, please!"

"I apologize," her cousin said, appearing a bit distracted. "It wouldn't have been proper for you to inquire."

Alyssa could see the workings of her friend's

mind. As she'd dreaded, Mr. Yates had landed squarely into her schemes. If Violet deemed him a wealthy enough target, he'd be in love with her by Christmas morning. Since childhood, she'd learned that anything Violet desired was almost always hers for the taking. "I'm sure Mrs. Wolfe has the answers you seek. Matchmaking or not, she's unlikely to let a bachelor escape inquiry. She'll be having tea in the drawing room with Mrs. Cunningham, and I know they'd love the diversion. I'll join you there after I see my father, all right?"

"Yes, please!" Violet kissed her on the cheek and left her in a happy rush to learn more about the handsome Mr. Yates.

Her father smiled as she entered, and Alyssa basked in the security and welcome of his presence. "Am I disturbing your work, Papa?"

"If you are, I am happy for it. A man can turn gray over columns and figures, and where is the glory in that?" He abandoned his desk and came round to take her hands.

Alyssa pretended to scrutinize his hair and face. "I see no gray." The lie was lovingly told and earned the laughter she'd expected.

"You have a loving daughter's gift for not seeing what the world sees, and I won't scold you for it." He pulled her toward the cushioned bench near the room's fireplace, where they settled comfortably. "Now, tell me. Are you enjoying your holiday and your cousin's visit?"

"Yes, of course!"

His scrutiny was much more honest. "Alyssa, your eyes betray you, my dear."

"It's not the holiday. I'm thrilled to be home and to

spend time with you. I'm sure it's just . . . perhaps it's nerves over my debut."

He shook his head. "There's no cause for concern, then. What's a quick curtsy at St. James and a few minutes with some crumbling dowagers? The court's a formality and nothing more for a beautiful girl like you."

"A formality I would prefer to miss."

"Every girl dreams of the chance. Besides, how will all those handsome lords and dashing earls discover you if not for a royal presentation and a lovely social season?"

Alyssa reached for his hand. "Father, please. I know you've done so much to give me this debut. But I've been unofficially out for a while—as your hostess and companion." She smiled. "You're very easy to keep house for."

He shook his head. "Alyssa, you're too young and beautiful to spend the best years of your life looking after your dusty father."

"Are you so eager to see me gone?"

"Hardly!" He laughed. "And don't think I'll allow the first man who asks to whisk you away! I have high hopes for you, dearest."

Alyssa sighed, but did her best to appear cheered at her father's pronouncement. There was no sense in belaboring the issue. "Mrs. Wolfe said you wanted to see me?"

"Oh . . . yes! It wasn't anything pressing really. It's just that Mrs. Wolfe has offered to accompany us to London to assist in outfitting you for your launch and I thought since Mrs. Hale might not be in a position to continue as your chaperone, this might present the perfect solution."

"Oh!"

"You seem surprised. But you've known dear Mrs.

Wolfe for some time, and she assures me that such familiarity can be a great comfort. Especially as you've admitted to suffering some nerves—"

"No! I mean, yes, of course, I did say that I was a little . . . nervous. But Mrs. Hale hasn't indicated that she won't be back before . . . I mean, I already have a chaperone, Father."

"But her sister is ill enough to keep her at her side, and I'm sure she would be relieved to be released from her responsibilities here. We cannot take her from her family at such a time."

His argument was sincere and Alyssa felt heartless to contest the point. Mrs. Hale was a good friend but she could hardly insist that her debut was more important than an ailing sister. However, the thought of Mrs. Wolfe hovering over her for her first Season was unacceptable and a guarantee of incidents beyond reckoning!

Before she could compose a diplomatic reply, her father went on. "I know Mrs. Wolfe may seem a bit effusive, but I truly believe she has your best interests at heart."

I'd rather have Lady Peabody.

"I'm sure she does."

He beamed at her, as if she'd declared an end to taxation. "It will be a Season to remember, I promise you!"

He drew her into an embrace and Alyssa could only smile over his shoulder.

Oh, Father, I can make the same promise.

Five

$\mathcal{T}$he pugs created quite a stir the following day.

The ringleader, Binkley, disappeared from his doting owner's rooms and the search for him was nothing less than a catastrophe in motion. In despair at the loss of her favorite dearling, Mrs. Wolfe suffered an attack of the vapors and took to her bed, while guests and staff were charged with his recovery and safe return. Alyssa quickly volunteered to look outside. She was sure that Violet would latch onto Mr. Yates, and she was in no mood to watch their romance unfold.

Now she had a wonderful excuse to escape the house. Or at least to take a brisk walk to clear her head of dreary fancies about Violet's perfect face being kissed by Mr. Yates or his lean strong hands unpinning Violet's brunette curls.

"Binkley!" she called out, but not with any urgency. *I'd have run away too, little man.* Poor Binkums might have had his fill of little sweaters and his mistress's endless attentions. Then again, he might just be planning another ambush. The image of him lurking in the hedgerows like a black-masked highwayman made her laugh.

"Where are you, Binkley? I'm wearing my best boots! Yummy footwear and tender ankles!" She pulled her muffler a little tighter, and kept up her pace. The snow had receded to small drifts under the trees, leaving the lanes muddy and slick. Alyssa tried to concentrate on her path and avoid dwelling on how many times Violet had innocently managed to touch Mr. Yates during lunch. At least Alyssa tried until a blur of yipping black and tan burst from the undergrowth. She gave a startled cry and the chase was on. Alyssa tried to catch him before he disappeared, but Binkley was enjoying himself far too much to allow for a quick end to the game.

It was like trying to catch a greased pig. Down the lane and around trees they ran until she was dizzy and short of breath. Still, she wasn't going to let her nemesis win, so she tried a new tactic by running around the opposite way to catch the little bounder before he realized she wasn't still on his heels.

The strategy was flawless, except for her narrow concentration on her quarry and not the ground beneath her. The puddle was deep and icy cold, and before she could alter course to minimize the damage, she lost her footing on the slick ground and landed on her rump smack in the middle of the mess. A squeak of surprise and dismay gave way to laughter, as she admitted to the disgraceful finish of her short career as dogcatcher.

"And what exactly is so amusing?"

Alyssa instantly quieted in astonishment, and gained her feet in embarrassment. "Mr. Yates!"

My God, the man has a gift for seeing me at my worst, doesn't he?

"Are you all right, or is the laughter perhaps a first sign of illness?"

She reached up to straighten her muffler and soggy coat, and stepped out of the mire. "I'm fine! I was picturing the headmistress of my school and wondering what she would say about ladies and mud puddles."

"She would have something to say, I take it?" He was impossibly handsome and undisturbed by her mishap.

"Undoubtedly something about ladies steering clear of mud puddles in the first place."

"Not something about waiting for men to lay their coats down before attempting to cross one?"

"Oh, no!" she corrected him playfully. "Mrs. Harris would never advise such a missish display. It isn't in keeping with the curriculum of her School for Young Ladies."

"Exactly what kind of lessons are you receiving at this school?"

She shrugged and gave him a mischievous smile. "The usual lessons, I'm sure."

He laughed. "I doubt that anything about your life qualifies as 'usual,' Miss Martin."

Alyssa glanced down at her muddy coat and skirts before perching with a resounding squish on a nearby stone outcropping. "As a confirmed bachelor, wouldn't the life of young ladies fall outside your area of expertise?"

Leland watched her and knew she was unaware of the muddy smudge on her nose—and of the fetching picture she made. He couldn't think of a woman he had ever met who wouldn't have been a screeching harpy at this moment. Instead, Alyssa was a cheerful mess.

"True enough. From a distance, I suppose I've made some assumptions."

"And what did you assume?"

"You might take offense as a representative of your gender." He was stalling, enjoying the conversation more than he wanted to acknowledge. After their ride yesterday during which he'd uncharacteristically let his desires overrule his good sense, he was relieved to find her once again relaxed in his company.

"I'm afraid you'll have to take the risk. How can I assure you of my 'usual' life if I don't know what you consider to be 'usual' for a young lady?"

"Very well," he said, leaning against a tree. "I'd always heard that young ladies spend more time at their dressing tables than anywhere else. That their interests and topics of conversation were limited to fashion, baubles and gossip. I imagined they embroidered and painted watercolors all day."

Her mirth was obvious, as she clapped her hands. "Helpless and hopeless!"

"And so I take it that young ladies are not?" he deliberately baited her.

"Well, *I* am not, though I suppose my tumble into the puddle may not bode well for my defense. Or at least I don't aspire to be helpless."

"And other young ladies do?"

"They might because they believe that that is exactly what men desire," she conceded.

"It is our fault, then?"

"Not that all men have the same opinions, but not all young ladies are in a dire state of constant fainting, chained to their vanities, Mr. Yates. If they feign weakness, I'm sure it's only because it's expected of them."

"A prevarication you don't attempt?"

She blushed, but didn't drop her gaze. "I have no talent for it. I am well versed in most of the required skills thought necessary for a refined young lady, but I'm afraid I will never master myself entirely." Her voice lowered theatrically. "I'm dreadful at watercolors and I have no patience for embroidery and I have never fainted in my life."

He made a great show of mock horror and shock at her confession, striving not to laugh. "You *are* unusual!"

She leapt from her perch to give him a playful punch on his shoulder. "Wretched man!"

He caught her hand and the warmth of laughter yielded to something much more powerful. Slowly

Leland drew on each wet tip of her glove, peeling the leather from her wrist to soothe the sensitive skin. Frosted clouds of their breath intermingled and disappeared and Leland knew the thrill of a dangerous heat and desire.

Kiss her.

Release her.

The conflicting impulses kept him in place but only for a fleeting moment, her fingers imprisoned against the rhythm of his heart. She didn't shy away from him; her face was tipped up toward his, waiting innocently for another taste of the maelstrom that kicked up whenever they were close to each other. But with every indulgence, he found it harder and harder to let her go. The title of gentleman was everything he'd measured himself and others by, but whenever she was near, it was the last thing he aspired to. When her father had requested that they ride together, it had been too easy to accept the gift of fate. He'd meant to apologize for his blackmail kiss in the library, but there was little he regretted. When she'd tangled herself in the thicket, regret had been even harder to summon.

Regret or restraint. I seem to be in short supply of both when it comes to this woman.

Her eyelids lowered, and he gave in to the primal impulse to possess her. He leaned in to kiss her, anticipation stoking the fire as his blood surged and his cock hardened. Desire dictated his actions, and Leland drew her into his arms for a hungry kiss. Her mouth parted at the onslaught, and her sighs whipped him on as he savored the soft sweetness of her lips and tongue, devouring and tasting, exploring each texture of her until he lost track of where he ended and she began. He'd called her a siren, but it was his own body that seemed to sing with every breath she took. Feminine curves beckoned, and his hands moved of their own volition down her back to her tiny waist, then to the firm mound of her bottom. Fingers splayed, he lifted her up against him, deliberately pressing his hardened length against her, relishing the friction of the clothes that constrained them and all too aware of the luxurious heat between her legs.

"Leland?" she managed breathlessly, her lips grazing the sensitive shell of his ear and sending shock waves down his spine. "The mud . . . you'll ruin your coat . . ."

He smiled, reveling in the odd twists of logic in that beautiful head of hers. He bent over to release her briefly only to sweep her off her feet, lifting her into his arms to cradle her against his chest. "I'm not sure that's the ruin we should be worrying about, sweetling."

"Oh," she whispered, and he savored the heated and dazed look in her eyes as she struggled for composure in the wake of his attentions.

"Alyssa!" Violet squealed as she came around the path, her eyes wide in shock.

Leland froze instantly, loathing the intrusion and the change in Alyssa's countenance, the horror and shame that flooded her eyes, but there was no doubt the damage was done.

Unless . . . He decided to brazen it out.

"I've got you," he whispered, making no move to put her down. Alyssa squeaked in surprise, and he went on more loudly to Miss Horner before the performance was spoiled, "She fell and was unsteady on her feet. Thank goodness you arrived when you did, Miss Horner."

"I . . . I came to tell you that we found Binkley in the garden . . ." She gave the pair an assessing look, but clearly felt more comfortable focusing on her cousin. "You're filthy!"

"I hardly think that matters," he interjected sternly. "She may be hurt!"

"N-no!" Alyssa protested, but her confusion and flushed color only gave his lie more momentum. "I'm fine, really!"

"Here, let's set you down and make sure." He gently rested her back on her stone perch, risking a small conspiratorial wink once his back was turned to Violet. He knelt in front of Alyssa. "Feeling better?"

"Yes, thank you," Alyssa replied. "I feel so foolish for slipping."

Violet's cheeks colored, her vexation apparent. She stepped forward, her eyes narrowing with displeasure. She reached inside her coat pocket and withdrew a handkerchief. Violet used it to wipe the dirt off of her cousin's nose, then turned the cloth to be sure that Alyssa could see the results.

Leland clenched his jaw in frustration as the last hint of confidence in Alyssa's eyes vanished.

Alyssa shook her head, snatching the telltale cloth from Violet's fingers, "I should go back to the house and change out of these clothes. Mr. Yates, thank you for your assistance."

She turned swiftly, Violet following, and he was left to watch the two women head up the path. In the winter sunlight, his gaze was drawn to Alyssa. She walked slightly ahead of her cousin, a queen unaffected by the scolding creature in her wake. Leland suspected that her feelings were not as untouched by Violet's censure as she pretended. Nor by anyone else's censure, he was sure.

What a tangle she presented. It shouldn't matter to him, none of it. She would have her debut and marry some crusty blueblood, and the thought of it made his stomach churn. In rooms where using the wrong fork meant banishment, how would such a sweet sprite fare? How long before the mischievous light in her eyes gave way to miserable quiet?

He had never envisioned Alyssa Martin when conjuring his ideal. She was none of the things he had listed as necessary in a wife. Instead, every moment with her was an adventure and every conversation was unpredictable and entertaining. She defied convention, but he could think of nothing unladylike about her. Every time he touched her, she was like a living flame in his arms and he lost all control.

Compared to her, all other women were pale, demure shadows.

It shouldn't matter.

But God help him, he was actually beginning to accept that she mattered to him more than he wished. And there was nothing he could do about it.

"You were practically throwing yourself at him!" Violet spat out the words.

Alyssa kept her pace up until she reached her rooms, unwilling to have this quarrel in the public rooms of her father's home. "Your unexpected arrival gave you the wrong impression, cousin. I was hardly throwing—"

"He was holding you and it looked very much as if you were going to kiss him!"

Alyssa's cheeks colored furiously. Still, she could hardly let Violet know the worst. "I'd slipped, as you can plainly see"—she pointed to her muddied skirts—"and he had thought to steady me. Mr. Yates is a gentleman and was only being courteous. You are confusing, I suspect, my actions with your own feelings in this instance."

Violet pursed her lips. "Perhaps."

"There, you see?" Alyssa turned to her mirror, her dismay renewed as the impact of her appearance hit home. Oh, God, he'd been about to kiss her again—and they'd come dangerous seconds away from total disgrace. She'd been a breath away from ruin and hadn't cared a whit.

My goodness, I look like a mud rat. How in the world could he possibly wish to kiss a mud rat?

Violet stood next to her, and the contrast between them was painfully obvious. Violet was the ultimate vision of beauty and the feminine arts while she looked like a dirty child. Alyssa abandoned the mirror, and allowed Violet to make her own judgments.

Violet was silent for the briefest span, then she sighed. "It's just that . . . he's always so serious. And when I saw him smiling at you . . ."

"It's hard to keep a sober expression around girls in mud puddles, cousin. I would hardly blame the man."

"And I can barely get ten words out of him, yet there he is apparently comfortable enough with you." Violet's pout was more evident now, and Alyssa gritted her teeth in frustration.

"What are you saying?"

"I'm saying that . . . you should be more careful. Anyone less understanding might read things into your behavior and misinterpret your actions. I mean, for a girl who has declared little interest in landing a husband, one might wonder what exactly you are after in your attentions to Mr. Yates."

"You can't be serious!"

"You aren't out yet. Perhaps you don't understand the rules."

"I know the rules!"

"Good." Violet's smile didn't quite reach her eyes. "You are dear to me, cousin. And I should hate to see you unknowingly disgrace yourself or your father."

Alyssa found it difficult to breathe, she was so furious.

"I thank you for the advice," she replied before she could think better of it. "Especially from someone who has openly declared her desire to land a husband at any price. A few weeks more, and I'm sure I'll think more of my prized dancing slippers than anything else. Not even how ignorant and desperate I look chasing after a man simply because he is the only openly eligible one within reach! You care nothing for him, Violet! You only care that you win him!"

"How dare you!" Her cousin stomped her foot.

"Well, you've won! There's no competition for you to destroy or outwit here! Wrangle the man, as you wish! Out or not, I can assure you that I am the last woman on earth Mr. Yates would choose."

Violet's mouth fell open and closed, a shocked imitation of a fish out of water.

"Now if you'll excuse me, I'm going to have my maid draw a hot bath and help me change clothes before supper." Alyssa watched her cousin storm from the room, and instantly her bravado and fury wilted. It had been a petty catfight and now she feared she'd lost more than her cousin's friendship.

Nothing Violet had accused her of had been unwarranted, even if she had been less than gracious in her tone. Alyssa had been caught up once again in Mr. Yates's hypnotic gaze and warm embrace, eager to experience the pleasure he gave her. Her behavior had been beyond thoughtless and undeniably wanton.

She yanked on the bellpull, and sat on a wooden trunk with a sodden plop. If there was a line to be crossed, she couldn't remember seeing it in the wake of his heavenly caresses, but she knew she was well beyond the pale. Leland Yates was a force to be reckoned with, and nothing Mrs. Harris had mentioned had even come close to arming Alyssa against his kisses. Only one thing was not in doubt. She was in terrible danger of forming an attachment that had no hope of success and would only break her heart. How was that for an "incident"?

Six

"Violet?" Alyssa knocked softly on the door again. The hot bath and change of clothes had settled her nerves considerably. If only she could manage an apology to Violet before dinner . . . She needed an ally, not a rival, and the argument had been entirely her fault. No matter what effect Mr. Yates had on her senses, she had no right to lash out at Violet. Her cousin had always been a loyal confidante and quick with sage advice. She longed to tell Violet of her father's invitation to Mrs. Wolfe, and receive some friendly sympathy to bolster her courage.

Instead there was no response to her knock.

"Beg pardon, Miss Martin, but she's already gone downstairs," one of the maids said as she passed her in the hall, and Alyssa conceded defeat.

"Thank you, Betsy. I'll be sure to join her."

Betsy curtsied and disappeared quickly back down the corridor, and Alyssa was left to make her own way downstairs. Perhaps she might still find Violet alone for an opportune moment to repair some of the damage. She composed a speech as she went, but lost her train of thought just outside of the sitting room. She was brought to an abrupt standstill as she realized that the door had been left ajar. Mrs. Wolfe's voice was unmistakable.

"I tell you in sincere confidence, Mrs. Cunningham, that no man should be left to raise a daughter alone! Oh, he has done his best and been forced to turn to strangers and tutors, but where is the help there?"

"Oh, I'm sure it is not so dire. She is—"

Mrs. Wolfe interrupted, having paused only for breath. "What are strangers compared to a mother's loving guidance? Miss Martin has been overindulged and, I fear, overeducated, as any only child might be. It is only natural for poor Mr. Martin to do so, without a woman's wisdom and restraint to temper his generosity."

"Oh!" Mrs. Cunningham exclaimed.

From Alyssa's vantage point on the other side of the door, it sounded as if Mrs. Cunningham had wisely decided not to reply. Eavesdropping was a terrible act, but Alyssa couldn't bring herself to move.

"At least I can offer him assistance now with her debut." She lowered her voice slightly, and Alyssa blushed to realize she was leaning forward to catch her next words. "It's an important time in a young woman's life. I'd be honored to help Re—Mr. Martin steer his daughter toward matrimonial happiness."

It's hopeless. Four weeks of her company and I'll be willing to marry the first man who asks me—just to escape her!

"Miss Martin!" Mr. Cunningham hailed her cheerfully as he came up behind her. "Are the ladies not yet within?"

"Yes, of course. I was just . . . wondering if I should have brought my wrap."

"The hall is far draftier than the sitting and dining rooms, I can assure you! Come, my dear, I'm sure everyone is waiting for us. Myself, I am notoriously late, so this is a happy chance for me to find you."

She was guided across the threshold, directly into the line of fire.

"Ah, there is my dearest girl!" Mrs. Wolfe stood to greet her with her usual effusive embrace. "I understand you made quite an effort this afternoon to find my lost Binkley. I want to thank you."

"No thanks are needed. I understand he was ultimately found in the garden."

"Can you imagine? All that running about and it was our timid Mrs. Cunningham who managed the feat! And by simply sitting very still!" Mrs. Wolfe marveled merrily, returning to her seat.

"I . . . I had the cook's help," Mrs. Cunningham confessed with a blush. "A bit of last night's squab wrapped in a napkin did most of the work."

"At least you accomplished his rescue without resorting to a swimming lesson," Violet added as she came into the room. She smiled as she went on. "But how clever of you to think of bait, Mrs. Cunningham."

"Yes, how clever," Alyssa echoed softly, conceding that there was no chance for a truce or apologies. She'd earned a miserable evening by misbehaving earlier.

"Our own dogs used to favor squab," Mrs. Cunningham supplied, "so it was just a guess."

"We had larger dogs, of course!" Mr. Cunningham chimed in, looking pleased that the topic was familiar to him. "Fit to hunt, but disciplined enough for the house."

Luckily, the conversation momentarily veered away from Violet's hint at Alyssa's earlier mishap to the subject of hounds and their preferences. Alyssa tried to catch her cousin's gaze, but without success. Then, upon the arrival of a very dashing Mr. Yates alongside her father, dinner was announced and they proceeded into the dining hall with minimal ceremony.

She did her best to ignore the livelier end of the table. It was hard to tell if Violet's charms were having any effect on Mr. Yates, but apparently there was no shortage of female merriment between Mrs. Wolfe and Violet. It was even harder to concentrate on Mr. Cunningham's discourse on the workings of his new mill when she realized that the subject of mud puddles was once again being broached.

"Now what was that earlier about swimming lessons?" Mrs. Wolfe asked.

"I'm afraid Alyssa tumbled into a mud puddle, poor thing!" Violet confided. "It's a wonder she didn't catch her death of cold."

"It was hardly a tumble," Mr. Yates countered, his expression stern with displeasure.

"Mr. Yates is being kind. He is too sweet a man to tell you that she was muddy from head to toe." Violet sighed. "She must have ruined your coat, Mr. Yates."

"Oh, my!" Mrs. Wolfe burst into laughter.

"I came upon them and was quite cross," Violet admitted, her brown eyes fastened on her quarry. "I owe Mr. Yates an apology. It's just that seeing my dear cousin in such a state—I was mortified on her behalf. I hope I didn't overstep, sir."

"How could you not be distressed?" Mrs. Wolfe said quickly. "But what a scene! I warrant it was richer even than that time our Miss Martin attempted to paint her kittens!" Across the length of the table, Mr. Martin cleared his throat and Mrs. Wolfe gave him a contrite smile. "But we can leave tales for another time . . ."

Violet brightened, and leaned toward Mr. Yates. "Has Mrs. Wolfe told you about our plans for the Christmas Eve party tomorrow night, sir?"

He shook his head. "She has not."

"I haven't had the chance!" Mrs. Wolfe spoke between bites. "You are most elusive, sir!"

"I'm sure he is simply occupied with his manly pursuits! You mustn't tease him, Mrs. Wolfe. Mr. Yates has better things to do than bother with our schemes." Violet brushed her arm against his as she reached for her glass. "But tomorrow night, we may yet win his attention."

He arched an eyebrow warily. "And how is this to be achieved?"

"Alyssa and I are going to perform a song. A carol for the season, and I guarantee you won't be able to take your eyes off of her!" Violet grinned. "It will be nothing short of memorable."

He looked down the table and caught Alyssa's gaze. Her last hope of escaping her musical performance was extinguished as the rest of the table added their endorsements.

"What a pleasure that will be!" Mrs. Cunningham said.

"Better our lovely Miss Martin and Miss Horner than myself," Mr. Cunningham jested. "My singing has been known to set dogs to howling!"

Everyone laughed, with one or two exceptions. Alyssa knew why she wasn't giggling, but why Mr. Yates missed the joke, she wasn't sure.

At last dinner was over, and the guests were dispersing to their own rooms and pursuits. Alyssa lingered to walk her father to his study, where his usual evening's routine dictated port and a cigar. At the door, she hesitated while she debated how to broach a new and delicate subject that had troubled her as she watched him at dinner. "Father, you . . . you're quite fond of Mrs. Wolfe, aren't you?"

He colored, his eyes dropping for a telltale second, and Alyssa was sure she had her answer. "She has been a good friend through the years and I won't deny that I admire her lively nature."

"I'm happy for you, then."

He shook his head. "You are as transparent as crystal, dearest. You cannot see how I can compromise after loving your mother as I did."

"No . . . well, perhaps. You always swore that no one could take her place, and while I'm not adverse to it, Mrs. Wolfe is just not . . . whom I'd imagined for you."

He laughed. "You sound like a perfect mother hen worrying over me as if I am a fledgling chick! I am not a young man and without experience, Alyssa. I shall leave great love to your generation. My happiness doesn't demand the same wonderful heights it once did."

"Are you sure?" She leaned forward, more worried now that he'd admitted his feelings were so tame. "Perhaps when we go to London, it will be you who will find a true match."

"Ah!" He tucked her hand into his. "You are a romantic, after all!"

"Hardly!" She smiled. "And you wouldn't want me to be, would you?"

"Oh, dear. You've become so serious." He squeezed her fingers gently. "What I want for you . . . is a *good* match."

She nodded, her own eyes dropping to study her hand in his. "And for you?"

"I am not making any desperate choices, I promise. If I marry again, it will be for all the best reasons. All right?"

"All right, Father." She kissed him on the cheek, and left him to his port.

Seven

The conversation with her father had left Alyssa even more confused and restless than she felt earlier. He'd teased her about not being a romantic and said that love was solely the territory of the young, but then stated again that he wanted her to achieve a good match.

She could hear echoes of Mrs. Harris even now. *"A woman of sense and fortune can ignore those who would poach on her future."* Was Mr. Yates one of the men that Mrs. Harris had warned them about?

She repositioned her pillow for the countless time, and wondered which was doing her more harm: thinking about Mr. Yates or trying *not* to think about Mr. Yates.

She decided on the latter and kicked off her covers to sit up with a frustrated groan. *Very well, since not thinking about him is robbing me of my peace, let's have at it!*

She took a deep breath and allowed herself to draw him completely to mind. How firm and serious he'd been that night compared to everyone else; how playful and relaxed he'd been when he'd found her alone in her muddy splendor. They were almost like two different men, but instead of bothering her, she felt an odd bit of pride in her ability to make him laugh and draw him out of his taciturn ways.

I have that talent, if none other. And he didn't seem to mind a lack of embroidering skills . . . or the chaos that coalesced in my wake.

She stood, and began the search for her robe and slippers. *What is it about this man that unwinds me?*

She placed cold fingers to her forehead and waited for the inevitable answer. *He laughs at all the right moments and never at my expense. He defends me, even when I'm up to my muddy skirts in foolishness. And when he touches me . . . I only want him to touch more of me.*

There! Am I sleepy yet?

She smiled at her own failed experiment.

Hardly. Now all I can think about is returning Lady Peabody to her spot on the shelf and hoping he'll be there in the library again.

But at last, reason reasserted itself. She left the room, most decidedly without the lackluster Lady Peabody's advice on flower arrangement; instead, she had a few Christmas gifts tucked under her arm. The hour was late and she didn't even bother with a candle.

The music room that adjoined the green salon had been decorated for the party, and even in the moonlight, it conveyed an inviting warmth. Evergreen garlands were strung over the mantel and the heavier furniture, and it was easy to imagine how the room would appear within hours with all the candles lit and the crystal sparkling. There was nothing like the festive elegance of a Christmas gathering.

There were already a few gifts on a side table, so she added hers to the pile. She'd gotten Violet some imported lace and a hair comb, but now wasn't sure her gift would suit. She could only hope that her cousin would accept them as a sign of her admiration—and not as another ill-intended point about vanity.

Light entered the room as Mr. Yates came through the far door. "You're following me, aren't you?"

She was instantly thrilled that he'd found her again. "I . . . I could accuse you of the same thing, sir!"

He shook his head, holding his ground just inside the doorway. "Not this time."

She crossed her arms. "I was here first, so that would make you appear more suspicious, I'd say."

"I was having trouble sleeping and thought I heard a noise down here. If I suspected or hoped it might be you, well, that is information I shall keep to myself." He was smiling as he set his candleholder on the table, and Alyssa's breath caught in her throat at the sight of him in the glow.

At Mrs. Harris's weekly teas, she'd been lectured repeatedly on the dangers of looking only at a handsome face—Mrs. Harris had assured them all that a monster often lurked beneath the surface. Staring now at Leland, she wondered what lay beneath his own hypnotic façade. If one peeled it away, like a great overcoat, what sort of monster would he be? It was hard to picture him with scales. She tilted her head to consider the puzzle, but realized that the thought of Leland shrugging off his coat had unexpectedly taken over.

Alyssa straightened instantly, amazed that her mind could be so wayward after a night of self-lecturing on discipline. Instead of an innocent philosophical internal debate on the nature of men, the image of Leland undoing the buttons of his shirt quickened her pulse and made her completely forget what they'd been talking about.

"Miss Martin?" he prompted gently, drawing a bit closer.

"I, umm, yes?" Her cheeks heated with embarrassment. "I'm sorry, my mind wandered for a moment."

"I think I would give anything to know where it went just then."

"I-I shouldn't say."

"If you wish . . . we'll let you keep your secrets then."
He sounded so formal, and she smiled. Only Mr. Yates
could address her in the middle of the night as if they
were in a solicitor's meeting—an aspect to his character
she found very charming.

"And what were you thinking?" she asked before she
could stop herself, curiosity overtaking her.

"I was thinking that I am extremely talented at catching you in your dressing gown in the unlikeliest of
places." His hand reached out to capture the trail of the
sash at her waist, gently holding her captive.

"Oh!" She blushed, unable to argue the point!

"But I was also thinking that I might be one of the
most selfish men I know." His fingers tugged on the
green satin, drawing her a few inches closer.

"Really?" She scrambled to follow his words, her
heart skipping a beat as she wondered if resistance
were really possible. It was as if they'd stepped into a
dream.

"I should have ushered you inside long before Violet
arrived. Instead I kept you there in wet, muddy
clothes . . . for my own indulgence." His fingers held the
tether between them but stopped their tugging to allow
her to keep a "safe" distance from him—for now.

"For your indulgence?"

"I was enjoying your company too much to end it. It
never seems to matter what you're wearing . . . I have a
selfish desire to keep you all to myself."

"Oh." Alyssa bit her lower lip. "Well, that is . . . selfish,
I suppose."

"Will you forgive me?" Leland began to smile.

"The rules are far too muddled for me." She
shrugged, unable to stop from returning his smile. "I'm
the one who was chasing that fat little bandit and

slipped in the mud. I warned you that I seem to attract mayhem."

"I'll never doubt you again."

A comfortable silence settled between them. Alyssa found herself openly studying his visage and trying to decipher the man behind those dark eyes. It came to her that Mrs. Harris might just be right. Any man handsome enough to make a lady forget modesty might be dangerous after all. But if she were in danger, why didn't she sense it? Why did she feel more alive when he was near—her body thrumming with an unchanneled energy she couldn't name or master?

"Mr. Yates?"

"Yes."

"Do you mind if I ask you something?"

He nodded gracefully. "Not at all."

"You see, it's just that I don't know very much about you."

"And what would you like to know?"

She hesitated a moment before she spoke. "Are you a fortune hunter?"

He choked and coughed for a moment, but to his credit, the poor man managed to regain his composure fairly quickly without relinquishing his hold on her sash. "What a thing to ask!"

"You're right. I shouldn't have—"

"And what exactly do you know of fortune hunters, Miss Martin?"

All the wisdom of her schooling suddenly seemed so hollow and fragile. "It's late and I'm tired . . . so I'm sure I meant to ask you why you're so . . . kind to me."

Instead of being insulted, Leland appeared bemused. "Are you insinuating that any gentleman who shows you regard must be a fortune hunter?"

"I suppose that would be foolish," she conceded.

"But I've learned that a young lady of fortune can never be too careful."

"Your logic doesn't hold, Miss Martin." He came a step closer, tracing a single finger along the line of her jaw. "You have beauty and charm enough to draw any man you desire to your side. You should have more confidence in your own womanly powers. Otherwise, when all of London is at your feet, what will you say? Or will you blame only your fortune to explain all the offers you receive?"

"You flatter—"

"No," he cut her off gently. "I never exaggerate and until I met you, I could have sworn I never would have been the kind of man to discuss the merits of fortune hunters."

"I was rude just then. I shouldn't have questioned you."

"Miss Martin. You have every right to your questions and I owe you a few answers." He drew her closer, gently allowing his fingers to move across her bare skin and trail along her throat. "At the moment, I hardly feel like a gentleman as I keep you here in a state of undress and can think only of kissing every inch of you."

"Oh, dear," she whispered, wishing he would proclaim himself a rogue and give in to his desires—and to hers. "Every . . . inch?"

He nodded, his expression enigmatic as he stepped closer, his breath fanning her forehead; the hair at the nape of her neck stood up in anticipation of his touch. He hovered, just an inch or two from her, the torture almost unbearable.

"Y-you have a talent for distracting me, sir." She swayed slightly, struggling not to give in to the impulse to tear the sash from his hand, untie the dress and let the lace fall to the floor.

His expression grew more solemn as he stepped back, releasing his tenuous hold on her and deliberately breaking the spell he'd cast on her. "My brother holds title, Miss Martin. As a second son, I am expected to seek a wife with a good dowry. But I have been unwilling to play the part. So you see, I disgraced my family by choosing commerce over matrimony. I have made my own way by sullying my hands in 'trade' and turning my back on what other men would consider an easier path."

"Oh," she said, crossing her arms over her chest to cover her dressing gown.

"I am *not* interested in promoting myself to your father through you," Leland continued, frustration creeping into his voice. "I am *not* interested in increasing my wealth through the acquisition of a wife."

"I see."

He shook his head, his eyes dark and unreadable in the candlelight. "I don't think you do. For you see, according to your schooling, I suppose I am exactly the man you ought to avoid. While I am no fortune hunter, I am hardly the gentleman you deserve."

Before she could gather her wits to protest, he took another step back into the shadows.

"I'm looking forward to hearing you sing at the party tomorrow night, Miss Martin."

He bowed gracefully before striding from the room.

Leland gritted his teeth as he made his way through the dark house back to his rooms. He'd told her the truth, but not all of it. For her own good, he told himself, but there was no comfort in the thought.

For days, he'd blatantly ignored the rules of conduct and lost himself in her sapphire blue eyes, seizing every opportunity to touch her. Tonight would have been no different, and visions of laying her out beneath him on the silk rug at their feet made his body tighten with need. But instead, she'd asked a simple question, and lust had given way to something else.

He had money enough, but from any vantage point, he was hardly the best candidate for her hand; no one would believe he hadn't pursued her with an eye on her father's deep pockets. Hell, his own family would be the first to applaud the maneuver.

And the greatest hidden truth of all?

"Are you a fortune hunter?" she asked.

Yes. Perhaps in a way I am. Yes, I want to ruin you and taste you and make you mine by any means necessary. Everything else be damned!

*C*hristmas Eve arrived without regard to Alyssa's sleepless night or her misery after her last meeting with Mr. Yates. As her maid finished fixing her hair, she tried not to keep replaying his words in her mind.

Was there no consolation in being so completely assured that he was not a fortune hunter?

Evidently not. Not when, God help her, his denial only made her want him more. As he'd spoken, she'd realized that she'd insulted him beyond repair while confirming that he was no villain. It was the worst kind of tangle. Whatever passing fascination he had with her was in ashes.

She swallowed briskly to keep her eyes from tearing again. *Well, at least I've learned a valuable lesson about asking direct questions, and that is that I'd better not venture them unless I'm prepared to accept the answers.*

A knock on the door provided a welcome distraction, and Alyssa called out, "Come in!"

Violet entered, a vision in a pale green dress with dark green ribbon work along the bodice and tiny matching bows at the sleeves. She looked very alluring in the gown's simple lines. "Oh, it's so exciting, Alyssa! The musicians have arrived and the other guests won't be far behind."

"You look so beautiful!" Alyssa rose to take her

hands, astonished at the mercurial change in her cousin. "I'm . . . I'm so glad that you're here with us, Violet. I hope you can forgive—"

"Say nothing of it! I've forgotten what we said and after all, it's Christmastime. Who quarrels at Christmas?" Violet embraced her and Alyssa sighed in deep relief. At least she hadn't sacrificed their friendship over Mr. Yates.

"Here, let me help you finish." Violet waved away the maid, and cheerfully took charge. "Your curls are so pretty. Let's see if we can tame them into order."

Alyssa laughed. "You'll have no luck." She stood, preventing Violet from making the attempt. She was already sure that she'd achieved as much order as the fates would allow her for one evening. Her own dress was ivory with an organza overlay. Delicate seed pearls scattered on the bodice and sleeves made her feel like a mermaid decorated with sea foam. But next to Violet's presence in the mirror, it was hard not to feel less than beautiful. "Besides, no one will be looking at me when you are in the room."

Violet shrugged gracefully, "You are kind, but come! Everything's arranged and we should go downstairs to be in place to greet your guests."

"Absolutely!"

Arm in arm, they descended and Alyssa felt a surge of nervous energy. It would be a lovely party and surviving it "without incident" was sure to prove the ultimate test.

Her strategy was simple. She would play the perfect lady, limit herself to one glass of punch and do her best to avoid Mr. Yates.

As the evening unfolded, her strategy seemed to be working. The guests all arrived safely, bringing their number to a fashionable eighteen. The rooms looked perfect, and she was delighted with the lively flow of laughter and the display of holiday finery against the candlelight. As she mingled and caught up with old acquaintances and neighbors, she noted that everyone seemed to be appropriately merry for the occasion.

Cider and wine flowed, and Alyssa made a point of tending to Mrs. Wolfe to ensure that she felt welcome and content. After all, if the woman made her father happy, who was she to pout? "Have you sampled the cake, Mrs. Wolfe? Can I fetch you something?"

Mrs. Wolfe smiled and patted her ample midsection. "I am not one to omit life's pleasures. I have already had two pieces, thank you, sweet girl! What a lovely party!"

Alyssa surveyed the scene again, and nodded. *At least Mr. Yates hadn't put in an appearance to spoil her show of confidence.* "Thank you for saying so."

Before long, Violet found her and tugged gently on her arm. "It's time for you to change."

"Already?"

Her cousin increased the pressure on her arm to prevent her escape. "Don't be a ninny! Come on." Violet began to guide her to the door to the green salon. "I put your costume in here so you wouldn't have to go all the way upstairs to change."

"I can't change my clothes in the salon!" *Another woman might manage it, but with my luck? I know better than to risk losing a single article of clothing within a mile of a public gathering!*

Violet giggled as she closed the door behind them. "You'll be fine, you goose! I'll be changing as well and here, I'll even lock the door so there's no chance we'll be disturbed."

"Oh, of course!" Alyssa gave in, unable to fault Violet's logic or obstruct her enthusiasm.

Violet drew her across the room, to an ornate oriental folding screen. "I'll change first."

Within moments, Violet emerged from behind the paneling, an exchange of overdress transforming her green gown into an angelic concoction. She turned to Alyssa. "Can you finish lacing me up?"

"Yes, of course." Alyssa tugged on the ivory ribbons, marveling at the work. "I can't believe you made this yourself. It's lovely, Violet."

It truly was. Delicate wings graced her back and the ivory organza made her a pastel green confection with lovely sweeping lines. The long sleeves were sheer, but puffed and tied with matching ribbons and little bells.

"Yours is the same and should go right over your gown. The ivory will be sublime!" Violet ushered her behind the screen and pointed out Alyssa's matching ivory confection. Just like Violet's, it was complete with wings and ribbons. "Here, I'll help you into it. I confess, I worked on them all night. See? This just slips over your head and then the sash will tie just under your bust. Here," Violet went on happily, "let me help you adjust your wings. Now, for the final chorus, be sure and lift your arms. It will be much more dramatic that way."

"Really?" Alyssa started to lift her arms to practice, but Violet caught her hands.

"Not now! I'm tying the bows on your sleeves!"

Within seconds, Alyssa was transformed from a mermaid into an angel. There were no mirrors in the salon, but she didn't need one. Despite all her misgivings about singing, she suddenly felt very festive and even a little brave.

"You look lovely!" Violet applauded her handiwork. "Every eye will be on you!"

"Oh!"

"Just follow my lead and do what I do, and you'll be brilliant!"

Before Alyssa could voice her anxiety about the duet or point out that she'd never been a "brilliant" performer, Violet had propelled her back through the doorway and into the music room. Conversations sputtered to an appreciative halt as the pair found their way to the pianoforte.

Alyssa nervously had time for one last regret that they'd hardly practiced, but then the music began and it was all she could do to follow Violet's lead. Luckily, Violet went first, singing in a lively soprano that honored the melody and beauty of the carol. At Alyssa's turn, she stepped forward, determined not to disappoint. Her voice was softer than her cousin's, a duskier alto that was less tailored to a salon performance, but Alyssa knew she could at least carry a tune. As she sang, her confidence grew a bit and she relaxed into the magic of the moment.

As she took a deep breath, that confidence wavered as she felt the unmistakable splitting of a seam. She only hoped it wasn't too visible. But at the final chorus, when she raised her arms as Violet had suggested, the problem became more than evident. Both seams gave way easily under her arms, and her sleeves slid off. She tried to catch them, but the quick movement made the back of the costume disintegrate and one of the wings dangled comically behind her. Alyssa was not immune to the chuckles and open looks of amusement at her appearance. The sight of a girl in some kind of disappearing angel costume singing a Yule tune was too ridiculous, and the giggling swelled as she curtsied after the final chord.

Out of the corner of her eye, she recognized the painfully handsome figure of Mr. Yates and steeled herself not to risk a single glance toward him, just in case he, too, was struggling to hide his mirth.

Polite applause made her knees feel rubbery, but before she could ask Violet to untie the sash and free her from the torn fabric, her cousin was leading her toward her father in the heart of the gathering. "He'll want to embrace you. Go on!"

"I don't—"

Her father was red-faced from attempting not to laugh, and stepped forward to offer encouragement. "My dear! You were lovely."

"You're too kind. It seems I grew more than Violet estimated since she saw me last." She turned with the question, but a bit too quickly and struck her father and the gentleman next to him with a *fwap* from one of her loose wings.

At the jolting contact, she attempted to correct the error and instead struck another guest, Mrs. Colter, who squealed in amusement.

Mrs. Wolfe approached to attempt a rescue and met with a similar fate. "Here, dear, let me get that."

But Alyssa's composure had crumbled. Gasps and giggles were interspersed with outright laughter at the novel spectacle of a fallen angel in their midst and it was more than her taut nerves could manage. She caught sight of Mr. Yates moving toward her, and decided that she'd suffered enough embarrassment for one evening.

"If you'll excuse me, Mrs. Wolfe, I'll just change in the salon." Alyssa finally made her way to the salon door, retreating with tears of humiliation in her eyes.

She swallowed hard and leaned for a moment against the door as the sound of muffled laughter reached her through the thick door. *Oh, God. Word of this will reach every corner of England before New Year's . . . and to think I was worried about wearing the wrong color slippers!*

The battle against her tears was lost, and Alyssa just let them fall.

"Oh, my!" Violet gasped, putting a hand over her lips to hide her smile. "I did promise everyone it would be a memorable performance."

A few guests laughed at the cutting comment, but quieted as Leland approached. "Miss Horner, that was unforgivable."

Her amusement gave way to an icy expression of disregard. "I've done nothing wrong!"

Without a word, Reid Martin turned his back on her and headed to the salon. Leland went after him and caught his arm. Reid looked back, outraged at being restrained. "I must see to my daughter!"

"Please, sir," Leland said, loosening his grip. "I would ask for that honor."

Outrage gave way to curiosity. "Would you?"

Leland held his gaze, praying that somehow Martin would see past the chaos of the moment and allow him to go to her. "I want nothing more."

The man's glance moved briefly to the door, his concern and care for his only child evident. But then he looked back at Leland, this time more closely, as if truly taking stock of him for the first time. "You didn't laugh, did you, Mr. Yates?"

"Tonight? No, of course not, but—"

"No. Not tonight. I meant at dinner, last night. When everyone else was enjoying themselves about the mud puddle and her kittens . . . you didn't join in."

It was a statement, not a question. Leland could only nod in admission, before Reid went on. "Even that first day, when Mrs. Wolfe shared too freely regarding my daughter's mishap in the vicar's garden, I don't recall your laughing."

"It was a sweet memory, but clearly not one I would have wanted to hear in jest." Leland shifted his weight, unsure if he was about to be lectured or praised. In either case, he was painfully aware of every second that Alyssa suffered alone on the other side of that door. "Please, sir. I'm not sure I'm making sense of this. If you'd allow me to just—"

Reid nodded and lowered his voice so that only Leland could hear him. "You remind me of myself at your age. And I shall tell you that Alyssa's mother ruled me with smiles and silly feminine pursuits that mystify me to this very day—but I would not trade an instant of it for a more sensible choice." The older man's eyes misted with emotion. "Go to her."

Leland didn't hesitate, not even to absorb the impact of Reid's blessing. Instead, he moved quickly to the door. Relieved to find it unlocked, he let himself in. The cheerful noise of the party was shut out instantly, and he spotted her—a fallen angel in tears by the fireplace.

"Miss Martin . . ." He knelt in front of her, tenderly assessing her state.

"Th-the . . . knot . . . i-is . . . too t-tight," she whispered, her breath hitching between sobs and making the loose wings bobble in chorus. "It w-won't . . . come . . . o-off."

She was so vulnerable, and his chest ached to see her brought so low. "There, now. I'm sure it's not permanently attached. I'll help you." He reached out to brush her cheek, unable to not touch her. "You're too wonderful to cry."

Her breath hitched one last time, but her shock at his words seemed to help her steady herself. "Y-you've had too much punch, Mr. Yates."

He smiled. It was the last thing he'd have expected her to say. "I haven't had a single glass, Miss Martin."

"Oh." She risked a shy smile of her own. "Then you're just saying nice things to keep me from molting any further."

She was too close and too funny and too impossible not to kiss. Pent-up desire was unleashed as he drew her into his arms and tasted her. Her response was an intoxicating ether that wrested away the last of his control. Her lips parted beneath his, allowing him the access he craved to tease and stroke every sensitive curve and texture of her sweet mouth. She mirrored his movements and when her tongue met his, the room spun. His cock tightened, a spasm of need rippled through his frame. The angel in his arms shivered when his teeth grazed her lips and he swallowed her soft sighs and moans and then released her mouth only to trail whisper-light kisses down her bare throat. *What sounds would his angel make when she climaxed against his mouth?*

Every inch of her. Mine.

"M-Mr. Yates?"

Oh, God. No conversation. Please don't . . .

"Is something burning?"

He lifted his head slowly and realized that the evening's mischief wasn't quite over—one of her wings had trailed too close to the fire. The flames were spreading quickly and within moments she could be in mortal danger. He reacted instantly. He pushed her over onto the carpet and beat at the organza wings with his sleeves; then, using his body to protect her, he rolled them over and over across the room to ensure that the flames were suffocated.

The maneuver happened so fast, she simply clung to him in astonishment as he lay over her. "Well, that was more than I'd expected."

"Really? They didn't cover this at school?"

Then they were both laughing, at least until the intimate nature of their embrace sifted back into Leland's awareness. She was nestled quite contentedly beneath him, his upper body supported by his arms, the rest of his length firmly between her thighs, his arousal throbbing. Her father had given his blessing to comfort her, but Leland was fairly sure this was a bit more than Reid Martin had had in mind.

"Happy Christmas, Miss Martin."

"You say that to all the flaming angels, I'm sure, sir."

"I have a weakness for angels like you."

He began to shift his weight off of her, but the friction proved to be his undoing. His world narrowed to the pulse of his own heart and the need to kiss her again.

Just one more kiss.

He lowered his mouth to hers. A grazing touch at first, teasing and featherlight, he explored each corner of her mouth and sensitive ripe lips, until she was trembling underneath him. Her hands fluttered against his chest, then began to explore, slipping under his coat and roaming over his chest. His skin ached to be free of the barrier that kept her fingertips from gliding against him. He deepened his kiss, and a new fire overtook them both. Though new to passion, she was proving to be an apt student, driving him on and beginning to take the lead. Her hands slid down to his waist and hips, exploring and pleasuring; Leland caught her wrist before she innocently strayed too far and he relinquished his sanity altogether.

This is very dangerous. The party was only yards away and—

"Alyssa?" Violet's voice was like a bucket of icy water on them both. Leland instinctively put his fingertips to her mouth to urge her to silence and they both froze in place—too paralyzed at the thought of discovery to move.

"Are you in here, dearest?"

At the question, they both risked a quick peek at where they'd landed. Apparently, for once, trouble had decided to allow Miss Martin a lucky circumstance; they'd ended up on the floor behind the settee—temporarily out of sight from the doorway.

"Cousin?" Violet called again, halfheartedly this time, though her footsteps drew nearer.

Hearts pounding, they could only wait as long seconds dragged by until at last, Violet's footsteps retreated, the door shut and they were once again alone.

He removed his fingers. "Are you all right?"

She grinned at him, nodding. Once again, they were co-conspirators, and she looked entirely unrepentant. "Are you trying to take advantage of me, sir?"

The question chilled him. *God, yes! And if your father and an entire Christmas party weren't on the other side of that door . . .*

He began to extricate himself. "No."

She sat up and caught his shoulder, her other hand gripping his coat to prevent his complete withdrawal. "That wasn't the right answer, Mr. Yates."

"No?" He gently shook his head. "I—despite how this appears . . ."

She pushed against him, until they were both on their knees, her body so close that when she took a breath her breasts brushed against his chest. "I already understand what you are *not* interested in. Please, just tell me what you *are* interested in."

He obeyed the command without hesitation. "I am interested in attempting to discover exactly how that mind of yours works. I am interested in learning that there is more to life than my business. I am interested in your talent for making me laugh and I am very interested in spoiling the hopes of every other man in England who will want you and love you the instant he sees you."

"That was a much better answer, Mr. Yates," she said with a satisfied smile as she brushed his mussed-up hair off his forehead. "Is there any chance you might help me out of this dreadful costume?"

"I beg your pardon?" He arched an eyebrow and gave her a telling look full of erotic promise. "Are you asking me to help you undress?"

"The knots . . . if you could help me get this wretched thing off." She started to stand so that he might oblige her. "It's a bit uncomfortable."

"Of course." He stood easily and turned her around to make quick work of the knots, indulging in a few light caresses of her bared neck and shoulders as he did so. "There! You are mortal again, Miss Martin."

"Thank you, sir."

Leland readjusted his coat. "Shall we return to the gathering?"

"You're not embarrassed to be seen with me after . . . everything?" She pointed to her charred and discarded wings.

"Never." Leland reached into his coat pocket and withdrew his handkerchief. Slowly and tenderly, he worked the cloth across the tip of her nose to remove a smudge of soot. "Never, my love."

Epilogue

*D*ear Mrs. Harris,

   While I have applied myself with utmost concentration and great effort to my last holiday assignment, I confess I may have failed. I can assure you I did my best to mind my surroundings and behave at all times as a true lady. Though no serious public scandal or destruction occurred in my wake, I did, in retrospect, manage the following:

— To become quite stuck in a carriage window;
— To have a run-in with a pack of ravenous pugs, resulting in the loss of one shoe;
— To trap myself in tree branches and ruin a perfectly good bonnet;
— To receive a singular mud bath behind my father's gardens;
— To experience a minor brush with the combustibility of angel wings (truly I was only singed a bit);

And finally,

— To gladly accept a proposal of marriage from Mr. Leland Yates of London, a fine man of outstanding character and disposi-

tion whom I madly and absolutely
adore.

I hope you aren't too disappointed, as I remain . . .
Your affectionate student,
Miss Alyssa Martin

The past burns with passion...

Bestselling historical romance from Pocket Books!

The Highlander's Stolen Bride
Melanie George

A sexy highlander vows to defend a proper English lady—
but who will protect her from her protector?

Never Seduce a Scoundrel
The *School for Heiresses* Series
Sabrina Jeffries

Good girls follow the rules...heiresses follow their hearts.

Three Little Secrets
Liz Carlyle

Promise not to tell.... Bestselling author Liz Carlyle
concludes her scandalous new trilogy with a sensuous
novel of two star-crossed lovers who share a secret
or two—or three.

Marriage Most Scandalous
Johanna Lindsey

Passion. Intrigue. Scandal. Some marriages have it all...

Available wherever books are sold
or at www.simonsayslove.com.